MARY DONOVAN

Mary Donovan

ANNE MILLER DOWNES

Chicago
PEOPLES BOOK CLUB

Go from me. Yet I feel that I shall stand
Henceforward in thy shadow. Nevermore
Alone upon the threshold of my door
Of individual life, I shall command
The uses of my soul, nor lift my hand
Serenely in the sunshine as before,
Without the sense of that which I forebore,—
Thy touch upon the palm. The widest land
Doom takes to part us, leaves thy heart in mine
With pulses that beat double. What I do
And what I dream include thee, as the wine
Must taste of its own grapes. And when I sue
God for myself, He hears that name of thine,
And sees within my eyes the tears of two.

E.B.B.

CONTENTS

MARY KENT

CHAPTER I

The Indians called it Oo-hoosk-ah, meaning, "It slips"; the scientists called it *Ulmus americana;* the early settlers of the eastern shores of our country called it the American elm and transplanted it from the low rich forest land to the dooryard, to the village Common, to narrow street; then, as cities grew, they lined long avenues with Lowell's loved "abbey arches."

Even at the turn of our century, men in the back country still used the hard, strong, tough wood for hubs for wheels, frames for chairs, sills for buildings and rails for fences.

Today, the motorist speeding over cement highways sometimes glances at a tiny cottage or low-roofed farmhouse dwarfed to insignificance by protecting elms towering fifty to a hundred feet into the sky. Sometimes he looks admiringly at some solitary elm, alone in a wide meadow—alone but somehow never lonely; yet in large sections of his home town he has cleared away every vestige of the noble tree as he has cleared away other forms of gracious living; and in small villages, as the cement roads multiply, he ruthlessly removes this symbol of beauty, dignity and leisure to make way for speed, noise and foul air.

In the fourth decade of this century the face of a woman who walked alone, and lonely, under a cathedral arch of elms in a Massachusetts city, was often saddened as she glanced up at the trees. She wondered if some philosopher in the future would find the apathy to the American elm's fate symbolical of the American spirit's decay.

Not a vestige of Dutch elm disease had touched our shores when, as a young girl, in the year 1919, she stood one fall morning on the curbstone in front of her home looking up into the branches of a tree, laughing as her father shouted to some workmen perched on a telegraph pole. "Hold off," he called. "Some tree-men are coming to cut that limb."

"Heavens, Dad, tell them to hold *on*. He'll fall off trying to hear you." She cupped her hands around her mouth and called shrilly, "Hold *on*."

The workmen grinned and nodded. Above their heads a branch of an elm had been torn off during a storm of the previous night and menaced their wires as it teetered on one of the lower branches.

On either side of the avenue, men passing remarked to companions, "That's J.R.'s daughter come home from boarding school to take her mother's place. Mighty pretty, isn't she?"

Joseph Rutherford Kent. In the professional and business life of the city few faces were more familiar than his whether he was sitting at a directors' meeting, advising on a hospital board, discussing political candidates at public meetings, pleading a case in court or driving his new automobile along country roads; a hulking figure of a man with heavy shoulders, thick hair once blond but now graying, plus what the family always spoke of, apologetically, as the large Kent nose, a nose honorably bequeathed to him by his father, the eminent jurist, Judge Kent.

His daughter listened carefully as he gave her instructions for the tree-men, then watched him as he started toward the business section of the city with the easy long-legged stride of a man used to cross-country walking. Avoiding the thick carpet of wet leaves on the lawn and the stream of water still running in the gutter, she picked her way along the stone curb, glancing up as a young man turned into the avenue from the entrance of an estate directly across the corner.

Bill Carter was remembering his mother's remark at the breakfast table: "Mary Kent's staying home with her father. She's inherited the Farnsworth hair." Now he was looking at the Farnsworth hair. And Mary Kent waved her hand in a manner half shy, half friendly and remembered her father saying at their breakfast table: "Young Bill Carter's doing well—soon be in line for a judge-ship. They've got a young baby over there; saw them walking him about the lawn yesterday." Mary wanted to see the baby being walked across the lawn.

She was about to turn toward the house when she saw the young man seem to hesitate and then, after a milk cart passed, come quickly across the road. Although she was of average height he towered above her as he shook hands and told her how surprised he was to see her so grown up.

Old J.R. called the Farnsworth hair simply, "Red—sandy," the red of the Farnsworth tribe imposed on the blond of the Kents. However, Bill Carter thought Mary's eyes even lovelier than her hair. He remembered her as a little child often smiling up at him, her older brother Gordon's friend, with those laughing yet shy eyes. Now, with a manner indicating grave reserve she looked away and he examined the delicate profile as he answered her questions about his baby. "His name? We called him Hunt for my mother's family. You must come over and see him and—" he hesitated noticeably, "and get acquainted with my wife, Mazie."

He watched the laughter give way to an expression sober and level as they spoke of Gordon whose plane had been shot down over German territory nearly two years before.

For a moment she turned her face farther away as he said, "It must be tough on your father. I know how Gordon was working with him expecting to take his place someday. I always saw them walking home together at night. It's mighty lucky he has you."

She turned quickly and smiled up into his eyes. "It's luckier he has Lawrence." Lawrence was established in the English depart-ment of a small college a few miles distant. "He and Cathey have bought a little house near the campus."

"I must see him. All the Kents go to Harvard and all the Carters go to Princeton. Besides, I've lost track of him a little. I'm older, you know."

He started down the street, but he turned to call, "Don't forget to come over."

She followed the path around the big brick house to the side door. Her head drooped a little and once her eyes filled with tears. Gordon. His death had killed her mother. The doctor may have diagnosed her illness differently but no one could persuade her to leave her husband and go to a warmer climate that winter. She died in the spring and Mary came home from her New York school.

She had said simply, "Daddy, I'm going to stay home with you now. Mother always told me never to wear black. Would you mind if we had no mourning?"

"No mourning, Pettie."

"Only—we can be quiet when we feel like it? We won't have to pretend and do things?"

"We'll be quiet when we feel like it. No pretending."

Now people smiled indulgently at old J. R. Kent's adoration of his slender, blond daughter. He always called her Pettie both while speaking to her and of her, and the boys in his office said if Pettie wanted the moon old J.R. would trade in a city block and try to get it for her. However, Pettie never seemed to want much of anything until she saw Tom Donovan. Then she wanted Tom.

CHAPTER II

The tree experts removed the limb which was dangling dangerously above the heads of pedestrians. They were giving scientific treatment to the ugly gash in the old elm when another shower forced everyone to scurry for shelter.

Down in the business section of the city, white-coated street cleaners retired philosophically to watch the rain clean the center of the streets for them; from the rivers forming in their tracks the wheels of trolley cars sent out sprays that rivaled the summer water-wagons. It was shortly before noon when the storm passed, the sun appeared and the streets again filled with people hurrying here and there to make up for lost time.

Some years ago J.R. had taken over a cousin's real estate and bond business, combining it with his more important legal practice and the venture had turned out to be both interesting and lucrative. On this rainy morning, the boys (so-called although some of them were gray-haired) were sitting at their desks behind the large plate-glass windows of the real estate office busily engaged with papers or account books when the door opened and a young man drifted in. Nearly a dozen pairs of eyes scrutinized him.

There was the matter of the raincoat. They studied it as the wearer studied them. On that early fall morning when he opened the door and stepped into their midst, Tom Donovan stood a moment with head held far back, chin raised, his eyes half laughing but sharp and darting about the office as though making a rapid but comprehensive inventory. The water dripped from the rim of his soft hat and when he took it off and shook it, he laughed, revealing unusually even white teeth. He held the hat gingerly and asked if Mr. Kent were in.

Yes, he was in his private office. The name? Tom Donovan.

Someone went in to announce him and, as he passed down the center of the room, one and all examined and memorized that raincoat. It was not only manufactured of a fawn-colored cravenette but it was obviously manufactured in England for a trade called "class." The sleeves were full and folded at the wrists under beautifully contrived bands; the belt was outrageously wide and confined the folds of the garment luxuriously about Tom's slender waist, then fastened with a remarkable buckle. The collar was turned up and another handsome buckle secured it at one side.

When he disappeared into the private office they discussed the coat and wondered if the "Earl of Donovan" would get the waiting job, for two men had been transferred to the bond department and there was an obvious vacancy.

Later, when the coat was hanging beside their own commonplace garments in the cloakroom and Tom Donovan had been given a desk, they received a shock, for the newcomer was wearing a blue serge suit with sleeves nearly frayed at the wrists, with trousers shiny and visibly thin in the seat. The shoes were resoled, much worn but highly polished. The shirt was cheap enough but stylish, deep blue with matching collar. After the first surprise and amusement wore off, the coat was relegated to the realm labeled "mystery" and the shabby suit and shoes won instant sympathy and friendliness.

They won sympathy from every man in the room except Warren, the cashier, who looked with a jealous eye on any newcomer who might have more than a nodding acquaintance with J.R. who, with his daughter, had usurped the place of religion in Warren's life. Warren had been in love with Mary since she was a little girl with curls hanging to her waist. Warren of all people! Such a plain little insignificant man, supporting a mother and two sisters, with no prospects of marrying anyone, a singed-cat sort of man with no redeeming features except his clear brown eyes.

In the months following Tom Donovan's appearance in their office, Warren, because jealousy sharpened his observation and prejudiced his judgment, came to hate the newcomer bitterly.

Except for him, the decision that Donovan was the man for the place was unanimous. He had seen service in France and that weighed heavily with J.R. He was good-looking but not handsome or "prettyish," with regular features and dark hair far thinner at the temples than his age of twenty-six seemed to warrant.

Somehow Warren was suspicious of that averred age; he was suspicious of the flush that often overspread Donovan's high cheekbones; he was suspicious of the hollows under his eyes in the morning. The other boys were charitable and suspected he had been half starved, needy and poor like his suit. They watched him as he sat at his desk when his thin face settled into lines a little old and hard, but when he walked briskly through the room, or jumped into one of the company cars, they saw his hazel eyes bright under the long lashes, his even teeth showing, and he appeared young and eager. And then there was his voice; such a pleasant voice, meticulous in enunciation, clear-toned and resonant. He was fluent and yet not glib, surely a perfect equipment.

They soon discovered that the mysterious raincoat was the only coat he possessed and even a shadow of cloud in the sky brought it out. On sunny days he must have shivered in his thin blue suit for with his first pay-check he bought shoes—a near necessity—shirts and handkerchiefs; then, at the end of the month, a gray tweed suit. It was not until late October that he bought a handsome topcoat but by that time J.R. was increasing his salary generously because he not only had made sizable commissions on the sale of two large houses but he had become a frequent visitor at J.R.'s home.

For years a certain spinster, blessed with the fine old British name of Hogg, had wanted to dispose of two mansions on the main street, classified as hopeless white elephants by the boys in the office.

Jokingly they turned the buildings over to Donovan who called on the lady and persuaded her to scale down her asking price.

The boys joked, "It's the flattering way you pronounce her name, Tom. Let's hear it."

Lightly and crisply, "Miss Hogg."

They laughed. They laughed again in a few days. "You have the old girl eating out of your hand." They laughed even more when he found a business client and sold both mansions. Everyone but Warren was pleased and no one could quite decide whether it was luck or his engaging smile or charming voice or, conceivably, some marvelous business acumen. In the full flush of excitement engendered by this sale, he stopped one afternoon to "take a look at the boss' home."

It had been a full day for Mary Kent. She had played some finals in tennis at the Country Club, she had had her first professional lesson in driving, all in the beauty of the bright October weather that she loved. She had noted how the green of the elms was turning to yellow and brown, the sumac was burning crimson on the hills, the beauty of the high-bush cranberry compelled attention from the most casual passer-by, the petals of the hydrangeas were glowing flakes of copper-brown. In the late afternoon she leisurely crossed her lawn, scissors in hand, toward her garden where the chrysanthemums were in bloom, and robins were gorging themselves on the honeysuckle berries.

She stopped to watch their man, Ben Tilden, patching and seeding some bad spots in the lawn. "How quickly the weather changed, Ben. It looks like rain."

Ben, a tall, gangling, loose-jointed Negro, had always been part of her life. He kept the walks clean in winter, looked after the one good horse J.R. still kept in his stable, mowed lawns, raked leaves, chopped wood, kept the fireplace baskets filled with kindling and logs. One of her mother's luxuries was having a fire in her bedroom and she always said she opened one eye when Ben slipped in on cold mornings and started the fire, then listened for his "Morning Mis' Kent" as he left which meant, "Now you keep an eye on that fireplace."

"How's Kit and Henry?"

"Just fit, Miss Mary." He looked up at the sky where the October blue was fast disappearing beneath heavy black clouds.

She walked around to the side, opened a lattice gate and called into the kitchen window, "Mattie, either you or Fanny better get in the clothes. It's going to rain."

"I'm watching it." A fine-looking woman of some thirty years stepped out on the kitchen porch, her eyes resting affectionately on the girl who had run to her as a baby and now, as mistress of the place, depended on her still. "That's a pretty suit, Mary."

It was lovely; a wool jersey with blended shades from gray-green to copper-brown. Mary looked off down the path. "It was the last suit Mother bought me." She and her mother used to go to New York and revel in soft wools and silks—jade-greens, dark hunting-green, green-blues, sand color, mauves, tans that melted into burnished browns and blues as soft as sky tones. The last thing J.R. cared about was the price of those costumes; they delighted his eyes and that was all that mattered.

Today, the colors of her wool jersey blended into the riot of color in the garden as she walked down the grass paths clipping dahlias, chrysanthemums and late asters. With her hands full of flowers she wandered toward the barn where the Virginia creeper flamed along the stone wall. As she came back she looked at the big red brick house set far back from the avenue among lawns that merited the word "spacious." Born under its roof, knowing no other home, she seldom saw it objectively; but today she did look at it. All the comfortable verandahs were at the sides and the back leaving the formal doorway uncluttered at the front. On the drawingroom side the windows extended nearly to the floor and up above the dormers with their tiny panes of glass indicated age.

The sky was growing darker and Ben with rake and shovel over his shoulder was making his way to the barn. She saw Mattie and the maid, Fanny, hurrying in the wash; then she looked up with casual interest as one of her father's Fords turned into the drive and stopped near the side entrance. A young man jumped out, stood a moment looking toward her and then slowly approached.

Step by step they came nearer, each looking steadily at the other. She would always remember. With head slightly lifted, his dark eyes smiling under long lashes, with some light grace in his step, Tom Donovan came within speaking distance. "Miss Kent?" She nodded rather gravely.

"I'm Tom Donovan from your father's office. I've never been here before. It's a beautiful place. That garden's wonderful." He glanced around as he spoke.

She looked pleased. Immediately she liked his good manners, his fine voice and the enthusiastic but quite impersonal way in which he looked about him.

"I can't shake hands—"

"Do let me help you." He took some of the flowers from her arms, and as they turned to the porch large drops of rain began to fall.

"You'd better close the windows in your car and come in."

The breeze had loosened some strands of her hair and brought color into her cheeks and she looked young and sweet and very pretty as he helped her arrange the flowers in vases which stood on a table in the porch. When she picked up a small mauve chrysanthemum and remarked, "This is the first time I've raised these," he smiled. "I suppose you mean your gardener raised them?"

She laughed gaily. "You don't know us. Father and I wear the most disreputable old slacks and we dig and plant and work like regular farmers. Why, I was given my own little plot of land when I was not much more than a baby." Her laughing eyes looked into his. "Haven't you ever owned a garden?"

For a moment the hard lines which Warren had noticed appeared in his face. "I consider myself lucky when I can pay the rent for a place to sleep." He laughed the remark off quickly and with a most engaging, boyish smile said, "I don't think you get all your exercise farming. I hear you're a crackajack tennis player."

She was leading the way into the sittingroom as she replied, "Oh, my brothers taught me to play tennis and golf. I had my first lesson in driving a car today. I loved that." She turned to him, her eyes full of laughter. "Our housekeeper is teaching me to cook and once I made a dress and I love to trim hats. There. That's the sum total of my accomplishments. Now tell me what you do."

Ben had lighted the fire in the sittingroom. For a moment they silently watched the crackling flames wrap themselves about the heavy logs. She offered him a chair. He stood a moment hesitating. "May I smoke?"

"Oh, certainly." She would remember him always, standing by the mantle, lighting his cigarette, flicking the match into the flames. She noticed his hands with their long, sensitive fingers, his strong wrists. She liked those hands. She liked also the awareness of his eyes, his quick graceful motions, even the nervous way he jerked his shoulders. He did not answer her challenge; instead he smiled at her again half mockingly, "You may like to play at farming but your brother Lawrence is a college professor of English and your father is a distinguished lawyer and you've come home from one of the most fashionable boarding schools in New York."

She looked up at him as if startled, but dropped her eyes quickly before his gaze which had suddenly became penetratingly personal. However, he still spoke lightly and gaily. "I heard all this at the office, of course, but," he stopped to laugh, "I wasn't even interested. I just thought I'd take a look at the boss' place today—I didn't even want to see you. But now—"

She glanced up quickly as he finished. "You see you're not the boss' daughter now. You're an unusual person I've met." He shrugged his shoulders. "I don't believe in you but I'd like to make sure."

She was amused, half embarrassed, but she asked eagerly, "Make sure of what?" She did not get an answer for the door opened and her father came in.

J.R. himself invited Tom Donovan to stay to supper. It was a warmly pleasant meal. J.R. asked questions all of which seemed to be frankly, readily answered. "Tom, you came from Boston?"

"Born there. I've lived either there or in New York most of my life."

To an inquiry about his people, Tom answered with appealing candor. "Few boys ever knew less about their family. I'm one of that army of children who graduated from an orphan asylum directly into a business career—the business of keeping myself alive—at the age of thirteen. I managed to earn, then get some education, then earn, then get more education, even a smattering of college."

"Your parents had died? You had no relatives?"

There was that quick graceful toss of head and shrug of shoulders. "I looked up graves in a Dorchester cemetery with the name Donovan on them but I have no way of connecting myself with any of them. My father apparently was nonexistent. Once I went back to the asylum and was told that my mother was a very refined lady and I have made what I could out of that. They 'understood' she had died."

He spoke lightly, charmingly, but when he glanced at Mary sitting opposite him, he saw her face tense, her eyes fill with wondering pity. He smiled directly into those wide eyes. "It sounds horrible to you, doesn't it? Don't mind. I'm so used to it I wouldn't know how to live except as a tramp."

Through the next hour, J.R. often looked thoughtfully at the young man but he was kind and cordial, even remarking as Tom was leaving, "Drop in again when you get tired of restaurant suppers."

Mary followed him out to the porch. They saw that a light rain was still falling. Laughingly she said, "I still want to know what you don't believe in and what you want to make sure about."

For a moment he narrowed his eyes and turned his head away. "I don't believe in you. I can't." He called, "Good night. Thanks for everything," and ran down the steps.

A perplexed expression in her eyes, she stood by the door until the Ford disappeared into darkness down the avenue.

CHAPTER III

Never in her life would Mary Kent be one who subscribed to the doctrine that all things were ruled by an inevitable necessity; fatalism had no part in her creed; planning or contriving was one thing; accidents were accidents. She knew it was accidental when she saw a Ford following her car up the steep road to Carter's woodland. The mechanic who was teaching her to drive said, "Stop. We'll practice turning."

The Ford stopped behind and Tom Donovan jumped out. He looked young and eager and boyishly happy. "A bright pupil?" he quipped.

The mechanic grinned and color rose in Mary's cheeks as her eyes laughed. She found it difficult for a moment to concentrate on the directions but presently Tom looked at his watch, called, "Good luck" and drove off up the steep hill. That was all; but she would always remember the sunlit hill, the narrow road twisting between two sycamore-maples, the shining, breezy morning and Tom Donovan's smile.

On the following afternoon Mary was called to the telephone. "This is Tom Donovan. I have to drive out to Camden, about twelve miles. There are nice, back-country roads; don't you want to come and practice driving? Who was that old codger—the kindergarten expert who said 'learn to do by doing'?"

"Pestalozzi? So you think I'm a kindergarten pupil?" She laughed and hesitated. "I'd have to change an engagement at the Country Club."

She changed the engagement. She saw the expression of surprise faintly tinged with disapproval in Mattie Briggs' face as she stepped into the Ford and drove off with "that new fellow from the office." When Fanny remarked about it, Mattie Briggs replied with dignity, "Probably J.R. sent him up."

Tom Donovan drove rapidly and expertly through the city but out on a country dirt road he stopped and let her take the wheel. Trees overhung the road; bars of sun and shadow lay across the brown dirt; on either side the stubble in the fields glowed golden while beyond were the blue hills.

It was exhilarating. When they came to a village, he laughed, "Go on; got to get used to traffic—two grocery wagons." Then, "Stop speeding; you were up to fifteen miles." Again, "Now you're up against it—a wagonload of hay. Creep along. Here's the main hazard of the fall."

He laid his hand on her wrist. "Relax. You must keep your hands relaxed." He left his hand there and the feel of his palm was perilously sweet. She liked him. He was friendly, yet reserved. He was full of fun. They found laughter and good comradeship all the way. He was successful in getting his papers signed in Camden but halfway home she said, "You'd better drive. We're having company for dinner and it's getting late."

He left her at the curb. When she looked back to say, "Thanks a lot," he replied, "You're unbelievable." It was the only personal thing he said to her throughout the afternoon.

Again it was "routine" that business took J.R. to Washington on the following week end. He would be gone four or five days. Late Friday afternoon, Mary was in the sittingroom when she heard steps crossing the porch. Tom Donovan was "just passing." They sat by the fire and Mary would have been a little hazy about what they talked about had she been questioned. She also would have been confused to explain why she woke in the night filled with some sense of sweetness and anticipation. They took a long ride on Saturday.

On the following Tuesday there came a telegram saying her father was unavoidably detained in Washington. The same message had been sent to the office.

She found herself refusing invitations to go out and in the late afternoon haunting the front windows, restless, filled with an undefined longing that bewildered her. When the little Ford turned into the drive her heart pounded and she held her breath listening for his step across the side porch.

On the stage, in New York, she had watched tap-dancers. She remembered that light, staccato step of theirs as they crossed the boards. That was Tom Donovan's step and from her throat down through her body to her finger tips and toes she seemed to tremble with delight when she heard it. She opened the door, always, before he could ring and it was then she first learned to love that little mannerism of his. He would stop, lift his head, look at her from under his long lashes and, with a delicate rising inflection say, "Mary?" That was all. "Mary?"

One day they drove off into the country beyond the Country Club. At the bottom of a hill in a sunny hollow they saw an enticing little lane. They parked the car and walked. In the woods it was cool, dark and quiet as a cloister, only bright patches of sunlight here and there lighting the gray barks of silver birches. They walked on a carpet of fir needles and breathed deeply of the aromatic scent. They were stopped by a turbulent brook and standing there, his toes kicking the stones, he spoke suddenly. "Mary, we ought not to be here together. I have no right to bring you here. You and I can never be anything to each other. I know that. I wish you would kick me out. Something has happened that I don't want to happen. I can never be anything to you so perhaps you won't mind my telling you this. I'm falling in love with you.

I don't want to." He laughed at that. "I've had more damned affairs in my life with women than my years would indicate but I've never been—in love. Tell me to go away and mind my own business."

In the depths of her eyes there was a look suddenly level, intense. She was trembling as she turned her head away and bit her lips. "I don't want you to go away, Tom, but I'm afraid."

"Afraid?"

"Yes. I don't know anything about being in love but I know the way I feel about you—for you—when you come in—"

"Go on, Mary."

"I know I'd be sick—if you didn't come. That's the way it seems to me. Your coming is all I care about any more." She hesitated a long time and as he didn't speak, she finished, "I feel as though it would kill me if you didn't come."

"But you would get over feeling that way if I went away and minded my own business."

She turned and looked into his eyes. "No. I don't think I would ever get over it."

She was trembling visibly as he took her into his arms, pushing back her hair and kissing her lips. "Mary, I didn't mean this to happen. You must believe that. I swear to you I never meant this to happen. To touch that hair. You are so beautiful, so wonderful. Good God, I should never have seen you."

A few moments later she raised her head and laughter filled her shining eyes. "Are you going to believe in me now? Are you going to be sure of what you wanted to be sure about?"

He looked grave. "No. I don't think I could ever quite believe that you could love *me*."

Day by day they went into the country to talk it over. Now Mattie Briggs openly remonstrated but she was answered only by shining eyes and trembling, smiling lips.

Again and again they found their cloistered hollow by the brook. They must know all about each other's lives. Hers was so simple, so quickly told. His?

Horror seemed fairly to freeze her as she listened to his sketchy dismissal of life in an orphan asylum. "We were toughs. Sometimes rotten."

"But you had school and—religion?"

"Oh, yes. School and religion and discipline and potatoes and skimmed milk and uniforms and rows of beds."

"Oh Tom. And after?"

"After? There have been thirteen years after, Mary. I'm twenty-six years old. I'm too old for you."

"Tell me about them."

"How can I? From thirteen to seventeen I lived a gutter existence, tough and hard. I was a wiry kid and could stand almost any kind of hardship. One winter I worked for a grocer and he was the best friend I ever had. He sent me to school, letting me work after school hours and on Saturdays. I went to live in his house and it was the teacher in school that year who gave me some longing for education and books and such things. Those three years from fourteen to seventeen are the only years in my life I am proud of, the only ones I like to remember. I got any idea I have of decency and any respect I have for religion from them."

"But what happened?"

"His wife died, the home was broken up and I got a job as a salesman, traveling around the country. Can't we stop?"

"But you're only seventeen."

For the first time she heard the bitterness in his laugh. "I wish I were still seventeen. I'm not." The narrative grew sketchy again. "One summer, I was selling up in Canada. I brought a girl back to Boston. The next year I met a woman—"

The muscles in her face grew tense and she watched him with wide wondering eyes. "A woman who influenced your life?"

He threw his head back and laughed, "Mary! what a way to put it! Yes, she not only influenced my life, she took it in her hands as though it were a piece of putty and used it whenever and however it suited her purpose. You see, Mary, I had got fired with a burning desire to be educated, to belong to the world of books and learning. She was thirty years old, had a position on a magazine and," he stopped to laugh, "she finished my education. She took me to New York with her and from then on it is a story that you would never understand. Ups and downs. Then a settled hell—poverty, drinking, and then one day a homesick longing for Boston. To start over—work up again from the beginning. I didn't reach Boston. A truck driver gave me a ride—here." He spoke lightly, "Do you know I didn't eat the first two days—not until Warren passed me out some money."

He did not wait for her to speak. "Now you know why this is utterly impossible. Like two fools we have fallen in love with each other. It was my fault. I am entirely to blame but I'll have the decency to clear out. Why, I'm almost rich with the money from those commissions. I'll go to Boston."

For a moment she sat rigid and silent, then her eyes looked into his with that level, intense expression. "Don't, Tom. I love you all the more for all you've told me. I won't care what anyone thinks. I'm going to give you everything—everything you've never had. Nothing can change me. I love you and I'm going to love you always. Let's put a blotter over all that past. Let's start now together."

"Your father will raise hell. If I were he I wouldn't let you look at me. I'd do the kicking out and in a hurry too."

She laughed aloud.

However, she was not laughing one evening soon after J.R. returned from Washington, when she followed him into his study after dinner.

He had picked up the evening paper and she took the chair opposite him, saying quietly, "Daddy, I have something I want to tell you right away. I have been seeing a great deal of Tom during the last few weeks. I want to tell you that we are in love with each other. We are engaged and I want to be married quite soon."

He laid the paper down and looked at her. How long it seemed to take and how many times she had to repeat the words before they seemed to sink in. Slowly his face grew gray-white. He looked haggard and old as he murmured, "Oh, no, Pettie, that could never be."

CHAPTER IV

J. R. Kent was confronted by a *fait accompli*. Over and over he thought bitterly, "If her mother had only lived, this never would have happened. I failed her." He felt that he had somehow done an evil thing when he had first invited Tom Donovan to stay to supper, when he had been gracious and friendly.

He had always prided himself on his lack of snobbery. He believed he was democratic. The mere fact that he and his father and his father's father had been Harvard men made him even more sympathetic to the man who never had a chance at college. Everything had been made easy for him and he admired the man who gained success wholly by his own efforts. He not only had nothing against a self-made man, even for a son-in-law, but he would have wanted in any case to give Tom Donovan every chance—and he had done so.

He brought every decent pressure to bear on Mary. He held a nerve-racking session with Tom who looked at him steadily and answered him soberly. "No, Mr. Kent, I'm not Mary's equal regardless of opportunity. I don't expect you to think I'm a suitable match for her. I'll do anything Mary says to do. I'll go away if she tells me to."

Mary's eyes, hurt, pleading, followed him in agonized entreaty day and night. He had never denied her anything—but Mary had never been a "wanting" person. When he deplored her youth— she was only eighteen—she smiled with disconcerting dignity. "I love Tom, Father." When he suggested that he arrange a job for Tom in Boston, sending him away for a year, she looked at her father in astonishment. "Would you want me sitting here for a year waiting for Tom to come back?"

Angrily, "He probably wouldn't come back."

"He would come back, Father. He loves me."

One day she stood at the side of his desk, her lips quivering with emotion. "Daddy, dear, why do you do this to me? I was so happy. I'm not going to send Tom away but, if you'd rather,

I'll go away with him and I don't want one single penny. You don't seem to understand that we love each other."

It was too much for J.R. One afternoon he stood in his sitting-room talking with his son. Lawrence pulled on his pipe and he did not affect any cheerfulness; it wasn't his way. "He isn't congenial to us, Father, but there's more than that worrying you."

"Yes, Lawrence, there's much more than that troubling me." He added slowly, "It's the family."

The family. For some nine generations the Kent-Farnsworth tribe had grown on New England or New York soil. They were comfortable people, never particularly luxurious, never playboys, but hard workers. Fathers expected sons to grow up and fill their shoes, take over their professions or mills or positions of respon-sibility in the community. Mistakes had been made in marriages but somehow the family, tribal strength had never been seriously weakened.

J.R. was already face to face with two tragedies; the loss of his eldest son, and the knowledge that Cathey would have no children. Her life had barely been saved in a railroad accident after which her first child, a boy, had been born dead. There was little hope of another child.

Lawrence placed a log on the fire, remarking, "I think the words 'madly in love' mean something now. Mary's a red-headed Farnsworth and she's a little mad. You could forbid the marriage and I don't think she would elope; neither would she ever get over it."

He relighted his pipe and looked at his father. "About his family, I'd guess he has good and bad blood but he's a tramp and it's uncanny to watch how cleverly he manages to avoid explain-ing his personal connections with either persons or places." He thought a moment, then smiled. "However, Father, I think you feel worse about this than you need to."

J.R. looked up expectantly.

Lawrence spoke slowly. "In spite of this 'madness' I pin my faith on Mary Kent. I don't think that either you, Father, or Gordon or I can match Mary in her love of family, the home, children and all the traditions that mean so much to you. She'll fight to the death for them."

J.R. raised his head and spoke more cheerfully. "Your great-aunt, Letitia, over in Albany, married badly but her line held strong. One of her sons is a prominent surgeon and the other is in the legislature. Isn't her daughter becoming a fair writer?"

"More than fair, she's distinguished." Lawrence looked amused. "You know, Father, the strength of the family, the tribe kept Rome flourishing for a thousand years; while here in New England, the family has been the strength of society for at least three hundred. Study the history of central or western New York State, or up and down the Hudson—how the families dug into the soil there. Just now we're suffering from the moral decline which follows all wars and the family solidarity seems to be disintegrating, but I can't believe it will be permanent.

"Suppose we face facts. You can't wreck Mary's life. She's chosen Tom Donovan. I believe he loves Mary. I mean that. I honestly don't believe he was drawn to her because of money or position. I may be wrong but I think they merely fell in love with each other. I'm frank to say he is an enigma to me; his seeming candor is a clever restraint. He drinks too much, but then—that may be merely a reaction to his thwarted ambitions. You say he is not drinking now."

"No. I can't find fault with his behavior or his work. It's just—"

"I know. You merely don't like him—but Mary does. I think he has a good mind, quick and smart. Can't you give him training and responsibility and gradually work him into a partnership? He's never had a real chance, I'm sure of that. Can't *you* bring yourself to giving him that chance?"

That was practical and J.R. felt comfortable again. They would stand by Tom and take him in and stand by Mary.

That was the big thing, but he often wondered if it were not the little things which annoyed him most. He, with his hearty, rather rough voice, found himself hating Tom's accent which seemed to be progressing to an exaggerated Harvard "a." He hated his mannerisms—like kissing Pettie in public. He fairly ex-

ploded when he found the men joking because Tom had told
them he was a "minor poet."

At the supper table he growled, "What in hell does Tom mean
by telling everyone he is a minor poet?"

"Oh, Daddy, don't most people have a try at poetry sometime
in their lives? Tom has a book full but he says he wouldn't think
of showing them to Lawrence or even to me because they aren't
that good. Come, Daddy, didn't you ever write a poem?"

"I did not. God knows I've been a fool often enough in my life
but something has preserved me from talking like one."

She looked at him with grave eyes. "Daddy, you must learn
to like Tom."

"You mean love him. Fathers should love their children."

A deep color flushed her cheeks. "I mean *like* him, Daddy."

There was a painful silence, then she spoke bravely, "We were
discussing a date for our wedding. Because it hasn't been a year
since Mother's death, it must be a quiet affair. I would like to be
married at Christmas time."

He softened a little. "You see, Pettie, I'm making plans for you
too. I'm going to make Tom a partner in the real estate business.
I am going to try out his ability and train him. He will have great
responsibility when I am gone and a great opportunity."

The glow of happiness that made her face radiant thanked him
more than words.

He finished, "I've one remarkably good man down there; in
fact I'm just finding out how good. Warren. He's been running
the financial end quietly for a long time and I find he knows the
business through and through and he has good judgment. I want
Tom to work with him."

Now the mellow days of fall had passed. There was no bird
song in the frosty mornings; merely the rat-a-tat-tat of the wood-
pecker, the cawing of the crows and the constant scolding of the
bluejays. No more the katydids either did or didn't; the squirrels
had finished the task of hoarding nuts; scarlet and russet and crimson had faded and over the meadows lay a blanket of snow. The

tall elms lining the avenue were silhouetted starkly against gray sky, their long slender branches swaying in the wind.

Mink coat and sealskin came out of mothproof bags. Fresh curtains hung at the windows, winter draperies elegantly swept in velvet folds to the floor. Mattie Briggs' cellar was stacked with rows of canned fruit and vegetables, barrels of apples, pumpkins, squash and jars of pickles and relishes.

J.R. sat at his desk thinking back through the years, thinking of the Farnsworths and Kents, jotting down the names of the friends whose prominence and social standing were not of the city or county, but of the state. Unconsciously he was heaping respectability, family, tradition and honor on one side of the scales to balance the lamentable lack on the other side.

The old house was beautiful on the night of the "quiet" wedding, with light streaming out of every window from cellar to attic. The awning reached from the severe Colonial doorway down the steps along the walk cleaned of snow which was banked high on either side.

Automobiles and carriages waited in line to discharge guests, the ladies wearing sealskin or lamb or mink or quilted velvet wraps, the gentlemen equally elegant in formal tails. The tall, rather handsome Lawrence was Tom's best man.

Mary Kent wore her mother's wedding gown and a grandmother's lace veil and collar. People noticed that old J.R. was getting a little stooped. Of course it was hard for him to give Mary away. They must get acquainted with this nice-looking young man—quite charming, wasn't he? Beautifully spoken. From Boston? His parents not living? They must entertain them soon.

When old J.R. handed his daughter to Tom Donovan and stepped back he was compelled to chew his lips. It had been more difficult to go through the ordeal than he had expected it to be.

CHAPTER V

When the storms and zero temperatures of January became their daily fare, the big brick house seemed like a fortress to the members of the family who were trying hard to think of Mary Kent as Mrs. Tom Donovan. The words always caused Mary's eyes to fill with laughter and her cheeks with color. When they had been home several weeks after their short southern honeymoon, Lawrence remarked to his father, "The 'poetry of the first passionate illusion.'"

J.R. looked up from his paper. "Yes, she is happy." Then he added, "He's happy too. I see now, nothing could have stopped it. It looks like the real thing."

"Cathey says one can scent the atmosphere from the curbstone." They both smiled as Lawrence continued, "The adjustments haven't bothered you too much?"

"Oh no. Pettie plans everything. He's always quiet and pleasant. They fixed up the west room. I offered to give them my room but Pettie wouldn't hear of my moving. After all I was born in that big bed and I've slept in it most of my life." He stopped abruptly and Lawrence, looking down on his father's bent head knew how empty the bed must seem without his mother, Louise Farnsworth. He knew more; he felt how lonely an older man could be in his own home. But J.R. was speaking cheerfully, "Tom's agreeable and quiet but he's a damned nervous chap, a bundle of nerves."

"Mattie? How does she really feel?"

"Oh—Mattie's reconciled. Wonderful woman. I gave her the chance to make a change; she says she expects to end her days with Pettie."

Lawrence's face expressed deep satisfaction and relief. "How's the business going?"

"All right. Warren bothers me a little. Sort of resented a newcomer at first but I think that'll work out in time. I took Tom around one day and showed him all that land I've bought and the property downtown. Little by little I'll hope to train him to develop that with me. Can't expect too much of him in a few months."

On that same evening, Tom Donovan was standing by a window in the west room measuring with his eye the depth of the window seat. "They certainly built these old houses with walls like forts." He turned to Mary who was sitting in a low chair pulling on evening slippers. His eyes were intensely bright and there was a light, mocking quality in his voice as he laughed, "You don't realize how surprised I am about twenty-four hours of every day to find myself *inside* the fortress." As she looked up, smiling, he went on quickly, "It isn't this house alone; it's all the fortresses in all the cities in the country. I've always lived on the outside looking at the strong walls but never expecting or hoping to be inside. When I was a kid I dreamed of it—homes, wealth, happy married life, children, prestige."

"Oh no, Tom, you're wrong there. Wealth or no wealth makes no difference. Next summer we'll go out to Mr. Glover's farm— you know, the man who brings our eggs and butter? Four generations have lived in that farmhouse and earned their living from three hundred acres of land and this Jim Glover has six children. It's the same up and down all our streets—just plain, everyday, substantial family life, mostly far from rich; but I love your word for it—the fortress of America."

"Well, darling, I've always been one of the tramps, part of the flotsam and jetsam; the millions of lonely immigrants, the orphan asylum graduates, the drunks, morons, weaklings—all outside."

She was slipping a gray velvet evening dress over her head and when he fastened the catches at the back she felt his fingers icy cold on her bare neck. He laughed. "That's the way my hands felt when I dropped the fork at the great Lucy's dinner party and nearly smashed a priceless dinner plate handed down from some great-aunt Petunia." Then he changed the subject again, lightly, "That color's not exactly gray, is it?"

She looked down at the soft folds about her ankles. "No, far from it. Came from France. They're experts at weaving in mauve or rose threads to give a subtle glow."

"It's beautiful, so simple."

She smiled mischievously at him. "That's what you pay so much for. Simple and subtle costs money."

"Simple and subtle like you, darling. Watching you dress fascinates me. You wash your face, put a touch of powder on your nose, brush you hair thoroughly then coil it up rather carelessly and there you are. No make-up, no camouflage."

"Leave out the subtle, dear. Your wife's plain simple. Transparent as a windowpane and so much in love she couldn't hide it from a man in an airplane."

She was fastening a necklace. With that quick, nervous fling of shoulders he bent toward her and, taking both of her hands in his cold ones, he looked into her eyes. "Mary, can you understand? I'm crazy about you. Sometimes—now you'll think I *am* crazy— sometimes I wish there was some way it could be just you and *me* alone in the world, even out in the hinterland if it would prove—"

"But you wanted to come here to live, Tom. Father would let us build a little house—"

"It isn't that, darling." He laughed, "No matter where we live you've got to tell me a hundred times a day that you really love me."

Her face sobered and her voice became tremulous. "There's only one thing I want in the world—that's to give you everything. I value all 'this' as you call it—my home, my friends—all the fortress, because I can give you all the things you never have had. And the one greatest thing you've never known—love. It wouldn't matter if we were out among the flotsam and jetsam or here; I'm completely and wholly yours, dear. Nothing in the world is ever going to change that." Then she drew back from his lips, laughing. "But if we're going to the Butlers' dinner party, we'd better get there before the soup's cold. I can't say I'll be sorry when all Mother's friends in this county get through inspecting us."

He was holding her wrap. "You honestly think I've passed so far?"

She looked him over from head to foot seeing how handsome he appeared in evening clothes. "You're fishing for compliments and I won't bite. Yes, I will. You know quite well that I'm sinfully proud of you and you know that you're getting downright popular."

"As J. R. Kent's son-in-law?"

"You're still fishing." She turned on the stairs and smiled up at him. "But you exert that charm of yours on the *old* ladies."

"As though I ever see any females old or young when you're in the room. I'll promise, little lady, if you'll promise never again to dance three times with that Bill Carter. I don't like the way he looks at you, as though you belonged specially to him."

"Silly. He's an old married man with a family and he's rather shy and heavy and feels at home with a girl he's known from a baby."

"Keep it to one dance."

J.R. looked up at their happy faces, their glowing eyes, as he bade them good night before they went out to the car where Ben had been waiting a half hour.

Snow fell on snow and most of the feet that passed up and down the avenue were encased in heavy overshoes and the fortress walls held out the cold as, day by day, Ben laid the logs that blazed and crackled cheerfully in the sittingroom.

Often after J.R. had retired for the night, Tom and Mary sat before that fireplace, feet toasting. Perhaps a little jealously he was watching a new radiance in her face as more than once she counted off the months on her fingers. "It will be late September or early October."

When she had first told him he had turned his head away quickly, an almost hurt look in his eyes as he ejaculated, "My God, so soon?"

One night she reached out for his hand. "Tom, dear, sometimes I think you are not so deliriously happy as I am about a baby coming. You do want him, don't you, darling?"

He held the hand in a grasp that almost hurt. "I want you. Of course I see that you being you— An heir, a son or daughter, for the family, the future, you know what I mean, all that seems inevitable. Don't ask me to get deliriously happy about sharing you, Mary."

"With your own son or daughter? Tom, its *your* baby."

He smiled into her eyes. "Give me time, Mary. I'll work up to it. The one thing you don't want me to do—the thing you hate is pretending."

"Heavens no. Never pretend, Tom." She suddenly laughed aloud. "Wait someday until a little fellow says, 'Daddy'; I can fairly hear you bragging about him, talking about 'my son, Joseph.' We will name him for Father, won't we? Joseph Kent Donovan?"

He gazed at her in amazement. "Good Lord, you even have him named. He's a reality to you. I haven't got to the point of believing in him yet."

She rose and wound her arms tightly about his neck. "Oh, Tom, you're a bit jealous."

"You know why."

"I know why, dear, but it is never going to make the slightest difference in our closeness. Nothing can ever change that. A dozen children around and still there would be you and me— really one, alone in the world. You know that?"

"Last fall when I first saw you, I wouldn't have believed such a thing possible. I know now."

"You're sure of all you wanted to be sure of?"

"I'm sure." He looked up at her soberly. "We'll accept Joseph or Louise or a little Mary but let's cut out that dozen."

Upstairs in his big bed, J.R. heard her laughing.

Sometimes in the late afternoon while he sat in the library reading his paper, J.R. again heard her laughing as they pelted each other with snowballs out in the drive. For a moment his eyes stared blankly at the newsprint as he murmured, "She is so young."

In the first week of April one began to see patches of brown earth or moist lawn as snowbanks melted. One early morning the sun had seemed bright but with the unpredictable changes of an April day, a light rain began to fall, forming a coat of ice on sidewalk and road. Mary happened to look out of a bedroom window as Tom's car turned with what seemed reckless speed into their drive. She saw him jump out, clear the steps almost in a bound and then, in what seemed but a moment, there were his steps on the stair, his voice calling, "Mary? Mary?"

She met him in the hall. Quickly and tenderly he took her in his arms. He was somewhat out of breath and waited a moment before answering her anxious, "Tom, you hardly made that turn. I was scared—"

He interrupted, "Mary, I've only seen you when everything has been happy. I'm not sure how you'll take other things." Gently he told her of an accident to her father, explaining details; how he was driving up the steep road back of the Post Office, how a coal truck skidded and smashed into his car. "The people who saw the accident got Dr. Porter and then came for me. We took him to the hospital. At first he was unconscious but he's all right now except that his right leg and right arm are pretty badly smashed up. Now put your coat on and I'll take you." He kissed her. "He'll want to see you immediately."

She remembered afterward that it was Tom who found her overshoes and helped her put on each garment. At the hospital door he parked, then turned to her. "You mustn't look scared. He's going to depend on you. Can't you pinch your cheeks a little?"

She smiled and looked gratefully at him.

A few weeks later J.R. was so homesick for the old house that they brought him home. A nurse was installed for he had no use of one arm and needed considerable help but he fought valiantly and by the time of the long summer days, he was managing crutches with help. Out on the porch where he could look across his lawn and enjoy his garden he received many visitors; Warren came nearly every evening, Lawrence canceled his usual vacation and Tom seemed always on the alert for any opportunity to assist him.

When Mary lay in bed beside Tom she felt as though some deep river flowed through her; she felt this yearning that became an ache low between her breasts until it became part of her heartbeats. It was a sort of ecstasy, part of her love for Tom. Creation? Out of her womb? Was this as near as any human being could come to knowing God?

Long before he was born, her love for her baby was so deep and so happy a thing that her face was physically changed. Sitting by her father, she talked of it to him. "If it is a boy we will name him Joseph Kent Donovan and I'll pray that he'll grow up to be like you, Daddy. Tom and I both want that."

Tom and I. J.R. watched them walking together in the garden on summer evenings; his eyes following them down the path, watching until they reappeared. One night as Mary came up the porch steps he looked at her strangely. When he murmured, "How are those zinnias doing, the ones old Carter gave you, Louise?" it was Tom who saw his fever and helped him to bed.

When a summer cold developed into pneumonia, J.R. seemed suddenly to have a premonition of the end. He talked to Pettie as her small hand clung to his arm. Of course he had expected to live many more years. Had he dreamed that his days of life and hard work were nearing an end he would not have gone into those new business ventures—matters that would need careful handling and negotiating. He needed another year or two.

He sent for Tom. With eyes fastened pleadingly on the young man's face he talked kindly. "Work closely with Warren, Tom. Keep this old house always for Pettie and her children."

Then he was struggling in an oxygen tent. One day when Mary looked through the little window he turned to her and she opened the small door. "Yes, Daddy, do you feel better?"

He smiled at her. "This fall, Pettie, have your mother's rose bushes hoed up and covered properly. I've always done it myself."

"Yes, Daddy."

He began, "Pettie—" He did not finish. No one would ever call her Pettie again.

PART II

DONOVAN'S WIFE

CHAPTER VI

There had always been an awkward constraint between Tom Donovan and his brother-in-law, Professor Lawrence Kent. One cold winter's day they stood a few feet apart before the fireplace in the sittingroom of the old brick house, watching Mary's laughing struggles to get the squirming baby's arms into the sleeves of a knitted jacket.

His lifelong affection for his younger sister shone in Lawrence's eyes as he smiled, "She has a merry love of little things."

There was undisguised irritation in Tom Donovan's voice. "You professors with your damned erudition should be compelled to indicate quotation marks when you talk."

Lawrence held up crooked fingers in good-natured mockery. "You poets are sensitive. It's a quote all right but my erudition falls short of knowing who is the author of the line. However, it fits Mary." He repeated, "She has a merry love of little things."

Tom Donovan extracted a cigarette from a newly opened pack, lighted it, threw the burning match into the grate fire and, with a characteristic upward toss of his head, swung quickly out of the room. From the hall he called, "I must get back to the office."

The laughter faded from Mary's face as she asked anxiously, "You'll be here for supper, Tom?"

He was getting into his great-coat with the beaver collar, pulling on his overshoes. Holding in one hand a cap from which dangled fur ear-pads—Tom hated the cold—he re-entered the room. Placing one arm possessively about Mary's shoulders, he bent over her, smiling as he laid his mouth against hers in a long,

41

an embarrassingly long, kiss. As she drew back, her eyes looking affectionately into his, he again pulled her close, kissing her several times. "You'll be here for supper, Tom?"

"I'll telephone about five." Then the quick, light step across the hall, the unnecessary slamming of the front door and presently the sound of a motor.

The jacket was but half on, yet her hands lay heavily resting against the baby's shoulder as she knitted her fine brows above troubled eyes. "Lawrence, this worries me. Tom doesn't like the baby. I don't think it's only that he doesn't like Joseph; I think he doesn't like babies."

Lawrence looked sharply at her as she sat in the low chair before the fire. There were red-yellow lights in her hair not unlike the sharp tongues of flame leaping up in the grate, licking at the black coals. Since her pregnancy and the birth of her baby, he had watched her change from a pretty girl into a beautiful young woman. Now there was a quizzical smile in his eyes, knowing how naturally she thought aloud when they were together. Queer thing about the Kents. Outside of their filial and brotherly relationships each member of the family had found himself friends with the others. It was nothing for which they felt they deserved the slightest credit. It did not always happen in other families; in fact, Lawrence gathered from his personal observations, that it did not happen often enough. The family blood-tie usually bound men through their lives and often through their final rest in the family burying ground, but the binding too often rubbed sensitive flesh into sore spots; sometimes into the tragedy of festering hate. The records of family lawsuits, the insidious motivation for suicide attested to that.

Mary added, "At first I thought that like some men, Tom didn't take to an infant; but now Joseph's a big boy, four months old; he has individuality; he's a special person and Tom doesn't like him."

He made a mistake. Used to unreserved expression between them he said, "Some men prefer the bower to the nursery." Seeing a shadow gather in her eyes, he jokingly held up two fingers, again crooking them, "Oh, I forgot. Melville, author of *Moby Dick* said that."

"Did he? I think I know exactly what he meant." She thought deeply a moment then, with a shrug she turned to the table and picked up a photograph, handing it to her brother.

He read at the bottom of the card, "Joseph Donovan, aged four months and twelve days—weight twenty-two and one half pounds." He laughed as he looked from the photograph to the baby. "What a pushover Father would have been for his name-sake. You know that boy's a spitting image of Grandfather Kent. A judicial expression on his wise little face, pugilistic shoulders bulging through all that finery. Embroidery's a joke on that mas-culine little fellow."

"Of course he isn't pretty—"

"Heaven forbid."

She rested her chin on the top of the baby's head and looked into the fire. "Lawrence, now that you're here for a few minutes, I want to ask you something. Now that I have a son to help inherit the earth, I wish I knew more about what the earth is likely to become. Of course I know about Mendel and the Men-delian Law; everyone knows that."

"Not quite everyone."

"Well, most of the reading public. Does all this knowledge of genes and chromosomes give us hope for bettering the human race?"

"Do you remember, Mary, one day Mother came home from a meeting of the Y.W.C.A. board? And how we laughed when she told us she had turned from a 'lady'-member into a red-headed Farnsworth? She had fought to have the place opened to the mill-girls, Poles, Lithuanians, Jews, Negroes. Do you remember how Mother loved this city? She loved its streets and houses and busi-ness enterprises and parks and trees and most of all its people. And did she know them! She knew them from Lucy's estate to the Negroes down on Pell Street. That afternoon when she had the fight with the board, she won. This is what she told them. 'Keeping the nails polished won't save the hand if paralysis is creeping down the arm.' Remember? That is the way she saw her city, her state and her country."

"Yes, I remember."

"Do you remember that Abraham Lincoln said the nation could not endure half slave and half free?"

"Of course. It took a civil war to make it endure."

"That's the whole answer, my dear. That's what your son is going to inherit—the new vision of man. The human race is more like a human body than we like to believe. A cancer in the Balkans, or in China, or Russia, or in South America is going to affect us, eventually destroy us if we don't cut that cancer out in time."

Mary smiled, "It's a wonderful vision, Lawrence. I'd still be inclined to start with the United States. Remember that old German adage? 'If each before his own door swept, the village would be clean.'"

"True enough but half the human race can't buy a broom. I'll bring you some good books to read."

"I'll read them; so will Mattie. She's a feminist. She believes in women."

"Don't you?"

She laughed merrily. "Mattie can tell you exactly what percent of the wealth of the United States is owned by women. It is a staggering figure. She can tell you by what alarming figures the women's vote now exceeds the men's vote. She then proves that all women have to do is unite and work together—organize like a union and take over the country, lock, stock and barrel. Little things like aptitude, training, even experience sound as easy to acquire as a new hat." Her merriment gave way to an expression of cold, sober disgust. "I'm afraid I see too clearly *how* women have acquired much of that wealth; what they have bartered on the open market in exchange for the gold. We have our own Milly Vaughan. She's about thirty, married to old Hiram near seventy. She keeps him very 'fond' of her and calculates when she'll be one of the richest women in the state. I don't think obtaining either a percentage of wealth or a percentage of votes is going to give women a majority percentage of influence."

Lawrence laughed heartily and turned away to find his hat and coat. At the door he looked back and remarked with studied casualness, "Some day soon, when you feel in the mood, Mr. Wainwright wants you to come down to the bank and discuss your own wealth. The final papers in the settlement are ready for your signature."

She looked up uneasily, "Is there going to be plenty of money? Father was worried about finances just before he died. Will there be enough money for Tom? He says he is going to need a lot to hold those investments of Father's?"

"Why try to hold them?"

She looked perplexed. "Of course, that would be my reaction but Tom feels quite strongly about holding onto them. He says those investments involve a lot of money which we ought not to lose."

He continued to speak lightly. "Father left this house to you, dear, and with it a very substantial income from money invested in bonds, stocks and real estate. Watch out about that income. If you leave the principal intact you will always have your home and be comfortably well off. Added to that, if Tom brings in a good amount from the business you will be more than easy in money matters."

"That is very comforting." She smiled brightly. "Perhaps, Lawrence, if you or I were in the business we would feel differently about trying to hold these investments."

He was fastening the buckle on his overshoe. He finished, then looked at her earnestly. "*No*, Mary." He went on with a note of pleading in his voice. "Now listen carefully, for this may affect your entire future. A few years before Father's death, he had the opportunity to take over what must eventually become an addition to the business section of Main Street. He also bought up a fairly large tract of land in the suburbs. He would have, in the course of a few years, torn down old tenements as leases matured, put up modern buildings, carried the property in the meantime, paying taxes and assessments of various kinds.

"He was a lawyer and a trusted business man. He would have

built roads, opened the land, built and sold houses and little by little consolidated his holdings and neither you nor I would have known why we were richer.

"Neither Tom nor Warren can take his place. Already, they are having difficulty meeting the tax bills. In no time they will want more money and more money to hold on. Don't jeopardize what you have. You do understand?"

"Why, even Joseph could understand that. I'll go soon to see Mr. Wainwright. The truth is—I can't bear an hour away from this little 'brute' as you call him. I'm jealous of nurse when she wheels him up and down the avenue."

He took a step toward her and spoke gravely. "I understand that. Any Kent would understand it but, Mary, remember Tom is not a Kent. That sort of thing was all right with our parents but with another sort of man it won't do. Forgive my clumsy butting in."

She looked astonished. "First, Lawrence, you couldn't butt in. Say whatever's on your mind. Second, don't you know that Tom is always first? He will always be first."

He said gently, "We've all known that for a long time, Mary."

He was gone. She held the baby tightly in her arms, her lips pressed against the soft skin of his cheek. Over his head her eyes stared into the fire and in those eyes there was growing uncertainty. She knew the implications in those words, "Some men prefer the bower to the nursery." She had learned much since she had loved and married Tom Donovan.

CHAPTER VII

She did not need the maid to call her to the phone. She was listening for the ring as five o'clock approached. Almost as in the first days of their courtship, the warmth of her love seemed to permeate not only her heart but every fiber of her body as she heard the clear tones of his voice, "Mary?" He pronounced it as though it had three syllables, "Ma-a-ry?"

"Yes, dear."

"I'll be up in half an hour. What about an early dinner? This cold makes me ravenous."

"I'll tell cook."

"Just you and me alone, darling?"

"Yes, dear."

For a moment she sat smiling at the impersonal mechanism. Who were these old cynics who said the glamour wore off after the first baby came? She jumped up, looked again at the clock and calculated. No, there would not be time for her to give Joseph his bath. She must leave for nurse that coveted pleasure tonight. She must dress for Tom.

Personally she would have enjoyed wrapping a rubber apron over her warm wool dress, and letting Tom find her in the nursery soaping the husky boy as he blinked and gurgled and kicked in his tub. Tom would kiss her and they would quarrel over which one would carry him to his crib. That was the picture clear in her mind which she had hitherto imagined natural, even inevitable; now, as she opened her closet door, scanning the gowns, her lips twisted into something less than a smile. That was not what Tom wanted. He was always so pleased when he came home and found her waiting, unemployed, "dressed" for him as in the days when they first met.

It was curious about Tom. Although she would not allow the words to form definitely in her mind, she knew that he was assertively and aggressively taking over the role of "lord of the manor." He walked through the large rooms filled with old mahogany, rich rugs, costly hangings and fine paintings, not to mention her father's and grandfather's library, quite as though he were inspecting a collection which he had himself assembled. At the table he demanded more formal service than the Kents had ever cared about. He spoke sharply if Ben allowed the heat to diminish in the evening or failed to provide sufficient logs for their bedroom fireplace.

Then there was the matter of clothes—the splendid great-coat with an ostentatious beaver collar, the fine suits and assortments of shoes, ties and initialed handkerchiefs. Once when she had teased him and accused him of vanity, he had turned quickly, taking her into his arms. "Don't, Mary. Don't laugh at that. Only you could understand, darling, that I've never had anything in my life. You're the only person I've ever seen who could know that and not look down at me. You're the only person who could love a man so much as not to see his shabby clothes. I can tell you and only you that when one shirt wore out I could never be sure there would be another to replace it. I've had shoes resoled until the uppers wouldn't hold the stitches; I've watched the seat of my trousers daily, dreading to see the light of day through the cloth. Darling, do you grudge me the joy of owning two shirts?"

Her arms had strained about his shoulders. "Oh, Tom, always explain to me when I don't understand."

Now, on this cold winter night, her fingers pulled and pushed at the skirts. She chose one of her loveliest silks, a copper-colored gown that Tom loved. She would shiver all evening after taking off her wool dress. What of that?

She was standing near the fireplace when he came in. Instead of coming directly to her, he stopped at the door and stood looking at her, his head tipped back, eyes smiling under his long lashes. "Don't move a step. If I were only an artist and could paint you in that gown with that light on your hair. My Mary, I love you."

Her cheeks flushed, partly with pleasure and partly with embarrassment for fear Fanny, passing through the hall, had heard him talk like that. Under this old roof where love had always dwelt, no one had ever talked out loud about love or lovers.

No one had ever talked at the old mahogany table as Tom did on that cold winter night when Mary sat in her mother's place and tried not to shiver in her copper-colored silk dress.

It happened that Mattie had used the remainder of a roast to make a stew, one of those tasty, hearty stews that would have made J.R.'s eyes light up with pleasurable anticipation as he removed the cover from the old blue and white tureen and savored the fragrance of the steaming dish. Mattie never trusted that tureen to a serving maid but carried it in herself. How confidently she had stood, planted firmly on her low-heeled shoes, amply filling her starched blue gingham dress, explaining what herbs she had used for flavoring.

One could remember J.R.'s smile as he asked, "Plenty of barley, Mattie?" The heavy silver ladle was an adequate tool for his man's hand as he filled plate after plate and Fanny carried them about the table. How hungrily the eyes of the boys followed the dishes; how gently but firmly Mother said, "Don't wolf your food, Gordon." Gordon had wolfed everything in life—food, sleep, work, play, college, his crew, his races, his dances, then war and flying. . . .

Memories were suddenly sharp in Mary's eyes as they two, alone, took their places at the old table.

Judge Kent, sitting in his library far into the night, fuming with righteous anger because there was such a thing as a retirement age. "Imbeciles! What difference does it make whether a man is seventy or one hundred and seventy if he is on his toes and knows his stuff. As soon as he has proved that he knows something about Law and human nature, he is retired and some youngster who has to start from scratch is put in his place."

As her fingers grew awkward and numb with cold, her eyes were curiously bright and there was a glint of laughter in them. She knew that through every fiber of her being she too was steeped in that zest for life—the homely, the vital, the everyday, the essential, yes, all the little things that added up to the big things. Lawrence had said it, she had "a merry love of little things."

Mattie did not come in tonight. It was Fanny, in black uniform and dainty white apron and cap who carefully set the tureen before Tom. Her voice expressed timidity, "Mattie says, would you prefer to have the stew served in the kitchen?"

"Stew! Stew again? My Lord, we live on leftovers. Stews and bread-pudding. Well, leave it."

When Fanny hurried from the room, Mary's brows were puckered. "Tom, dear, you scared Fanny half out of her wits."

"Aren't we feeding four or five adults besides ourselves? Why in hell can't they eat up the scraps? Five adults and a baby."

She laughed, "We can't feed the stew or bread-pudding to the baby quite yet."

"It's the *pièce de résistance* of Child's and the Automats. I've come direct from New York stew to Massachusetts stew; from Boston beans to what seems to be the original home of beans. Can't we have any decent food on our menus?"

"We'll avoid it after this, only—"

"Only what?"

"I think I'm partial to stew. My entire family liked stew."

"Darling! With all your wealth and position what country bumpkins your whole family have been. To a cosmopolite, you can't believe how provincial you are. Up and down this supposedly aristocratic avenue they're one and all as bucolic as cows." He tilted back his head as if appraising her. "Yes, my darling, if you will keep looking as beautiful as you are tonight, I'll count the days and nights until I can show you off in certain places in New York. They don't feed on stew. At present Warren would collapse if I suggested leaving that office for two days."

He talked of the food served in some famous hotels and night clubs; he tossed the word "caviar" about lightly.

"You're a red-head; you dote on salads and cold dishes, just like Cleopatra, the famous red-headed beauty of the world. Her hair was, I believe, dark red; yours is sandy-red but very beautiful. I wonder if she had your creamy white skin—satin on every inch of your body." Fanny came in with the salad bowl, unavoidably hearing the last remark.

"Do you know what Cleopatra ate? A chilled melon with sugar-filled, tiny silver onions and eaten with a one-pronged golden fork."

He rubbed a hand across his eyes as though obliterating a painful vision. "You and your father and your plain lettuce! I've seen your father cut up a dish of lettuce, put on milk and sugar and eat it like porridge. Turning a salad into a pudding!"

He talked of lettuce cups filled with crab meat or the white meat of chicken, of molds of grapes in gelatine served with watercress, anchovy paste, chives and parsley, of avocado pears. "Someday you and I will eat where salad is an art, not a pudding."

However, they were both eating their stew as he talked fluently. He turned to other manifestations of provincialism. "Look at that Carter across the avenue. He was offered a junior partnership in one of the big firms in New York and refused the offer because he preferred to hang out his shingle in his home town. Didn't want to leave Mama I suppose. Look at our own brother, Lawrence. No one to see him standing in that sittingroom today, wearing baggy trousers that hadn't been pressed for six months, would dream he was a Phi Beta Kappa, Harvard-crew man. He takes a job in a little fresh-water college to be near Mama. The only party he has given in a year was one to see his night-blooming cereus, and they served hot cocoa for refreshments. Hot cocoa! Someday I'll write Lawrence up in a funny story. The only trouble would be lack of action. He never *does* anything, never gets anywhere. He thinks but he doesn't feel."

In the passing of a second, with startling clearness, she saw Lawrence standing at the library door looking at J.R.'s head bent over the telegram. She heard his one word, "Gordon?" She had listened to him crying in the night. And Lawrence, choking over the words, before their mother's funeral: "It's her hair, Mary, on her forehead. It isn't natural; can't you fix it?" She wasn't sure that Lawrence now might not be refusing offers of positions merely to be near her, Mary, if she needed help. She said sharply, "Tom, please *never* discuss Lawrence." Then she laughed. "You've gone on a rampage tonight. I wonder if I'll ever dare look at stew again. Here's some fresh apple pie; perhaps that will redeem the meal."

In all their previous bucolic life, the Kents had had tea with their evening "supper" but now coffee was served before the fireplace, with cognac which Tom procured from some secret source at some fabulous price.

As she stood a moment before the blazing fire, she remembered Lawrence in that very spot telling them he had enlisted. "I'm going to take Gordon's place." Her mother's head dropped forward as though the neck had been broken. Her father stared at the boy, then answered evenly, "Of course; I'm too old."

Now she sat close to the fire. She was dressed for Tom tonight so she would be beautiful and gay—and cold.

He lit a cigarette and handed it to her. He was pleased. "You smoke like a veteran, charmingly." He poured cognac into her glass and stood before the fire, coffee cup in hand, smiling down at her. "Forgive me, darling. I was an awful grouch through dinner."

"I understand, Tom. You have lived out in the world and never been used to family life. I suppose families that are closely knit together, I mean families where there are grandparents down to babies and death and birth—long years and life close together, they get to be a little world by themselves, especially if they are all congenial friends. They never realize they are provincial. Now we have our own little family, you'll begin to feel differently about many things. I do understand, dear."

"You understand so little, you innocent! We're not going to be like that at all." There was a glint of amusement in his eyes. "I honestly begin to think you would have welcomed being a bride in your grandmother's age when a girl married, put on a cap and long skirt, retired from 'conquest to the cradle-side.' She bore a dozen children, lived the life of a drudge and died at fifty or under, an old woman."

She was amused. "The ones I've known and heard about lived to be eighty or ninety and managed to be mighty important, some of them too important for comfort—like Aunt Letitia Farnsworth." There was still gaiety in her laugh. "Do you know, Tom, you are completely adolescent in your view of marriage?"

"Now really!"

"Yes."

He laid his hands tenderly on her shoulders, looking into her eyes. "Really!"

"I mean it. You are looking at marriage with the eyes of a schoolboy. He sees only the falling in love, the thrill of the beginning, half a dozen beginnings. He never does see—" Her eyes widened as the glow deepened in them.

"The what?"

"The deep, steady, really wonderful companionship and—I'd call it partnership, that grows and grows through troubles and happiness and sorrow. I grew up in such a home. Daddy was always lonesome for Mother no matter how hard I tried to fill her place." She wound her arms about his neck and laid her cheek against his. "Tom, dear, that's what I want for us. We won't always have to use words. I want to be sure, day and night, that the something my mother and father had will be ours."

He walked to the table, lit another cigarette and extinguished the match. He stood for some time pounding the stub on the tray, then he turned, looking searchingly at her. "You know, my Mary, I've told you that I never fell in love before. It's a funny thing about you. I'm most in love with you when I'm away from you."

"How awful, Tom!"

"You don't get it. When I'm with you, I can hardly keep my hands off you. I tell you the truth. I love you, I adore you. But —when I'm away, you haunt me. I get panicky. I don't believe you love me. I'm terrified you love your ideal of what I ought to be."

"You're crazy. I loved even the grouch at the dinner table. I'm hopeless."

"Stay hopeless, Mary. Promise me?"

"Until death do us part."

They sat before the fire but, even as he glanced over the paper, she picked up none of her books. He did not like to have her lose herself in a book; he found it boring to listen to a recital of the cunning things the baby did; he could get irritable in a moment if she asked questions about Warren, the business and the office, snapping, "Do I have to live through hell all day with that tight-fisted boob, Warren, then come home to go over it all with you at night?"

Setting down her glass, she smiled, "That cognac burns. I'm afraid your bootlegger's filling it with red pepper. Lawrence says all the business about the will is finished. I can come in to sign papers any day now. Because I own this house and the double house and two small houses, I'm going to get a ledger, be methodical and keep my books and accounts as Father did."

He asked pleasantly, "You have stocks and bonds which could be liquidated if we can't save those investments any other way?"

"I don't know what I have yet. I know it takes a great deal of money to run this place and be ready for taxes, repairs, wages, food bills, clothing bills and—" she thought deeply —"and I must never forget that I must preserve everything for Joseph and for other children we may have."

He rose, leaving her abruptly and went into the library. She waited a while then, when he did not return, she walked through the hall and looked into the room. He was sitting at old Judge Kent's desk writing on a sheet of paper. He looked up at her. "Forgive me, darling. I wanted to put something down."

It had happened before. She knew it was a poem. What right had Lawrence to smile? He had never read one of Tom's poems; neither had she.

After J.R.'s death, Tom had appropriated the old desk. In one of the deep drawers he kept a large green-covered scrapbook and an assortment of pads and pencils and various notebooks and, in his pocket, he carried the key.

Now, standing in the doorway, she watched him close the notebook. She said wonderingly, "But, Tom, I can't imagine your having anything in your life that seems to mean so much to you as your poems and never show them to me. If you love them, I'd love them."

"I don't love them, Mary. Perhaps someday I'll learn how to write what I want to write." He looked down at the book. "They're not your kind of thought."

"I don't want to read my kind of thought. I can understand Shakespeare and Browning and Amy Lowell and James Whitcomb Riley and Edgar Guest and Gertrude Stein. Why not try me on Tom Donovan? I'm not supposed to be dumb."

"You're sometimes not dumb enough. You're not dumb but you're puritanical and narrow and—" seeing the color flame in her face—"and a red-head. See, you were angry, furiously angry with me in that second. Wait, darling, I'll polish them and show them to you."

"Now I'm consumed with curiosity."

He looked up teasingly at her. "You've been trained all through your life to be a lady—controlled, soft-spoken, gentle. That's all an aristocratic veneer. Underneath you're a hot-blooded red-head. Don't I sleep with you?"

She listened, her eyes glistening, a deep burning reaching down into her throat and chest. The mockery in her voice just escaped sarcasm. "While you're writing an ode to Cleopatra and her silver onions, I'll look in the nursery at Joseph."

"Get ready for bed, darling. I'll be up in a few minutes. You know I'm in love with you."

Yes, she knew. She mounted the stairs slowly.

CHAPTER VIII

She stopped at the nursery door but it was too late. Nurse had put the light out which meant that she and the baby were both asleep. For the second time that evening she felt that her desire to see and touch the baby had become a need. Suddenly the want tortured her, the want to look a moment at the little fellow, listen to his breathing, find a physical outlet for the surge of emotion that, in her mind, she could liken only to a river flowing down through her. Her love for them both. Sometimes the river flowed through a deep, quiet channel; then, without warning, it flooded and her chest could not compass the riotous element.

She smiled at her own foolishness thinking of him lying half turned on his full, round stomach. She saw his fist stuck out. He wasn't pretty and that knowledge intensified her love for him a hundredfold. She bit her lips hard as she thought, "How I love them both. When he gets a little older his father will feel this way about him."

She went into the master bedroom, the large room which she and Tom had taken over after J.R.'s death. There were the windows on two sides with the English cretonne draperies reaching to the floor. In winter that floor was covered with a dark red velvet carpet but in summer this was taken up and blue cotton scatter rugs took its place.

She had been pleased because the room seemed to fascinate Tom. She had been amused when he stood studying the bed. "Lawrence says that bed wasn't made; it was built—like a house. I remember Grandmother telling us that on bitter nights before they put in central heating, you could find her and Grandfather, the nursing baby and the next larger child all snuggled up together."

Tom had nodded and stared at the bed. "What's the wood?"

"Cherry. The chest of drawers, bureau, the chairs and I think loveliest of all this dressing table, were made to order. In those days people ordered their furniture made. This was made by a Scotch cabinet maker but the carving was done by an Italian from New York."

"You mean some ordered furniture made and some did the making. Yes, it's like a house, built for the entire family. Your great-grandfather is the pompous ass in the oil over the mantel in the diningroom?"

"Yes. Only I don't think he was really a pompous ass at all. Those were his Sunday clothes and I'm sure his hair was not combed like that five minutes before or five minutes after his sittings for the portrait. He was a pioneer in these parts. He pushed his own plow behind his own work horses when he came into what they called the West, meaning any place west of Boston.

His brother who settled in the Mohawk Valley had gone much farther west."

There had been an edge in her voice. "Anyway he and Great-grandfather Farnsworth gave this community two things of importance—"

There had been an irritable note in his voice, "What two things?"

"The cotton mills and the elms. You know the pioneers planted the elms; they didn't just cover the land like dandelions. Even these long avenues were planted—probably with many a back-ache."

"The cotton mills turned out to be the really important thing. Don't maples grow faster, give as much shade and sugar besides?"

"Yes—but there's nothing quite like an elm." A little stubbornly she had held out for her favorite tree.

"So you worship your elm and you worship the old man who gave you the mills and the money." He had been studying the bed, his hands sliding along the smooth footboard; then he turned to her with something of insolence in his eyes. "That's what I'm trying to tell you. All you Kents and Farnsworths are, at heart, snobs, looking down at people whose grandfathers didn't start the mills but now work in them."

"Tom!" Her eyes had suddenly filled with tears. "What's the matter with you? How can you say that to me? I married you and I love you."

Flinging himself around, he seized her and almost smothered her with passionate kisses. "Mary," he had breathed hard into her neck, "I'm the very Devil. Lord! you are wonderful. You are the most wonderful person I've ever known on earth. Sometimes I can't believe you. I'm not worth your little finger, dear."

"If you were a little boy, I'd use the slipper on you, Tom Donovan."

A few minutes later they were laughing uproariously at three oil paintings—standing with shoulders touching, fingers inter-twined. He asked, "'Who did them?"

"Grandmother Farnsworth. She wasn't a 'master,' was she?"

"I like them. Damn it, they look modern. They are done with a dash and abandon, free, impressionistic and a riot of color. Look at that rakish leghorn hat with the funny fruit for trimming. She had a sense of humor. I like this woman under the umbrella, sitting on the sand by the sea."

She laughed, "We always called her the drunken idiot. One cheek's bashed in and she lacks an ear. I think Grandmother did like her toddy. She always called it sherry."

"What was her name?"

"Nancy Farnsworth." She had added, "I'm sure she'd say, 'Off to the attic with them.'"

"Nothing of the kind. I'm all for the old lady who could paint them. They'll be nice warm spots of color when the thermometer drops below zero."

Now, it was the second winter and Mary's eyes happened to rest on those warm spots of color as she began to unfasten her dress, standing as close to the burning logs as she dared. Carefully she smoothed the copper-colored silk and hung it in the closet. Again she stood under the oil and examined it. Gordon had been an adept at imitating the intoning of some rector who read to them at prep school. She could almost hear his voice, "The drunken idiot of a one-eared woman with the bashed-in face in the bright red dress under the purple umbrella by the blue-green sea under the blue sky dreaming of a dark lover with her feeble brain." She chuckled, "I'm another drunken idiot of a woman. It's something to know it; I wouldn't have it otherwise."

She had put on the warmest nightgown she could find, wrapped a warm flannel bathrobe about her and was slipping her feet into fleece-lined bedroom booties when the door opened and Tom came in carrying a tray. Long afterward she would remember that there were on the tray a cut lemon, a jug steaming vapor and a brown bottle of whiskey.

As he pushed the door with his foot until it slammed shut, his eyes, smiling, almost feverishly bright, met and held hers. Not with thought but with all her senses she knew that unashamed sex, an integral part of their love, had preceded him into the room.

She saw the next two hours as though they were already in the past.

His face was flushed—he had already been sampling the drink—his eyes wavered, then steadied as he stood looking at her. Why did her brain suddenly clear and become soberly active? She turned away and stood looking down into the fire. Why, in that moment, did she find herself hungering to be something more to her husband than a drunken idiot of a woman? As clearly as though it were a tangible thing, she wanted to go quietly to bed, rest in his arms, talk as fathers and mothers talk about their children, their plans, their dreams, then sleep in deep security and peace.

He set the tray down and looked at her. "For god's sake, Mary, it's warm as toast here. I just sent that lazy coon to stir up the fire. Take off that old woman's flannel." He turned around and flung open her bureau drawer. "You have these gorgeous negligees and you keep them in bureau drawers. Saving them for Joseph?"

She tried to smile but the implications made her cringe. Roughly, with hands not too steady, he stripped off the flannel and kicked it across the room. "Let me look at you while I undress."

"You'll look at me in a hospital if I get pneumonia."

"There's no ice water in your veins."

A few minutes later he was dressing her in the exquisite lingerie, pulling the pins out of her hair, running his hands lovingly through the red-blond shower, pushing it back from her forehead then, after pulling her down into the armchair by the fire, he began to pour drinks.

"Just hot water and lemon for me, please, Tom."

He poured some whiskey into her glass smiling, "Who is it that is always saying that we must do everything together?"

"Not drink whiskey."

"Everything, darling."

"Even read your poems?"

"Some day soon. I'm going to begin to educate you for them."

The hot drink was good. When he put the glasses and tray aside he stood looking at her. "Mary, that's the way I'd like to keep you looking every day of our lives." Between his passionate kisses he murmured, "That firelight on your hair and that color in your face and that light in your eyes. Do you know, darling, that you have the most beautiful eyes I've ever looked into? Do you know I love you? Do you know you are my *woman?* A million wives can't hear their husbands say that."

She laughed aloud. "Perhaps a million wives neither expect nor want to hear their husbands say that. We take some things for granted."

"Darling, don't forget that a wife has to work hard—sometimes damned hard—to keep her husband saying that."

Her hand was too steady as she smoothed his hair and her voice too light as she laughed, "It would be a pity to waste a valuable education on me. Now don't start in with all that about what French women or sophisticated New York women do and say. In the first place I don't believe you know half you pretend to know about women and love and I don't believe any of it anyway. I don't believe French women or German women or Russian or Hindoo or New York or Greenwich Village women are much different the world over. Anyway—I'm just an average, loving wife so don't—"

"Don't what?"

It was as though she were living on two planes. Her lips pressed against his forehead. "What I mean, dear, is that we must be really and truly everything to each other. Lovers of course but we're father and mother—"

"Forget that tonight. You're mine, not Joseph's. Any real woman would tell you that she'd rather part with six children than with her lover."

"That's that mythical French woman of yours talking now." She laughed again, "Or perhaps that idiot up there under the purple umbrella said that."

He stopped her lips with a pressure that pushed her head far back. "Mary? Ma-a-ry? You love me? You want me?" She would hear that sudden tremulous earnestness in his voice, some pathetic yearning for her to want him, as long as she lived. Her face grew sober and she answered gently, "Yes, Tom dear, I want you. I love you. I'll want you and love you all my life. I'm that kind of person." Then she repeated softly, "Through sickness and health, for better or worse, till death do us part. I promise you." With every pulse beat, with all her being she must hold those words close. Nothing—nothing must change that.

An hour later he was lying with his head pillowed on her breast. He was panting, exhausted, and again it was as though she were two creatures each living on a different plane. When and where had she heard Lawrence talking about "passion and death"? What did he mean when he said they went hand in hand? She remembered; he had been explaining some scientific study of suicide—uncontrolled emotions, unbridled passion—passion and death—hand in hand.

She shivered a little. "Tom, dear, sleepy? Talk to me."

"What do you want to talk about?"

"Our children and our home."

"Our children? You have him."

"*We* have Joseph but of course we're going to have other children. In fact, I want my next baby. I think it is wonderful to have children near an age."

How quickly an edge could come in his voice. "There's nothing wonderful about it. It ruins a woman, turns her into a dull, domestic animal—a cow. Having children's a disgusting procedure, dangerous and terrifying. I never want to risk you again. I never want to live through another night like that when that brat wouldn't get born and every minute I thought that old fool of a doctor would come out to tell me you were dead. It's terrifying."

She laughed gaily. "Leave the terror for me, dear. I never had the slightest fear and Dr. Porter said I was as stoical about pain as a Japanese woman and I guess that's high praise. You don't have the babies."

"You're not going to again. Do you want a lover or a boarder called Papa?"

"I want both."

"To hell with it. Let the cats and pigs breed. There are too many people on the earth now."

"Where would you be if your father and mother had said that?"

"Except for you, I'd be where and what I'd prefer to be—nonexistent."

She answered quietly, "We'll talk it over someday soon. Better get to sleep."

"Yes. Warren will be displeased with his errand boy if he's not bright in the morning." He added slowly, "Until I knew you there never was a year or day in my life when I wouldn't have been better off if my father and mother hadn't bred. You're not such an imbecile as to imagine they ever wanted me, are you?"

"You don't know."

"The orphan asylum said she was a refined lady—there was no father. I'm not a blockhead."

"Go to sleep, dear."

Soon he lay breathing evenly and she knew he slept. When her arm grew numb she gently removed his head; then she lay with wide-open eyes staring at faint shadows wavering across the ceiling as the branches of the tall elms were whipped by the icy wind outside.

Love. Could the word connote two different worlds of meaning to two people? Love. She saw her father and mother sleeping in this bed together through most of a lifetime, getting to look alike, talk alike, think alike, living for each other. She saw her father come in at supper time, hanging up his coat as her mother called, "Well, Jo, did it go all right?" Her father would lean over, touch Mother's cheek with his lips, open his paper and smile at her, "Everything's signed and sealed." That was love. Her father and mother taking turns sitting night after night by Grandfather toward the last, helping him; someone close by as he crossed the bar. That was love.

She saw a children's playground down near the cotton mills.

That grandmother, Nancy Farnsworth, who had painted the idiot woman, had bought four old tenement buildings, had them demolished, built a fence around the block and filled the space with swings, trapezes, sand boxes. That was love. It was big; it was sure, penetrating, all-embracing.

Then the personal love between a man and woman. From a bewildering, breath-taking wonder in the beginning, it grew through the years and finally became part of the very breath one drew; permeated every thought and heartbeat. Cognac, negligees and passion seemed like a sideshow.

Restlessly she turned. Some time ago, Lawrence had published an article examining the source materials of the mediaeval tale of Tristram and Iseult. He traced its influence through the centuries as it was used by poets greater than the original authors. He spoke of Shelley, Montaigne, Browning, Tennyson, Anatole France and our own Robinson. But, Lawrence questioned, had it ever been a love story at all? It had come from the outside not from within. It had been born of a love potion which they drank. Passion and death. Humorously he had asked why someone did not write of Tristram the great liar. He had compared the tale to the great love stories; how Aucassin's "heart was ever set on his fair friend, Nicolette."

Mary turned restlessly on her pillow. Her heart warmed to those words, "his fair friend." She smiled as she remembered, "'Elaine beheld Sir Launcelot *wonderingly*." That was love—something from within—palm touching palm, eyes meeting eyes. Romeo did not need a love potion. Tonight she repeated,

> "Sleep dwell upon thine eyes, peace in thy breast!
> Would I were sleep and peace, so sweet to rest!"

Fire is a beautiful spectacle but one does not want it to consume one's house.

She was very young. Tom was still young and all their life lay before them. She would, day by day, show her husband what she meant by love. She reasoned clearly that it was always the things he had never had, the life he had never experienced, that he resented. It was not her great-greats, as he called them, but his lack of great-greats that he hated. How trivial was all that compared to their love for each other!

CHAPTER IX

Sometime during the night the bitter wind had died down and snow was now falling steadily. Mary waked to an instant sense of quiet as though the entire world were hushed with snow.

The door opened softly and Ben tiptoed in carrying a large basket. Mary watched him gently ease the window shut, then lay first his kindlings then his three logs in the grate, light the paper and set the screen in place.

"Thanks, Ben."

"You're welcome Miss Mary."

"How's the baby?"

"Just fine. The new formula works all right."

"Joseph and your baby are almost twins."

He smiled as he tiptoed out of the room.

Lying with head propped high on the pillow, Mary watched the kindlings ignite, then the little curls of flame lick the logs. She knew there was more difference between two black men or two white men than between a black and a white man, scientifically, biologically, emotionally. There was Ben. His grandfather had been a fugitive slave during the Civil War, passed through New York State, up through that Mohawk Valley underground to Canada but whether he ever reached Canada or not would never be known because he was not heard from again. Ben, an ignorant boy, had made his way north and finally found employment with J.R. Now he was married, had a little house and two boys, his baby fed from the same formula as the doctor prescribed for Joseph. His children would be educated. Mary would see that this "twin" of Joseph's, little Monty, would get all the education he could take.

She was dressing by the warm fire as Tom sat up in bed, stretched and looked at her through half-closed eyes. "You wake up like an eager, excited child."

"That's the way I feel."

"I suppose you love this snow."

"Guilty. I even love what someone labeled, 'this wonderful thing called a day.'"

He watched her as he repeated, "'This wonderful thing called a day.' You're making a fool of me. I swear I never dreamed I could be in love with a woman before breakfast."

It was a morning crowded full of happiness; there was no grouch at the breakfast table. Tom smiled at her, "Buckwheat cakes and maple syrup. Taste that and see if there's anything left to say for your elms. Maples for me."

Ben got the drive shoveled out in time and Tom held her close in his arms and kissed her before he drove away. She went with him to the side door. He whispered, "You were wonderful last night."

"What about this morning?"

"I tell you, you're making a fool of me. I love you even in the morning."

She ran lightly up to the nursery.

Later, men and boys were shoveling the walks, and the plow went up and down the avenue noisily whirring as the brushes tossed the snow, heaping it into piles on either side of the road. She raised the window and called down to Ben, "Are the trolleys running?"

"Oh yes, Miss Mary."

She put on her fur coat, her overshoes and, with hands snug in her muff, she walked and slid over the snow-packed walks to the trolley car which ran on a parallel street below them.

One could walk miles, without fatigue, on such a day and think clearly. Tom had never known love. With infinite patience she would change his attitude toward Joseph, toward companionship, toward children in a home. Passing a large, white Colonial house, someone rapped on a window and waved to her. In reply, she threw a kiss to one of her girlhood friends. Her face sobered as she thought how too many of these friends were disappearing from her life because of Tom's possessive, "just you and me alone, darling?"

On the few occasions when they went out to some dinner or reception, people were most cordial to Tom. Men seemed eager to know him better for, after all, hadn't he stepped into J. R. Kent's shoes and money? She had had a slight twinge of jealousy, one evening at a dance when Milly Vaughan, had flirted outrageously with him. She had been shocked later, when, after she mentioned Milly, he answered, "Oh, yes, I know that kind. Your so-called good society is full to overflowing with women hanging on, like leeches, to the old money-bags they have married while they hunt like cats after birds, for affairs with some younger man. To hell with them."

She must gradually resume social life because, as her children grew up, they must enjoy friendships and the companionship of boys and girls in their own set just as she had. Her children. As naturally as breathing she thought of herself as the mother of children.

After passing through the depths and heights of that experience —conception, the carrying, the birth of Joseph and now her love for him, she knew something which she could not explain to anyone. It was merely a conceit of her own mind yet she felt that somewhere in the very depths of her flowed that river, quiet in its channel now. The river was love. It encompassed Tom, her home, her child, even her city with its people.

She had come to the bank, a large building dignifying one of the busy corners of the city. She paused a moment before passing between two marble columns at the entrance, to readjust her mind to the realities of business. Rivers of love and stocks and bonds and rentals from double houses and small single houses somehow did not mix. Perhaps Tom was right when he so often called her "terribly young."

No. Standing aside near one of the pillars, she watched the activities of the street for a moment. That which she had experienced in burying her father and mother, giving birth to her child, was old. Even her thoughts were old, old as life itself. Her face grew serious. That river deep down in a woman was creation—was God. God is love. She watched the people passing. Only a few years before, the World War had ended. There were widows passing, widows with empty hearts and toilworn hands. There were men passing whose sons lay moldering in foreign soil. There was Gordon, not forgotten. One heart could not bear to know all the sorrow hidden under tweed coats and fur jackets.

An attendant turned the revolving door and a few minutes later she was seated opposite Mr. Wainwright in his private office. Of course they talked first of J.R., then of the will and his plans, then of the papers before her. The signing over, he spoke again of the business and, with sharp eyes watching her from under heavy eyebrows, he frankly talked about her husband.

"Tom has taken"—he emphasized the word "taken"—"authority which J.R. intended his sharing with Warren. Warren has grown up in the business, always known the money end and he's a man of good judgment. He may seem rather commonplace personally and he's slow and methodical and cautious and probably exasperates your nervous, impetuous husband."

Mary smiled pleasantly. "I know, Mr. Wainwright. Probably Warren finds Tom unpredictable also. Sometimes I do myself."

"The point is, Mary, you have one of two courses to pursue. First, as his confidant I know that, in spite of difficult financial times, J.R. could have held that investment. Had he lived he would have greatly increased his wealth. That's water over the dam. Here are your two courses. Either take what seems to me an unjustifiable risk and try to hold it or take the loss, forget it and hang onto what you have. Your stocks and bonds and rents are gilt-edged investments. You can surely keep your home and live comfortably. Business will pick up again and Tom is a good salesman. That charming voice of his can bamboozle a woman into buying an acre of rock or swamp.

"This is my advice: keep the real estate business going; keep Warren at the books. Everything else is in your name. Keep it there for your security and for your children." He laid his hand on hers. "You know I'm thinking of J. R. Kent as I talk."

She walked out into the noonday bustle of the street where the sun on the snow was almost blinding. Perhaps the plunge into the reality of business was a greater shock than she had anticipated. At any rate, she felt confused, worried and suddenly impatient to have the entire matter settled. She was like J.R. in her dislike of indecision.

She would do that which she had not done since her father's death; she would go to the office and get Tom and Warren to go over matters with her and make that decision now. Yes, this very day, this minute. In fact, she had already decided.

Between the snappy cold of the day and her excitement her cheeks flamed with color as she stepped into the office. A young man fairly sprang to attention. His words halted her. "Mr. Donovan is not here today."

"Oh," she stopped. "He is out to lunch?"

"He hasn't been in today."

Without a moment's hesitation, "I want to see Mr. Warren."

She and Warren both needed time to gain composure as he led her into a private office.

"Where's Tom?"

He cleared his throat ineffectually several times. "He didn't come in this morning. About a half hour ago he telephoned from Fayettville that he would not be in today. He asked us to telephone the house and tell you he would not be back for dinner. We called but you were out so we left word. I was going to call again later and be sure you got the message."

"Fayettville?"

He nodded.

Concisely, she repeated Mr. Wainwright's exposition of the two courses open to her. She had made her decision. Let the investments go, take the losses, carry on the real estate business. Mr. Warren could go ahead directly and arrange with Mr. Wainwright. "I hope you will stick with us, Mr. Warren. My father had complete trust in you and admiration for your ability."

The brown eyes looked into hers. "I've been here a long time. Why, I could pretty near tell what J.R. was thinking before he spoke. We won't see his like again. I've lain awake nights trying to manipulate this problem but I can't see how we can meet the next payment coming due. You've taken a load off my mind today. I've been so worried about you—sending good money after bad and finally losing everything. That's what happens. I've wanted so much to talk with you just the way Wainwright has."

"Why haven't you?"

"Oh, Tom wouldn't stand for that."

She rose. She stood for some minutes resting her little round muff on the desk, her eyes downcast, then she looked up into his face with level, serious gaze. "Mr. Warren, I know that you and Tom are very different—temperaments." She spoke earnestly, "When you have something to say to me, you say it." She held out her hand. "I have confidence in you."

She walked slowly for a few blocks until she came to the corner where she could find a streetcar. Finally it came clamoring along the steel tracks that shone like burnished silver in the sun. The conductor turned a switch, readjusted the trolley overhead, the people pushed on. As she sat on the long side seat, she felt unhappy. In her mind were unpleasant misgivings about those interviews. Had she implied any distrust of her husband in her conversations with Warren and Mr. Wainwright? She could not endure such a thought and after this, she would rectify any such impression.

As she climbed the hill to the avenue above, her eyes rested on the big brick house. She saw the starched white muslin curtains at the nursery windows and quickened her steps.

Mattie was keeping some lunch warm. She remarked casually, "You probably know Mr. Donovan won't be home for dinner. I had a leg of lamb. I could keep it for tomorrow." Then, with a twinkle in her eye, "I have quite a lot of stew left over."

Mary laughed. "All right, Mattie. Stew." She added, "And lettuce."

With the rubber apron wrapped around her wool dress, she

bathed and fed the baby and settled him in his crib. When Ben looked in to ask if they would want more logs or a late furnace, she sent him home. "Nothing more tonight, Ben."

Fayettville; eight miles out on the west road. Once her grandfather had run the cotton mills there but she had been a baby when they were closed and the business had been consolidated with the mills down by their river. There was nothing there now but a dilapidated general store, a few occupied houses. It was a squalid remnant of a place, a ghost town with an unsavory reputation. Tom must have merely stopped there to use a phone.

At midnight she went to bed, slept fitfully, waking to switch on the light and watch the clock. It was nearly four when he came in quietly, undressing in the warm bathroom.

There was a strong smell of whiskey on his breath as he lay by her side. She tried to speak lightly, "I'm so glad you're back safe. What in the world took you way out through the snow to Fayettville?"

"Fayettville!" He jerked around on his pillow. "How in hell did you know I was in Fayettville?"

"Why, Warren told me. I stopped to see you at the office. I had been to see Mr. Wainwright."

"I never thought he would be such a damned sneak. He had that call traced."

"You probably mentioned it without remembering." She was puzzled. "I'm surprised you could even find a phone in that place. Isn't it a ghost town?"

He was silent for some time, then he laughed harshly. "Yes, it's a *ghost* town. I hate ghosts." Before she could ask, he went on, "You want me to tell you 'all about my day' I know." She waited silently.

"I've told you before that there were thirteen years from the day I walked out of that asylum until the day I walked into your father's office. I thought I could forget them, blot them out. We decided on that together. The blotter slipped today. An old friend has bought a house in Fayettville, the house that was owned by your grandfather's superintendent."

"The house way up on the cliff above the mill stream?"

"Yes. She's ill, came here for her health. She telephoned me. I didn't want her coming here so I went to see her and tell her so. Now can we put the blotter back, darling? I'm sick and tired and I've got to get some sleep."

She laid her arm across his chest and her cheek against his. "Go to sleep, Tom. The blotter's back. Only, dear, I wish you wouldn't drink so much whiskey when you're upset."

When she waked, she was surprised to find that he was up and dressed. She thought of it as a "dragged and drained" look on his face as he hurriedly ate some toast, then refused his usual second cup of coffee. She heard him in the hall, stamping as he put on his overshoes but she did not move from her seat at the breakfast table. He came back and from behind her chair he pressed his hand hard on her shoulder and said brokenly, "Mary." His hand remained there but there was only the one word, "Ma-a-ry."

He was gone. She lifted her cup, unconsciously seeking relief in the physical reaction from the hot liquid; relief from some sense of fear. But fear of what? She knew. Of pity. That was what was in his voice. When dozens of episodes in their life had been forgotten, that moment would stand out. He loved her and pitied her.

Sometime in the afternoon, while the nurse was busy elsewhere, she slipped quietly into the nursery to close the window as Joseph slept, for the sun had departed from that side of the house and a bitter wind was blowing from the northeast, the harbinger of more snow and storm. Gently she rearranged the blanket, bending over the little boy as she thought, "He's no Reynolds' angel with delicate, triangular face. His face is broad and his nose is rather large."

The door had opened but, thinking it was the nurse, she had not looked around. Now she was startled to turn and find her husband standing a few feet back of her. Impulsively she reached out for his hand and drew him to the side of the crib, whispering, "Our son, Tom."

"You do like that little fellow a lot, don't you, Mary?"

"So do you, only you haven't discovered it yet."

Later, she found him in the sittingroom standing before the fire. He was chewing his lips nervously as he gazed intently into the flames.

She picked up her mending and sat down in a low rocker but her fingers took no stitches. She listened to his quick, audible breathing as he began to pace up and down the room. His motions would have been funny had they not so clearly been a manifestation of mental disturbance for he would stride rapidly to one end of the room then, as though the wall had stopped him unexpectedly, he would whirl around and return for all the world like a lion in a cage.

He repeated, "You do think a lot of that little fellow, don't you, Mary?"

"So do you, Tom. I remember Grandmother Farnsworth saying once that life always moves forward, never backward. You love your children more than you love your parents. Your children, no matter how devoted they appear to be, will love their children more than they ever can love you. Better face it. Life and love move forward. Now I know what she meant. She said that life and everything connected with Nature is change. Even death isn't static; we decay and fertilize the ground becoming part of new growth. I hated the idea then, now I like it."

He chewed his lips. "Mary, you've ruined everything in business for me. You were a damned fool yesterday. Warren and Wainwright didn't waste a moment. They've brought our financial embarrassment out in the open, told the whole world. You've by one stroke destroyed the confidence the business men of the city had in me; you've ruined our prospects of holding that investment."

"What prospects had we?"

"Why in hell didn't you ask that before?"

Her anger flamed. "My Heaven, why didn't you talk to me? I've tried to discuss business with you. What prospects could we have except risking all my income?"

"I have friends—I have ways of doing things—ways you wouldn't understand."

Was it her hidden fears that increased her anger, her hot, red-headed temper? She asked icily, "In Fayettville?"

"Yes, I've friends even in Fayettville. Friends who were working on something in New York to save our investments."

The color left her face. So that blotter had been removed before yesterday! She sat very still looking into the fire.

The minutes ticked away. It was so quiet in the room that she turned to see if he were still there. He was standing at the window looking out into the snowy street. His thin face looked tired and so utterly sad that her heart ached. She spoke quickly, the words almost tremulous on her lips, "Tom, I'm afraid it would have been doing the dangerous thing. Risking too much. Forgive me for saying that I rely on Warren and Mr. Wainwright when they agree without a question. I'm terribly sorry. I went to the office to see you. Of course I didn't know you had plans. I'm terribly sorry. Now let's forget it all and go on safe and sound."

Always unpredictable, he came to her and, as he had in the morning, he pressed his hand hard on her shoulder. His voice was low and he spoke slowly, "Mary, if anything ever happened—if I ever left you—if I died or anything else happened—I wanted to do two things for you."

She looked up into his face. "What two things, Tom?"

"I wanted to save your fortune for you. . . ."

"What was the other thing?"

He turned away. "Oh, it was merely my quixotic idea that I could give you what your father wanted you to have—and give you Joseph. Two things from me that you would never despise."

Her hands had been clasped tightly about her knees, the fingers tensely intertwined; now she leaned back passing her hand across her forehead and eyes as she told him everything Mr. Wainwright had said. "That's all I want, Tom. We will always have a comfortable living. You will do well, I'm sure, in your business. Let's forget it all." She smiled up at him, "And don't you dare put Joseph in the same class as money. All the fortunes in the world don't balance the scales with him or with you." She reached for his hand, repeating, "Or with you, dear."

He was still twisting and chewing at his lips, looking at her through half-closed eyes.

She looked up smiling. "You were terribly upset about it, and my horrid temper didn't help but after we get used to it, we'll both be glad it's settled. Do you know, Tom, I sometimes believe that I don't care half as much about money as you do. I believe, today, I could get along better without money than you could."

He walked away as he answered, "You've never tried it." A few minutes later, she again heard him in the hall stamping into his boots. She rose and hurried out to see him putting on his great-coat with the fur collar.

"Where are you going? Surely there's no business at the office so urgent that you can't take care of it over the telephone. There's a fearful gale and I'm sure more snow and sleet are on the way."

"I'm not going to the office. I'm driving out to that damned Fayettville."

"Tom!" She did not mean it to sound like a hurt cry. "Tom, are you crazy? Eight miles on the poorest road out of the city and a nor'easter blowing up."

"I'll have to go to straighten things out, stop negotiations and explain. I probably won't be back tonight if the roads get too bad."

"Where will you stay?"

"I'll be taken care of." The tone was half mocking, half bitter.

Without pride, she pleaded, "Don't go. Tom, you *can't* go."

His hand was on the doorknob as she asked, "What is your friend's name?"

He laughed. "I've forgotten whether it's Astor, Carnegie or Morgan."

He slammed the door. She walked blindly back into the sitting-room, suffering in some manner that she couldn't endure. Over and over she told herself that she couldn't endure it.

She couldn't endure the remainder of the afternoon before her, or sitting down to the leg of lamb at the dinner table, or living through the endless hours of the evening. The wind howled and the snow piled up on the window sill. When Ben came in she asked him to fix a blind that had blown loose. He got a heavy cord and tied it.

She knew something about prayer. That night she prayed for but one thing—the safety of Tom Donovan.

Before she slept she thought quietly, "It's only a storm, for all the world like this wild wind and storm outside tonight. We won't allow this to get set into the pattern of our lives. Like the storm, it's terrific while it lasts, then tomorrow, probably, will be calm and sunny. Nothing can really matter because I love him. He loves me." She could hear his voice, "Mary. My Mary." This storm would pass.

More beautiful than she could have imagined it, the morning sun glistened through tree and shrub where the branches hung heavy with wet snow, snow heaped on even the smallest twig. Somewhere near ten o'clock he called her. His voice was light and crisp, "Just to tell you I'm here at the office."

"Thanks, Tom."

That evening he stood before the fireplace, coffee cup in his hand. He drank it quickly and held out his cup for more. Her hand was unsteady and she spilled some. In the same light, crisp tone he had used in the morning, he remarked, "You're tired; we'd better get to bed early tonight."

"No, I'm a little too happy in having you here; that's all."

He had been avoiding her eyes. Now he walked over to the table, set down his cup and, as he lighted his cigarette, he said, still lightly, "The money that was to be used for us, has gone back to its original purpose; it will be used to start a new magazine in New York. It may amuse you—I'm sure it would astonish my compatriots down at the office—to know that your husband has been offered a position. The prodigal son has been invited to come home." He turned and watched her.

She looked bewildered. "I know you told me that you've worked on papers or magazines but—but—I don't understand; you were poor and unhappy—"

He came over quickly and kissed her lips. "Don't try to understand, darling. The blotter's down for good now. All right? Can
we turn the page?"

"But wait, Tom. You say the blotter's down for good now.
That means you would not consider leaving your home and going
to New York? You refused? You—"

Again he kissed her. "Leave you? Don't be silly. I refused
every offer, every enticement. Nothing and nobody can separate
us."

She laid her cheek against his hand which she was holding
tightly in both of hers.

CHAPTER X

Somewhere in her reading Mary Donovan had come across the
statement, "When Shakespeare was a little boy, Roger Ascham
wrote: 'The hole yere is deuided into iiii partes, Spring time,
Somer, faule of the leafe and winter.'"

As she walked across the lawn with her son, she told him, "Long
ago the English adopted the word 'autumn'; but in our American
language, we often find the older words. They don't know when
they laugh at us for calling this season the 'fall' that we are using
the pre-Shakespearean word with the exact meaning."

"I'm glad my birthday comes in the 'faule of the leafe.' It's my
favorite season too."

They pointed out to each other the brilliant red of the sumacs
near the barn, the gorgeous colors of the poison ivy mixing with
the Virginia creeper along the old stone wall in spite of all their
efforts to eradicate it, the brilliant scarlet of a native maple and
the soft yellow of the great elms. They were conscious of a fragrance they both loved more than any perfume—the penetrating
odor of burning leaves for Ben had raked the lawn and the bonfire
still smoldered, filling the air with a smoky haze.

In the wide grape arbor where a long table had been set up by placing planks on sawhorses, Mattie had finished spreading a white cloth and, as he set down the heavy tray he had carried from the house the boy said, "The only thing I have against fall is the way the birds stop singing. Daddy says they only sing when they're making love. By fall they're old married couples just looking for a snug place to keep warm through the winter."

He lingered a moment until Mattie went back to the kitchen then, kicking at the grass, he frowned. "Do you want to know what I think? I think it's mean of Uncle Lawrence to go to Chicago to teach and leave right before my birthday. What about when I get in High School?"

She smiled at him. "What about it? You're only nine years old today. You're not going through school tied to Uncle Lawrence's coattails—or any coattails for that matter. You have books and brains and you'll get from the books what you need, that's that."

"Perhaps I'll go to Chicago instead of Harvard."

"We won't decide that today. I rather think he knew what was best for him. He'll miss you more than you'll miss him. Now go up and scrub for dear life and look out for those black fingernails. I've laid your clothes out on the bed." He turned away and she called after him, "Don't wake Sandra if she's still sleeping."

"O.K." He started across the lawn, then stopped. "She has to keep with her own baby gang if she's coming to my party."

"I'll watch out."

"O.K." He took a few steps, coming nearer to her. "You're sure, Mother, that Daddy'll get here in time? It's getting awful late."

Her smile reassured him. "Stop worrying so about him. He wired he'd be here. He's never missed one of your birthday parties yet."

"He missed Sandra's."

"He'll get here today." Mary Donovan's hands rested on the table as she watched him saunter toward the house. He never hurried when soap and water were waiting at the terminus of the trip.

Glancing at him as he strode across the lawn, a stranger might have taken him for a large boy of twelve. He was tall, broad shouldered; the nose that had promised to be large, was large; the face was broad and the jaw strong and square. The head appeared large also, because of the heavy blond hair. But in spite of his size he was a nine-year-old little boy when he snuggled his nose into his mother's neck or waited for her good night kiss. Mary liked to quote Mattie's oft repeated remark, "That boy has a smile that goes right to the bottom of your heart." He was precocious in his studies. Lawrence had chuckled with delight when he had him reading aloud at four years old. By the time the boy was nine, Lawrence had tried all sorts of experiments with mathematics and Latin.

Now, as Mary watched him bang clumsily into the balustrade by the side door, she sighed, "Perhaps what he needs most is dancing school." He had always been awkward. More than once his father had jumped nervously when he knocked over some apparently solid piece of furniture. Tom said, "Can't he ever learn to walk forward instead of backward? He slides to the dinner table as though he were making second base with the ball in the air. I have to sit with my feet under a chair if I don't want them kicked."

He was awkward but he might make the crew at Harvard like Lawrence and Gordon. Would he take dancing lessons? At present his scorn of girls was so colossal that he might prove to be more of an antagonist than a partner.

Her face sobered. It was a futile conjecture about the dancing school for there would be no extra money for that "trimming" as she called it. She had told Joseph that, with Lawrence gone, he was "on his own"; they were both on their own in more ways than she liked to acknowledge.

Like a cosmorama the sequence of events since the day when Tom Donovan had first walked up that side path unrolled before her eyes.

Looking back through the years she realized that had she been a shrewd business woman instead of a frank, open-hearted, impetuous young girl, she would have cleverly made it appear that her

husband had made that decision to take the loss on those investments. Tom had been right when he said that she had hurt him,
undermined his standing with the business men of the city. Never
for a moment would she forgive herself for that blunder. Never
for a moment would she forget Tom's attitude toward that blunder. After that one bitter, angry outburst, in the hard months
which followed he never again referred to her action. One night
when he had spoken of the dropping off of business and said that
Warren had suggested liquidation, she had mentioned her unhap-
piness over that first mistake of hers.

He had whirled around, surprise in his eyes; then, taking her
in his arms he had kissed her again and again. "Forget it. I know
my Mary. What you did, you did exactly in character. See what
I mean? If you had done it some other way, I wouldn't be sure I
know you. That is my anchor in life; I know you and I love you,
my Mary." And he had repeated, "Nothing and no one can ever
separate us." Unpredictable as usual.

But quite as unpredictable in its consequences was the ever-in-
creasing antagonism between Tom and Warren. Once when Tom
was out of town on a business trip, Warren had come to the house
where he spent an entire evening showing her frightful discrep-
ancies in his accounts. "He is the boss, Mary, and I have to take
orders. One by one the men are leaving as the business falls off.
Tom is a damned good salesman but he conducts each transaction
as though the entire business was his private possession. I can't
trust him. No one knows what he's doing. I never thought the
time would come when I'd say this—I'm through. I'm leaving you.
He owns the place.

"I've stuck with you a long time but now I know even old J.R.
would say there's no use trying to take it another day. Tell him
I came up here to see you while he was away. He'll be so mad
he'll fire me. I'd rather have it that way. It will be better for the
business to say he fired me than to say I quit."

Hot tears had stung her eyes that night when Warren went out
of her house.

He was fired and Tom found someone else to take his place

and for a few months there appeared to be some renewed confidence for it was springtime and Tom made several sales. Also he was in a happier frame of mind about the entire business, a happiness which was directly reflected in his moods at home.

Then came a winter that appeared in retrospect like a nightmare. If nothing succeeds like success surely nothing fails as quickly and surely as failure. Within the year after Warren's leaving, the entire business was so deeply in the red that it was necessary for Mary to sell stocks in order honorably to meet their obligations, pay off indebtedness and liquidate.

Tom was home; and now there came a period of hourly railing against all business. He would wash the taint of the buying and selling world off his hands.

Quite accurately he had drawn the picture. Here in their city, as in every other town and city and village in the land, from row after row of houses men get up by the clock, take a trolley or subway to work, go into offices or factories to grub like worms, back for lunch, back for dinner, eat supper with a wife they never really see, slave for commonplace children, go to sleep, get up by the clock and repeat. He was not made for that deadening routine.

It had been a relief after the harrowing fear of gossip and disgrace at the office, to have him home. Mary had understood the mood, sympathized with him and even forgiven his bitterness against the business life in which he had been such a conspicuous failure. She had suffered as keenly as he when it had become apparent that the name, Mary Kent Donovan, could command credit and respect in the business life of the city while the name, Tom Donovan was suspect.

There had come happy months after the debts had been paid and all obligations had been liquidated, when he had stayed home. At first, he worked on his poems and experimented with short stories, writing some days furiously, feverishly. Once he said, "Mary, when I learn to write the way I want to write, I'm going to do a book. I'm going to write the story of my life. I'm going to turn a searchlight on every damned woman in it including my mother whom I never knew. It will end with you."

She had stood beside him, her fingers smoothing his dark hair. "I couldn't bear to read it."

"Nonsense. It would sell."

She had realized that that was the quality of nebulousness in all their plans.

Afternoons, they had driven out to the Country Club and had played golf for needed exercise. She treasured the memory of those months when he played the role of the country gentleman for he had been a success in the part, perfecting his already good game, improving his health as they tramped over the rolling hills and through fragrant pine and hemlock forests. They had been popular and sought after by the group which gathered around the stone fireplace in the late afternoon, drinking bootlegged cocktails. To the gay set they had been "that rich young couple, living on income"; and to the more substantial set they had been "Mary Kent."

He had excelled also in the role of the perfect lover; but she was no longer the inexperienced young girl who had trembled with ecstasy in his arms, she was the mother of Joseph and the woman who stubbornly wanted other children. Nevertheless it had taken courage to tell him, when Joseph was something over three years old, that she was again pregnant. She braced herself for the deluge of protestations and arguments.

"We don't want our lives cluttered up with children. Look what Joseph's done to you; he absorbs half your day and three fourths of your mind. A baby would keep you a prisoner in the house. I've been planning a trip for us. Let's get away for a while. Let's go to New York, stay at a hotel, see some plays and night clubs, look at some live people and get in touch with the human race again. Here you see the same faces over and over."

She had been delighted. "Let's! I'd love it. You plan the trip, get the reservations and I'll pack. Mattie will look after Joseph and I won't have a worry."

He had leaned over to kiss her lips. "Or the baby?"

"I'll have the baby too." She laughed excitedly, "You're right about the trip. It's exactly what we both need and I want some new clothes and won't I enjoy buying them in New York!"

She had not bought clothes in New York. He took the trip alone, the trip that later proved to be the turning point in the road of their life together. That clumsy, awkward Joseph had come down with scarlet fever and Tom packed and got out only a few hours before the house was quarantined.

The weeks had turned into a month, the month to two months, three months, four months. At first he wrote love letters daily, then less and less often. She had grown large with child, physically well but mentally worried, bewildered and, she constantly told herself, needlessly apprehensive.

She could hardly endure her loneliness—their first separation! When the heavy snows of winter blanketed their world, she took walks holding her sturdy little boy by the hand. Sometimes she stood at the door hesitating to re-enter her house. The rooms were so large, so empty.

Twice she had written suggesting that she join him but when he had replied "In a few weeks; I'm deep in plans just now," her pride forbade her mentioning it again.

She found herself watching for his letters like a love-sick girl. Then one day, there had come a telegram announcing his return for the "week end." She had never forgotten that first telegram, "for the week end." She would get used to the words, later.

She always thought of her behavior during his three days at home as the summation of the assinine. He had told her frankly that he must live in a cosmopolitan atmosphere; that life in a smaller city was worse than existence in a goldfish bowl. Back among his old friends and among fascinating new friends, where he had been once deserted and thrown out he was now wanted. Perhaps she remembered his speaking of a friend who had once come up to the superintendent's old house in Fayettville to recuperate from an illness? She remembered. What was her name? He had shrugged. "Everyone calls her Marta."

This woman who had been an editor of one of the leading women's magazines, had had her ups and downs too, had suffered

from failures as he had; now, fed up with trite stuff, she was starting—at last, after several years of planning—a small magazine of
opinion and short stories, and poetry, modern of course, none of
the stupid pollyanna stuff she had been forced to handle in the
past. Art.

Mary suggested that there were already many really fine, small
literary magazines, one in particular edited by a friend of Lawrence's.

This was to be different. There was room for an exceptional
one, a magazine "of opinion."

"Of course. Only, whose opinions?"

He had brushed aside all her silly and wet-blanket questions.
At last he felt that he had found something he wanted and had
been searching for for years. He was in on the ground floor.
They must buy a partnership.

He admitted that he realized she must have the baby. After it
came they would arrange somehow, get rid of all this property
which was an elephant in their lives, then wipe the dust of Massachusetts off their feet. They would go to New York and live
an exciting life together. It would be lonely for them both for
only a short time. "My Mary, I still love you. You are and you're
going to be, my only woman. Life just now consists only of writing and business when I'm away from you. When we get going,
once you get into our crowd, once you feel part of us—they'll
seem a little bohemian to you at first because your life has been
so narrow—once you're with us, you'll love it. You see, darling,
it's my chance. I've got to succeed."

Yes, she had seen that, somehow, he must succeed; but she had
seen more. She had seen a precipice opening at her feet. She must
bridge it. She must become part of this new life which filled him
with such excitement and happiness.

Throughout those two nights when he had slept and she had
lain wide-eyed beside him, there were times when cold, practical
thoughts seemed to dissolve the mists of emotion and excitement
and she knew that she was a fool to have any traffic with the
venture. The welfare of her children, the security of her home

and children must come first. Then she saw the chasm widening. An army of doubts, fears, hopes and despairs followed every attempt to simplify her problem.

In the calm of daylight she had tried argument but, after all, what had she to suggest, to offer in its stead? He had spoken eloquently. "A man must have work. Isn't that your own preaching? A man's wife is bound to follow him wherever his work takes him. Isn't that your creed? Yes, in time, I'll take the entire family. We'll make it the home you want."

There could be no plan for moving until after the baby came. In the meantime her longing to please him, to help him, to be part of his life overwhelmed her. She had no sum of money large enough for what he wanted but she could sell stocks or one of the small houses.

He had been so tender, so grateful. He looked at her in wonder. "It's the damned truth, Mary. You don't love money. Money never means a thing to you except what you can do with it for your home and family and for those you love. There is no one in the world like you, my Mary."

Those last words were to become like the refrain of a song, to ring in her ears throughout her life.

Now the baby, Sandra, was five years old.

There was the sound of a car stopping at the curb. She saw her husband jump out, pay the driver and start up the path toward the front door. Halfway up the walk he saw her and, with that familiar quick, nervous swing of the shoulders and head, he changed his course and came across the lawn toward her.

He carried a briefcase and small overnight bag both made of handsome calfskin. He set them down on the side step, threw his raincoat over them and approached her. When a few feet from her he stopped, tipped back his head and looked into her eyes. "Well, Mary?"

She had not moved. Her hands were still resting on the table. Quickly he stepped into the arbor, took her into his arms and pressed a hard kiss on her lips. Again and again he kissed her then, with fingers under her chin, he tipped back her head and looked into her eyes. "Are you glad to see me, Mary?"

A deep flush that suggested anger spread into her cheeks and forehead as she answered, "You know quite well that I am always glad to see you, Tom. Too glad."

She saw how rapidly his dark hair was thinning at the temples; saw the touches of gray above his ears. She thought, "He is frightfully thin, the skin drawn over the cheekbones; and that flush is increasing. Does he live on whiskey and cigarettes?" There were tired lines, tired, bitter lines at his mouth and a redness about his eyes. She laid her hand against the side of his face. "Tired?"

"I came by way of Boston—stopped there overnight. Yes, I'm tired."

She pulled away as Mattie approached, carrying a large tray of sandwiches covered with a napkin. She and Tom greeted each other politely but with strict formality.

He turned to Mary and together they walked slowly toward the house. "Where's Joseph?"

"Scrubbing, I hope. He was so worried for fear you would not get here."

"Why, I wired—"

"I know. I assured him you would come."

He did not ask for Sandra but turned again to her. "You look lovely. You look as fresh and sweet as a girl of twenty."

She was already dressed for the party, wearing a silk sport-dress under a gray-green sweater, a color which enhanced the beauty of her eyes. She answered indifferently, "Thanks," and added, "You'll want to take a shower, perhaps? I have things to do with Mattie and Sandra."

"Who's coming? I suppose all the best mamas and best papas and the best children from the best houses from the best neighborhood in the best of cities, meaning our own."

"Not all the best—only Joseph's friends. At that he seems to have quite a few. Then I did, rather casually, tell mamas and papas to drop in. A few may do so."

She stopped at the side porch and, with a curious movement

of her hand that somehow indicated a sharp dismissal, she went toward the kitchen.

Tom went directly to his room and Joseph, splashing in the tub, did not hear him, so it happened that Mary was ascending the stairs to wake Sandra when they met.

It was curious to watch Joseph. He had worried for days for fear his father would not arrive. Now he came hurriedly out of the bathroom, hair in wet strings hanging in his eyes, shuffling in bath-slippers and holding a towel quite insecurely about his middle. He looked up and saw his father; and Mary, watching, saw all the relief and pure joy and pride in the boy's heart burst like sunlight into his smile. Then, instantly, he turned shy and awkward.

He merely muttered in reply to his father's pleasant, "Congratulations, sonny. Thanks for your invitation to the party. We all thought you said it neatly even though the scrawl was hardly legible."

Muttering and ducking his head as though in painful embarrassment, the boy edged around by the wall and, when the path was clear ahead, he fairly dove into a doorway sending a small object, dressed in drawers, sprawling on the floor. There was a sharp crack as the little girl's head hit something and then there was a howling, wailing, screaming crescendo of sound which brought Mattie on the run, panting up the stairs.

From within the door came a high-pitched, angry voice, "Shut up! I say, shut up! You're not killed or you couldn't yell like that. Girls!" The boy's voice was mixed with Mattie's indignant, "Her head's bleeding. How did she fall?" But above the babel of noise, Mary heard the aloof individual with the charming voice remark, "Good Lord!"

So this was the family beauty, the little girl of fairy-like loveliness. As Mary stood her on her feet, instead of a rosebud mouth, her most conspicuous feature was a veritable cavern from which came the almost unbelievable howls. Four front teeth were missing; her eyes were screwed shut yet the tears streamed down her red face. She dug one small hand into her hair and pulled it away quickly. For an instant she looked at her hand and, when she saw blood, her screams grew higher and louder and before Mary could grab the fingers they were tight on her blue silk skirt.

A few minutes later from the bathroom Mary spoke to Mattie who was skillfully dabbing at the stains on the dress. "She must have hit the metal door-stop." She was parting blond curls as she whispered, "Needs stitches. Telephone and see if Dr. Porter's home."

"Leave it to me"; and Mattie disappeared down the long stairway.

Somehow in ways inscrutable to the uninitiated, Mary managed to dress Sandra after Dr. Porter's ministrations, partially dry the wet spots in her skirt, smooth her own hair, inspect and improve Joseph, tidy two bedrooms, get into the kitchen for last minute suggestions and appear on the lawn to greet her guests, looking quite as lovely as Tom had said.

Many more came than she had expected. She had said casually, "If you feel like it, come and watch the children. The garden's still quite lovely. There hasn't been a heavy frost to take the dahlias." And now Mattie was boiling more water for tea. Even Milly Vaughan, the handsome brunette who had so determinedly flirted with Tom, appeared.

Some of the old shyness mingled with the warmth of Mary's smile as she welcomed the Carters from the estate across the way. People addressed the tall man as Judge Carter for the first time but glanced pityingly at the children knowing the mother lay in a new-made grave and a hearty infant, the innocent cause of the tragedy, was being cared for by an aunt. Mary was conscious of the warmth and duration of Bill Carter's handclasp, of too intimate an ardor and eagerness in his eyes, and drew back, laughing but with a slightly heightened color, to talk rather hurriedly about the baby, his son, Hunt, and his daughter, Mazie.

He called to Hunt and a tall youth approached with the awkward shyness of any boy who knows he is being inspected. He was too tall for his age, his legs seeming to hang loosely and his arms almost insecurely; but he had fine steady eyes. He squatted down to Sandra's level to examine her head.

The little girl, just turned five, stood in the midst of them all, exquisite in her simple white dress. With pride she spoke to Hunt. "I had to be sewed."

He parted the beautiful blond hair as he asked, "What happened?"

"Joseph knocked me down." Mary added, "Quite accidentally."

Hunt asked, "Want me to knock Joseph down?"

Sandra's emphatic "no" brought laughter from the watching group.

A flood of sunlight came slantingly across the lawn, laying patches of yellow among the shadows of the elms, turning the crimson and purple, yellow and blue of the garden into a riotous blend of giddy coloring. The guests milled about and Mary with the trained eye of a born hostess seemed to speak to everyone and see everything and never appear to be seeing anything but the person to whom she happened to be speaking.

At every moment she was observant of her husband, wishing he would shed that slightly superior, slightly arrogant manner, suggesting boredom among the bucolic. She slipped her arm through his, leaning lightly against his shoulder when he was forced to talk to some of the plain women; women who didn't seem to know anything about hair-dos or style; women who, as Tom once said, "Gaze down their homely noses at rouge and lipstick and allow their figures to look like mattresses and don't give a damn because, 'My mother was a Lowell you know!'" She had admitted that some took advantage of positions not achieved by either brains, work or character; however, she had stood up and fought valiantly for the plain old women who were too busy doing worthwhile things to bother much with "looks."

Once she whispered, "You *must* remember Miss Simmons. She's the principal of the Grade School—Joseph's teacher." She left him with the estimable spinster and did not hear the severe-looking woman's first question, "Exactly what *do* you do in New York,

Mr. Donovan? I shall be interested to know about your poetry and other writing."

It was plain that Mr. Donovan would not discuss his writing for he wheeled on his heel and joined several men deep in a discussion of the stock market. They drew Tom in eagerly and Mary, catching a word now and then, gathered that these "authorities" saw no end in sight for this phenomenal boom. Desperately she wished she knew about all that for she was sure Tom would want more money before he went back to the city.

Her thoughts of money were interrupted as, apparently without looking, she saw Milly Vaughan pass the group of men to enter the side garden path. Deliberately, Milly called, "Tom, where do you get your roots? I must have some of those yellow dahlias. Come show them to me. What do we care about stocks or money —we artists?"

There was a hearty laugh from the men, glances exchanged, even some admiration of her frank boldness. Tom, with his most malicious smile, joined her.

A few minutes later a large car stopped at the street curb and a liveried chauffeur helped out a feeble, elderly gentleman who steadied himself with the aid of a cane. Mary crossed the lawn to meet him wondering who had suggested old Mr. Vaughan's coming to the party. As he bent and kissed her cheek, he spoke of old J.R. then asked briskly, "Where's the boy? Show me the boy."

When Joseph came to them, he clutched his shoulder and shook him vigorously, "You hulking monster! I expected to see a little Lord Fauntleroy. You're a Kent through and through. If you don't look like the old Judge!"

Joseph liked the treatment and smiled and chatted with his best manners.

The old man's deformed, rheumatic fingers were searching in his vest pocket as he talked. Finally he extracted a small envelope and handed it to the boy. "There you are. Open it and see if you want it. Do you know, Mary, this is the first time I've been invited to a boy's birthday party since I wore short pants myself.

That was about seventy-five years ago but I remembered a present was expected. Now do I get some ice cream?"

Joseph opened the sealed envelope. His eyes grew wide with astonishment. "Two of them! Gee!" He held up two ten dollar gold pieces. The youngsters swarmed around examining the treasure, and then helped the senile old man to the arbor, pushing him at times rather perilously. He seemed to be in high spirits as he ate his ice cream.

Glancing down the garden path, Mary thought, "She won't have long to wait for freedom and the money," and she felt a little sick, for Tom and Milly Vaughan were nowhere in sight.

Casually she passed Ben, whispering, "Go around by the barn and tell Mrs. Vaughan her husband is waiting for her." Laughingly she took Ben's place by the fast emptying ice-cream pail.

Later that evening, Mary recognized Tom's nervous, restless mood when he said sneeringly, "Milly Vaughan suggested a movie party—all stop there for a little dancing and a snack later. To hell with her." He whirled around. "I'll get out the car. Let's run out on some country road, get away from the house."

She answered, "That's impossible. Mattie's worked from daylight. She's too tired to be asked to sit up. I couldn't afford Fanny so I let her go and I have Ben only part time, sharing him with Judge Carter."

"The children sleep like logs; they'll be perfectly safe."

"No. They are too young to be left alone."

He took a few turns about the room. "You're tied down like a servant girl."

"I don't mind, Tom, except when you're home. I'm so busy all day. I have an hour or two for reading at night, sometimes. At other times I'm glad to go to sleep almost as soon as the children do." She smiled at him.

"What a life." He took the chair near her as he repeated, "What a life."

She laid her head against the chairback and looked steadily at him through half-closed eyes. "Tell me a little about your life."

He stood up. "I've a lot of things to look after in the morning.

Shall we go up now, with the children and chickens? We can rest if we don't sleep."

"In a few moments." He walked about the room as she said, "Joseph is so happy about his party—those wonderful gold pieces that Mr. Vaughan brought him. What pleased me was that he valued them for their beauty and unusualness. He says he doesn't want twenty dirty greenbacks instead of them."

He leaned his elbow on the mantel and watched her. "My dear Mary! Joseph. The very way in which you speak his name. You, with your youth and beauty. And Sandra. The way all those damn fool women rave about her beauty."

"She is beautiful, Tom. I think that beauty is something a mother and father have to take into consideration. Even I, seeing her every day, am astonished when I look into those violet-gray eyes. They're unusual."

He interrupted, "So am I astonished. She's no doll. She can look a person right through and through without a sign of a smile. I've seen you do it when you're angry. As for Joseph, he's beginning to interest me. I meant to buy him a present in New York but I had neither time—nor money."

"Having you here was his choicest present. He adores you, Tom. I was so glad you sent the telegram to *him*."

He leaned nearer her. "Mary, don't be a fool about those two children. Joseph would be better off in boarding school next year. It's time you quit the coddling. They haven't lived an hour without your direction and your thoughts. That petting ruins a boy."

She moved impatiently in her chair. "From what you've told me of your boyhood, I don't think you qualify as an expert in passing judgment on the evil effects of mother-love. Really. As you say—really! Let me bring up my children in my own way for I have faith in that way and I'm willing to sacrifice less important things—"

His interruption was sharp and bitter. "Like your husband?"

She smiled wearily. "Don't be absurd. You're too intelligent to talk like that."

"Why is it absurd to ask you to send the children to good boarding schools, get rid of this place which eats up all your income and come and live with me in New York? I think even the preacher says your first duty is to your husband."

She laughed as she rose. "Where's your sense of humor, Tom? I think the preacher would offer a few duties for the husband's contemplation."

There were no logs burning in the bedroom fireplace now. However, the night was not too chilly and she undressed leisurely. As she approached the side of the bed, he gathered her with all the old tenderness into his arms. "Mary, I'm dead serious about this. I've been in New York five years and I'm still living alone. My God, that's a tribute to a wife. I'm always honest with you. I'm still waiting for you."

He pulled up her bent head and looked into her eyes. "I want the truth. You still love me?"

Instead of the old excited flush, her face grew white and her eyes steady and level. "After ten years, no husband needs to ask his wife if she loves him. Perhaps all he wants to know is how far she is still willing to sacrifice herself and all those about her, for him. You know I loved you the first day—like this day—when you walked up that side path. I wanted to give you *everything*. I have. I may love you to the last day of my life but I often wish I were not made that way because you take unscrupulous advantage of it. You are an utterly unscrupulous person—"

"Go on. I love to watch you when you're angry. I'm 'selfish, unstable, unpredictable'—but you love me; so who cares? Come with me, darling. Leave this mess of house and children. Just you and I alone—"

"Tom," as she drew back from him, "Tom—you are so honest —did you kiss Milly Vaughan this afternoon?"

He laughed aloud. "What did you expect?"

"I expected—" she turned away.

"Your husband to be the perfect host? Even to the damnedest female you invited?"

"I didn't invite her or her husband. I expected you to be an adolescent. You were."

He was suddenly sober. "Mary, what's all that to do with us?" He pulled her down beside him on the edge of the bed. "Come with me. Leave this mess before it's too late."

She spoke slowly, "After ten years you don't even know what I mean by love. I was once so sure I could teach you. A home, children, husband—it's all part of a whole. It's the family." She clenched her hands and he felt her trembling. "If I had lived in pioneer days I would have taken my household goods and my children and have put them in a covered wagon and gone with you to the ends of the earth. We would still have been intact, a whole. I could give you everything I possess—if it were for our family. What are you asking? You want me to get rid of my home, separate myself from my children, leave them in the hands of strangers. You want me to come into a life where I would never fit, a bohemian life in New York. You and I alone in a little apartment, mixing with strangers, people who are never anything but strangers if you know them for years. It is all so adolescent, like kissing Milly Vaughan."

She was angry and she spoke rapidly. "I admit I wouldn't be afraid now to send Joseph out into the world at his age—and I'd do it if I found I could no longer control the atmosphere of the home. Nothing can undo these most formative years that are passed. However, I'm not going to do anything of the kind. I'm not going to give up the fight to keep us all together—just yet. I want you to understand."

"I understand. You belong to a tribe, the Kent-Farnsworth tribe. You are part and parcel of a family. Its traditions, its honor, the old homes, the fathers, mothers, children and even servants are part of your blood. I understand it's tearing you to pieces to tear you away from any part of it."

"Then why do you want to tear me to pieces?"

He laughed bitterly. "I don't know. I merely know I want *you*."

He walked to the table, found a cigarette and lighted it. He laughed again. "And how you Kents have traveled—Europe, summer after summer. You've seen Africa. Lawrence took a trip around the world but I don't believe one of you would have taken a train as far as Boston if you hadn't looked forward to coming straight back to this house at the end of the journey."

"Perhaps not." She spoke more slowly now. "You're missing the point, Tom. I don't care so much about where I live as you think I do. I could tear up and build a new home in New York City or Albany—as Aunt Letitia did. Cathey was born three blocks from here and she willingly and happily broke up and went with Lawrence to Chicago. I would take my home almost anywhere to be with you if you wanted that home—almost anywhere—but you don't want a home. You want to destroy a home."

He did not answer, though she waited; so she finished, "You would tear me to pieces."

He had walked to the side of the room and now he stood pressing his back hard against the marble mantel as he watched her. There was no levity in his smile as he said, "It never occurs to you that you tear me to pieces also. Do you know, Mary, no matter where I am, talking to anyone—you walk in, we look at each other— You know as damned well as I do, it's like an electric current." There was tenderness in his voice. "I didn't fall in love with this house, or your position or your money or J.R.'s office. It was you and, by God, you know that's true."

Her head was bent and she almost whispered, "I know, Tom."

Later, as he lay with head pillowed on her shoulder, he murmured, "There's no one in all the world like you, my Mary." Then he slept.

She moved over to the edge of the bed. For the first time, for the very first time, she wept. Never had she, like so many women, found quick relief in tears. She remembered an expression of her father's. "Things eat into me." She was like that. Things ate into her, gnawed and burrowed. Her love for Tom had eaten into her, had become part of the fiber of heart and brain. First, her fight for that love, against everything and everybody; then her fight for faith in that love. Through all those early years, filled as they were with fears, shocks and uncertainties, she had always had a serene sense of peace, a sense of oneness, something very sweet in her inmost thoughts after the consummation of their love. Always her faith in him, her love for him had been renewed and she had known a deep, quiet happiness. He was the father of her loved children and she found peace before she slept. Tonight, for the first time, she wept. The river was there but it was a river of sadness. She wept as though the flood of tears would never cease because she saw no way out.

CHAPTER XI

On the Sunday morning following the day of the birthday party, the weathercock on the red barn told those who took the trouble to look, that the wind was shifting to east-northeast. However, the sun was still warm and bright and Joseph and Sandra sat in sunshine on the lowest step leading to the kitchen porch.

This comfortable spot was on the opposite side of the house from their father's room and here they could talk out loud and not be hushed by Mattie every few minutes. They were trained not to disturb their papa.

When old J.R. had slept in the big bed in the front room, Sunday mornings often witnessed a wild scene; Lawrence and Gordon in pajamas and little Mary in nightgown, waiting a given signal, then rushing him, sitting on his chest, smothering him under pillows until he roared like a lion and scared them out, locking the door behind them.

Joseph and Sandra were unaware of the difference in papas. They adored this remote and important person whose business compelled him to live in New York and when he came home they were filled with pride and boastfulness.

The boy had risen with the sun; had managed his feet very well, neither banging nor kicking over furniture as he went about the house gathering his scattered birthday presents, to arrange them on the steps for Sandra's inspection. "They left these around though Mother asked them not to bring any."

Sandra looked them over. "But they put their names on so you'd know who gave them."

When in company, he spoke to this little girl, and of her, disdainfully as "Toots"; but when she was his sole companion he affectionately called her "Sandy" and explained the universe to her. Docilely, she now listened to his ravings about the white leather baseball, his bat, the football, the books and boxing glove. She eyed two large boxes of candy. He pushed them aside. "Mother said we'll have to wait." Then, in his most expansive mood, he reached into his pocket and took out the gold pieces, letting her hold one.

Solemnly she sat with her small hand stiffly outstretched and gazed admiringly at the shining beauty of the coin. "Is it a lot of money, Joseph?"

"I'll say." At that moment she was exactly where his masculine ego most enjoyed her. She was soft, tractable, tamely acknowledging his superior wisdom, humbly ready to learn; so he explained about the United States government and gold. Uncle Lawrence had made it clear to him long ago. He left her with a vague impression that government gold was added to the dependable things like God, Mother, Father and Mattie.

Then he added smiling, "One of these is going to be for you. Do you like that?"

She handed it back. "Yes, Joseph."

He put them in his jacket pocket. Then they looked up and saw their mother standing above them, gazing at them intently. She had been up almost as early as Joseph, straightening up the house, planning meals, and now she looked tired and there was an unusual heaviness about her eyes. She had shears in her hand for she was going to pick the choicest flowers before frost should injure them.

All three went down one path and up another, chatting and enjoying the quiet of the Sabbath morning. They arranged gorgeous bouquets for the sittingroom and dinner table and a small one for the breakfast table. "For Papa," Sandra said; but they could not wait for his reaction for it was time to dress for Sunday School; and besides, he was not going to eat yet. He was having a bromo seltzer, having waked with one of his "beastly headaches."

As they went upstairs to dress, Sandra asked in her most wondering tone, "Did you ever drink one of those, Joseph?"

"No, but I'm going to have plenty if I ever get a beastly headache." He swung his shoulders and tried to step lightly like his father as he said, "When we're going to Sunday School, if any fellows I know come along, don't you walk *with* us."

She didn't. When Hunt Carter joined them, trying with his skinny fingers to pull her bangs, she darted across the street and walked the few blocks to the big stone church without glancing over, once.

She looked so small across the broad avenue under the tall elms. Knowing their responsibility for her, they both watched a little nervously at crossings but neither discussed her independence.

At the breakfast table, Mary was refilling Tom's coffee cup. He had eaten his breakfast of ham and eggs, toast and marmalade. Now he picked up the newspaper and turned to the stock market report. He looked up after a while, lit a cigarette and, as he smoked, he told her of petty clerks in drygoods stores, of hairdressers in beauty shops, of teachers, of bakers and plumbers, all borrowing a few hundreds here and there and watching it grow into tidy sums.

She spoke indifferently, "I suppose gambling is a natural instinct; an instinct apparently left out of me."

He smiled; no, while others were turning hundreds into thousands, she had taken all the money she could lay hands on and done what? Bought annuities for her old age. "Forgetting your children."

Her elbow on the table, her chin resting in the palm of her hand, she looked tired as she answered pleasantly enough: "For *our* old age. They are transferable. It's because I am thinking of my children that I've done what I've done. I have some ideas about children that may not be quite orthodox. Quite contrary to your idea of me, I don't believe in coddling and I don't think love of home and parents and coddling are the same thing."

"What are your unorthodox ideas?"

"I hardly believe in inheritance. Of course I must keep this property for Joseph or Sandra whichever one wants it—nothing can replace an old family home—but I think each generation should work for its own living. I must have money to educate them but after that, they are on their own. Also I wish to be on my own. I don't believe in parents looking forward to living on their children. Some people talk about children as they do life insurance."

She smiled, "What would become of robins if they expected to find nests waiting and an inheritance of worms? I suspect, like every creature in the natural world, they still exist because they get strong digging like mad for those worms and building their own homes. Every baby robin has to start at scratch."

He looked amused. "So you think each generation should have a try at shirtsleeves. What about the scholar, the artist, the musician?"

Anger darkened her eyes. "What about them? Your men's wars, your men's slavery, your men's poverty and disease," her eyes looked steadily at him, "yes, even your gadgets and senseless luxury and drinking and debauchery—especially your wars—have destroyed more scholars, scientists, musicians and artists than all the overalls in the history of the world. Work doesn't kill genius."

"My Lord, I started something. Of course you're right." Then tantalizingly, "What about your own inheritance from your father?"

"There isn't so much of it left to talk about. He expected to leave a tidy fortune but—'the best laid schemes o' mice and men gang aft agley.'" She was lost in thought a moment, then she added slowly, "We often talked together and his ideas were not so different from mine. He educated his boys then expected each to make his own way. I'm sure Gordon would have been as independent as Lawrence."

"Lawrence has never needed much money for the kind of life he wants to live."

"No, he works hard but not for money. He's getting what he values—and that's success." A smile crept about her lips. "As for me, I never got started. I'm sure I would have done something." She raised her head and smiled into his eyes. "Didn't I get the job I wanted? I wanted you. I wanted children. I got both. If I don't make a success of my job it will be, like any other man or woman, because I didn't have what it takes. At least I'm working at it."

He rose and, walking around the table, he bent and kissed her neck. "My Mary, somewhere hidden under that soft, pretty exterior of yours, is enough stubborn cussedness to supply all the mules from Florida to Maine." He pressed his hands on her shoulders. "You think too much, my darling. Eventually it can spoil a woman. Emotion is woman's charm. Leave the thinking to men."

"Then stay home and do my thinking for me. My life is getting filled with so much aloneness—I'm finding thinking can be quite an exciting and interesting occupation."

He moved his hand several times over the soft hair then abruptly went into the library.

She sat quite still for several moments gazing at the tablecloth before she carried the dishes out. "Hold dinner back until two-thirty, Mattie."

He called her as she passed through the hall. "Darling, have you a few moments for some business talk?"

She stopped, passed her hand across her forehead. She had dreaded this moment. "Of course." She straightened her shoulders and entered the library.

CHAPTER XII

She seated herself in one of the leather armchairs and he took the chair opposite her. How inadequately he filled that chair. For a moment, more vividly than she saw Tom Donovan, she seemed to see her father's heavy shoulders, his broad face with the large Kent nose and his thick gray hair.

Curious what tricks memory plays on one. Vividly, at that moment, she remembered his agonized expression in that hour when she demanded marriage with a man he did not trust, a man whom he called a stranger. How completely she had been swept away with passionate love for this man now sitting before her. How little she had cared about the opinion of the world or her family; how little she had cared about her education or any future except with Tom Donovan.

And this was the end of ten years. As on the night before when she had edged over to the side of the big bed, some devastating sense of sadness seemed to overwhelm her. Tears which she stubbornly controlled seemed to burn behind her eyeballs. Her hands lay on the carved arms of the big chair; her head was bent forward and she did not know that her sensitive face expressed a sadness that made her husband so uneasy that he went to his desk and began needlessly arranging papers, searching in pigeonholes, clearing his throat as he glanced at her now and then.

She must not give way to anger as she had in the past when she had spoken bitterly. "Art magazines! You and your friends use the word 'art' like an umbrella. The word is about as all-embracing as the word 'God.' It covers whatever any lunatic wants covered. And friends. Year after year you are less anxious that I should know your 'friends.' "

She braced herself for the moment she had dreaded. Her tears, her sadness, were under perfect control as she looked up at him with a cool smile. "Tom, you want more money to sink into that magazine."

"Another three months—then my personal expenses—I've sacrificed everything."

"I can't give you any. I could sell this property—real estate is selling at high prices I know—but, with my cussed stubbornness—or is it stubborn cussedness?—I'm not going to part with my home. I'm still determined to keep it for Joseph and Sandra. Three times I've sold valuable stock or houses to 'lend' money to you and your friends and partners. I will never sell the double house next door. It is, as Father told me, a good investment and will always rent well."

She took a deep breath, "I'm getting down to rather close calculations in money matters. The rent from that double house and the interest from my stocks and bonds keep me going. I can't jeopardize one cent of that income. If it were cut badly I couldn't make ends meet. I couldn't live here."

He was standing with his back half turned toward her. She wet her lips, thought a moment and, as he did not speak, she went on, "I did put away money for the children's education and buy those annuities while I had the larger income. I'm glad I had that much sense. Anyway"—she rose—"that's that. That's the whole story. I'm sorry but from now on I'm frank to say you're on your own."

He did not look at her. She waited. With his nervous fingers he snapped at some papers, picked up and threw down a pen. As she started to leave the room, he turned. "Mary, come here."

She came up to him, laying her hands lightly on his shoulders, looking up with what was now a miserable attempt to smile. "I suppose, Tom, there always must come an end. Why, oh, why, do we have to have these cruelly unhappy crises in our lives—always over money?"

Her fingers traced the line of his dark hair along the temples, touched the gray above his ears. He looked old, worn, dissipated. There was an anxious note in her voice, "Tom, how much do you drink?"

"I'll drink less if you'll get rid of all this past and come and make your life with me."

For a moment his arms tightened about her shoulders. He did not kiss her, merely looked into her eyes and there was something in his face that frightened her.

There was a duet of voices in the hall as little feet stamped on the floor. She loosened his arms, kissed his cheek lightly and turned to greet her children.

Throughout the fried chicken dinner which Mattie had prepared because it was his favorite meal, he appeared gloomy and depressed. He glanced at the children, even at her as though he were hardly sensible of their nearness. Again her heart began that aching for him; that old choking pity began to suffocate her. She saw he was worried, greatly worried. She was sure he needed money desperately. She would give him all she could spare. She must spare some.

While they were eating, the room grew so dark that lights had to be switched on and they could see gusts of wind blowing down the tops of the tall elms. She spoke of the east-northeast breeze in the morning and the promise of the weathercock.

Joseph asked, "Did you notice it, Father?"

"No."

"Neither did I. Mother sees everything but I don't notice so much."

Tom laughed heartily and Joseph looked pleased. Mary noticed that throughout the dessert his father looked often at the boy with a sometimes speculative, sometimes inscrutable smile. She was in the kitchen wiping dishes so Mattie could get out for her Sunday afternoon, when she heard the sound of a motor and, looking up, saw Tom drive from the barn.

He stopped at the side door and, a moment later, Joseph rushed in almost breathless with eagerness and excitement. "I'm going with Father. He said to tell you."

"With a storm threatening?" She went out on the porch. "Tom! What are you thinking of?"

He jumped out, speaking lightly, "I'm thinking of your idolatry of your son. It's time he and his father became friends. I'll get my raincoat."

Joseph was already in the front seat, his face fairly illumined with joy. His father inviting him to go with him on a "business trip"! Tom returned, tossed the old English raincoat into the back seat, stepped into the car, started the motor and, with scarcely a glance at Mary, "Don't get worried if we are a little late. I have some business calls to make."

He was driving down the roadway. She watched them turn

into the avenue and head toward the city center; then she walked slowly back to the kitchen, her brows meeting in a perplexed frown.

Mattie spoke soothingly, "I wouldn't worry. It may be only a windstorm. Tom is an expert driver. Notice how carefully he took the curve. Nothing makes a father doubly cautious like having his son in the car with him. My land! You'd have thought the gate of Heaven had opened for Joseph."

An hour later her voice still carried the soothing "don't worry" notes as she stopped in the hall. "I could come back and get the supper. They'll likely come in hungry as wolves. I don't mind at all."

"Of course you'll do nothing of the kind." Then she made the remark which Mattie was waiting for. "You look so nice, Mattie."

Had Mattie been told that, like the last mastodon, she represented a vanishing era, she would have been astonished. She pulled good quality black silk gloves over her hands; she buttoned her good black wool coat and gave one last glance at her hat in the mirror. As she adjusted the hat to as near a horizontal position as possible, there was an expression of serene contentment in her face.

She did not know that Mary thought of her as one of the most "emancipated" women, one of the most "advanced" women in her country. She was actually so independent that she lived the kind of a life she liked to live; she even went so far as to wear the kind of a hat she liked to wear. She liked a brim, a sailor with a brim, white in summer and black in winter. That was what she liked and that was what she wore.

She liked a good wool coat and she had a best and second-best. She liked a bank account and she was possessed of a substantial one. She liked politics; she liked to read her newspaper every day and, unlike some of her radical and superior sisters, she had never missed casting her vote whether it was for local, state or national figures.

She was a feminist. She had faith in her sex, never dreaming that that faith had been fostered by her own integrity. Sometimes, when she was up to her ears in work, sliding pies into the oven, filling the cookie jar or preparing a roast, she would go "on the stump." "Give us time, Mary. We're only starting. Politics is a tricky business and we haven't learned the tricks yet. I'll vote for a woman for senator from Massachusetts someday and I won't be surprised if she doesn't do so well, either. Someday, women will scrub off the paint, wash their fingernails, give their bridge cards to children for toys and tackle the world's business."

"What about motherhood, bearing children?"

She would stop, rest her hands on her hips and shake her head. "Mary Kent, aren't there more women without children than with them now? It isn't husbands and children that have held women back. They're holding themselves back. They've always crippled themselves by clothes, styles, parties and plain silliness. They've got the money now; they've got the vote. They'll wake up."

She was a spinster and was too honest to pretend that some Barkis had been "willin'." There had been no Barkis in her life and still her brow was serene and she was not suffering from any form of frustration.

She expected to hear Mary say, "You look nice," and Mary said it and meant it. They were friends.

Now Mattie pushed her umbrella securely under her arm, grasped her handbag and with, "Don't you worry about Joseph; his father'll look after *him*. I'll be back direct from evening service," she went out.

Mary watched the solid, substantial figure turn into the avenue. The woman walked with head held high; with a long easy stride made possible by her "sensible" shoes. There was pride in the bearing of this New England spinster, the housekeeper of the Kents.

When Sandra slept, Mary lay down on the sofa in the big bedroom. She was no feminist like Mattie. She knew plenty of women who had fine jobs with splendid salaries and they were spending them on clothes, hotels, jewelry, social life and synthetic "beauty." Perhaps Mattie who saw them marching was right. Mary saw them marching into lives of supreme selfishness. Independent of men? Well, she frankly wanted the love of men. She had possessed that love from her babyhood. With Tom? Her eyes grew dark with fear. There couldn't come an end. She couldn't endure it. She couldn't endure any more of this kind of half-living. She was young, full-blooded; she wanted love—passionate love, children love, home love.

She must have slept, for Sandra's fingers on her face wakened her. She dressed the little girl and then, with her old instinct to please her husband, she chose for herself a new, soft-gray dress.

Together, she and Sandra prepared the evening meal.

The light faded early; the wind died down and a heavy blanket of clouds seemed to rest almost on the treetops. At six o'clock she began to watch anxiously down the avenue; at six-thirty, she fed Sandra; at seven she read aloud and at eight she put the child to bed.

Pressing her face against the windowpane, she could see nothing except the flickering, now inadequate street lights. Even as she looked out the rain began to splash against the window.

Sitting by the unlighted grate, she laid her head back against the cushion. In her eyes anger grew as half hour was added to half hour.

Once she went upstairs, took out her account book and separated some dividend checks. She carefully set down the amounts and added for the total. She calculated. Perhaps by rigid economy, she could do without these until her January first checks came in.

Her lips were pressed hard together. She endorsed them to her husband and put them in an envelope.

She went back to the sittingroom where the rain was beating against the windows. Clearly, over and over, she heard Tom Donovan's words, "I'm thinking of your idolatry of your son. It's time he and his father became friends." Some nebulous fear of she knew not what ate into her. She shivered as the rain slashed in sheets against the house. There was nothing she could do but wait.

CHAPTER XIII

As carefully as he had made the turn from the driveway, Tom with Joseph by his side, had driven into the business section of the city, through the streets with their deserted, quiet, Sunday atmosphere, out to the west end where he stopped before an apartment house. All the way he had chatted in his most ingratiating, comradely manner with his son and that son's heart-warming smile had responded to every sentence.

Stopping at the curb, Tom said, "I'll be here only a few minutes; don't get out."

He was as good as his word and, before Joseph expected him, he was again in the car. There was a slight smile on his lips as he took a wallet out of his pocket, inserted some bills, replaced it and started the motor. They made two such stops, always in neighborhoods and houses totally strange to the boy; and always they were getting farther and farther out toward the west road.

At last they were in the country and Tom was fascinating as he discussed both the World Series and the football line-up of the various colleges for the approaching season. He knew the names of all the players, the scheduled games and the sporting chances, even the odds on betting. It was wonderful.

It was so wonderful that Joseph lost track of road and direction and was surprised when he found they were climbing a very long, very steep, winding hill. Tom shifted into second, laughing, "This car hates this hill so it grunts and groans but it always gets there."

They stopped before a large, flat-roofed, square house, a singularly ugly house, now needing paint. Even Joseph noticed and remembered it as a dingy, forbidding place apparently stuck on the edge of a cliff high above the mill stream below. It looked especially gloomy and uninviting on this dark, cloudy day.

Tom pulled the breaks securely, locked the ignition and, appearing to smile as though at some inner amusement, he turned to the boy, "Come on."

Joseph jumped out joyfully and tried to get in step with his father as they went up a winding, rocky path. Tom stopped. "Quite a view. You'd hardly believe we'd climbed so high."

They looked back over the valley below. Deep down there was a small river meandering out of a clump of woods, twisting into an S-turn through the village center; then, after winding down the valley, it found itself confined in a canal between solidly built stone walls. Along the banks of this canal was an old factory with the windows and doors boarded, with weeds covering the old yards and with gates barred.

"Didn't you ever see these old factories before?"

Joseph looked sharply at the scene and answered, "No, I guess not." He saw it now and didn't like it.

"That's where the Farnsworth fortune was built."

Joseph scowled. "Why I thought one of my grandfathers owned the factories down by our own river. He died but they're still kept up and running."

"The old man moved from here; closed this place up like a jackknife and the village died."

Years after, when Joseph studied the place from that same height, he realized that there never had been much in this village except the first small factory and little frame houses for the help. Grandfather had built large brick factories by their river and, at the time, modern homes. Yet, on that gloomy Sunday afternoon, the dilapidated buildings and his father's manner of stating the history gave him a sense of guilt and shame which he would never forget. He was relieved when Tom turned and, without either ringing the bell or knocking, opened a heavy front door and they stepped into a square hall.

For a moment they listened. Tom said quite loud, "Pretty quiet for this family."

A moment or two later no one would have called the place quiet. The hall led directly into a room which extended across the middle of the house. Later one noticed that a partition had been removed to make this long, narrow room which appeared to be an art gallery because the walls were covered with pictures.

Big oils and smaller water colors were both hung and stacked against the walls, set on tops of tables and even on chairs. There was a large window on the valley side and there must have been an enormous drop to the river below; but on the hill side the long windows and the side door were almost on ground level.

The first person whom Joseph was conscious of seeing plainly was a woman rocking in a sheltered corner near the door. He thought her queer and was not surprised when they called her something that sounded like "Gran-dam."

During the weeks that followed when Mary questioned him about the old woman, asking, "A grandmother? You mean really old like Grandmother Furgeson down the street?" He had answered, "Oh no, Mother. This was a New York grandmother. The others called her Gran-dam but I think Father called her Marta. She had a terrible cold in her head and sore feet and every time anyone left the door open she would yell way down in her throat like a man, 'Shet that door!' That was supposed to be funny. It made you jump. Gee, how she could make you jump. When we had supper Father carried her to the table—you know, because of her sore feet."

"I see. Was she fat? Did she wear a gingham dress?"

"No, she was so thin that she looked like a stick. She had red hair."

"Red hair?"

"Not like yours. Hers was dark red. You know—queer hair."

"I think I know. And no gingham dress?"

"I guess I don't remember her dress but she had bare feet in sandals. I don't notice so much." But he remembered how his father walked straight across the room with his hand on Joseph's shoulder and stood smiling at the woman. "You're going to get the surprise of your life, Marta."

The woman with the "queer" hair was holding Tom's hand as she stared at the boy. Then she fairly shouted, "You damned fool!"

It wasn't so bad for, almost instantly, Joseph saw that, while she was staring at him, she was really fooling with his father.

Two other women crowded against them, two odd-looking women, a thin one and a tall, fat one and soon Joseph noticed that the thin one was like a shadow; she followed the big woman, laughed when she laughed, agreed with all she said, got up when she got up and sat down when she sat down. It was something like the game of Follow-the-leader. He wasn't sure that he liked the big General (they called her "General") and he didn't like her shadow at all. It gave him no pleasure when he learned that the General really owned the house and invited all her friends from the city to come up and rest and get country air. She said they could rusticate with clothes on or off. They laughed when she said that.

There was a heavily built young man who stopped to stare at the boy, then took his hat and presently Joseph saw him climbing over the hill. He never came back.

They sat down in a circle about Marta who was waving a copy of what Joseph thought of as "his father's magazine." They all talked at once but Marta talked loudest and seemed frantic about its being the best issue they had ever put out and its being so deep "in the red." But almost at once, Tom jumped up and, standing before a water color, peered down at the name; then asked, "Who's Bel—D-y-n-i-t-c-h?"

There was a subdued "sshing" sound and the General pointed up at the ceiling. "Dynitch. Father Serbian, mother American, taking a nap, delicate, sick, probably incipient tuberculosis, bright —Marta's newest protégé—all run down—worse shape than Grandam—going back tonight—been here a month."

"Awful daubs." Tom glanced at three or four other water colors and seemed to shudder.

The General laughed. "She's a starry-eyed adolescent, crazy as a bedbug. She can write though. You'd better take her on your lousy magazine."

Marta replied hoarsely, "I would but the pay-roll won't support the addition of a flea. She's a nice, sensible girl, high-strung and nervous but very refined. She's got to earn her living sooner or later and she knows she can't sell enough of this stuff so she's

going back to New York to take a job as a stenographer. Clarence
is bothering her. She can type, take shorthand and she can spell.
God knows none of us but Tom can do that—spell. Her figure's
good enough for a model but she wants none of that."

Joseph began to like the old woman; he could see she had a
kind heart and felt sorry for the orphan.

When she added, "She's a virgin," they laughed uproariously.
Joseph's prowess in Latin or mental arithmetic was inadequate to
help him understand the laughter. The word "virgin" meant one
of two things—either the mother of Jesus or a girl who was not
old enough to be married yet.

As though to prove Marta's description as accurate, the door
from the hall opened and a young girl hesitantly, bashfully, entered the room.

Immediately, Joseph was filled with pity and a great sympathy
for her for he knew how painful it was to be talked about and
stared at. Besides, she had been represented as a complete failure
and this girl might starve to death if she couldn't earn her living.
The idea of starvation came to him naturally when he looked at
her for, if Marta was a stick, she was a mere sliver.

She was introduced and, when she looked at Joseph, her smile
was very pleasant. "Your *son?*" She seemed to find him astonishing.

It was the boy's turn to be astonished when his father began
to praise her water colors. "Freshness, originality, impressionistic." They all agreed that they were "individual" and poured
on the praise like syrup over pancakes. It was bewildering after
the previous shuddering and words like "awful daubs."

Everything was bewildering, amazing but exciting. At first one
noticed the constraint, the timidity of the girl's glances, the wonder in her up-turned eyes, the diffident but pitifully eager manner
in which she tried to explain what was in her mind as she painted
the big oil, resting against the legs of a chair. Tom seemed to
understand; Joseph did not. He tried hard and he saw horses'
hoofs, a saddle, blue plates, the hands of a clock without the clock,
half a woman's face and, down in a corner, an engine and part

of a train, steam up. He got so excited when he was sure it was a train that he joined in the praising chorus and he told her he thought it was a fine train. She put her arm around his shoulders and gave him a squeeze but he noticed her hand was icy cold and wet when it touched his.

She was getting excited; yes, it was plain that she was excitable. She said that, in this picture, she had shown the progress of women, where she is and where she is going and Tom gave the picture flattering attention.

They looked at other pictures. There were landscapes painted by the General but again, they were not fully appreciated by the galleries; there were portraits done by the thin woman, lucrative work but a bore and beneath her talent. They talked of Art, endlessly of Art. Then the General told Tom to mix some cocktails. He stopped at the door and told the General he would like milk for Joseph.

"Milk! Bel had the last drop." They all discussed having no milk and Tom made them laugh when he said, "What, no milk!"

They all got to laughing almost hysterically at the idea of *that* family having no milk and in the midst of the uproar, the General ordered, "All hands turn to and clear this table. Goulash for supper." All hands turned to, Joseph overdoing his part. Had he stayed on the chair near Marta (like the queen bee she never moved) the accident would not have occurred. He, in his excitement, forgot his clumsy feet and, stepping back from the table, he put his heel right through the picture, the picture symbolic of the growth of a woman's soul.

He bit his lips hard and tears stung his eyes as his father explained, "Sorry, I forgot to warn you that he always walks backward."

Feeling frightfully sick in the middle of his stomach, he sat down on a sofa and instantly Bel came and put her arm around his shoulders, whispering, "Thanks, Joseph. I *hated* that picture. I've wanted to do that myself."

Instantly, his wonderful smile illumined his face. He was so sick that he couldn't speak yet but he looked his gratitude as she whispered in his ear, "You're a darling. We—you and I—must be real friends." She left her arm resting against his back and then and there he knew that he and Bel would always be friends. He knew exactly what he meant by that. He was not too young to know that a friend was a person who was always *for* you and you were always *for* him. He glanced at Bel's thin little face with the feverishly bright eyes; felt her arm against his back, heard her friendly, whispered words and was happy again.

If that ambrosial odor, wafting in from the back of the house, was something called goulash, he could hardly wait for supper. It was. A man servant whom they called Peter-the-Great, came in and scrubbed the table, then set blue plates on the wooden surface. In trip after trip, he brought food; what looked like half a cheese, a loaf of bread with a knife to cut it; then came pickles and sweets. Later, after instructions from the General, this old man set a cup of cocoa before Joseph. It was made with water, was almost as thick as a mud pie and he must have forgotten the sugar. The boy was watching his manners carefully now so he drank it heroically and felt he had performed no mean feat.

They all spoke gratefully of Clarence who had supplied the bottles out of which Tom filled and refilled their glasses.

At first, Bel looked frightened when Tom coaxed her to try a cocktail; then she took a second and when it was followed by a third, it was something to watch her. She had very dark, naturally curly hair which had been freshly combed when she first came into the room. Now she began to run her thin fingers through it, finally snatching at it with clawlike hands, leaving it standing out every which way. Her thin little face with the narrow chin became flushed, her eyes got darker and brighter and she talked eloquently about Serbia, about oppression and liberty, about writers and then about the old stand-by, Art.

About a hundred times she said that only sincerity counted. She loved the word "sincerity," although it was getting difficult to enunciate every syllable and Tom evidently loved to hear her talk about sincerity for he changed his seat to be next to her and gave her the same flattering attention he had given her pictures.

Once in a while, he caressed the back of her neck with his fingers just the way he often did Mother's. Once Marta reached over and pulled his hand away although she laughed as she did it.

Long since, darkness had closed down outside; the lights were on and they drank and talked and talked. They went into near-hysterics over jokes which Joseph missed. When Peter-the-Great asked if they would save goulash for Clarence, the General said, "No, scrape the dish." Then she looked angry as she added, "He's got a woman in the village."

Bel suddenly looked alarmed. "He promised to drive me into the city for my train. There's no other way I can get there." She had reservations and must be in the new office job in the morning. Jobs were not easy to get. She was on the verge of tears when Tom said what Joseph was longing to say, "Forget Clarence, stop worrying. I'll take care of you. There's loads of time. I'll get you to the train."

She thanked him and looked up into his eyes and for quite a long minute she did not look away; then she blushed and dropped her head, murmuring, "Thanks. That will be wonderful."

Marta said, "Don't take too good care of her, Tom," and ordered him to help her back into her rocker. Then she showed him her bare feet and red, sore spots which she called something like rheumatic-inflammation. He seemed greatly concerned and, while the General and the old man were clearing the table, Marta patted Tom's face and they held a whispered conversation after which she reached into her dress and took out some money. She counted out bills and gave him a lot.

Joseph heard her say, "You see I can't go. You'll have to be there tomorrow."

Everyone kissed everyone. Some must have got themselves kissed several times for there seemed no end to the affectionate good byes. Tom kissed Marta, then Marta kissed Joseph, then Tom again. Even the General kissed them both and when Peter-the-Great put the bags in the car Joseph dodged quickly for he felt certain he might try to kiss him next.

At first Joseph sat in the middle, all three crowding on the front seat but soon the rain started to come down in earnest. Tom stopped the car, got the raincoat and, putting Bel in the middle he covered them all with it. The rain slashed and beat in mostly on Joseph's side and he was glad it wasn't on Bel for she was going on a train but he could go right to bed. They took it as a joke and made up their minds to enjoy the "pure water, straight from Heaven."

Every so often Tom would say, "Can you see the time on my wrist watch?" She would lean over him and, forgetting to sit up again right away, she wiped the glass and told the time.

Sometimes they did not talk at all and, in spite of manly efforts to control his eyelids, Joseph would wake with a start, perhaps when some freshet of cold water started down his neck.

On the whole the trip seemed very short. Bel kept her arm about his shoulders much of the time, holding the raincoat almost over his head. In spite of puddles and slippery roads they reached the station long before schedule. Under the shed roof, Tom got out and took her bags. She kissed Joseph several times, hugged him and rubbed her cheek against his, then ran quickly after Tom.

They were gone some time while valiantly Joseph fought to keep his eyes open. At last his father appeared, spoke a moment with a public cabman, stopped to put some railroad tickets in his pocket and then they drove home.

When the car stopped at the side door, there was his mother standing in a flood of light, waiting. His father said, "Jump out. I'm putting the car up."

In the side porch, Joseph dropped the raincoat to the floor and shook himself as he smiled up at her, "I'm drenched but it's only at the top. I've been to a wonderful party."

She did not smile. "Tell me in the morning. Mattie's waiting with a hot bath. After your bath, get right into bed. She'll bring you a mug of warm milk."

He ran up the stairs. "Aren't you surprised, Mattie?" If Mattie was surprised she did not show it.

It was his turn to be surprised, even completely dumfounded for after his bath, while Mattie was gone for the milk, he went down the hall where he heard voices. He came to his mother's door and stopped.

His father was standing by the bureau wearing his overcoat. On a chair by his side were his bag and briefcase. His mother opened her little desk drawer, took out an envelope and handed it to him. Joseph instinctively knew he must not intrude for his mother's face was deadly white and strange, and she spoke with some fearful weight of sadness in her voice. "If you must go, Tom, here are some checks I've endorsed to you. It will mean rigid economy here for us until January. I'm sorry you're doing this."

Joseph ran back where Mattie was waiting, thinking, "Everyone gives my father money. Gee, it's wonderful." He got into bed, drank the milk and was so sleepy he did not know when Mattie put the light out and he scarcely remembered the incident the next morning.

The full impact of the knowledge that his father had actually gone back to New York on that night train did not strike him until that next day.

He excused and explained it all to his mother. "I think he was going instead of Marta because her feet are sore and I think he was afraid to let Bel go all alone to New York. She's too young and excitable."

"Bel?"

"I can't spell her last name. You have to be particular about Bel—just three letters." He seemed to like Bel, his friend. He poured out all kinds of information about her; she was so young, so excitable, so poor, so run-down; then, about her job, Clarence's disappearance, his father's kindness to her. He even told of the shameful accident when he kicked a hole in her picture. He remembered Marta's words of description—she was a nice, sensible young girl and a virgin.

His mother seemed dazed and sad and silent and soon he felt only hurt and bitter disappointment because his father had gone away again.

CHAPTER XIV

For several days Joseph continued to pour into his mother's ears details of his experience at the wonderful party in Fayettville.

"My, she could make you jump. Once she threw that magazine across the room and it hit the wall a wallop."

"You're sure it was the old woman who was called both Grandam and Marta?"

"Oh, yes."

His mother was always a good listener, sitting quietly, looking directly into his face and paying attention to every word. If Sandra spoke she turned to her and listened just as closely, knowing quite well that to them both she was a sort of safety-valve; after any trouble, any quarrel, any triumph, any joy, they poured the tale into her attentive ears, then, straightway, forgot it.

When she saw the boy's troubled expression in speaking of the old factories, she explained carefully what that grandfather had achieved by closing the poor little mill and building a fine new one where the waterpower was sufficient. She told him of the new houses and how he had moved the workmen from Fayettville into them.

One evening when she opened his window, she spoke cheerfully to Joseph, "You have had two exciting parties. It's all over and now we must get down to regular business which is fun too. There was a letter from Uncle Lawrence today. He's anxious to know if you can skip another grade. He thinks with a little tutoring you can. What do you think? And he asks if your tennis is improving."

Joseph scowled, "Not much. Who would tutor me?"

"Either Miss Simmons—she's very good—or your Latin professor."

"O.K."

Faster and faster the leaves fell, sifting down through days of cold rain and days of mellow sunshine. Hard frosts came early on shriveled leaves and full seed pod and the flower stalks in the garden hung their heads as though mourning the glory that was departed.

Now Ben came regularly to stoke the furnace while, in his spare time, he began to adjust double windows and storm doors and generally prepare a defense against the storms of winter. Inside the house, Mattie was equally busy, getting blankets and winter clothes out of moth balls and giving curtains and draperies a last chance at sunshine.

The faule of the leafe. The days were so full of activity that there was little time except for practical thinking, but the nights were long.

In November, late one evening, Mary sat before her desk reading three letters which she had but glanced at when they arrived on the noonday mail. Her fingers moved nervously back and forth over a letter from her husband addressed to her son. Would she hand it to the boy or open it? She tore it open. It was short, affectionate, presumptuous: "Hello, there. How are you? Here's a surprise for you. I (Marta and Bel also) want you to come to New York for your Thanksgiving holiday. Father's too busy to get home but a big fellow like you ought to begin to learn to travel alone. . . ." For only a moment she looked at it, then she tore it into many small pieces and threw them in her wastepaper basket. A flush of anger reddened even her forehead. Not another step would the boy take, if she could prevent it, on that road which looked so dark and dangerous to her. She was sorry to deprive him of the pleasure of receiving a letter from his father but she saw no other way.

The angry flush did not recede and her eyes held their level steady expression as they moved quickly from line to line in Tom's letter to her.

He had written four letters to her since that September night of the party, some of abject contrition, begging her forgiveness: "I'm what you call me, Mary, a lunatic, a madman, an absolute idiot, running off like that when we had dozens of matters to discuss. Besides it was not so necessary as I thought at the time." Later, letters of anger because she did not write. "Even a housemaid gets a few minutes off. Write me or I'll go out of my mind. Your love is the only thing I'm sure of in the universe."

She was half frightened at herself for she could not and did not write. She must think out what she wanted to say before she said it.

Now she threw his long, pleading letter aside and read an even longer one from Lawrence. Three entire pages given over to an analysis of the financial situation because he was worried about her future income. All through October the value of stocks had been going down, dropping as though into a bottomless pit. He begged her to husband every dollar and write, immediately, giving him a financial statement. Then came suggestions about Joseph's school work. "Keep him on his toes." Then his and Cathey's love to them all.

The reserve, sincerity, deep devotion and care for them all, almost unnerved her. It was as though she were quite suddenly assailed with homesickness. She had been the baby surrounded with what had seemed an impregnable fortress of big brothers, father and mother and now, twenty-eight years old, she was alone. She must adjust her mind to that idea—she, the head, obliged to shoulder the responsibility. She wrote at the top of a sheet of paper, "My dear brother," but she could not go on. She could not put into words the thoughts and suffering which were the only realities in life.

She pushed away the paper and sat lost in thought. She remembered Tolstoy had written, "Man survives earthquakes, epidemics, terrible illness and every kind of spiritual suffering but always the most poignant tragedy was, is, and ever will be the tragedy of the bedroom."

She smiled with twisted lips. For a long time she allowed her mind to play with those words, "the tragedy of the bedroom." The frights, mistakes and disillusionments of the young; the ecstasy, the indescribable wonder—physical, mental and spiritual—in the fulfillment of the union where the river of life and love flowed deep and joined in both man and woman. The millions of spinsters, the dammed-up streams; the hellish variety of perversions.

The noble saint, passion changed into love for all humanity, nurses, teachers; the locked doors in thousands of homes where secrets black and devastating ate into lives; the age-old cancer of prostitution.

She suddenly saw all life as individually lonely, deeply secretive. As mysterious as God was that soul of man. Why should God seem any more mysterious to man than man's own soul to man?

She rose, walked to the mirror and stood before it looking at herself appraisingly. In one of Tom's letters he had stated—and embroidered the statement—"You say you want our life together. Come. I want you, you want me. We were born to be lovers. Get rid of that encumbrance (you call it a home), put the children in boarding schools. I can't stand them about. They drive me mad. When I came to New York, I expected you to follow soon. Then Joseph was five and there was no Sandra. I can't forgive your being a mother before a wife. Surely you wouldn't (with your eyes open) desert your husband for a son who will grow up and leave you. Come to me, my Mary."

She ran both hands up through her hair. She narrowed her eyes and saw the regular features of her still pretty face. She was pale.

She was growing painfully thin; all that rosy roundness that had been so becoming to her after the birth of her children was disappearing. If she couldn't find an appetite and eat more she would look like a stick.

She looked at the old cherry bed, the bed "built" for a family. Before drawing the curtains she pressed her face against the cold windowpane. What was the truth about her? About Tom Donovan? Did his very birth begin with the tragedy of the bedroom?

She gazed again at the pretty woman in the mirror and smiled bitterly. It didn't just happen that people used the words, "a damned fool." The qualifying word was well chosen. To be a fool was to be damned.

She threw herself down on the sofa and buried her face in the pillow. What a fool she had been—trying to save even his cheap, pretentious and unimportant magazine—and now she was to be damned. Not one tear would she shed in self-pity. If she ever started to cry she would weep until her heart should break for a million men, a million women, for untold numbers of children, born and unborn.

She lay until the house grew cold then, pulling on a heavy robe, she wrote Lawrence a brief note of thanks and the promise of a financial statement in a few days. She wrote a short note to her husband asking him to refrain from writing to Joseph for what he had requested was out of the question. He, Tom, would doubtless reconsider and find he had time for coming home at least for Thanksgiving dinner. Whatever they had to say to each other had better be said in the privacy of their own room, not on letter paper.

In the morning she had a sniveling cold in her head. However, she telephoned to Warren who said he would come up that afternoon.

They sat before the grate fire as she read to him the parts of Lawrence's letter concerned with the financial situation; she listened to his detailed description of the local conditions and saw that he too was frightened.

When he said almost casually, "The mills will be closing before January. Your dividends will be cut. . . ." she clasped her hands tightly around her knees and spoke almost angrily, "The mills? Closing? My dividends cut? What do *my* dividends matter?" She bit her lips hard. "Those are wicked words. They mean that the fathers, men I know, come home one day and set their dinner pails aside and can't—no, they can't look into their wives' eyes. The older children stop drinking milk and then there is no milk for the baby. Soon there is no way to resole the shoes. They are sick and hungry but they don't see a doctor.

"You have to know each man and each woman to visualize what it means. The families in the company houses can stay there but those who have bought homes can't pay the taxes or interest on their mortgages. Old Miss Jennings—you remember her?—she was my teacher. She put her savings in a little two-family house. The rent from one half is her living income. She can't put the poor things out who live downstairs; she will be hungry and the days of her old age will become a nightmare. Those are such cruel wicked words, 'the mills are closing.'"

His brown eyes watched her unsmilingly. "Yes, Mary, you have to know each man and woman and child to see the picture but the men at the top who gamble with human life see it as impersonally as they do the men in a game of chess."

"The men at the top! Men who have obtained money and power! They are often the lowest moral layer in our society—or in any society. They talk about mill-hands, Negroes, Jews, miners, housewives—" More tightly her clasped hands held her knees for she was trembling.

Her loneliness, her hunger for mental companionship found relief in talking unreservedly to Warren. She missed all the strong masculine minds that had formed so integral a part of her young life. When she had fallen in love with Tom Donovan she had been unconscious of his shabby blue suit; now she was unconscious of the little man's narrow shoulders, his bald head, his singed-cat appearance. She looked into his grave, steady brown eyes and knew they spoke the same language; he would understand. Like Mattie Briggs he would know everything.

"Mr. Warren, I've never been concerned with the literal meaning of the words, 'But the very hairs of your head are all numbered,' but the idea—my brother says it is the most revolutionary idea ever presented—the *idea* is my religion. I think it must have been the religion of Abraham Lincoln, and great men like him. If you once accept the Christian teaching you never again see men as classes, as groups of slaves, groups of 'middle-class,' as groups called labor unions, as mill-hands." She threw her head back against the cushion and gazed into the fire. "Once—oh, I must have been about fourteen—I came home from Europe with my mother and father and Gordon on one of the most luxurious ocean liners. Some two weeks later, I took my first motor trip with Father. One fall night we drove through a mining center in Pennsylvania when the men were coming out of the ground. I saw their grimy faces, the lanterns pushed up on their foreheads. It was dark. They had gone in while it was still dark in the morning. I remember crying. That evening I thought, 'But the very hairs of your head are all numbered.' I wanted Father to explain the contrast of that group of men and the people on the ship—explain it away. He couldn't." She turned to look into Warren's eyes. "I never forgot. I don't understand, I can't put it into words but it often makes seemingly important things appear quite trivial to me."

"Everyone doesn't care as you do, Mary. I think you care too much. There's trouble ahead and you'll have enough on your shoulders without suffering for everybody."

When he rose, he cleared his throat several times, then spoke sternly, "I guess I don't have to mince words about Tom, do I?" A deep red flushed his face. "You had better have poured your money down the kitchen drain than let him bleed you as he has. He's bled you and all his friends and acquaintances."

He spoke in his usual quiet, unimpassioned voice, even coldly and deliberately but the words stung her. "Some men spend all their lives living by pipe-dreams. Your Presbyterian Church supports that Rescue Mission down on Water Street. You draw a check and mail it in to help feed and clothe and give a bed to the people who come there. You don't follow the bums into saloons and listen to their talk. Everyone of them has his own pipe-dream. Everyone can tell you who is to blame for his condition. When he gets soused, the dream gets rosy. None of them are capable of coming to grips with reality. I'm not blaming them. At heart, I can often imagine joining them."

She was resting her arms on a chair back. Now, her hands clutched lightly as she bent her head and listened.

"At the office, I think I was the only one—except your father—who understood Tom from the beginning. If he'd gone out and honestly sold real estate—or buttons or manure—he could have earned a good salary as a salesman. No, he must be a literary man. He's a panhandler and there are different kinds of panhandlers."

Her eyes were downcast for his outburst had shocked her. Then, with a quick straightening of her shoulders, she spoke rapidly, "Mr. Warren, I think we can leave Tom out of our plans and calculations just now. The point is, I have to preserve the integrity of my own life and my children's lives."

She thought deeply while he waited. "The last thing my father would have been capable of was to paralyze me so I could not act freely and according to what I consider right. Of course I expected to keep this old home for my children. I love it." She smiled with a sudden radiance. "The brick and mortar and lawns and gardens are not the home. I shall keep my family intact. Perhaps, God willing, I may be able to keep what Father called *the line* strong. I belong to the Kent-Farnsworth tribe, if you want to call it that." She laughed, "I belong. I can't change that. I can't change my belief in that."

She rested easily now against the arm of the chair. "I told you that seemingly important things appear trivial to me. Debt and living beyond my means don't seem trivial. All right. You and Mr. Wainwright can go over my affairs. If I can't hold on here, will you sell the property for me? I can move into this side of the double house; it will be vacant."

She said the words as quietly as when she had asked him to sell her small houses some years ago; but her face was white and she held her lips firm with pressure from her teeth.

He turned his face away and answered huskily, "It won't bring what it would have two years ago; but—I'll see—I'll let you know. Give me time to think it over and talk to Wainwright."

Warren turned his back and did not look at her again as he hurried out, walking quickly to his car. He leaned over the wheel and for some time gazed at the big house, the tall elms, the shrubbery, the spacious lawns and gardens; then he started the motor and drove rapidly down the avenue.

As soulless, as superficial as the newspaper headline, "the mills are closing" were the words in her letter to her husband, some weeks later. "We are moving the first of February." The offer to buy had come unexpectedly from a distant cousin by marriage, a daughter in the Boston branch of the family. "We did not dare refuse the sale."

To Mattie, "We'll manage if we take one thing at a time."

They took one thing at a time, the attic before the bitter weather set in, the cellar, the unused bedrooms, the contents of closets and old bureaus. No one now had money to buy at prices commensurate with the value so she sacrificed a cartload of antiques to a dealer. There were the various asylums and Homes which needed furniture and Mary laughed, "Thank God for the Salvation Army. If it were not for them we'd have to pile furniture in the side garden over there."

She forced herself to laugh a great deal in those weeks; not only because it kept the children laughing, maintained a generally cheerful atmosphere, disposed of any commiserations, but also because she found the petty discipline personally helpful.

She laughed at Ben as he carried to his small house load after load of this and that. She laughed as Mattie said for the twentieth time, "I'm thankful *he* isn't here. He wouldn't be of as much help as Joseph and we'd have to stop to wait on him."

How she hated Mattie's using that pronoun "he" instead of her husband's name. However, she laughed, "Yes, this is no place for parlor ornaments."

At Thanksgiving time he had written that he had a severe cold, added to his financial worries. Early in December he wrote that he was confined to bed. He was very sick. The doctor called it some kind of intestinal flu.

Sleep would not come in the night after she had read that note, reread it, tossed it down, then picked it up and crushed it in her hand. He was sick. Warren was right; she cared too much.

She slept, then waked with a start, the victim of a terrifying dream that haunted her for days. She was stumbling alone over a rocky field in a twilight atmosphere that was strangely beautiful yet subtly menacing. Far in the distance she heard bells ringing and, with the inconsistency of a dream, the bells rang out words. The words frightened her. "For better for worse, for richer for poorer, in sickness as in health, until death do us part."

She sat up in bed and found her nightgown wet with perspiration. Tom was sick. She tossed in the big bed that had been built for a family, feeling as alone as when she struggled across the endless expanse of field in her dream.

At Christmas time, he said he was wracked by a cough but could not get away because they were liquidating the magazine; their offices would be vacated by the first of the year. "I am looking for another opening." Then, in the early part of January he wrote briefly, "I am going to Florida as the guest of a friend. I have been in bed again with this beastly Flu."

Tom Donovan saw nothing of the moving.

CHAPTER XV

Mattie said afterward that the getting ready was so much worse than the moving. Instead of his hour in the morning and his brief chores in the evening, Ben worked all day. When Mary remonstrated, he replied, "The Judge sent me over. He says, 'You pitch in there and don't let those women do any lifting or hauling. It's my time and you spend it over there.' He's the boss."

Joyce, the decorator who had always done their work, had the entire house painted and papered before they came in. Only the previous summer Mary had had the pure white of the exterior and the dark, rich green of the blinds renewed. That was as J.R. had always kept it—something pleasant and clean to look at across his lawns.

Now, if the rooms seemed small and cluttered, if the large paintings went to the attic and those that were hung appeared still too massive, if the grand piano seemed to sulk like an elephant in too small a cage, Mary merely laughed and assured the others they would soon get used to it, which was true. It was also true that Joseph and Sandra enjoyed it all. They loved the little white house with the green blinds.

Sometimes, during the weeks of February, Mattie Briggs would stand in the middle of the floor, clapping her hands to the sides of her head, exclaiming, "My land, I get dizzy trying to make decisions—a dozen things for one spot."

Mary smiled, "I expect it's more fun to expand than to contract. Still, this is a beautiful big kitchen, Mattie." Some premonition of the years ahead when she would learn to know that kitchen intimately, caused her to appraise the room with keen eyes. How different from the kitchen "over there." This was not a remote place inhabited by cooks and maids, a distant section of the house always spoken of as "down in the kitchen"; this room proclaimed itself to be the heart of the house.

It was one of those large pleasant rooms so often found in New England homes. Although a modern gas stove was used for most of the cooking, the old coal range with its shining nickel trimming still sat enthroned on its zinc platform, a solid bulwark of comfort against the cold of the long northern winter. Already, Mattie's pots of soup or stew simmered on its commodious top; crocks containing pork, molasses and beans were stowed away for twenty-four hours of slow cooking in its oven depths. At the open oven door chilled feet or legs were warmed and snow-soaked stockings and leggings were thrown over that same oven door to dry.

Hot air or the newer oil heating did very well for the remainder of a house but many northerners would as soon face the winter without coat, boots or cap as dispose of the cheer and comfort and sense of safety emanating from the big kitchen range. At any moment, winter or summer, storms might bring down the wires or disable the electric power plants but there was the good old woodpile and well-filled coal bin dependable day and night through every season.

One might search in vain for a picture of the old range in any modern magazine; it was relegated to antiquity by the designers of "laboratory" kitchens, yet, even as Mattie settled the cupboards, the crackle and blaze of wood in the morning, the steady glow of hot coals throughout the day, brought comfort to the spirit as well as to the body.

Then too, Mattie had placed an inviting round table in the center of her room, a couple of rocking chairs, one in the bay. She had placed pretty blue dishes in the sturdy corner cupboard and geraniums and begonias on a small table to get full sunlight. But Mattie would have none of the usual rag carpet. The floor was covered from baseboard to baseboard with a fine-patterned linoleum of her own choosing.

It was an integral part of those New England kitchens to have the door open into an invaluable old woodshed where one saw the planked floor, the snug roof, the beams and rafters proving the sturdiness of the whole building.

All this kitchen and woodshed comfort was duplicated in the other half of the double house; a low railing separated the two parts of the commodious front porch and a picket fence divided the deep narrow garden.

Vaguely, Mary could remember when her father bought this place to control it and protect his own property, how he took down an ugly high-board fence; how he planted perennials and annuals and came over every summer to praise the rich blooming of phlox, sweet william, baby's-breath, hollyhock, delphinium and foxglove and spared some of his precious manure for the place.

He set out some fine plum trees along the back fence, some pear and apple trees and a grape arbor. Often he sent over his gardener in the spring to plow up the vegetable patches. Mary was often to see Joseph sink his teeth into those juicy plums and wish his grandfather could see him and know, as she knew, what a beautiful memorial of a man a tree could be.

One thing they all thought very fortunate; their rooms were on the sunny side of the house and there were large bay windows. One could stand in a bay, look across the narrow drive, the side yard, then over the low fence into the spacious grounds of the old place.

Mattie remarked, "Upon my honor, I see more of the garden and lawns than I could from my old kitchen over there." As she had come to refer to Tom Donovan as "he," so she now referred to the old home as "over there."

Mary did not answer. She would need more months of discipline before she could enjoy that vista.

Of course the remainder of the house was also important. She arranged and rearranged and yet she thought the rosewood sofas, high-backed chairs and tables cluttered up rather than furnished the double parlors.

Mattie stood with palms of hands resting easily on hips as she surveyed the rooms. "In no time we'll be calling it cosy."

One bitter night in late February, they again applied the word "cosy" as Mary joined Mattie and the children who were sitting close to the big kitchen range. She entertained them with a description of a visit which she and her mother had once made to Scotland. She told them of the wee cottage with its "but an' ben," the kitchen and sittingroom; how a guest was warmly welcomed with the words, "Come awa ben."

There was a knocking at the side door. Mattie hastened to open it and, as she said later, "I guess my eyes fairly popped when I saw Judge Carter, standing as tall as a giant, his shoulders covered with snow."

He had been walking home, saw their lights, wondered how they looked in the new home.

Mattie carried his coat to the kitchen to shake off the snow as Mary explained their "cosy" occupation. Sandra, now turning six years old, watched them from the doorway; then, suddenly, with a burst of infectious laughter, she called, "Come awa ben."

Could he come into the kitchen and warm his feet at the range? His head came rather close to the ceiling, a fact he demonstrated to Sandra's delight. He proved that his feet could well-nigh fill the oven door. She allowed him to lift her to his knee and measure her tiny foot against his. She turned her violet-gray eyes and looked up into his as he asked, "May I put a tag on this big rocker and come over and sit in it when I can't stand that big, empty house?" He was asking Sandra but he glanced sharply at Mary whose cheeks flushed as deep a pink as the child's. He quickly spoke of Hunt and Mazie at their boarding schools, of Willie asleep and the aunt in Florida.

When Mattie took the children upstairs, Mary walked through the rooms with him. Judge Carter. William Higginson Carter.

Though a few years older than her brothers, they had all been friends. Mary had always known him; had always known his place, the finest estate on the long avenue, running back over the hill into something of a small farm. More vaguely still, she had known his wife, Mazie Templeton. Was gossip correct in labeling the marriage a tragic misalliance? The wife flitting about the fashion centers of Europe, secure in the wealth and prestige of her husband but bored with him, his mother, their children and home? At any rate it was something of a tragedy that she had died giving birth to this child, Willie.

The color had not left Mary's cheeks for a woman knows when a man is watching her instead of what she is showing him. She spoke lightly and gaily of his kindness in lending them Ben. As she talked she looked very pretty and avoided his eyes.

He found his coat and was putting it on as he said, "Your children have something in this little house my children have never known—a home." Then he added, "That child, Sandra. She is like you—the way I remember you until I saw you—grown up. Where did you hide between times?" He smiled. "And now? Thanks for letting me sit in Mattie's rocker. I know I mustn't intrude here but remember I'll *always* be just across the corner."

When she closed the door after him, she stood a moment with her back pressed against it as a sensation of warmth, protection— even a wistful eagerness for his friendship swept through her. She avoided Mattie's eyes when she came downstairs. That woman saw and understood everything.

The snows of February deepened; the banks along the sidewalks were waist high and almost daily the great snow-plows roared down the avenue leveling the ruts and smoothing roads for automobile safety. When school was out, pedestrians ducked the children's snowballs that flew about recklessly, walked warily for fear of sleds bumping into ankles. Sometimes icy winds bent the tall elms, whipping the branches angrily and there were long dark nights when the snow fell in sheets rather than in flakes.

On such a night early in March, Mattie, leaving a clean and orderly kitchen, was ready to follow the children to bed. Two

events of the day had disturbed her. In the afternoon the postman had handed Mary a postal. She had hurried to her room with
it and when she came down to supper there was that in her face
and eyes which Mattie could not bear to see. She pretended not
to notice Mary's mere pretence at eating.

Now, on the stairs she stopped a moment, a heavy frown mar-
ring her usually pleasant face. She muttered, "If I wasn't a Christian, I'd say, 'Damn him to hell'; but I suppose I have to say, 'God
forgive him,' instead." She took a few steps, then her frown increased. She retraced her steps. "I guess I'll have my say. You
can't keep bottled up all your life."

Back in the sittingroom she stood a little back of Mary whose
head was bent over the newspaper. She began as though she were
continuing a conversation.

"As a matter of fact, it is your fault, Mary Kent. The whole
problem of marriage is always the woman's fault and marriage is
always a problem."

Mary turned, smiling quietly into Mattie's scowling face. "*Always* a problem?"

"Beginning with Adam and Eve. Lawrence is right about the
Bible. The facts might not be historically true but, as he says, it's
the truth of life in the Bible." She sighed, "Do you know where
Eve made her mistake?"

"No. Where?"

"In telling Adam about the apple; in letting him in on the taste
of it. She should have kept the knowledge to herself. Every
woman knows that it's taken them some thousands of years to learn
that. Now the wise ones keep their secrets."

"You think women keep secrets better than men?"

"Men are open books. Women keep secrets locked in their
hearts until death. You'll keep yours. Judge Carter is an open
book."

"But—your wonderful, advanced, emancipated women haven't
learned to solve the problem of marriage yet?"

Mattie sat down on the edge of a chair. "Can I speak my mind,
Mary?"

"Go ahead." Mary dropped her eyes and looked steadily at Mattie's feet, seeing the high shoes, neatly laced to the top, the strings wound about the ankles. Mattie was large, heavy, and often said that her foundation must be solid. Now as she was silent, Mary looked up, "Go ahead old wise-woman."

"You laugh at me, Mary Kent, because I say women are marching. It's the biggest army the sun ever shone on and naturally there are whole battalions of damned fools, some imbeciles, some conceited jays. A lot are merely Follow-the-leader, you know, the kind that trot after any new fashion in clothes or ideas. Some are so weak you could blow them over. I see all that but the point is they are marching into the light.

"You see they're not marching down a road paved with smooth asphalt, they're spread out over the whole world; they go slow up a hill and they flounder in a swamp. Just now the women of America are in a swamp when it comes to the point of solving the question of marriage and divorce. The swamp is divorce and the capital city is Reno."

Mary's eyes narrowed as she looked steadily into Mattie's face. "It's a tough problem, Mattie, if you believe in home—especially if the woman is entirely to blame—a spoiled child who always got what she wanted."

"I knew you'd say that. A woman almost always gets what she's after when she wants it bad enough. That's not the point."

"What is the point?"

"The point is—no one on earth ever marries the sort of person she thinks she's marrying. A man marries a girl but only *after* does he ever find out what he's married. She may be wonderful but you take my word, she isn't what he thought she was."

"The same with a woman."

"Of course. He may turn out to be a prince but he is never what she expects whether better or worse."

"Well, you promise 'for better or worse.' It isn't that you promise God; that doesn't mean so much to me as it might to someone more orthodox, I'm afraid. It's more important; it's one's own integrity."

Mattie's well-shod foot tapped the floor. "That's just what I know about you, Mary Kent. I think you are up in the front line of those who are marching. Your head is in the light. You know Good and you know Love and that's knowing God." The foot tapped harder. "But your marriage is resting on quicksand. You hate getting in the swamp. Divorce is all right for the silly, shallow women. Those who can take one divorce after another are merely the water spiders skimming over the surface of life. They have no depth. Divorce can't wound them."

Mary jumped up and walked rapidly up and down the room. "Well, it would *wound* me. You are a wise woman, Mattie Briggs. You know it would wound me. I hate it. I hate the whole sordid, despicable business. It's defeat."

"That's your pride."

"All right. That's my pride. I hate defeat. And besides I *care* about Tom Donovan. He isn't what you think he is. He isn't what Warren thinks he is. He isn't what Lawrence thinks he is. I know him and I *care* about him." She stood a moment with her fingers tight against closed eyes. "Oh, Mattie, I expected so confidently to have what my mother and father had. No other thought ever entered my mind. I still want so terribly what they had, what Lawrence and Cathey have. I want so terribly to keep my home, a home for my children, a background, a heritage of decency, uprightness, a home where there is confidence, security and love. It's precious for children to grow up in that simple happiness.

"This little house doesn't matter. Losing my beautiful home doesn't matter. They still have everything. If I can hang on until they are old enough to be formed—don't you see? What does it matter about me?"

She stopped behind Mattie's chair and her small hand clenched the strong shoulder. "Don't you see, Mattie, I still have something. I still hope to save something?"

"That's what I know, Mary. That's what I call the quicksand of it. You're clinging to an idea."

"But do you want me to divorce my husband?" She stood in front of the woman now looking searchingly into her face.

"I did until this minute. I thought of it as defeat, as you say; but I told myself you had better say as some great general said—I don't remember who—you've lost a battle but you could still win a war. See?"

"Why do you say—until this minute?"

"Well, to tell the truth, I guess my mind was on Judge Carter. You can have that man by just looking up into his eyes and saying, 'Yes.' I was mapping out the rest of your life and I liked the landscape."

Mattie rose heavily as though struggling with a weight. "You being you, you can't divorce Tom Donovan until you give up. I see pretty clearly that you won't give up until you stop caring about him. When that happens it will *wound you more than divorce.* My Heaven! You're strong like J.R. You're like him."

She stood at the door. "You're a loving heart, Mary. You're no water spider." She opened the door. "Well, we didn't solve any problem, did we?" She smiled.

She still smiled as she climbed the stairs. Standing before her bureau she shook her head slowly from side to side. It was too perplexing; so she did up her front hair, hurried into her long-sleeved flannel nightgown and got into bed. A little worried, she slid out again to take a look at Sandra. Sometimes the child restlessly threw off the quilts. Mattie leaned over the bed and saw her sleeping quietly. She pulled down the window "just a trifle" for she and Mary could not agree about night air. For herself, she'd as soon sleep on the roof as open a window on such a night. Back in bed, she concentrated on her baking for the next day—graham bread. Otherwise she would never get to sleep.

Below, Mary went about putting out lights, checking the furnace. Then she opened the door of the upper front chamber softly, switched on the lights and stood looking about her. The bed, built for a family, looked like a monster to her, half filling the space—what space was left from bureau, chest, desk and small table. She had kept even the picture of the idiot woman and now she raised her eyes and looked at it.

She smiled a little as she turned to her desk. She too had been imagining something of that "landscape" that had pleased Mattie. She laughed as she remembered Mattie's words, "I was mapping out the rest of your life and I liked the landscape." She opened the desk and took out the postal that had come that afternoon. It was postmarked Florida and he had not hesitated to use the feminine pronoun. He had been in the hospital again but was now in Florida resting with a friend at her home.

She sat looking at the card until she shivered with cold. Was she still being an idiot woman?

She stood a moment after putting out the light and watched the storm. The street lights flickered through the swaying of tree branches. The avenue was deserted, not a man passing, not a car. Over at Judge Carter's the lighted windows gleamed through the snow like friendly beacon lights. She laid her cheek against the cold pane before she opened the window.

Almost at once, under the down quilt in the big bed, she felt a delicious drowsiness. She was young. She felt young and eager and filled with a hunger for life. Yes, she had a loving heart and —a loving body.

She could not have told why, in the morning, the world seemed a brighter, fresher place. She went about her tasks humming. She took a brisk walk in the snow, meeting the postman on her return.

"The idiot woman," she smiled, as her heart beat fast seeing her husband's handwriting and the Florida postmark. She took the letter to her room. Sitting by her desk, still wearing her fur coat and hat, she tore it open.

He reminded her that on that morning after Joseph's birthday it was she who had said "there must come an end." He supposed that she had willed long since to bring that end. He knew that divorce had been formerly distasteful to her but doubtless now she would welcome a clear-cut decision. He was not living alone. There were girls and women who valued love; who would follow a man to the ends of the earth. As usual he was being honest with her. There were three pages detailing his business reverses, his ambition, his debts and worries. Perhaps the only gift he could make her was her freedom. That and Joseph and Sandra were the best of him.

She rose, walked to the door and locked it. She read again every word in the long letter then she folded it neatly and locked it away in her desk. She sat by the window looking out into the street. The children came home from school, shouting and playing. Judge Carter's car turned into his drive. She merely stared at one spot.

She remembered attending a funeral where two friends had lost an only son. She had watched the women cry; she had watched the men sit with dry eyes and wondered, as a child could, if men were not allowed to cry. She had thought the expression on the father's face so much worse than tears.

She did not cry. She was afraid of tears. She sat with that man's expression on her face.

She behaved rather well at the supper table, actually hearing what the children were saying and making satisfactory answers. Late that night she wrote Lawrence. Perhaps he could plan to come at Easter time. She needed his advice. She finally acknowledged defeat. However, there was no great hurry. She must have time to clarify her thoughts.

During the next few days there was the matter of a cold and sore throat which kept Joseph in bed. This was so unusual as to be disturbing. Dr. Porter came and there were some days of nursing, reading aloud and carrying trays.

Through the last days of March, the snow fell more gently. There were fewer and fewer of the terrific blasts from the north. Then as April days arrived the sun again asserted itself and claimed its high position in the sky, lengthening the days, thawing the snowbanks, causing little brooks to flow in the gutters through which the children waded.

On such an April day, tired after a long walk from the business center where she had managed some necessary shopping, Mary came in, took off overshoes and coat and sat down to rest in the rocker by the sittingroom window. Beside her on a table was a basket piled high with stockings waiting for her needle. She reached for it, then pushed it away, allowing her hands to drop listlessly in her lap.

She was unconscionably tired. Perhaps she would ask Dr. Porter for a tonic. She smiled. She probably would not ask him because he would sagely advise her to eat more food. She sat thinking about him. He was an old man who had a right to be tired but who had no intention of asserting his right. He had been one of her father's best friends. She liked to think he was one of her best friends. Nevertheless, she did not want to encounter his penetrating eyes and brutal words. He might again say as he had in the past, "Get rid of Tom Donovan. Get some flesh on your bones, some brightness back in your face; get yourself a proper husband. I'll be specific—Carter there across the street. I sometimes wonder if the Judge comes in to see me to talk about his health, politics, the stock market or you. I'll produce at least two other suitors if you give me a commission." Then his probing eyes seemed to look through her. "You don't even blush. Hell and damnation! I think I know women's insides pretty well but I certainly can't get head or tail to what's in their hearts and minds. I'd like to take you over my knee and wallop you. I've wanted to do that for ten years."

Once he had barked at her, "Haven't you got enough of J.R. in you to face it? Will you get anywhere by drifting along like this?"

She wasn't drifting. She was waiting. She heard the children's voices laughing, calling, often screaming in noisy play in the garden; then as they all ran down the street and turned the corner, a peaceful quiet pervaded the house. Mattie went out to purchase groceries. Alone, Mary listened to the sound of creaking rocker and ticking clock.

She stopped the rocker and bent over her head listening to the quiet. She loved the stillness. She understood how one might come to enjoy living alone; she even understood how a man or woman might become a recluse. The great Chinese philosophers named peace of mind as the greatest blessing, far greater than wealth or fame. Did one gain peace of mind more easily living alone? A man did not live alone because he necessarily feared the world or was unable to cope with it. It could be because he did not want to.

With head resting on the high back of the chair, she could see through the window the gray clouds slowly drifting across the blue of the sky. Infinity. The infinity of time and space. The utter insignificance of the earth, its affairs, the speck called man. Property, money, position, all eventually swallowed up in six feet of earth. Only there was that something called a soul. She smiled. Queer little four-letter word, without definite meaning, without location, boundaries, compass, beginning or end. The heart was a marvelous little physical pump and people located their soul in that pump because the ache, the hope, the despair, the joy and pain seemed to be there.

She noticed the light fading in the sky. She knew that soon the children would come in with all the accompanying noise and confusion, that soon Mattie would return and prepare their supper; knew that soon this moment of quiet and peace would be gone.

For, strange to her, it was a new peace. Almost unbelieving in her own mind, she felt that it would be better for them all to know that he would never return. They had not seen him for six months. Alone, she would fight to regain a healthy atmosphere, her lost dignity. Let him live with his women—this one and that one—apparently he felt no need of marriage.

Clear-cut plans began to shape themselves in her mind and then—on the walk—even out on the street—was she imagining? —she heard his light step, the tap of his shoe, that step the sound of which had once filled her entire being with sweet anticipation. Her heart seemed to jump and throb; her hands clutched the arms of the chair as she sat tense listening.

The steps turned onto their own sidewalk; a man's figure passed her window hurriedly and he did not turn his head. He stopped at the side door, opened it; there was his quick step across the vestibule, then he stood in the doorway and her heart contracted with pain.

The thin face, the eyes slightly red-rimmed, the hair, gray, receding at the temples, the flushed cheeks not hiding the drab-white skin that was beginning to show blotches. She saw it all at a glance. She saw the age and at the same time that apparently indestructible aura of youthfulness. The old graceful charm, the head drawn back, the raised chin, the long black eyelashes and the hazel eyes; eyes now shamed, meek, begging as he whispered in a hoarse voice, "Mary?"

She shook like a dried leaf in an autumn storm as she rose with hands clinging to the arms of the chair. "Mary?" He came toward her and then, like a child, he dropped his head onto her neck and cried.

Hearing children's voices and steps in the woodshed, she took his hand and hurried him into the front hall, up the long, narrow stairs. Her trembling hands turned the key in the bedroom door, then she found towels and warm running water and soothingly, as she would talk to a child in an accident, she fixed him up and got him into a clean shirt and a good suit.

Long before she had finished, little hands were pounding at the bedroom door; then, after she had controlled her voice and offered an explanation, two pairs of young feet were running pell-mell down the stairs, Joseph's voice loud with excitement calling to Mattie, "Our father is home from New York."

CHAPTER XVI

When they came down into the brightly lighted diningroom, Mary had the curious sensation that the whole house was shaking. She swayed a little as she walked across the floor which seemed unsteady under her feet. She saw that Mattie's complexion resembled that of a cabbage rose as she shook hands with "him," turning her eyes away even as she smiled politely. Joseph also was exhibiting the clumsiness that always accompanied intense excitement. He threw himself against his father with force enough to send him reeling into a small table, then stepped heavily on his mother's foot as he bounced back and forth.

Only Sandra peered up from under her blond bangs and waited wonderingly for her turn. Tom smoothed her hair and kissed her cheek with a tenderness he had never shown her before. He called her "my baby," an appellation she had never coveted so she whisked about and ran for her seat at the table. Nevertheless her eyes were shining with the excitement and she seldom removed them from her father's face throughout the meal.

It was a good meal. Could he have a second helping of the bean soup? The omelet folded on Mattie's canned tomatoes was delicious; so was the hot cornbread of which he could not get enough. When Joseph questioned him, he was vague about when he had eaten last; in fact, Mary was constantly parrying the boy's questions and she was relieved when Tom began to entertain them with descriptions of crocodiles, snakes and birds of Florida. She drank two cups of strong tea when Mattie brought it in and, little by little, found the house, the table, her voice and her hands growing steady again.

It was Joseph who ran from room to room switching on the ceiling lights and showing his father every closet, even to pantry and woodshed.

Later, in the bedroom, Mary saw his shoulders drooping with fatigue as he stood at the foot of the bed, running his nervous fingers back and forth. He looked ill and his voice was growing hoarser. She suggested medicine but he begged, "No, no, if I can only lie down."

Under the down quilt, he stretched out and closed his eyes, murmuring words she did not catch. She lay beside him, silent, waiting. He reached out, found her hand, pressed it to his lips then lay holding it tightly resting on his chest. She heard his words, "Oh, God, what it meant to be able to come home to you."

Presently she heard his regular breathing and knew he slept. She withdrew her hand and turned her face into the pillow.

Sometime in the night her whole frame began to shake. It was as though an uncontrollable shudder had started somewhere in the depths of her being and circled outward until it encompassed her whole body. It frightened her as no nightmare ever had for she was saying, "I do not want him here."

She tried to shut out the thoughts. How long she lay shaking she would never know; asleep or awake she would never be sure; but as clearly as any experience of her life, she felt herself standing on the tennis court. She walked to the net where Gordon, that brother killed in France, was waiting for her. He took her hand, showing her how to hold the racket but, instead of proper words about tennis, he smiled and said, "Don't worry so, Mary. Of course you want him. No one can kill a miracle. Men don't believe in God nowadays. They say they can't know Him or explain Him. They can't put Him in a test tube or under a microscope—as though they ever could in times past!"

Strange, he was there only a few inches from her eyes, speaking in that simple boy's voice. "Man can't kill the miracles. I'll tell you what I know. The miracles are Birth, Love, Procreation, Death. Can any man with all the guns, all the planes, all the poison gas kill Birth? Kill Love or Death? Perhaps these scientists—they are boasting of this now—will find some secret with which they can destroy the earth. What about it? They would only destroy less than a speck in the universe. What of it? They would only destroy their personal manifestation of Birth and Death. They can't destroy Birth or Death itself. They didn't destroy me, Mary. They only got rid of a hulking human who ate and slept. Go to sleep, Mary."

She closed her eyes and felt the softness of the mattress but even clearer came the boy's voice, "One man for his moment of time on this speck of an earth is a drunkard, one a libertine, one a coward, one brave, one a wily politician, one a miser, one a cheat and a liar, one a saint; what about it? It is nothing. Time, Space, Infinity, God is not destroyed. God is Love. You can't kill Love. Go to sleep, Mary."

Her lips relaxed and a delicious drowsiness crept over her eyes.

When she woke, the sun was streaming into the room. She slid out of the big bed so as not to wake her husband. More real than he or her children or her household was that strange experience of the night. It was hours, even days before the tones of Gordon's voice grew dimmer. She wanted to tell Mattie. No, smilingly she thought, "Mattie's right; there are secrets in women's hearts."

The first days and weeks were difficult. This shamed, meek, apologetic person was no one she had ever dealt with before. He kept to the house, sometimes lying for hours on the couch or on the big bed upstairs. He looked ill, sometimes desperately ill but when she wanted to send for a doctor, he protested. "I'm tired. Give me a few days to rest. I'll be all right when I get over this cough."

She was grateful for sunny days when she could keep the children out of doors. Here there was no distant nursery to which to banish them and, willy-nilly, one was forced to live with one's family in a small house. He said he didn't mind.

For days it was difficult for him to speak because of his cough and hoarseness but he must talk: no dam could hold back his usual fluent speech.

She tried to quiet him because he was running a temperature. "Tom, don't let's talk about the past. Don't you want to forget it all, bury the memory of the magazine, forget the losses and bitter disappointment? Can't we start right from today? I don't live in the other house over there; I live here. Can't you do the same?

"It's like this. I've invested my money so as to insure the children's education and assure me of a modest, adequate income. I accept that. I'm willing to forget."

No; he had to tell her. He began talking about the dead magazine exactly as one speaks of a corpse lying in the next room. It never had amounted to much. That was Marta's fault. His hatred of Marta, his bitterness against Marta appalled her. Marta had lied to him about her capital; she had got him back only because she saw a source of money.

"But wasn't she a capable editor? Hadn't she held some important position on a large magazine?"

That question loosed a torrent. He must make her understand. "As an editor for women, when she was younger, she was a marvel. She knew exactly how to chose the pretty story—the girl sacrificing a pretty dress to take Grandma to the play—the girl meets pretty boy, boy meets pretty girl thing—as thin and superficial and clever as she could find them—baby-pink stories—society notes—sweet, inspiring sermons. Oh, yes, that was when she was a big shot—a petty, pin-brained ass sits at a desk and feels like God Almighty because she can make or destroy some human being who has put his life blood into years of work. She could boast of throwing out two stories of Galsworthy in one day."

Mary tried laughing. "Oh, Tom, there are pompous asses in every line of work."

"She was worse than that. She couldn't be satisfied with that. She had to have an intellectual 'little' magazine of opinion. If she had honestly written one opinion she had of God, man, woman, home or money, she would have had a public. No, she was simply a liar. She followed the so-called intellectual crowd, bought the bilge—"

He drew himself up on his elbow and the red blotches became prominent on his skin. Sometimes there were really beautiful intonations in his charming voice, sometimes he hesitated, then fairly blurted out his venom. "Christ forgave the thief nailed on the cross. That thief stole silver. Marta steals both money and human souls. Once, Mary, you called me an adept lover; Marta taught me that."

She looked into his hazel eyes now filmed and sunken, with bloodshot whites, noticed his heavy breathing and now she listened intently to every word. Perhaps he was right; she had better know about Marta.

"Marta taught me what she knew when she got her claws into me when I was a boy in Boston. Do you know that a boy of seventeen or eighteen can be putty in the hands of a woman of thirty? Did you ever read Colette? She knew a thing or two. I had got my first good job as a salesman. I was living with a girl who had come back from Canada with me. I had almost decided to marry her for we were fairly happy and she expected a baby. Oh, I wasn't brought up like Lawrence. I wasn't brought up at all.

"Marta got rid of that girl, gave her money and sent her home. She was a big shot then, had lived years in France and Italy. She was smart. She could write interviews with rich and prominent nincompoops; could advise young girls three hundred and sixty-five times a year how to powder their noses, how to make up, how to get husbands, and say it every time as though it were new.

"She took me to New York for education with her. I was educated. When she got her big position, she threw me out. I got to drinking. That's when I came here. I had on my last suit and my feet were nearly on the ground and I was twenty-six years old."

She spoke with a calmness and quiet that surprised even herself. "What became of the girl, Tom?"

"What girl? Oh—Elizabeth? Lord! I don't know. I don't know to this day. She started back to her father and mother in Canada. She was just an ignorant, healthy little cow who had got herself pregnant."

He went on talking but she hardly heard him. Was that the beginning of his complex, that furious hatred of pregnancy? Or was it what he so often said—his own unwanted birth? Or was it an integral part of Marta's creed?

He was telling of Marta's cashing in, selling her stocks before they knew what she was doing, in December, getting out of the country, living now in France, "Swinging high again while everyone else was sinking into the abyss. A new man is like a tonic to her. She has no loyalty, no care for anyone—for any of them." He spoke of "them" as though speaking of a family.

After some of the furious bursts of confidence, after torrents of words, he would lie exhausted, ill and weak. Down in the kitchen, Mattie almost ran from butcher to market, from cupboard to stove, planning, cooking delicious meals to build him up.

One day he stood at the window, studying the drive. "I think I'll tackle those last cakes of ice today, Mary; get the drive cleared."

"Don't overdo." She watched him pick the ice, scatter it about in the sun and get the garage doors open. There was a day of tinkering, the mechanic getting it in order, the trial of the car on the road, then he came in smiling, "Now we can get out into the world again."

The beauty of the spring came with the bright May days. Sometimes with the children, sometimes alone, they rode out to the country, watched the buds swell on the trees, the tender green leaves unfurl, the grass grow green, the farmers laboring at the plows.

The smell of the good earth. When they were alone, he talked fluently of impersonal things—of poetry and nature. His long years with Marta and her magazine had not been fruitless for he had attained an amount of erudition that secretly astonished her. Once he spoke of a certain novel. He smiled at her, "I read that —I read dozens of books because I had heard you speak of them, Mary. You never knew how it used to burn me up when you and Lawrence flaunted your wide reading—"

"Tom! Did we ever *flaunt* anything?"

"I'm teasing you. I'll admit—though he hates me—Lawrence is modest, too modest for his own good; but I was insanely jealous when you looked at him and referred to some book or poem or character I didn't know."

There was, during those bright days, some mental companionship with him which she had never experienced before. And yet —why was she always straining so hard to stop thinking? It was, she thought as she looked back at those days in later years, as though she were standing with her back against a closed door, always knowing what was behind it but never allowing herself to look.

She often told herself that he was her husband, the father of her two fine children. It had been all through the years "for worse"; now, wasn't there a chance? Wasn't there a chance for its being "for better"? Was it too late? Not for him but for her?

They passed a little box-like house on a back-country road. The roof was half covered with new shingles and the sun shone on the glistening hammer as a young man, on a ladder, tore off the old gray rotted ones and fitted in the new. Near him on the ground, a girl was picking up broken bits for kindling, filling an apron. She looked up at the passing of the car and Mary saw she was thick with child, her face lineless, placid, smiling, and Mary's eyes suddenly felt hot with unshed tears.

Tom looked at her. "What's the matter?"

"Nothing."

Long before the end of June she would wonder if this could be the same man who with hanging, shamed head, sick and broken, had shambled in on that early April day. There was now the old jaunty swing to his shoulders, the resonance to his voice, the cleared eye and the hearty appetite. He even strutted as he walked about the house, saying he too thought it cosy. He was getting to like it.

But behind that closed bedroom door, was lost forever the ecstasy of a young girl experiencing the holy miracle of love. No more would her entire being seem part of the very source of life, a deep flowing river, an endless stream of love, something beautiful and eternal.

She was his wife. Now she told herself that if she were to keep the father of her children in their home, she must set herself certain tasks. She must be his wife and painstakingly avoid having a child. Somehow she must also find work for him to do.

Almost impossible to endure was a sense of shame which lived with her through those days. She was not used to feeling shame. It was not from knowing of gossip, of prying, curious eyes. She couldn't define it until she knew she was pregnant, then she understood. She was ashamed because she did not want this baby. She was ashamed because she could not bring herself to tell Tom Donovan. Day by day she waited for some felicitous moment to break the news but the moment never seemed to come. The days went by and then an hour of catastrophe struck.

Almost as lightning demolishes a tall, gracious elm standing in solitary beauty in a low pasture, tearing away its limbs, so black-hooded tragedy entered their door and struck at the solitary woman who was so close a part of the structure of Mary Dono-van's life.

On the morning of the Fourth of July, Tom had the car out, ready to take them all down to see the parade. At the last moment Mattie, who always enjoyed sitting in the back seat with the chil-dren, refused to go. Mary was puzzled and, as she walked toward the car, she remembered how flushed Mattie's face was and how she had evaded answering when asked why she was prowling around downstairs in the night.

Turning, Mary retraced her steps and entered the house. What was that sound? She followed it to the kitchen where Mattie sat by the center round table, head pillowed on her arms.

In the minutes that followed, Mary sent Tom off with the chil-dren, telephoned Dr. Porter, and had Mattie lying on the sofa with loosened clothes. Half an hour after Dr. Porter arrived an am-bulance stopped at the door, men in white carried the large woman out on a stretcher, and Mary climbed into the vehicle by her side as Dr. Porter went ahead in his car.

The hospial was but half a mile from the business center, a gloomy old building with long narrow windows set deeply in the brown brick walls. As the ambulance turned into the court, they heard the parade a few blocks distant, heard the band playing "The Stars and Stripes Forever," and the cheering crowds.

Mary hurried into an office to make arrangements for there was not a minute to be wasted when a burst appendix threatened a life. The patient must have a private room. "Don't spare any-thing that is necessary. Yes, I will be responsible for any expense." She signed a check; one paid in advance for a room here.

There were interminable delays and more examinations. With apprehension, Mary at last learned that the doctors too celebrated their country's birthday. The case needed an experienced man and someone was driving in from the Country Club.

At last Mary was leaning over Mattie's bed as they put a shot in her arm. "I'll be right here to watch for everything, Mattie. I won't leave."

"I had biscuits raising."

"They'll be nice and light." And they both laughed.

They both laughed, the merriment lingering on their faces as the door closed behind the wheeled bed.

Mary telephoned home and Joseph answered that Mrs. Fuller had seen Mattie taken out in an ambulance, watched for Father and told him.

Then she talked to her husband. "Tom, can you keep things going? I can't leave here."

"Of course we'll manage. Don't think of us. We're all scared to death though; we're whispering. You should see the size of Sandra's eyes. We never saw the house before without you or Mattie. Call me when you can get away and I'll come for you."

She only got away for changes of clothes, baths and short rests. Again she watched close to the miracle Death. She sat with her arm circled around Mattie's head seeing what she had seen in her father's face. She was so close she could catch Mattie's whispered words, "They were such beautiful babies, Joseph and Sandra."

Mary said, "Remember, Mattie, how we argued when you said Joseph was beautiful. I knew he was a big clumsy, broad-faced boy with the large Kent nose. I knew it and wanted him that way." They laughed. Again the merriment lingered on their faces. Once Mattie whispered, her voice dying away with the last words, "We've been such friends, Mary."

Mattie Briggs was dead. It couldn't be, because the mind could not accept it and yet it could be because you were following the line of behavior that she would have wanted.

Days before, Mary had telegraphed Lawrence and he got there too late, although he came directly from the train to the hospital. Early the next morning, before they brought Mattie home, Mary stood in the front parlor waiting for her brother's answer to a request. "Of course I could send Sandra to some friends but I thought if you wanted her—she is young—"

"Please let me take them both, Mary. Cathey will love having them. It will give you time."

"No, not both, not Joseph."

She wanted to drive to the station with them but she could not leave the house now and teeth clenched into her lips as she watched Lawrence carrying the bags, holding Sandra's hand as the little girl's tiny feet skipped and ran keeping up with him. They waved from the cab, Sandra looking back at her mother a little wonderingly. There would most certainly be trouble with her later but Lawrence would know what to do.

It was as Mattie would have wanted it. At the funeral in her own parlor were her pastor, all her church friends, neighbors who respected or loved her. On the sofa sitting close together shoulder touching shoulder, were Joseph and Ben's boy, one with thick blond hair, the other with black kinky curls, two friends who had known Mattie from their babyhood. The small white hands and the small black hands had clung to her skirts, reached for her cookies, dodged her tongue and her slaps after perpetrating some annoying mischief; two little friends, wide-eyed, seeing Death but with no understanding, only vaguely troubled.

There was Ben who had toted for her, hurried for her, eaten from her table and served her. Now Ben sang at her funeral. He was soloist in the African church and he said, "I know what to sing."

It was the only unendurable thing at the funeral—that music. Big Ben stood by the piano and his wife, Kit, played the accompaniment. His rich voice was steady, full, golden in tone and weighted with emotion, the words pregnant with meaning.

"I have come to the end of my journey."

The day held warm and clear; the light slanting across the Kent-Farnsworth burial plot where they laid her beside her father and mother. Martha Briggs.

CHAPTER XVII

For a few days, except for breakfast, there was hardly reason to go into the kitchen. The invitations poured in. Sunday dinner was eaten with one of the homeliest of the old women whose nose was not only long but bumpy. While he dressed in his light-colored palm-beach suit, Tom looked gay and youthful. "Remember the first time we ever dined there? I wasn't sure whether I ought to be up on James Russell or Amy, so I read them both until I was groggy; then old Lucy talked for two hours about growing herbs and making soap and Cal Coolidge. I couldn't even get to her book shelves."

They drove back from the rambling old white house far out in a suburb, slowly because the long July evening was cool and refreshing after the heat of the day. For a few minutes, after Tom put the car up, and Joseph had been sent up to bed, they walked back and forth in their own little garden. Once he put his arms about her shoulders. "Why don't you have one good cry, dear?"

"Why don't I?" She smiled. "Because I'm trying to think out what to do, how to manage. Crying makes me feel weak and useless."

"Well, there isn't another Martha Briggs but there are women who can cook and clean."

"Yes, I told Kit, Ben's wife, she could come by the day. She asked for the job."

"What smells so sweet?"

"It's those white roses. I've never had roses with a heavier perfume." She laid her hands against his chest and looked up into his face. He was very attractive tonight, looking almost handsome in his light suit, his eyes bright but with a calm, happy, affectionate expression in them as he pulled her close to him. She said, "Tom, in spite of all the rough and ugly spots in the road, we've had something rather wonderful, haven't we? I'm beginning to have faith that it's nearly indestructible."

He kissed her. "We've had *you*." He added lightly, "I'm every kind of a damned fool; I've dragged you through hell. It's of no comfort but it's the truth, you're the only person I've ever loved."

"You have been so kind and understanding through every minute of this awful week, I wonder if you will be equally kind and understanding when I tell you that I expect another baby."

She dropped the bomb and watched breathlessly for the result.

He did not show either surprise or anger but she saw an expression of disgust creep into his face. He looked away as he said, "Just when I was thinking—'at last!' Joseph so grown up he can be *sent* to bed, Sandra sent to Lawrence and you and I alone. . . . When will it be?"

"March, I expect." Then she added pleadingly, "Why do you only want 'you and me alone'?"

He loosed her arms abruptly and walked away. He called, "The telephone. I'll answer."

She heard him talking to someone he called "Mr. Graham." He ended, "Make it any time you like, nine, ten—all right, I'll be down at ten."

He showed excitement as he explained that Graham was the biggest—well, one of the biggest newspaper men in New England. "Rather curious, it wasn't a definite offer, sort of a try-out. Anything I wanted to do, they need help even in editorial work."

The calm was gone; he walked about, paced back and forth, lit one cigarette from another, shoulders jerking as he turned, all the old nervous motions apparent. Once he laughed, "You know, the Catholics, with their funeral wakes, have something that we Protestant New Englanders missed. Haven't we some whiskey in the house?"

Her quick-drawn breath was a fervent prayer. She smoothed back his hair, tenderness in her face and voice and hand. "Tom, dear, let's be old-fashioned New Englanders tonight. You'll need a clear cool head in the morning. Why, do you know you're really handsome tonight. You have that clean, youthful, energetic look you had when we first met."

"All right. You win. Shall I lock up?"

Behind the closed bedroom door, he laughed, "Your old-fashioned New Englanders could drink us under the bed with their gin and hard cider."

She laughed but stopped when she saw him standing by the bureau, narrowed eyes staring at one spot. She did not like the tone of his voice as he asked, "You know that Carter owns or practically controls this morning and evening paper? I suppose

he owns Graham. The great Judge happens to drive by the cemetery, stands at Martha Briggs' grave, sends a priceless bunch of
lilies and orchids—"

"He raises orchids in his greenhouse—"

"And walks across the graveyard in intimate conversation with
my wife. Joseph prattles about his sitting in our kitchen. I've
never had occasion but I could be infernally jealous of you."

"You've never faced the fact, but you have been rather jealous
of Joseph and Sandra." She tried making light of the idea, making his jealousy an amusing characteristic.

"While I was begging for one letter. I didn't miss the way he
looked at you. A man means only one thing by that look—"

"Tom! Stop it."

"Six months. Now—" he turned to her, "did you ask him for
this job?"

"No, I did not. He asked me if you would consider staying
here and accepting newspaper work."

"Why in hell didn't you tell me? Was it a secret between you?"

"Snap out of it, Tom. I had no idea what he had in mind, or,
for that matter, whether he had anything in mind. If you will
come to your senses you'll remember that I've had other things
on my own mind."

He was silent then. He put out the lights and got into bed. He
turned on his side and did not speak again.

So there was to be more rough road. She arrived nowhere by
thinking: Was it the baby? Would she talk to him and tell him,
with shame, that she did not want it either? She heard his even
breathing and knew he was asleep. She felt only sad and bewildered. Was marriage still, to him, only what an adolescent
boy dreams of?

In the morning, she was standing by the stove as Joseph came
into the kitchen. She had been standing there for some time looking about the room. How immaculately clean, in what perfect
order Mattie had always kept that large, pleasant kitchen. Now
the sun was slanting in; later it would flood that bay window.

The boy stood beside her and to her eyes, he was not unlike

the fresh morning sun. She smiled, "What's the schedule for today?"

"We play Winton High this afternoon."

"Your tutoring?"

"He says just an hour—ten o'clock. Can I have cornflakes?"

He brought the milk bottles, turning one upside down on the table. Steadying it with his hand, he glanced at her. "Mattie never let us pour off the cream. We won't have to have someone else here, will we, Mother? I think you are just as good a cook as Mattie."

She smiled. "I have learned a lot since we lived in this little house. I'm thankful for that, but I'm afraid I'll need help with the hard work. Cooking an occasional supper and serving three meals a day are two different things. Try to remember all the things Mattie taught you, Joseph. It will help Mother. I'll write a list while you're eating and see how well you can do some marketing."

"What about Sandy?"

"What about her?"

"Why did you do it? Send her away?"

"I thought it best." She watched his face down near the cornflakes. "Don't wolf your food."

"I thought I'd write to her. Could I describe the funeral?"

"Write anything you please."

He fastened the wire basket on his bicycle, rode pell-mell down the walk, pedaling mightily, his face lifted into the sun, as he bumped over the curbstone.

She made black coffee for her husband.

Before noon he telephoned her. She asked, "How did it go, Tom?"

"There was nothing to it. All cut and dried, decided before I heard of it—a job for *your* husband, my darling. I won't be home for lunch."

"If you're not using it, I'd like the car this afternoon."

"I'll send it up with one of the boys." He hung up abruptly.

The hot July day was what they called a "scorcher" but, under the great arch formed by four rows of tall elms where the branches interlaced over her head, she was conscious of the coolness, as she drove down the long avenue, the majestic beauty of the trees, the exquisite tracery of deep shadow on the pavement.

She slowed down as she approached a group of boys riding bicycles. There was the disheveled blond head of Joseph. There was black Monty with his kinky hair. There was Hunt Carter to act as referee, home for vacation, still skinny. Others she knew by name or family. She drove slowly, keeping well behind them until they turned up a hill where they stood on their pedals pumping vigorously, swaying from side to side, shouting at each other.

Reluctantly, she turned off at a street leading to a fairly new development far out on the river road. Here she entered a small community of Negroes and parked her car before a yellow house. Ben, who was working in his potato patch, hurried to open the door as widely as his mouth was flung open in a great welcoming smile. Kit was swinging a broom, her girth fairly filling the small hall. What a mountain of a woman and what it must take in food to feed her and Ben and the two growing boys!

The smiles disappeared as she sat in the little parlor furnished almost entirely with gifts from the big house. Kit's equally huge brother, LaFayette, sat with them. He was the father of six children, had also started to buy one of the small frame houses and was now idle. His mill had closed and trouble had taken up its abode under both roofs. In Wall Street, in New York, a mythical place to them, a stock market had collapsed and in a Massachusetts city a Negro couple sat with tears in their eyes.

The rich people were laying off extras, not taking them on. The October mortgage would be on them, the winter was coming.

Mary sat with tense face listening.

"Folks are all scared about something. What is it, Miss Mary?"

She said that frankly she did not know. She would take Kit on for so much a day and she could help LaFayette. Even as she walked down the path to her car after inspecting and praising every room in both houses, each garden, the canned fruit and vegetables, her sober common sense told her that she could not take on those families and be responsible for their sustenance, their mortgages, their taxes, their doctor bills; and some premonitory voice warned her that when she took Kit, she would take them all on.

She drove slowly down the avenue, trying to think things out. Her father would have taken over the mortgages and given LaFayette work. What was poverty anyhow? From all ordinary standards, Ben and Kit were very poor, he a laborer on an estate, she washing clothes. Poor? They had been prosperous happy people, aristocrats among their own people because they had inherited money from J.R. and bought a house. They were gardening, earning their way, laughing, eating, sleeping, feasting on special days, educating their children, all in confidence. Yes, in more than confidence. There was some exuberant joy in their living. What had been taken away from LaFayette? Merely a chance to work. What had been taken away from her with her money? A chance to help others.

She stopped the car at Dr. Porter's, her next appointment. She was not looking so "damned pretty" today. He looked into a pale face, troubled eyes and studied his blotter.

He handed her a prescription. "Begin this before dinner tonight."

She had plenty of time to go down to Fuller's Drug Store and get the prescription filled. As she entered her neighbor's drugstore situated where it had been for two generations on one of the busiest corners of their city, she glanced about with some curiosity. The plate-glass windows opened on two streets and their display could well have advertised a department store. Inside, the many tables recently crowded with lunchers now were given over to couples or groups sipping sodas or ice cream or lingering over cigarettes as they chatted or giggled.

Of course she realized that most northern cities became summer resorts in July and August and she found it easy enough to pick out the so-called New Yorkers. Slacks were coming into vogue, and fuzzy permanent waves, the combination ludicrous with high-heeled shoes.

She walked to the back of the store where one small counter was still serving as an apothecary shop. Mr. Fuller saw her and came immediately to take her prescription. She asked, "How long will it take?"

"About ten minutes. I can bring it up."

"Thanks. I think I'll wait."

He found a chair for her, thoughtfully pulling it back to a rather sheltered place half hidden by a revolving book shelf. There was a shout, in a familiar voice as bicycles were hoisted onto the step from the sidewalk and three boys burst in, scurrying for three vacant seats at the soda counter. Mary smiled but did not move as Joseph, Hunt Carter and a chubby boy grinned blissfully and wound their legs and feet about the pedestals of their stools.

Hunt in a large way, tossed his head. "Anything you want, boys. What about a banana split?"

"Twenty cents?" The chubby boy looked incredulous but hopeful.

"I say anything you want." They ordered banana splits from the pretty blond girl.

Still smiling, Mary watched the activity of the soda counter which, after all, was the heart of the establishment, occupying one entire side of the room. Two sallow, pimpled youths and two or three girls were moving as fast as young hands and feet could move, filling glasses, ladling out ice cream, wiping up, taking money, making change. It was a little world of its own.

"How he wolfs it," Mary thought as Joseph scarcely raised his head from the luscious-looking mass of banana, ice cream, nuts and whipped cream. Then he did raise his head. The spoon hung limp in his hand; his eyes opened wide and slowly a smile of excitement and pure joy lit up his countenance as he stared at a girl who had made her way down from the far end of the fountain.

A few minutes before the boys came in, Mary had noticed that girl. She would always remember that. There was something different about her. She was not pretty, no, not by any definition; but she was like an exotic flower among garden zinnias or geraniums.

She was dark, with almost brown skin and dark eyes so bright as to look almost feverish. Her hair was dark brown and banged, the bangs being constantly tossed back as she jerked her body about. One thought, "A bundle of nerves."

Now the dark eyes were looking into Joseph's face and if such were possible, they were growing momentarily brighter. Her small uneven teeth, stained with cigarette smoke, were held apart, her pink tongue darting in and out as she leaned toward him. "You remember me?"

"Sure."

The other two boys stopped eating to stare.

Mr. Fuller touched Mary's shoulder. The package was ready. Mechanically she opened her purse and paid him, looked back at the boys, hesitated, then decided it wise to go out the side door, get her car and drive home.

She prepared a simple supper and was irritated when both Joseph and her husband were late. Tom came first. He was in a cheerful mood and said he wanted to do some typing then go back to the office for perhaps a half hour. They did not wait and he was already eating dessert when Joseph noisily banged his bicycle against the woodshed wall, sketchily washed his hands, smacking a small amount of water on his hair, then slid into his seat at the table.

He was quite out of breath, excited as one seldom saw him. Tom looked at him and said severely, "Well, why are you late?"

Ignoring the question, with an ecstatic smile, he asked, "Have you seen her, Father?"

"Seen who?"

"Bel."

His father laid down his spoon. "What are you talking about?"

"Bel. You know the artist—the girl—the nice one who painted the funny pictures. She's in Fuller's Drug Store." Rather breathlessly, "It was like this she said. She lives in New York and she wasn't feeling well and the doctor told her to get up into the country for air and sunshine. She's still awfully poor and has to earn her way so she came here and Mr. Fuller gave her a job. She says she's good at soda-jerking. She has one afternoon and all day Sunday off for painting. She's specializing on cows."

He gulped a little to get his breath, then turned to his mother. "I didn't mean to be late. I just didn't notice the time. Hunt treated us and while we were eating she came over and I knew her right away. After we finished we waited for her and she came out with us. I wanted to ask her home for supper but I didn't know—I wasn't sure—without Mattie, you know—should I have asked her?"

At last, Mary glanced at her husband. He was rising from the table, throwing his napkin down unfolded. She saw his jaw rigid, the muscles of his face stiff and blotches of color in his skin.

Without speaking one word, he walked out the side door, went to the garage and presently drove swiftly into the street.

Joseph raised his head, sat with open mouth, the hurt look spreading over his entire countenance. "Gee! Father's jumpy!" He added nervously, "I think we ought to get Sandy home."

"Why?"

"I guess there aren't enough of us now—without Mattie."

Mary pushed back her plate and dropped her head into her hands. For a moment she closed her eyes then she pulled herself together and turned to her son. "It would help Mother if you would watch the time. Father started a new job today. That's rather trying and he didn't like your being late. Now tell me all about the ball game. Did you win or lose and by how much?"

On the following afternoon Joseph told her, "Bel isn't at Fuller's any more. Hunt and I went in and the girl told us she decided to give all her time to painting. She came in this morning only to get her pay. She wants to have an exhibition in New York, all cows, next fall and she'll need a lot of pictures ready so she's gone to paint all the time somewhere out in the country."

"I see."

"If I knew where she lived I could ask her to come and see you. I don't know. She didn't leave any word."

"She's probably gone away where there are more cows. Now I want you to do some errands for me."

"O.K."

CHAPTER XVIII

She counted the strokes of the clock to twelve as she sat at her dressing table brushing her hair. She heard the car turning into their drive and shortly afterward Tom entered the room. She glanced at the stern set of his features, then said, smiling, "That was a long half hour, dear. You must be tired after such a first day. Do you want to tell me what you think of the job or is it too soon to know?" She had determined to treat the matter of Bel as insignificant.

"I'm only rattling around, finding out what it's all about. I'm not tired and I do want to talk to you. I don't know what you're thinking of, Mary, letting that boy run wild."

"Joseph? Run wild? Whatever do you mean?"

"That's what I said—run wild. You've given him money to spend, a bicycle to ride and he's here, there and everywhere and no one knows—you less than anyone—what he's doing or where he is. You don't know what he's getting into. Perhaps it's some damned theory of yours but you'll ruin your son if you continue in it."

At first her amazement made her speechless; then two thoughts came clearly: first, "A year ago he was upbraiding me for coddling him"; second, "That boy has become of vital concern to Tom. He loves him."

She spoke slowly, sometimes stopping to think between sentences. "Of course he's running hard, as a strong, healthy boy of his age is bound to. I don't believe in coddling. My brothers weren't coddled. They never heard all this preaching about being democratic; they were democratic; they had friends, black and white, Jewish and gentile everywhere. Joseph has what they had

—one dollar a month as his own, no questions asked about how foolishly he spends it; but, out of it, he has to buy pencils, balls and the sort of things he'd lose too quickly if he didn't have to use his nickels to replace them.

"I don't know, in any day, every spot where he has stood or every road where he has ridden or every person to whom he has talked, but I know him. I know him closely, intimately. I know his eyes, his smile, his heart. I'm always here to come to, and he always comes to me.

"I would be scared to death of a straitjacket for a boy. He's going away some day, when he's still young in years, to college, away from home and away from me. I want him so self-reliant that he'll stand on his own feet wherever he goes. I want him to have liberty now and learn how to use it so he won't flounder when he's in a larger environment."

He was standing near her, his head bent, listening intently. She looked up into his face. "I don't want our son to be a plaster saint nor a sissy. I want him to be a big, rough-and-ready, strong, independent man, unafraid of other men and, in his inner life, a gentleman." She added, "I've even wanted to keep him proud of his father. In spite of the fact that you sometimes hurt him with sarcasm, he still adores you. You know how he has always adored you."

In one hand he lifted her long, shining, red-blond hair then let it drop. He turned away as he said, "I often think you both would be better off without me. I never should have come back."

She braided her hair and answered more lightly, "Leaving a void that never could be filled."

"I can hardly believe that."

She slipped off her kimono and got into bed. He went into the hall where he opened a door leading into an unused small bedroom at the top of the stairs. When he came back, he said, "I've got to have a place to work. I could clear out most of that stuff, put the big desk in, my cabinets and some book cases."

"I rather thought you would want that room." She was pleased. "Only don't start moving things at one o'clock in the morning."

Over the next week end he and Ben tugged and hoisted and toted, an electrician came to adjust lights, Joseph worked until he was panting and from all the effort a remarkably neat, pleasant and uncluttered office was created.

A box arrived from a New Jersey address; once before a box of clothes had come. He explained indifferently, "One of the boys stored my stuff in his attic."

"Why not send for everything?"

"I don't want to see the damned stuff. This is all I want."

He was sitting at his desk as she stood in the doorway looking about the room. "Now that it's done, suppose you relax a little. For ten days you haven't had a decent night's sleep or eaten many regular meals. Let's not undo all our three months' of building up."

"Don't expect a newspaper man to be as regular as a mill-hand." He looked up into her face and there was an expression in his eyes which made her uneasy. "Mary, do you think—" He began again, "If you had had me as a little boy—we'll say younger than Joseph, do you think you could have made a rough-and-ready man not afraid of other men and, within, a gentleman, out of me?"

She walked over, laughing a little, and laid her arms on his shoulders, resting her chin on the top of his head. "You're as unpredictable as an April day, Tom. I never know what you are thinking."

"Answer my question."

"I can't. I don't even know my husband; how could I know the boy he once was?"

His tone was mocking. "No family photographs to help you? Well I'm going to put some of those missing photographs into words. They won't make pretty stories but I think I know an editor who would publish them. I'll write them for you."

She slid around on the arm of his chair. "I know one thing; I would have made that little boy into the kind of person I could talk to freely—not be afraid of asking questions."

"What do you want to ask."

"Did you send that girl, Bel, away?"

He laughed aloud. "So *I'm* unpredictable. That little bitch! Mary, you don't know one damned thing about the different kinds of women in the world—the vultures, the leeches, the little mongrels—not one damned thing. At that I think I'd rather deal with a hard-boiled, mercenary adventuress than with a sniveling little faithful puppy that never gets out from under your feet."

She shivered a little and he could not see the expression in her eyes as she asked, "Tom, look this straight in the face and answer truthfully. Doesn't the faithful, little, sniveling puppy get that way because the man has fed her and petted her in the beginning?"

He turned and looked up into her face. "I'd hate to face you as a lawyer prosecuting me. Your inheritance counts, doesn't it?"

She told him in detail how she happened to be in the drugstore, how she had seen everything. "That girl is not a bitch, Tom. I felt sorry for her."

"You would. Now, can we turn another page?"

During July and August he often threw down a daily paper or the Sunday magazine section and carelessly indicated some editorial or article. She read every word avidly, greedily. There was a quality in his writing which instantly claimed attention; there was some sarcasm, a bitter, cutting phrase, then paragraphs of near-beauty. Jealously she cut them out and hoarded them.

One article ridiculed New England smugness but ended in a description of the Berkshire hillside, the elm-lined streets of its cities and villages, that brought a tightness to her throat. He had accurately described their own comfortable, beautiful old avenue.

When she praised it he said, "I wrote most of it last winter. No one ever described it that way, exactly, because no one with a roof over his head could feel so homesick to see it. You will never know what it was like, coming home to you."

Now big, black Kit came in from the trolley every morning, filling the house with her rich, soft laughter, her mistakes, her apologies; also with confusion. The orderly kitchen, Martha Briggs' pride, became a memory. Kit did put out a nice wash but she also put disorder into every corner of the house.

Ben found himself needed in more and more of Kit's "pinches," always arriving in time to help her cook and eat a hearty meal. Henry and Monty, between activities with Joseph, sat on the woodshed doorstep, a little roost which Monty seemed to love. Kit said with her soft laugh, what was the sense in her going home to cook another meal? And Ben was so spry in serving.

Lawrence brought home Sandra, open-eyed with wonder at the new people in the kitchen. She would glance shyly at Joseph or her father while she clung to her mother.

Then there were school days again and grapes, apples, plums and pears ripe from the garden. Soon the leaves were sifting down from the great elms; orange berries hung in heavy clusters on the ash and the pungent smell of bonfires filled the air.

One afternoon Mary sat by her bedroom window sewing on some small white garments. She heard Tom come in, go directly to his office and almost immediately there was the irregular clicking of typewriter keys. Presently Joseph passed through the hall, glancing at his father, then repassing. He had done this several times when Tom called, "Joseph."

The boy sprang to the doorway. "Yes, sir?"

"If you want to work here by Father, bring your books."

Astonished, Mary heard him give further directions. "You can use this drawer; never leave your stuff around; when you work, work."

Mary walked through the hall to look in at them sitting side by side.

She went back to her chair and for a few minutes her fingers patiently wove the needle in and out as she ran the seam; then her hands lay listlessly in her lap. Clearly she remembered her physical strength, her perfect health, her radiance when she was carrying Joseph and Sandra. Now she was sick. Weeks had dragged into months and still she suffered waves of nausea, weakness, depression. She jumped nervously as something rattled against the window. It was only a handful of dried leaves, sifting down from the trees, tossed by the wind.

Driven by a sudden longing to get out, get away from everyone, she went quietly downstairs, slipped on her tweed coat, not bothering with a hat.

Some friend of Kit's was in the kitchen and there was the sound of laughter and hilarious conversation; also the smell of coffee. In the side yard, Sandra, Monty and some half dozen youngsters were shrieking as they tumbled in and out of a pile of leaves.

Like all her family, she loved to walk, and on the avenue she stepped off the flagstone sidewalk, felt the earth under her feet, the leaves soft against her ankles. She raised her face to the breeze and breathed deeply. She merely nodded and smiled as she met chance acquaintances and passed on quickly.

Of course she reported regularly to the doctor but could he give her a ten-minutes-to-fill prescription for her mind? She slowed her steps because her breathing bothered her as she started up a long hill.

Not for years had she followed this road which wound through a small wood, over the crest and came out above Judge Carter's farm land. The light from a slowly sinking sun flooded the landscape. She was facing the light and its diffused radiance seemed to permeate her whole being, bringing a delightful sense of quiet and peace. But she was tired, unconscionably tired.

She stopped and looked down toward a hollow where greenhouses lay in open sunlight. Two young workmen on the road spoke to her by name. She smiled and told them she had come much farther than she had intended and was tired. Wasn't there a short cut through the woods?

They would show her; so she walked with them chatting about crops and the wonderful apple harvest. It was like a vacation. The wind blew her hair but she did not care. Now, walking easily, she felt happy and free.

Surprised, she found herself near the greenhouses, passing a group of men when Judge Carter came out of one of the doors. Lightly, and with all her old gaiety, she explained her presence and he explained his soiled slacks and leather jacket. He liked to get out and grub in the soil especially on fall days. Could he show her his work in the greenhouse?

The sun was dropping behind the hill. "Please, another day. I *am* tired and it's late." Then she mustn't walk home. He took a small Ford and insisted on driving her. They backed up the narrow lane, out into the road, then he drove slowly over the long hill, down side streets, through the avenue to her door. She thanked him and promised to see the greenhouses someday.

Hearing the car, Joseph looked out of the window. "Gee, there's Mother. She's been out driving with Judge Carter."

Tom jerked up his head, looked out, then turned to his typewriter without speaking.

Kit was announcing supper. They went down to find Mary already sitting at the table. She had not bothered to smooth her disheveled hair. The becoming color was still in her face as pleasantly she explained her walk, then changed the subject.

She was in her room again trying to make some headway with her sewing when Joseph was being sent to bed. She heard his "Good night, Dad," in a comradely tone of voice, then his retreating footsteps. He had forgotten to speak to her. A few moments later Tom stopped at her door, a light coat over his arm, hat and briefcase in hand. She was startled as she looked up into his eyes. There was the shamed, agonized expression. She tried to speak casually, "Out again tonight?"

His smile and light mocking tone belied the eyes. "How out of place you are here, Mary. You need a larger canvas. You would grace that estate. I see plainly that the most wonderful gift I could make you would be your freedom."

"Tom. Don't—" But he was gone.

Tired after her long walk, she slept soundly, both then and afterward unsconscious of a scene enacted when Tom returned somewhere near four o'clock in the morning.

A little girl who had proved her sturdy independence since Mattie Briggs was not there to hover over her in the night, woke uncomfortable and started down the hall toward the bathroom. Her father was coming up the stairs. He was merely going to care for her, offer her protection, but he lunged toward her drunkenly, calling, "Get back to bed, baby." She ran into the first open door, the door of his office; when he followed she was wedging herself in between the desk and the wall. Faintly he saw her frightened eyes staring at him and, when he grabbed at her, she slipped down to the floor and, on hands and knees, frantic with fear, crawled around the corner of the door, the bare feet and legs scurrying beneath the white nightgown. With unbelievable speed she got to her room, scampered into bed, pulling the quilts over her head. In the morning the child was hazy; "I had a bad dream." She did not tell her dream.

Then the winter closed in. Thanksgiving Day they all praised Kit's dinner but as Tom closed the door after that mountainous woman, he noted the full baskets she and Henry were toting. He said to Mary with a look of amusement, "It takes just about my salary to make up the extra, doesn't it? I see you working double time over that account book. You paid LaFayette's mortgage in October?"

"What can I do, Tom? This bitter winter. It's all wrong and I don't know how to right it. I'm really an utterly incompetent person. I'd gladly throw that account book into the garbage can if I dared. I realize how incapable I am, in the kitchen, everywhere, I guess."

He spoke quickly, earnestly, "Do nothing just now, Mary. The place has turned into a sort of bedlam. I've heard you trying but you can't re-train Kit at her age. Make the best of it for a while. My job seems secure enough so we'll manage."

"The house is small—"

"You are sick. You've never been sick like this before? You're finding it the hell I think it. All we need now is a brawling baby to finish the picture."

She bit her lips hard.

A few weeks later, on one of those stormy December days, just before Christmas, she was resting on the big bed upstairs during school hours. She heard Tom coming up the stairs after parking his car in front of the house. He opened the door of their room and instantly she felt some excitement in his voice as he asked, "Asleep?"

"Oh, no, just resting my back."

She turned to look at him. She was struck with that something she thought of as an aura of youthfulness. That fine old sealskin cap hid the receding hair while the gray at the temples seemed attractive. The upturned fur collar enhanced his high color and today his hazel eyes were exceedingly bright. He tossed his cap to the foot of the bed, came around to her side and held out a copy of one of the finest of the national magazines, open at a story by Tom Donovan.

She sat up, pushed a pillow into the hollow of her back and read every word, turning the pages as he watched. Every word, every paragraph she read and then she who never wept, who prided herself on her ability to curb "sniffling," let the tears flood her eyes and fall unheeded down her cheeks.

He said, "It's not pretty."

"It's beautiful and utterly cruel—wicked." She closed her eyes. "You must have known that old woman, and that tenement doorway. How could you know her fat was diseased bloat? How could you describe hands that had washed down tenement stairs and floors for years? How did you understand her cold despair while she waited for the men to come and take her to the poorhouse?"

"She had lived there with her son, the janitor of the place. It was her home. He was killed in an accident at one of the wharfs. I was with her when she identified the body."

"I could feel that cold, slow rain and the yellow mist and salt spray. But the boy—when she was going, he thought only of himself."

"Why not? She had let him sleep in that hallway. It was his only home. He got his little bundle out from under the stairs— all he owned. A new janitor was coming in. He had to get out."

"Oh, Tom."

"It's the first of the family photographs I promised you. There are two more scheduled."

"I can't bear it."

He laughed.

She asked, "You said you write your editorials and feature articles here; so that's what you've been doing nights downtown?"

"Sometimes, not always, Mary." He walked to the window and stood looking out. "Quite as often I'm playing poker in the back room of a saloon or occasionally spending the night—oh, here and there as better men than I do."

She looked through tears at his profile and the feeling that he didn't belong to her, choked her. She dried her eyes and spoke quietly. "You have some strange talent, Tom. Some remarks have come indirectly to my ears. Graham says you can do what he called—"

He whirled on his heel and interrupted her, "What he called the goddamned best editorials and feature articles the paper has carried in two decades. That's exactly what he said when he was drunk at a dinner. He retracted the next morning and told me to go to hell when I asked for five dollars a week more pay. Damn him." Then he cooled down and laughed again. "That thing's not bad but, see, it's only a try at what I have in my mind to do. There isn't anything in the world I see and know and understand like writing. I know talent. I know good stuff and I know hypocrisy and imitation and popular trash. I know writing but that isn't being a writer. I sweat over this thing. I sweat days and weeks."

"It shows it. What about your poems, Tom?"

"Someday I'll get at them again." He picked up his cap. "And write that biography filled with women as pretty as this old woman in the doorway."

He left the magazine on her bed and walked out. She heard the motor being started. Sometime in the later afternoon he telephoned. Joseph took the message, "Tell your mother I won't be home tonight."

She lay that night with her face turned into the pillow. She thought, "He is not what Lawrence thinks he is; he is not what Warren thinks he is. Divorce him? It's come to this; it would be only one form of suicide for me." Yet, even as she lay there with hunger for which there was no appeasement, with grief unassuaged, a cold, implacable anger was mounting in that heart. Neither Sandra, Joseph or the hilarious Kit could bring the old glint of laughter back into her eyes. Sometimes she shuddered at her capacity for anger, remembering that she was soon to give birth to a child.

Through January the snow deepened. There were days when neither Kit nor the trolley could quite make the trip, at least until the great plows had been through the roads. One morning she came puffing in several hours late. "You'll excuse me, Miss Mary, but I have to use language about this weather. I say enough is enough. And don't you consider going out for that walk today. It's just as smooth and slippery as the path to hell. I certainly could use language about it."

Tom Donovan used the language when he was forced to shovel snow for an hour before he could get his car out of the garage. But, less and less did it offend Mary's ears for less and less did she see of him. Sometimes he was half drunk, gay and debonair when he came in but far more often he came merely to change his clothes in a mood of unapproachable ugliness and she would lie on the big bed large with child and feel more alone than when he was in New York.

Just after the first of February a new sound was heard in the little white house—a new baby's cry. It had been scarcely daylight when she roused Tom, and within an hour after the arrival of the doctor and nurse the baby was born. Without breakfasting Tom got his car and drove away.

She was hardly conscious of his absence for all through the day she slept heavily in an acute exhaustion she had never before experienced. In the late afternoon, she waked to see her husband standing at the foot of the bed looking at her. She smiled weakly, "Have you seen her, Tom? I'm thanking God that she's all right. She's a perfect little girl and Dr. Porter says she's fine."

As he did not answer or come near her, she tried to see his face but the light was fading. "Will you put this light on?"

He came around by her table and switched on the light. Then she saw a bitter expression about his mouth.

She closed her own eyes and lay still for a moment feeling only her great weakness and telling herself that he felt like this about Joseph and now he loved the boy. She smiled bravely, "I would like to name her after my grandmother Farnsworth—Nancy Farnsworth—if you like the name."

"That's very pretty. Yes, I do like it."

"I know you will think it's silly but the nurse and Kit and I, all think she's an image of you. She looks nothing like Sandra or Joseph did." Her voice trailed off in weakness, "I'm so grateful that she's all right."

When Mary was able to look over her accounts she saw with frightening certainty that by no stretching or planning could she afford to feed and clothe them all. Now her dividends were being cut and Tom did not look amused when she explained conditions to him.

He thought a while. "I might squeeze a little more out of Graham. However I won't beg. I could try my hand at some 'pretty' stories but I'd probably fail. I never did have the knack."

"No, please. Give me a little time." Then she looked up brightly, "I discovered something for myself today. The baby does look like you. I saw it plainly this morning."

He turned away without interest.

With a burning sense of humiliation, she wrote to Lawrence early in March. "I can't express my mortification in having to ask you for money to see me through. When I regain my strength, I'm sure I can tackle the whole problem, systematize my house, telephone my friends and get enough washing jobs for Kit so I can get her off my hands. I must do that—God help them—and live within my means. I can do it but I must ask help now." The check came by return mail. "What are brothers for?" he asked.

Then came that last frightful winter storm. Old residents recalled none worse. All through the night, the branches of the elms were whipped mercilessly to and fro; the wind screamed as it blew the light, dry snow into drifts. All that night Mary listened and hoped to hear her husband, hoped to hear the closing of a door, his step, his voice. He did not come.

On the next morning, the sun shone and there was some thawing but by afternoon a disagreeable wet snow began to fall. The sky darkened and night closed in early. She had had a nerve-racking day, disciplining the children, and finally explaining to Kit her financial inability to care for them all and the offers from her friends of various washdays. She arranged to pay for coal and start them off, promising that Lawrence would help LaFayette with his mortgage and taxes.

Kit served her last supper in tears and Mary hired a cab to come and take her and her belongings away. It was better to make a clean, quick break.

Somewhere near midnight, she rose, cared for the baby and laid her back in her crib. How quiet was the house. No wind moved the elm branches and the outside world was as she loved it, hushed with snow. Inside there was warmth, peace again, and quiet.

It was not long after midnight when she heard Tom open the door, close it softly and come upstairs. There was as always, that feeling of relief, some sensation of warmth and happiness which swept through her when she heard his step on the stairs. She was glad she was wide awake for they could have a few moments of talk before he slept.

Usually when he came in, he undressed by the low light and slipped into bed so quietly as hardly to disturb her. Tonight, he stopped at the door, slid his hand along the wall until he touched the switch and snapped on the ceiling light—a light they seldom used—and instantly the baby sleeping in her crib began to whimper.

"Oh, Tom, don't do that. Turn out that light, please." Even as she spoke, Mary sat up in bed, reaching for her table lamp and lighting it.

He was standing in the middle of the room gazing at her and his eyes looked angry and sullen.

The baby's cries grew louder. "Tom! Please turn off that light.

What is the matter with you? What are you thinking of?" She put her bare feet out, reaching for her slippers as the infant's voice became more piercing. She was halfway up from pulling on the slippers when she felt his hands on her shoulders as he roughly pushed her back on the bed, pinning her down with fingers that dug into the flesh of her arms and hurt cruelly.

"What am I thinking of? What I'm always thinking of—you. I want to look at you." He stood gazing into her face while the baby's screaming close to his ears must have rasped his nerves.

Never before in all their hours and years together had he ever touched her except with tender, considerate hands. What had he once told her? "You never saw me drunk. I match the ugly world then." Was he drunk now? She tried to see his eyes. She looked up into his face and all that cold, implacable anger of months of accumulation suddenly took complete possession of her.

He bent down until his mouth reached hers with a pressure that hurt then, quickly releasing her, he stepped back. "Tend to it; tend to it. Stop that hellish noise. Tend to your unwanted baby."

Was she awake or was she enduring a frightful nightmare? She pulled on her robe. He stepped back to let her pass. She snapped off the ceiling light angrily before walking to the crib. Her hands lifting the baby, she looked up at him with a fury of scorn in her eyes. "She's not an unwanted baby now. I love her. I want her now. It's you I don't want."

Almost as she said it she felt herself consumed with an agony of remorse. Long after, she remembered that it was as though the words pierced her own heart and she would have given her life to recall them before they reached his ears. It wasn't true. In her anger and her horror of what she had said she felt the blood throbbing in her temples and she was shaking from head to foot.

Up and down she walked, patting the baby's back and little by little quieting the crying. Once she turned to him, her eyes imploring, "Oh, Tom!"

He was standing with his back against the bureau, his head thrust forward, looking at her. Perhaps he had "matched the ugly world" for that few moments but now he was sober. He watched her with a shamed, agonized expression in his eyes.

He turned away and spoke brokenly, "I've known that for a long time." He threw himself down on top of the quilts, his hands over his face.

She tried to control her voice and ask naturally, "Aren't you going to undress?" He did not answer or move.

Her throat aching, she begged, "Oh, Tom, Tom, dear, I can't endure this. Please, dear, stay awake and let me talk to you. You and I talking to each other like this! Please, don't go to sleep. This has been shameful, hideous. I can't endure it."

He did not speak and she could not go to him because of the still whimpering baby. She made all the customary changes, did everything she knew to quiet the child but each time she laid her in the crib she was forced to pick her up again.

Once she walked to the other side of the bed and pulled a quilt over her husband. Her hand touched his hair tenderly but he made no response.

At last she went to her side of the bed, snapped off the light, crept in and snuggled the baby in her arm. She whispered, "Tom, dear, won't you say something?"

Ominously he lay quiet and she could not tell whether or not he slept. Time passed: how many minutes or hours she would never know but slowly, more slowly than ever before, her muscles relaxed, the throbbing in her temples became less, the aching in her chest became more bearable and finally a blessed drowsiness began to steal over her.

She must have slept from sheer physical exhaustion. Was she dreaming that her baby was slipping out of her arms into some hideous danger? With a low frightened cry she sat up in bed searching for a small white bundle which was gone from her side. Then she heard her husband's voice muttering; she caught the words "—in the crib, in the crib," as, in the semi-darkness, she saw him moving.

She was snapping on the light, jumping out of bed when he stumbled over the blanket which was trailing on the floor. He clutched at the footboard to regain his balance as the baby was tossed across the open space hitting the metal castor of the bureau.

Through all the years of her life when she lived over and over every hour of that night she remembered the sense of confusion. It all happened in seconds. He was never to tell her but she assured her aching heart that he had only wanted to put the child back in the crib because he could not endure it between them in the bed; that his foot was caught in the blanket and later, when he lunged toward the bureau it was again mere accident that his foot shot out and seemed to kick the child toward her. She always remembered that even as she picked up the whining baby he threw himself on the bed and covered his face with his hands.

On her side of the bed she sat with the child in her arms assured that she was not hurt for almost immediately she closed her eyes and slept peacefully.

Completely sunk in some abyss of shame and sadness, Mary held the child until light began to creep into the small-paned windows. Tom moved restlessly. Once he muttered, "God, that was Mary." Again and again he murmured, "Mary." She rubbed her throat to control herself and force back tears.

Long before daylight she gathered together her clothes, went softly down the stairs and sat in the kitchen, her feet at the open oven door. She had left the baby sleeping quietly in her crib; she was not afraid for her. That person was not Tom Donovan. That soul-searing, degrading night! How could she go about washing the memory out of their hearts and minds? How could she go about making him believe, making him know that she could not mean those cruel words? She knew she could have poured torrents of abuse on his head, but she could not say those few words to him.

When the clock reminded her of feeding time, she went for the baby. She was surprised to see the empty bed and hear Tom in his office. The door was closed. For a moment she hesitated, then tapped lightly. There was no response and she turned away. Perhaps he needed a little time, so she prepared breakfast and dressed and fed the children.

It was a little after eight when she sent them off to school snugly protected with hoods and pulled-down caps, and overshoes.

She went up the backstairs to the upper hall and seeing his office door ajar, she looked in. One drawer of his desk was open and empty. She heard the latch on the front door click, then the sound of the door closing. Quickly she went to an upper window and looked down into the street.

It was snowing hard. Through the dark, bare branches of the elms, the flakes fell thickly and the walks were completely obliterated. She saw Tom on the steps, then on the sidewalk. He stood some time looking first up the street and then down as though undecided which direction to take. She wanted desperately to see his face but she could not for there was visible only the top of his fedora hat. She saw he had on neither his boots nor rubbers of any kind. Instead of his heavy coat, he was wearing his old raincoat. He stopped on the walk to turn up his collar and fasten the buckle, then pull the wide belt tight about his thin body.

Desperately she tugged at the window and finally raised it. She called, "Tom," and again and again, "Tom." He glanced up and she saw his face.

With lowered head he plunged forward into the whirling snow and howling wind. She watched the figure grow slighter. Now it was lost in the storm.

She closed her eyes and her features semed to take on the gray look of stone. She spoke aloud as though talking to him, "Tom, don't! You can't do this, Tom." Then, "He is going away. He is not coming back."

She had once said that if she ever started to weep she could never stop. She went into his office. She stretched her arms out across his desk, and then she laid her head down and wept.

PART III

LITTLE NAN

CHAPTER XIX

It was on Monday morning of Easter week in the year 1941. The postman, his hair graying, his shoulders hunched more and more, was making his way down the long avenue, grateful for the bright warmth of spring sunshine, for dry walks, the end of winter storm. Had he looked up to notice, he would have seen the faint color and thickness as buds began to swell on trees and shrubs. He did not look up. Day after day, month after month and year after year, he shifted his pack, sorted letters, scrutinized addresses, ascended steps, crossed porches, rang bells, descended and went on to the next number.

Long before he reached the double white house with the green blinds, Mary Donovan opened the front door and stepped out on the porch. As she waited at the railing, taking deep breaths of the fresh air, she raised her face to the brightness of the morning sun.

Ten years had dealt kindly with her. As she lifted her arms to replace some hair which the breeze had whipped into her face, one might notice some thickening of the waist; one might call her thin instead of slender; see, in the bright light of this morning's sunshine, the lines deepened about the mouth, the firmer set of lips and even a few scattered strands of gray hair among the heavy red-blond waves at the temples.

There was still the clear pale skin, the graceful curve of neck, the delicately formed profile which Tom Donovan had gazed at with such articulate ardor in their years of love.

In the expression of her eyes there had come the greatest change. If the eyes are the most direct mirror of the soul, then Mary Donovan had attained somewhat of that which the philosophers and teachers of all time have valued above all other earthly possessions —peace of mind. The peace of mind which she would aver no woman ever attains except through a purposeful life.

Once she wrote Lawrence that she was sailing a craft, a rather small boat but filled with precious cargo; there were storms and too deep water but she managed somehow to keep firm hold of the rudder and sail direct on the course.

Though they were not the laughing eyes of her girlhood, they were still beautiful and this morning they were filled with a bright expectancy as she watched the postman coming down the avenue for she was waiting for her usual Monday morning letter from Joseph. Mrs. Fuller glancing out of her window, the neighbor across the way, even the postman himself accepted as part of the usual neighborhood scene, Mary Donovan's eagerness for the letter from her son who was finishing his last year at the University, and planning for a law course the following year.

As the postman came nearer she smiled, thinking that he represented the government of the United States and, for the delivery of every letter he was responsible to that government, but neither the postman nor Uncle Sam was accountable if the white slips of paper in the envelopes brought happiness to a human soul, happiness that could make the whole day a singing beauty; or carried words that destroyed the last hope of a human heart. The lines tightened about her mouth as she finished her thought—or never brought a scrap of paper bearing the handwriting which her eyes hungered through the years to see.

She felt the chill of the early spring air as she took her mail, thanked the carrier, exchanged a few words and then went into the house.

She noted the thinness of the letter before she tore open the envelope as she stood in the bright light at the kitchen bay window. Of course the note would be short because he was coming home— Friday he had said—for his Easter vacation. Besides there had been examinations so she had not been concerned even though for some weeks now he had written singularly unsatisfactory letters. Like his father, Joseph was fluent in speech but sparing of words when he put them on paper, using concise, terse phrases always rounded out to a smooth completeness. She was proud of his writing.

She read: he might have to disappoint her about getting home, better explain when he saw her, had to ask Uncle Lawrence for money but she'd do the same, a jam just now but it couldn't help but come out all right, don't worry, love to Sandra and Nan.

The day was being taken out from the number of commonplace days in her life to be labeled, "The day Joseph wrote that he would not be home for his vacation." Every woman's life is highlighted by such days. Listen to the old women talk. "The day John got hurt in the accident at the mill," "the day my baby was taken with diphtheria," "the day my mother had her stroke," "the day we buried Walter—how it rained that day." There had been many labeled days in her own life but she was training herself to look forward, not read the old heart-breaking labels.

It was probably a girl again, one of his clumsy, hot-headed love affairs. He would "knock over a little furniture," "walk backwards," then come home smiling his wide smile as he poured the tale into her ears.

It was perhaps a violent one like that of two winters ago when he was wanted to take Sandra to the Carter's dance and couldn't possibly because *she* "demanded" that he come to Baltimore to meet her people and friends. Mary had managed a check for him but in the end, he had used much of it for carfare to get home for two last days. When she had asked sympathetically about the girl, he answered, "You know it was funny, Mother; I liked them all—society, plenty of dough, lots to do—but it *was* funny—when we weren't dancing, when we were alone—gosh!—after an hour—"

"Well?" she had smiled, "after an hour?"

"I guess church was out; so I came home."

She dismissed the anxiety from her mind and went about her many household tasks.

As she passed through the upper hall, she glanced at the closed door of the front bedroom. Some years ago she had had that room repapered and painted and had rented it to the principal of their local school, Miss Harriet Simmons. At the time, the advent of that middle-aged, gray-haired woman seemed a Heaven-sent gift. Mary never was sure whether her request to live with them was induced by her interest in Joseph whom she had often tutored, her desire to "help" Mary or, as she stated, her wish to get out of a boarding house into a spot where she could be alone.

Long since, Mary had learned how "to cut her pattern according to her cloth." She wanted plenty of money for Joseph's Harvard years and for his law course; she wanted a sum of money ready for Sandra and she would need plenty for little Nan. Surely the world could not have produced a more perfect tenant than Miss Simmons to help with current expenses. At least she thought that in the beginning.

The lady spent all her vacations including her long summer's rest on a farm with her people in Maine; she cooked her coffee in the morning on an electric plate, but ate lunches and dinners "out." She had said, "I like to make my own bed, do my light cleaning and be let alone." She stood in an open space in the room and looked about. "I want every drawer in the bureaus and I'm going to wedge in my own bookcase and my machine. Sewing is my hobby and that big bed will make a splendid place for cutting—lots of room."

There was a curious expression in Mary Donovan's eyes as she thought over this new use for the big bed.

Miss Simmons finished, "I get sick of children and adults. I'm a born old maid and I'm moving in to stay. I read and sew and sleep. I'm not unfriendly but, you understand, I'm coming here to be alone."

She was a large woman with a commanding presence—Mary thought of it as a platform presence—and when she stopped by, dressed in her modish green wool to leave the money for her rent, one could see that, like an accountant, she added up the sum total of inefficiency, by her standards, whose evidence lay all about Mary Donovan's house. But there was something deeper and more subtly disturbing. In the long hours when Mary worked and thought alone, she had time to reason about it. What colos-

sal self-sufficiency and self-righteousness that woman possessed!
And why not? She was a thoroughly fine person who had risen
to her present enviable position by reason of her own hard work,
good mind and blameless character; a country girl who had walked
miles to school and worked her way through college. She could
knit beautifully, she could sew, was well read, could review the
latest best-seller at the Woman's Club, could preside at a meeting
graciously and authoritatively, discuss the international needs of all
mankind and never, never in her whole life need she lie in bed with
aching heart, baffled, uncertain of her next step, wakening with
sickening hunger for the touch of a hand, the sound of a voice,
her ears straining to hear a light step that never came down her
walk; or, with life's blood ready to be sacrificed for three children.

Miss Simmons spoke of her own perfect health with a satisfied
smile. Mary also had hardly been in bed a day in ten years but
when her inefficient hands seemed ready to betray her, she knew
what it was like to breathe, "Dear God, give me strength, just to
see them through."

In the late afternoon of that Monday, after she had written to
Joseph and carried her letter to the postbox, she was sitting in the
rocker at the kitchen bay window, matching her yarn to darn
the knees of a stocking when she heard the sound of children's
voices, and presently she saw a small red cap pass directly under
her window.

The little red cap was not moving as caps usually move on a
child's head. This cap came up with the motion of the body as
though it were tracing an arc high in the air; then it sank down
almost out of Mary's sight; then up it came again with a singularly jerky motion. Had she not known the cap, she would have
known by the high arc which it traced that it was little Nan.

Mary Donovan set her work basket aside and looked toward
the back door. There was the sound of the latch at the woodshed,
a creaking sound as the heavy door was opened, then several slam-
mings for the latch was a trifle high and difficult for Nan to reach.
There was the sound caused by the pushing of a chair then the
kitchen door opened and a thin, eager face seemed to precede the

slender body as the child entered. Though she was ten years old she looked hardly more than six or seven, she was so small and fragile.

She pushed the door shut with her body and as she turned she swung one foot only the other resting heavily on an iron brace, and yet she made the motion with some charming bodily grace.

"Mothey?" How strange that a child who had never known a parent could inherit a motion of the hand. She had a charming little way of pulling her head way back, looking up with eyes shaded by long lashes. She repeated with that rising inflection of voice, "Mothey?"

Mary came to her side, lifted the cap and smoothed the hair. She unbuttoned the coat and threw it aside. Then, as little Nan sat down on a chair at the center round table, she removed a rubber from the normal shoe.

This routine was seldom varied. As Mary's eyes smiled down at the child, the hazel eyes looked up into hers glowing with serene happiness and contentment.

"Mothey, what do you think? I won a spelling match."

While she chattered, Mary set warm milk and a brown bread sandwich before her. When she had finished, her mother said briskly, "Now run to the bathroom then—out to play."

Instantly the entire atmosphere changed. The child stretched her right arm straight out on the table; then her head was dropped on to the arm as though all strength had departed from the muscles of the neck. In a high, petulant voice she whined, "I'm tired, Mothey, and I don't want to go out."

Again it was routine. "You know what the doctor says. You must go to play every sunny day, try every game even jumping rope. You won the spelling match because you tried. Now you will win this game if you stay out in the air and walk and play. You will grow strong and well like Sandra and Joseph."

"You come to walk with me."

"Not today. I'm going to make a nice meat pie for supper." She laughed. "You see, Nan, housework is Mother's game and she's going to play hard at it."

"Will you win?"

"Of course I'll win."

"What will you get?"

"Three fine healthy children, well educated and happy. Come now, hurry."

Reluctantly, whimpering a little, she struggled into the coat and soon Mary saw the little red cap pass the window and go bobbing down the street around the corner.

She was starting to clean up the untidy mess on the table after preparing the meat pie and salad and dessert when a slight rattling of a key told her Miss Simmons was letting herself in the front door. The clump of Nan's footstep and muffled sobbing were audible in spite of Miss Simmon's forceful voice.

As they entered the kitchen the child tore her hand away from the older woman's and lamely, blinded by tears, threw herself sobbing against her mother's knees. Above the noise of crying, Mary heard the collected voice saying something about finding her hurt and frightened, soaked with mud, her spine not strong enough, Nan can't cope with these rough boys, hysterical with fright and, "what are you thinking of?"

"Thank you Miss Simmons—if you will leave Nan to me now?"

"I'm always trying to help you, Mrs. Donovan."

Again Mary said, "Thank you," as Miss Simmons went out.

Lifting the hysterically sobbing child, she carried her to the rocker, unbuttoned and threw aside the mud-soaked coat then quickly removed the iron brace and shoe. She stripped off the wet stockings and rubbed the cold legs. Reaching for a woolen shawl she wrapped it around her, wiped the tears from her face, and murmured, "Now tell Mother."

"It was Willie Carter again. He knocked me down and hit me because he said I spoiled the game if I was on his side. Then he took my cap. My cap is gone. He wagged it at his dog and let the dog chew it up and when I tried to get it he threw it over the fence. My red cap, Mothey."

"Mother will buy you another cap."

"Red?"

"Yes, red."

"With a tassel?"

"With a pretty tassel." Mary rocked as she soothed and soon the long dark lashes drooped and regular breathing told her Nan had fallen asleep.

She could hardly discern the hands on the clock but she knew by the slanting sunlight that it was after five. She wished Sandra would come. She did not like her to stay so late at the High School. In the quiet of the room she listened to the slightly audible breathing and the creaking of the rocker. Tired, her own shoulders rested gratefully against the cushion. Once she laid her cheek down against the soft hair.

No one on earth but herself knew why that leg was shorter than the other. What had Martha Briggs said? Women went to the grave with secrets locked in their hearts. "You will keep yours, Mary."

She could still see Dr. Porter's face as he examined the baby girl who limped when she tried to walk, the baby who whined, and fretted and lacked appetite. "Now think back, Mary, and see if you can remember a serious fall or accident." She had felt sick and faint when she stumbled through the words, "Once—she—fell out of bed. I remember—something hit her—perhaps her back."

He had looked at her as though he were trying to look through her but he asked nothing more. A spot in her spine?

As she rocked, she thought what ugly secrets doctors must keep hidden in the labyrinthic depths of memory. The enigma of human behavior which so puzzled the onlooker often was not only intelligible but forgivable to the physician whose skillful hands and penetrating eyes probed deep into physical, mental and moral weakness and disease.

Dr. Porter was an oldtime family physician. In extreme suffering men could keep no secrets hidden from such eyes, for often the diseases of maturity revealed the indiscretions of youth. Faced by the old master, Death, they found themselves naked and exposed to the eyes of the physician.

Through the years how little she had told him but how much

he had seen and known. About Nan, he had seen her distress at his questioning. He asked no more and she had kept her secret.

Lawrence had been alarmed when the child began to limp. He wanted little Nan. "Give her to me, Mary. It will be so much less of burden for you. Let me take her to Chicago. Dr. Porter says it's a spot in her spine. Let me take her."

She could not. All that night, trying to decide, she had held the baby in her arms. In the morning she answered, "I can't part with this baby. Never."

Now, in this late afternoon, she rocked as her lips rested on the soft brown hair. The child was frail, "difficult," lame. Her arms tightened around the thin body.

The light was fading. The child moved then stretched and slowly looked up into her mother's face. She raised her hazel eyes with the long dark lashes and smiled. Pursing her lips she said with inimitable charm and that strange rising inflection of voice, "Mothey? You are going to get me a new cap?"

"Yes, darling."

"With a tassel?"

"Yes, sweet."

Nan suddenly sat bolt upright, her eyes sparkling with excitement as a light step came across the verandah and the side door was opened. She called joyfully, "Sandra?"

Then, "Quick, Mothey, put on my stockings. Sandra's here."

PART IV:

SANDRA

CHAPTER XX

"Sandra's here." The lights were flashed on. With her first step inside the door, her quick-motioned fingers had thrown the switch; hardly another second and equally swift feet had taken her to the rocker.

"Why are you sitting without a light?" Affectionately her lips touched her mother's cheek then, turning to Nan, she placed a hand on each side of the child's head, "Nancy, darling, you've been crying. Did you get hurt?"

Instantly Nan's eyes clouded, tears formed and she began to pour out the tale of misery and humiliation as her mother tugged at the stockings.

Knowing the little actress was enjoying her moment in the spotlight, perhaps sensing too sympathetically the child's satisfaction in being able to turn from the brutal conflict in the outer world to the warmth of love, even the "petting" of her sister, Mary pulled her rather roughly to her feet. "Sandra will fasten your shoe. Now stop whining. You are going to be a big, strong girl and you're going to play with all the children every afternoon."

But little Nan had come to the dramatic moment in her recital when the dog chewed the treasured cap and Willie Carter threw it over the high fence. "My red cap with the tassel, Sandra, the one Miss Simmons knit me for Christmas."

As Sandra rose, her eyes fell on the mud-stained coat still lying on the floor by the rocker. During Nan's recital, the brightness had faded from her face; now, she spoke undramatically but with an intensity which disturbed her mother. "I could kill Willie Carter. The bully! How I hate a bully. How I hate those Carters!"

Mary stopped in the doorway. She thought Sandra's "Farnsworth hair" lovelier than her own had ever been; she knew strangers turned on the street to look at it. Did she see the firm chin and disconcertingly direct eyes of her daughter? Of course she had always seen them and once in a while she had been startled when that pretty, "soft-looking" girl said something in a manner which was old J.R. himself.

In her childhood Tom Donovan had been annoyed and somewhat discomfited by the manner in which the little girl gazed so steadily at him, that level, fixed regard implying, not so much doubt as speculation. In either case it was disconcerting. In one of his most penetrating moods he had said, "Neither Joseph nor Sandra is going to enjoy the 'blessing of shallowness.'"

As the little girl grew older, she mingled happily with her companions in play, passed her grades easily in school, lived the simple, healthful life of any unobtrusively guided and sheltered child.

Quite often Mary failed to follow the mental processes taking place under the blond curls; but why should she be able to follow them? Sandra had always been an individual, retiring into her own small world, a world her mother believed she must respect, a world which must remain inviolate.

One morning months after their father had left them, Joseph rushed in from play, demanding to know if his father were coming back. Gossip from adults had filtered down to children who had stung him with the brutal callousness of which children are masters.

Mary laid her hands on his shoulders, talked gently but ended, "Joseph, your father is probably not coming back."

He had been playing baseball. He stood a moment, his eyes opening wide; then he choked, ran to the woodshed, dashed his bat onto the floor. He ran to the "office" and slammed the door shut.

There had been difficult days. One night Sandra whispered to her mother, "He didn't take our baby, did he? Aren't you glad he left us our baby?"

Mary understood Joseph. It was Sandra who puzzled her. For days there were stomach upsets, bad nights, even a temperature. No, they did not enjoy the "blessing of shallowness."

There came the grammar school years, the age of puberty. As for learning the "facts of life," a euphuism which amused Mary, she knew that boys and girls were cognizant of the exciting "facts" almost as soon as they reached the school yard and street. She was concerned only with their use and misuse of those facts.

In the previous fall, Ben had helped her pack a box of apples to send to Lawrence. Carefully they had examined each apple, wrapped it in tissue paper assuring its being uncontaminated. Well, no parent could so wrap his child and, she thought, no wise parent would try. She loved the whole man, his mind, his soul with its aspirations and yearnings, his body with his appetites and passions. She liked a hungry man and she liked to see him satisfy that hunger be it for learning, religion, food or love. She wanted her children to be strong, vital and hungry. But how do you teach them when to draw aside from the touch of the rotten apple?

One said little intimate things to Sandra without embarrassment. A flicker of her eyelids, a slight nod of her head and, even as she walked away, one felt she understood—understood everything; that is everything one sees like a chart drawn on paper and un-translated into the confusing pattern of living.

She was pretty, "soft-looking" and the boys' eyes were drawn to her. Mary saw them in the garden, on the street, heard the in-tonation of their voices always calling, "Sandra." Mary watched. How instinctively the bees go for their honey! She watched jealously, anxiously. She saw the girl climb trees, climb back fences with the boys, reaching for plums and pears, ride her bi-cycle fast and furiously with them, on rainy days sit in the house playing games, adding scores, always gay, sweet. Flirting a little? Of course, with laughter in her eyes. She was becoming conscious of her power. Vicariously, Mary lived again her own girlhood.

Occasionally there was a hot argument between Joseph and his sister, Joseph insisting he be told why some particular boy was to be ostracized. Sandra, looking at him levelly would end the argument with a few words delivered like blows. "He is *fresh* so he can't come here."

Then came High School but Sandra seemed scarcely conscious of the transition from the lower grades. The children's world was still limited but not yet was it muddled. What was right and what was wrong, what was clean and what was nasty, was clearly perceived. When the code was broken, they knew and were usually ashamed.

Sandra loved to dance. The children who received private instruction taught the others but no one could teach such lightsome grace, such instinctive mastery of intricate steps. In her junior year, paralleling Joseph's junior year at college, there came an invitation inviting them to a Christmas dance to be given by Mazie Carter. "Mother! It will be a real dance, in their ballroom with an orchestra." She added thoughtfully, "Of course I hardly know Mazie. She has always been away at boarding schools and she's three or four years older than I am. Probably it was only Joseph she wanted—an extra boy. I can't see why she thought of me—only it's wonderful. I've never been to a real dance. I can go?"

There was a night of thinking, after which Mary had one of her serious talks with Sandra. They must come to grips with some facts. They had been fortunate in owning this house in an aristocratic neighborhood. She and Joseph had been fortunate in their friends and schoolmates. "Let's look at the future. We are all going to be hard-working, democratic people. The struggle for an education for you and Joseph is not over. Getting into some profession with which to earn your living comes first. Mazie Carter's luxurious life, the endless frivolity and trivial interests, beaux, dances, travel, are not for us."

There was a long silence as Sandra sat with bent head, her keen disappointment showing in drooping lips and clouded eyes. Finally she looked up. "Just once? Please? Wouldn't it be part of my education?"

Mary smiled. "Very well, we'll take it that way—part of your education. If you are going you must be correctly dressed."

She was. Full long skirts were again fashionable and Mary took from a trunk one of her own gowns and remodeled it. She cleaned the ermine collar on a black velvet cape and knew the entire costume was stylish, simple and right.

Then came the dismaying letter from Joseph. He couldn't possibly come because he was going to Baltimore. "Anyway," he concluded, "as I remember her, Mazie Carter was an empty-headed, silly snob. Willie was a little brat and only Hunt was worth his salt. And since he went to Princeton we've hardly seen or heard of him. I wouldn't care about the affair if I were coming home."

Angrily Sandra threw down the letter. "I'll telephone Mazie." Unctuously, Mazie purred back over the telephone. "Oh, that's too bad but you come anyway. I've slews of boys. Hunt would be furious with me if I didn't get you."

Above the banks of snow, down the long avenue, the elms stood stark and cold, the stars visible in the midnight blue of the sky through the bare branches. The vapor from her breath showed on the frosty air as Sandra stepped across the porch and made her way past her mother's girlhood home to Judge Carter's house.

She lingered a moment in the dressingroom to glance in the long mirror. She knew how right she looked in the shell-pink taffeta, her hair smoothly brushed and falling nearly to her shoulders. She carried a small beaded bag, her mother's bag—a precious possession that J.R. had brought her from Paris—in one hand as she lifted the full skirt with the other and slowly descended the stairs, not only with confidence but with pure joy in her heart.

She loved the dress, the bag held tightly in her fingers, the feel of the thick velvet carpet under her slippers. She loved the spacious, richly furnished rooms and now, as she looked down, she saw young men in evening clothes and girls in dancing dresses and heard the scraping of violin strings as an orchestra tuned up. She wondered: What would Hunt be like? She remembered a tall skinny boy and that she had always crossed the street to avoid his teasing.

As she reached the lower floor she found Mazie's aunt and Judge Carter, tall, stoop-shouldered and rather ponderous but now unbending and enduring the ordeal of smiling into each young face as guests were presented.

When he turned to Sandra, he started visibly, held her hand, and looked searchingly into her face. "You—that child, Sandra, old enough to dance? I'm afraid I'm getting old. You see I remember your great-grandfather, Judge Kent and all the Farnsworths. What a damned shame J.R. isn't here to look at you now."

Sandra's head was held high as she walked away. She felt the earth firm under her feet. She was proud of being J.R.'s granddaughter.

The first uncertainty came when she entered the drawingroom. If Joseph hadn't let her down she would have had someone to walk with, to be with. She went in alone and for some minutes she stood alone. The girls seemed to be both older and strangers to her. Mazie was in the midst of a group and awkward minutes passed before she turned. Then she looked Sandra over appraisingly before she drawled, "You're Hunt's Sandra. I haven't seen you in years. You look lovely, Sandra." The tone suggested that it seemed incredible.

Sandra remembered Joseph's letter. "She's an empty-headed, silly snob." She thought quickly, "She hasn't any mother and she hasn't any manners." However, she knew that bad manners were fashionable, almost a pose with certain types of young people. She began to feel more uncomfortable as young men stared at her and girls looked her over. Then Mazie called, "Oh, here's Hunt." And in a high voice, "Hunt, here's your blond girl from across the street. He says he's had a crush on her since she was a baby."

With a curt, "Cut it, Mazie, don't be such an idiot," he came directly to Sandra as the orchestra began playing. He smiled and held out his hand. "Sorry about Jo. Let's dance."

They were the first couple on the ballroom floor. At first, shyly, silently she glanced up at him. He was tall, still lanky but he had nice eyes and she called him good-looking. Words formed in her mind—Princeton, travel, society man, sophisticated, out of her world—very wealthy, then again, she thought with a sigh, "so sophisticated."

He drew her closer. "Gosh, you can dance!" She smiled and again warmth flooded her heart. Almost as though she were part of him she followed steps new to her. He laughed, "Don't mind Mazie. She's a bla-bla. If you say one damned thing to her she makes you sorry you said it. It's the truth though. I was crazy about you when you were a little kid; then I saw you on the street last Thanksgiving. I told Mazie I'd come home for her fool dance if she got you over. How's that for being important?"

"Important for you or for me?"

He pulled her a little closer. "Perhaps for both of us."

She laughed, "I used to hate you. You pulled my hair. I used to cross the street when I saw you."

"You're on the right side of the street now. If this mob weren't around, I'd pull your hair now. I want to get my hands on it." He looked down into her eyes and she entered into what she thought was gay fooling as he asked, "Sandra. Gosh, I love that name. You haven't anyone? I mean—you know—you aren't engaged?"

She laughed outright, "Heavens! I'm all of sixteen. Of course I have plenty of friends. I know plenty of boys of my age."

He held her closely. Time after time, some boy touched his shoulder to cut in. When one was too insistent, Hunt turned savagely, "Go to hell. No cutting in on this trick."

It became embarrassing. She said sharply, "I'm not a trick. Let's stop and rest." She saw some men in the doorway. Only for a moment she saw Judge Carter towering above them, saw his eyes rest upon them briefly, then he turned away. She was not to see him again. A few ladies sat near the entrance to the little ballroom but apparently the aunt's friends preferred to gossip together in the parlors, leaving the dancers to themselves. Chaperoning had been out of fashion for a decade.

It was a pretty room. She thought how lovely it must be in

summer when those french windows were opened into the garden. Now they were covered with draperies. When the music stopped, he drew her into one of the small alcoves but still he did not introduce her and Mazie seemed to have forgotten her.

Again they danced and he held her more closely, so closely that she felt others would notice. Above the pink taffeta her cheeks were beginning to burn as his hand pressed too hard where his hand had no business to be. He smiled at her. "Tired? You're not tired. You and I could dance like this forever. We're going to. You're crazy about dancing, aren't you? So am I."

"That's why I came. I love to dance."

"I'm going to be home all week, angel. We'll dance everywhere. I've got a well-heated car. What about it? Is it a date? Seven days?"

She was adding another word to her list. She did not want to add it because she loved the dancing. To dance "everywhere" for a week?

The color deepened in her face. She couldn't endure to have him think she was a child or afraid or for that matter completely confused and too provincial and inexperienced to know how to handle the situation. She saw girls enviously watching, exchanging remarks. They wouldn't forgive her; neither would their mothers.

He spoke of Joseph again, then suddenly he asked, "By the way —you see I'm so seldom around here I don't keep up with the gossip—or—I mean news. Did your father come back? Is he living with you or did your mother divorce him?"

For an instant the entire room seemed to be obliterated in blackness; then she answered evenly, coldly. "No, he is not living with us."

He sensed his blunder. "I'm sorry. Forgive me. You see, most of the people I know are divorced. You'd need a blueprint to keep families straight. In fact, from what I've learned, my own mother and father were on the verge of divorce. It's funny to come back here and find the same middle-aged couples jogging along together and the old couples gumming it together—I suppose to the grave. Except the young set."

The orchestra stopped playing and set their instruments aside. Supper was being served. Older people were in the diningroom. She saw Milly Vaughan watching her. Now a tight knot was gathering in her chest and the smile was hard to summon to her lips. When she answered Hunt her voice trembled slightly.

She could scarcely swallow the food. Again the violins were being tuned. Milly came over and sat beside her, friendly, and Sandra stiffened for she knew her as a woman her mother disliked.

Hunt held out his hand. "Come—" He turned to answer his aunt who had spoken to him and Sandra rose, made some almost inaudible excuse, passed Milly and stopped by Mazie. "Thank you and good night, Mazie, I have to go now."

She ran up the stairs to the dressingroom, asked for her wraps and stood impatiently while the maid put on her overshoes. She knew it was a childish, inglorious thing to do but she couldn't handle it: she must go home. He was sophisticated, but—"He is *fresh*. I always hated him. He's fresh. Maizie's a silly snob. None of them have any manners and I'm not Milly Vaughan's special friend."

Below the dancing was in full swing. She went into the deserted upper hall only to face Hunt standing at the top of the stairs. Without speaking and with unexpected strength, he pulled her into what seemed an enormous room. She afterward remembered book cases and a desk besides two beds.

He laughingly began to argue about her leaving, ending, "Besides I want to take you home. I ought not to leave now."

At first she seemed gay and laughed and insisted she must go and she kept stepping back as he came too close. She tried to appear indifferent and what she would have considered "sophisticated" and endeavored to edge past him but soon she had to push away his strong arms. She was pulled farther back into the room and then she was suddenly and violently crushed against his body. "Let's quit the game, Sandra. We've only seven days, darling."

"You fresh thing." Even to her own ears, the childish appellation sounded silly and inadequate. He had found her lips, and now she fought him. In the struggle she lost hold of her bag and it dropped to the floor. With a sickening sense of tragedy she heard his heel crunching the beads as he stepped on it. His greedy lips reached her ears, her cheeks, her mouth, even into her teeth, as she tried to speak.

Long since her embarrassment had turned to hot anger; but above and through it all her brain held one thought. She must not cry out no matter how far he went. She must not let anyone know that she was alone in that room with Hunt. They must not know that he was treating her like a piece of baggage. She wouldn't have a ghost of a chance. They would say she had enticed him upstairs.

Her thoughts filled her with fury and, wrenching one arm loose, she tore at him, at his face, at his hair. She kicked furiously; she scratched. Hearing her dress tear, she also heard her own half sob.

She fell against the desk as he released her, almost throwing her aside. "You damned little tigress. You'd make a killer."

She darted across the room, picking up her bag and cape but, at the door, Hunt was before her. She saw blood on his face from her nails but she saw something else—complete amazement and now cold, sober, serious anger in his eyes. He barred her exit, staring at her. "So that's what you're like."

"I'm not what you take me for."

"I'm not what you take me for either, Sandra."

"I could kill you." Desperately she was trying to pass him. Her lips quivered like little Nan's as she begged, "Let me out."

"Sure, I'll let you out but I'll bring you back." He stepped aside.

She ran down the stairs. At the foot Milly Vaughan who had heard her good night to Mazie and had seen Hunt follow her upstairs, now blocked her way. Rudely, Sandra pushed past, knowing others saw, past the footman, out into the night, down the street, panting until she reached the ice-covered walk at the side of her own house; then she stood up tall and straight, smoothed her hair and walked across the side porch. She must save Mother from knowing.

She looked into the window. There was Mother sitting at the table reading, waiting for her grown-up little girl, wearing her first party dress, to come home from her first dance; the dance that was to be part of her education.

CHAPTER XXI

When Hunt Carter called on the following afternoon, Mary received him, explaining that Sandra was out. In the few moments that he was in the house, she watched a very serious young man, who asked, "Could I call her tonight?"

"Certainly." She liked him but she was not going to make it easier for him.

"I was a bounder last night, Mrs. Donovan, whether Sandra's told you or not. I want to apologize and talk to her."

"I'll tell her."

Sandra said coldly, when told of his call, "If he comes again give me time to disappear. I don't want to know him."

She had "saved Mother," telling her only part—about the dancing and not allowing boys to cut in, then, "Oh, you know, Mother, he got fresh and tried to kiss me and I tore my dress and dropped my bag."

"Where did all this happen?"

She hesitated, "Oh, in one of the big rooms."

When the telephone rang that night, Sandra said quickly, "I won't talk to him."

Quite pleasantly, Mary spoke over the phone, "I'm sorry, Hunt, but Sandra doesn't care to talk to you. I'm sorry." She heard something like a gulp as he said, "Thank you, Mrs. Donovan," and hung up.

Sandra jumped up and stood in the center of the room and there was that in her eyes which one did not trifle with as she said, "I hate the Carters." Then surprisingly she smiled, "Mother, I did get an education at that dance. I learned a lot. Men respected and loved my grandfather, didn't they? You know the way they say 'old J.R.' Do you know what I'd rather be than anything in the world?"

"What, dear?"

"I'd like to be a man and have people, while I'm living and after I'm dead, call me 'old Sandy' just the way they say 'old J.R.'"

Mary found her own heart beating fast and unaccountable tears in her eyes. She knew quite well that Sandra had received a wound which would not quickly heal. She could not follow the mental processes under the blond hair. She could not fathom the now increasing silences. Once she found her crying, holding the ruined bag in her hand. "I loved it, Mother." She sobbed convulsively.

Mary could not promise a new one and the beautiful old one was beyond mending.

A few days later, Sandra came in unexpectedly and found her mother pressing the pink dress after darning and repairing every rip. She leaned over, examining them closely. "Oh, Mother, you did that wonderfully."

Together they slipped the pink taffeta gown into a bag and hung it away in a closet. Mary remarked, "You'll wear it at happier occasions. Remember that."

"Yes." Sandra stood quietly, thinking. "Yes, I know I will, Mother." Then she added, "I want something very much."

"What, dear?"

"I want to wear suits and blouses." It was as though she had said, "I'm grown up."

Then Sandra's attitude toward her school and its various activities seemed to change. There had been a death in the faculty and a new professor had been chosen to fill out the term.

One day Mary asked, "You like this new teacher? I read about him in the newspaper. They seem to feel they were very fortunate in getting such a talented person to come here even temporarily."

"Of course I like him but he's like a person from another world. He jumps on us and wakes everyone up—says we mumble our words. You should hear him formally introducing us to consonants. He says we don't deserve our heritage of literacy or our literature. He is going to put on plays and teach us to act. Then he is taking over the athletics also—basketball and tennis and the baseball. He says he has written plays which have been produced. He is stimulating but I guess we're all a little afraid of him."

"Sort of a challenge?"

"That's just it. Makes me feel—'I'll show you.'" She laughed happily and her eyes were sparkling and eager.

Mary was pleased when Sandra was chosen for important parts in those plays, proud when her English compositions won high marks. She was more pleased when Professor Waring accepted the position for another year.

The next Christmas vacation was not clouded by any unhappy experiences like the dance at the Carter's. Sandra had won a play-writing contest and the play would be produced at Easter time.

In the weeks preceding the production of the play, the girl seemed happy, vibrant with the joy of creation. She fairly lived at the schoolhouse. "You see, Mother, the boys are making properties in the workshop, the sewing classes have to make the costumes, the orchestra is to produce the music. Why, even the lights are to be managed by boys. Besides we've got to get good marks in every other subject or we'll get thrown out. He keeps us on our toes. Everyone's working."

"He monopolizes your time. I don't want you to skimp your piano practice or walks."

"But we have our exercise on the tennis court or in the gym."

"I don't object, dear, but I'll be glad when the play is over."

Like little Nan she loved to hear the step on the porch and her heart had echoed Nan's excitement when she called, "Sandra's here." But, unlike Nan, she was disturbed by the violence of Sandra's reaction. "I could kill Willie Carter, how I hate a bully!"

Often when Sandra spoke Mary heard some of the beautiful intonations of her husband's voice. For those, she listened eagerly but, as she turned from the doorway and walked into the kitchen, she thought how often she had recoiled from the vehemence of his hatred of those who had hurt or wronged him. Now she saw that capacity for scorn and hate added to the rock-like strength of character which Lawrence long ago had seen hidden under that pretty, soft exterior. She stood a moment, hands resting on the round table, thinking, "After all a child has two parents and many grandparents. No wonder we seldom quite understand our children."

Sandra fastened little Nan's brace, again held the child's head between her hands, kissed her affectionately. She took off her jacket, rolled up the sleeves of her blouse and tied on a big apron, then began setting the diningroom table.

Because she was working with Sandra, helping with supper was a happy game for Nan and the arc curved high in the air as she limped about bringing knives and forks and napkins. "Do you smell your favorite meat pie, Sandra?"

"I smelled it the minute I opened the door. Don't forget the butter knives." Leaving the child intent on her work, Sandra walked into the kitchen. For a moment she watched her mother arranging the salad. She spoke as though weighing every word. "If my grandfather Kent were living, no bully would dare touch Nan or—" She left the sentence unfinished. Was she going to say "or me"?

Mary Donovan glanced up and there was sadness in her smile. She was acutely aware of the omission of "my father" and the substitution of "my grandfather Kent." She lowered her voice. "I have learned not to live by ifs, Sandra. The greatest kindness to Nan is to help her learn how to get along in the world with all kinds of children now and, later, with all kinds of people." She hurried her words, "Nan won't always have her mother's arms waiting. We can't guarantee her a sheltered life. My parents thought they could assure my future." With decision in every word, she went on, "Even if I could guarantee it, I wouldn't. I want my children to be wiser about life than I was. I want them to be able to face the world alone if they have to; and the world can be a hard battleground."

Sandra was helping arrange the sections of orange and grapefruit on the lettuce leaves. As she so often did at the most awkward, the most inopportune moments, she leaned toward her mother and asked a question that sent a crimson flood of color into Mary's cheeks. "Mother, I heard Dr. Porter talking once—talking to you—besides I've seen other things—wasn't Judge Carter in love with you? Didn't he ask you to get a divorce and marry him?"

There was a painful silence. Sandra smiled, "I know he did. We would have had everything, wouldn't we? I mean wealth and your old social position and—"

"Everything? We'll talk about that some other time."

"I didn't mean—"

"Call Nan for supper."

Sandra stood with a salad plate in either hand. Suddenly her happiest, most infectious laugh rang out. "Mother, you don't understand how glad I am. I bet the learned judge would have worked harder every day of his life at home than in the court-room. Six children! It is funny, Mother. Now that I know the crew. Imagine Hunt and Willie."

Mary looked into her daughter's eyes for a long minute. The relieving sense of fun. She said, "Call Nan."

Sandra stood still looking at her mother. "It isn't only because you're really awfully pretty, Mother, I think you're what Professor Waring describes as desirable. You've had other chances—"

"What people call chances—"

"So what?" Sandra turned away. "You—" She did not finish the sentence but set her plates on the table and went into the sittingroom. She knew Nan was "showing off" for her. The child was seated at the grand piano and her performance was astonishing. She was the only individual who had access and welcome to Miss Simmons' room and, after listening enraptured while Miss Simmons played a piece several times on the phonograph, Nan could play it on the piano with remarkable accuracy and feeling.

Now Sandra wound her arms about her sister's thin shoulders. "That's wonderful, Nancy. I love it. Come, darling, dinner's on the table."

Mary noticed an unusual tenseness and excitement in Sandra's face and eyes as she asked, "Did Joseph's letter come?"

"Yes. We're all going to be disappointed. Fetch it, Nan—there on the table."

Sandra read it aloud and Mary would remember much later the curious feeling she had that the substance of the letter was not 'news' to her daughter. At the moment she turned to comfort Nan whose lips were quivering. "I'm sure, dear, he'll manage to get here for Sandra's play. I'll write him again immediately."

Nan spoke excitedly, "After supper, Sandra, we can mark Monday off the calendar; then there'll be just Tuesday, Wednesday and Thursday. Only three days and we'll all go to the play on Friday. A seat way up front?"

"A seat way up front, seeing you're deaf and blind and very old."

As they laughed, there came Miss Simmons' authoritative tap at the door. Mary resented her coming in during their supper even though she kindly brought the evening paper.

She stood erect and quite handsome with her perfectly marcelled hair as she reminded Mary that this was the night of the important forum to be held at the High School. Mary acknowledged that she had forgotten the date.

Earnestly she regretted Mrs. Donovan's absence from lectures on international affairs. Was she going to be like most Americans, burying their heads in the sand like ostriches, not sensing that this war in Europe menaced us? Joseph and all the boys of his age might be fighting and dying on foreign battlefields again.

Sandra and Nan sat listening with bent heads. However, the subject tonight did not happen to be war; instead it was a subject which no parent could afford to miss—juvenile delinquency and the speakers were national authorities. A friend was to pick her up with her car and they would be happy to take Mrs. Donovan.

Sandra's gaze had been directed rather fixedly to a spot on the tablecloth. Now she looked at her mother. "Our Civics class is going to the forum." Her eyes were shining bright. "Professor Waring is going to stop for some of us at eight o'clock—"

Nan asked shrilly, "What's a juvenile, Mother?"

Mary turned to the child and smiled, "A juvenile's a childish person of any age."

Miss Simmons nodded, "A good definition." Then she turned to Sandra. "I often wonder when you do your homework, Sandra. I'm sure you could double your subjects without injury to your health and graduate a year or half year earlier. Tennis with Professor Waring, plays entailing endless rehearsals, basketball, now an evening spent at a forum intended for adults."

Sandra's head bent lower and she made no reply.

Miss Simmons continued, "Sandra, just what are you aiming at? Surely you're not going to join the army of female scribblers. I hope you have no silly notion of being an actress. Joseph is going to be a lawyer, what do you plan to be?"

Sandra spoke without hesitation, "I don't know what I shall be but I know what I'd like to be; I'd like to be a gardener."

"You mean a scientist? Perhaps a botanist?"

"No. A gardener."

"Oh. Like Sir John Forsythe?"

"Like John Forsythe. I don't like titles." She added politely, "I shall take Mother, Miss Simmons."

Miss Simmons smiled as though she had won some secret victory, spoke of hearing little Nan's playing earlier in the evening and withdrew.

Mary looked around. "She didn't leave a paper. I wanted to read the President's speech."

"You will come, Mother?"

"Of course. I'll speak to Mr. Ryder." Once in the prosperous years, Mr. Ryder had worked for her father. After the death of his wife, jobless and lonely, in the depression years he had come to her bringing some fine snapshots of J.R. Knowing his desperate need, she had offered him the room at the back of her house. Now he had a job as a petty clerk, a drab little man who liked to cut the grass and chop wood and begged often to "mind the baby."

When she started for the stairs to go to her room to dress,

Sandra spoke earnestly, "Mother, I'll get Nancy to bed. Please wear your nice hat and your good mink."

"If you want me to, Sandra."

CHAPTER XXII

Mary combed her long hair, smoothing it painstakingly, knowing it contrasted strikingly with the close-fitting black velvet hat. She put on a long dark coat, carefully fastening the mink collar about her throat.

She stopped to soothe and reason with Nan, then descended the stairs. It was fortunate that her hand was on the railing for near the bottom her heel caught. Sandra who was lighting the parlor ran into the hall. "Mother, did you fall?"

"No. These heels seem a little high." As she drew on her gloves she looked at her daughter who had made a quick change from a white cotton to a pink silk blouse, charming under the navy suit. She noticed the smoothly brushed hair and the tweed coat over her arm. "Where is your hat?"

Sandra walked to the window watching for Professor Waring's car. She answered casually, "I didn't wear it home."

"I noticed you wore your good beret this morning. Surely you wouldn't leave *that* hat on a cloakroom nail or in a desk?"

Never in executing any bit of millinery had Mary been so successful as in making that beret. She had used a navy broadcloth, had tailored it, then, on one side, she had appliqued soft gray-green worsted flowers. Perhaps she was right in thinking no Fifth Avenue milliner could have designed a more chic and charming beret to set on that golden head. Her voice sharpened, "Sandra, have you lost your beret?"

Sandra turned and with composure answered, "My beret isn't lost, Mother. You're pale since you stumbled, can I get you a drink of water?"

"I remember now, I didn't drink my tea." She passed through

the dark diningroom and went into the kitchen. She felt the sides of the teapot—still warm. It would be at least stimulating. As she stood drinking, she heard the front door being opened then voices in the parlor. She heard Sandra explaining that her mother would come with them. Putting the cup down, she turned out the light.

There was gay laughter and involuntarily she stopped in the dark sittingroom, looking into the brightly lighted parlor. Presently her figure stiffened, both hands grasped the table edge. The man was holding in his hands the beautiful beret as Sandra said, "Please, Mother asked about it. I must wear it."

He smiled. "Sorry. Let me put it on."

The girl bent her head, a deep flush in her cheeks, a slightly confused smile on her lips as his fingers expertly placed the beret upon the head, smoothing and tilting it perfectly with the appliqued flowers at the side and with the drape exactly right over the ear. Expertly! How familiar was that expert touch of a man's hands—the sort of man who was a past-master in adjusting any garment a woman wore. She saw his eyes close to the pretty head then his cool composure as he turned away with a careless, "There you are. Beret safe, not a wrinkle. That little cap has always fascinated me—guess you'll have to will it to me."

There was a happy but still confused smile on Sandra's lips as she answered, "Oh, I expect I'll wear it until it falls apart. I'll call Mother."

Her feet felt like leaden weights but Mary entered the room, shook hands with him and thanked him as he held her arm when she descended the steps. In what seemed but a curiously hazy moment they were seated in the coupé, Sandra nestled between them, and moving swiftly down the long avenue under the elms.

He left them at the entrance to the auditorium and drove off to park his car. It was Sandra who led the way to the main aisle of the already well-filled hall.

They sat at the end of a seat filled with strangers. Over at the right of the room, rows reserved for the Civics class were rapidly filling with adolescent girls and boys. Presently, Professor Waring took his place among them. He sat at the end with his arm carelessly thrown over the back of the seat as he scanned the audience until he located them. Mary knew the exact moment when he saw them and she knew that several other people about them also knew. It was as though her suddenly frightened heart were equipped with delicate antennae. They could call it woman's intuition but, name it what they wished, it was more accurate and authoritative than facts or logic. She knew there was gossip; she knew there were watchful eyes, sharp tongues waiting for the chance to lash out.

During the rather tedious introduction she had a chance to watch him surreptitiously. Athletic but lean rather than heavy; alert, darting eyes, sharp eyes, mocking eyes, eyes that could be full of fun, passing off any awkward moment with a laugh. Prematurely gray hair added to his distinction. One might like his clean-cut general appearance, have no doubt of his intelligence. His remarkable ability in choosing and producing plays had made drama important to both pupils and parents. He had awakened a live interest in government and civic questions. On the athletic field he was an enthusiast. A formidable antagonist.

Mary Donovan glanced at the girl sitting by her side and saw her with earnest, lifted face concentrating on every word coming from the first speaker. With a mental wrench, Mary tried to pull her own mind back to the subject under consideration.

There was a rising curve of crime among the young, an alarming lowering of the average age of juvenile delinquency which paralleled a disquieting increase in divorce and a growth of laxness in the relations of the sexes. The speaker marshaled figures and statistics, reports and reports and, before he finished, he had indicted practically everything in human society—the motion picture, the press, the tabloids, welfare groups, education boards, school teachers, social workers, children's courts and finally church and home.

When he sat down the audience turned and twisted in their seats uneasily.

It was hardly necessary for the chairman to introduce the young woman who followed as an authority for she exuded authority in every accent and gesture. Her subject was "The Motherless."

In spite of a foreign accent she spoke with precision, every word carved, clipped. It was with a sense of shame that she was obliged to state that their fair city was one of the few remaining in the state which tolerated an orphan asylum, a barracks-like building containing nearly fifty children wearing uniforms. She hoped public sentiment would be aroused to tear down that anachronism and, before she visited them again, every one of these "waifs of fate" would be found in private homes receiving some mother's care.

One could fairly feel the collective shame of the audience as, after applauding politely, each sat avoiding his neighbor's eyes.

A rather elderly British medical officer seemed a little more cheerful about them. He had visited their city and county jails and had found conditions sanitary, intelligently managed and not at all damning. With more figures and more statistics he knocked into a cocked hat the theory that ignorance produced crime. If anything the reverse was true. Morality is not increased by education. About the same proportions of ignorant and educated were found in prison and out. He actually smiled and the audience taking their courage in their hands, dared to smile also and look into each other's faces again. He received hearty applause.

At last they came to the final speaker—an Irishman from the lower west side of New York. Perhaps they had never heard of a *west* side. In a moment people were sitting up eagerly in their seats. With what he acknowledged as a "curbstone accent," he told them his personal experience in saving boys and girls from crime and degradation in his own Boys' Club. The details were specific, constructive, amusing and convincing. "Put a boys' club in every section of every city and town in this land where boys congregate. Put decent men and women in charge—volunteers— never pay a worker one damned cent—if a man or woman works for money, throw him out." Get together, start clubs, he'd come and help. Save their boys before they became criminals.

There was hearty and prolonged applause. Of course a forum must end with a question period. A spinster, a woman known to them all, stood up and crisply, using a very broad "a" stated that only thirty-three children, brought from all over the county, were left in that so-called barracks and five hundred and seventy-nine had been placed in homes. Her voice cracked toward the end of her speech.

Presently with compliments and thanks the celebrities on the platform and the audience were dismissed.

As they rose, Sandra drew a long sigh and took her mother's arm. They went out a side door and she quickly found Professor Waring already waiting in his car. On the drive home, Sandra asked him tentatively if he didn't think they tried to cover too much ground.

Contagiously, his hearty laugh rang out. "Gosh, we live in a vocal age. If talking can save America, we're headed straight for Heaven."

Mary Donovan joined in the laughter but again she thought, "A formidable opponent."

He walked to the door with them. She thanked him. "It was kind of you to take us."

Quickly he raised his hat and with a brief "good night," ran down the steps. For a moment Sandra looked after him, then she opened the door.

They decided they both were hungry and would get some warm milk. Sandra walked about the sittingroom, cup in hand.

Directly Mary asked, "Sandra, don't you think Professor Waring is making a little too much of you? Showing a partiality that may cause gossip? Also a partiality that I would call in very bad taste for a teacher."

"Can't a teacher be a friend?" She whirled around. "Perhaps some vulgar, gossipy people imagine he likes me because I am a girl—"

"A very pretty girl."

"Oh, Mother, you're not like that. We are friends and it's wonderful to have a friend like that. He says he likes to talk to me and I'd rather talk to him than to anyone I know. He makes boys seem shallow. I just can't tell you, Mother, I can't tell you how much it means to me. It's done so much for me, why, see how he's made me work."

"How old is he?"

"He's thirty."

"I believe he is married?"

"Oh, yes."

"Why doesn't his wife live here with him?"

"They have two children, three and seven. The seven-year-old has tuberculosis and the mother stays with him in Colorado. It was her home. They must save the boy's life and this was the only arrangement they could make."

Mary was silent a moment then she looked straight into Sandra's frank face. "Why did he have your beret tonight?"

Color rose in the cheeks as Sandra dropped her eyes. "I don't know, Mother. He never did anything like that before. Just before I came home, he took it off my head and walked off with it. Once in a while he fools a little but not often."

"What do you mean by 'fools a little'?"

"Mother! You talk like a judge. I mean he laughs and acts young and jolly. Mostly he doesn't."

"Never romantic?"

"Heavens, no!" She walked over and smiled into her mother's eyes. "He's nothing like that and, what's more, I wouldn't want him to be. I don't like—I don't want any man—unless I ever fall in love—I want to kill any man who touches me. I wanted to kill Hunt Carter." She smiled pleadingly, "Don't spoil my wonderful friendship, Mother. It's such a relief, it's so wonderful to be friends with an older man after—after Hunt."

"But you've always had nice boy friends of your own age."

"You don't know, Mother. They're silly and sentimental and they're always pawing you."

Long after Sandra went upstairs, Mary sat lost in thought. She hadn't had income enough to send Sandra away to school while money was still needed for Joseph. Back in her mind was a dearly treasured dream of sending her daughter to that old school in New York where she and her mother and aunts before her were educated. Family tradition. Once Tom had said to her, "You need a larger canvas." Now, clearly she saw her daughter's need of a larger canvas. This clean-cut, intellectual, talented man! She found herself murmuring, "If he doesn't make a mistake—was that matter of the beret his first slip?" How coolly and composedly he had passed that off. He was clever—a formidable opponent.

She found herself absorbed with thoughts of the seven-year-old boy, the wife in Colorado. Miss Simmons? Miss Simmons as usual was trying to help her.

Well, they would get through with this play and then she would see what she could plan. Joseph must come home Friday. She smiled a little bitterly. So one wants one's children to be wiser about life. She saw clearly that all the words ever written or spoken could not enable Sandra to see what her mother saw. Perhaps that was the tragedy of human life; one had to live and die a thousand deaths before knowledge came.

Sandra was up early Tuesday morning. She was in such a hurry that she hardly noticed little Nan who was dressing by the range. Pulling on a tweed coat and her green felt hat, she remarked briefly, "I may be late this afternoon. They need help with the costumes."

Nan stopped her struggle with a stocking to listen as the outside door closed. She sighed, "Sandra's gone." Mary bent over to fasten the brace. Her voice was as soft as a whisper as she repeated, "Yes, Sandra's gone." She thought of J.R., her father. So much went out of a room, out of a house with him. So much went out with Sandra.

CHAPTER XXIII

Here and there among the multitude of household duties was one which Mary loathed. One could positively enjoy creating a meat pie; setting a table, arranging flowers and dishes could be pleasure but, when she wrestled with a wet-wash in the woodshed, her soul was filled with loathing.

Kit was laid up with rheumatism so Mary pulled on an old sweater of Joseph's and never had she found it a more disheartening task than on this cold Tuesday with sleet and rain hammering on the roof.

In the afternoon, while Nan took a nap, she went through the beating rain to the grocer's for more lemons and oranges. She must stop Nan's cold. She squeezed fruit, then set up her ironing board.

It was only a few moments after three when she heard Miss Simmons arrive in a taxi. She was home very early indeed. Five minutes later, there was her sharp, authoritative knock at the door and her authoritative presence at the side of Mary's ironing board.

About Nan's absence from school? About Nan's cold? The questions all answered, she held out a hand which Nan eagerly grasped. "I'll take care of her until supper time. I have fruit." Then to Nan, "We'll put up the projection screen and see colored pictures."

"And play records?"

"Of course."

Leaning with all her strength, Mary pressed the iron back and forth over the damask napkin. About her lips hovered a smile. Miss Simmons was quite in love with Nan. Her brother Lawrence was in love with Nan. Sandra had always loved her completely. Her lips quivered a little like Nan's as she thought, Tom had left them the baby with his hazel eyes, his charm and some of his mannerisms.

Under her hot iron the second napkin grew smooth and carefully she folded and matched the corners neither knowing nor consciously seeing what she was doing. She was in the old brick house, hearing his step on the porch, seeing the door open. The way he raised his head looking from under dark lashes, that rising inflection in his voice, "Mary?" Now, Nan said, "Mothey?" It was a reaching out to her, "You see me? You want me?" "Mary?" "Mothey?"

She jumped so violently she nearly dropped the iron as the door-bell rang. Straightening her hair she went through the hall. At the curb she saw a car, the driver peering out as though waiting to see if his passenger had further need of him. A man was standing near the side of the porch. He was a young man and a stranger and, when she opened the door, she was sure in that first moment, that he was not only a stranger to her but a stranger to that community and even to the way of life in that community. How much one can see in a first concentrated inspection.

He was looking at her as sharply, as expectantly as she at him. He spoke in a heavy, coarse voice, "I'm looking for Mrs. Donovan."

"I'm Mrs. Donovan."

He smiled and the smile was so eager, so pleasant that it completely changed his heavy mouth and plain face. He called to the driver not to wait, then turned again to her. "May I come in and talk to you?"

She was naturally courteous yet she hesitated. "I'm afraid I can't place you. Should I know you?"

His smile broadened, "No, you don't know me; you've never heard of me but I know you. If you will please let me talk to you?"

Her thoughts were of Joseph as she opened the door wide, inclined her head and spoke graciously. "Come in." She led him into the parlor. She motioned to a large chair but when she crossed the room and sat down, he followed and seated himself on the sofa near her.

He seemed awkward and ill at ease and she felt that he was trying to gain control over some inward agitation as his eyes first stared hard at her then searched the room as though he were registering in his mind the appearance of every piece of furniture.

"Won't you lay your hat right there on the sofa?" He had been twirling it nervously in his hands. Now he laid it down. He had worn no overcoat and she noticed that his shoulders were damp and his shoes quite wet.

"The things in your house *are* beautiful." He was looking at the fine old rug on the floor.

She noted his emphasis on the word "are." As he still looked about the house, she had time to examine him. Heavy—that was the first general impression, heavy and coarse. But, by "coarse" she did not mean vulgar or low. A cloth of coarse weave could be substantial and, adapted for the proper use, could be as beautiful for its purpose as chiffon for its use. Standing, he had not appeared much taller than she; sitting he seemed almost squat. His feet were broad and the breadth was accentuated by heavy, square-toed shoes; his hands were broad and the fingers short and blunt. Perhaps that impression of bluntness was increased by the way he wore his hair. It was a wiry brush clipped into a pompadour above his forehead. She noticed the high cheekbones, the eyes open and frank and now directed toward her with an appealing expression.

The more she looked at him, the younger he seemed. Perhaps he might be twenty-eight or twenty-nine. She spoke pleasantly, "Will you please tell me your name and let me know why you wanted to talk with me?"

Presently she clasped her hands tightly together to steady herself and she found herself trembling as she slowly grasped the meaning of his answer.

"My name is John Donovan. I am Tom Donovan's son. I have learned about you from my father. I was sight-seeing in Boston and, all at once, I wanted to see you and talk to you so I got on the train and came here." He talked neither fluently nor easily and he looked at her soberly. "He told me so much about you. He said that you were the only beautiful woman he ever knew who was indifferent about her beauty." He smiled as he finished, "He doesn't think many women are beautiful *and good*."

He waited, watching her with frankly admiring eyes, then he stumbled on, "Being a poet, he isn't afraid of—saying fancy things. When you get used to it you know he is just honestly saying what he feels. I couldn't."

She found her voice and spoke evenly. "Most of us work very

hard to appear reserved and even," she smiled, "hard-boiled. We're terrified of appearing sentimental."

"He says things pretty neatly though. His big word for you is inviolate." Now he smiled and there was a glint of intelligent humor in his eyes. "He got out the dictionary and he made me learn what it means—unbroken, unpolluted, unprofaned. I see what he means. He read me some beautiful poems he wrote about you." He looked appealingly at her. "After I left him I told myself, I just had to see his wife."

"His wife." Outside the wind was blowing sheets of rain in fitful gusts; high over head the tops of the elms swayed and the branches were whipped and beaten as though by an angry antagonist. The heavy sky was growing darker and in the parlor it seemed as though daylight had suddenly vanished and night had closed down.

With conscious effort, Mary Donovan steadied herself and, with hand firmly grasping the arm of her chair, she managed to rise and walk to the table where she snapped on a light. She lit another lamp near her guest before she reseated herself. The words were clanging in her brain, "His wife."

She was amazed at the sound of her own quiet voice, "How old are you?"

"I am twenty-six."

A little more than five years older than Joseph. She raised her hand and held her throat as she controlled her voice to ask, "What do you do? Where do you live? Tell me about yourself."

"I am a miner."

She saw the men coming out of the mines with the lanterns pushed up on their foreheads as she had seen them so long ago with her father in Pennsylvania. That dark barren picture had haunted her all her life; but this was different; he was from the Canadian Rockies.

She interrupted, "What was your mother's name? Given name?"

"Elizabeth."

"You say she died? When you were a baby?"

"Oh, no. She died about six months ago. She was killed almost instantly in an automobile accident. She ran head-on into a bus. She often drank heavily and I'd beg her not to drive but no one could stop her doing anything. She was reckless. It was when I went through her things that I found a letter which proved I had a father living. She had told me all my life that he was dead. It was a shock, the biggest shock I ever had. I took all the money I had and went to New York and hunted him up."

"How did you find him?"

"The way she had, through a magazine. She had seen his name as a writer."

"He had never seen you?"

"He didn't know I existed. I never thought he would be friendly or even decent. I didn't expect that. I just had to see my own father. I'd thought he was dead all my life. I can't explain but, if he was living you had to see him."

She scarcely whispered, "I understand. And he?"

"He was awfully decent to me. He told me the truth, the whole truth."

"The whole truth?"

"Yes, mam. At first I thought he was lying because I was not his kind of gentleman. I had decided, in my own mind, that it might be because he had deserted her that she had gone to pieces morally. Perhaps that was the reason. I don't know. She had worked as a waitress in a restaurant where the miners ate and I think she got tired and found living with some man an easier way of life. When I was little she boarded me out with a nice family. As soon as I was big enough I went into the mines."

When he hesitated, she urged, "Tell me more."

"I always saw my mother and I lived with her off and on. Of course I see now why she always lied to me about my father. He told me. They were never married. I don't hold it against her. Only, it's no use, is it? The truth always comes out in the end, doesn't it? This took twenty-six years. Everyone up there thought she was a widow."

Mary was leaning far back in her chair and for a minute she closed her eyes. "You're right; it's no use."

He seemed eager as he bent forward. "I don't hold anything against him now. I can see what happened. I had to see him to understand him."

"You understand him?"

"Yes. I think he is a wonderful person. Men like that—"

"Men like that?"

"You see I can't talk easy like him. I never know how to say anything fancy."

Upstairs, directly over their heads, the record was being changed from a Schubert Impromptu to a waltz. The rhythmical strains were a maddeningly gay, light accompaniment to the conversation in the parlor. Suddenly there was a thumping, a curious sound coming always like a down-beat with the three-four measures. Nan had told her mother that sometimes she and Miss Simmons danced. Mary had never seen it; the imagined pathos and grotesqueness of the Junoesque woman and the child with the iron brace dancing, hitting the floor in perfect unison with the beat, somehow seemed too much.

Her guest looked up at the ceiling. She said quickly. "It is nothing—a child playing with the music." When he relapsed into silence, again looking from one piece of furniture to another, she urged, "Tell me more about your mother."

He groped for facts. Her people were Polish; she was seventeen when she ran away from home; she wrote back that she had been married in Boston. "Boys are thick-headed. I was brought up by religious people. They were very good people. I went into the mines young and I was always more interested in getting a good meal and seeing a show than in my parents. Now I see that she had a hard life."

"Yes, you are right. She had a hard life."

Now, another thought startled her. Sandra! She must get him out of the house before her daughter came in. Some day, in some understanding way, the girls must know this truth but she must have time to think. Almost as though it were a tangible thing she saw Sandra's pride. She must have time. Desperately she looked out of the window. The wind was blowing a gale but the rain seemed to have ceased falling and somewhere there must have been a rift in the leaden sky for a bright glow from the west was touching the opposite houses.

His eyes watching her face, he smiled, "I took all my money out of the savings bank and went to New York. I'll never be sorry I spent the money. I saw the city. He was wonderful to me, although at first I was an awful shock to him. I was there three days and we talked most through the nights. Even now I can hardly believe that he could be my father. He is such a wonderful person but I felt awfully sorry for him."

"Why?"

"I could see that he suffered for all he had done wrong in his life—living alone like that. He says himself that living alone with a bad conscience is hell."

"Alone?" By no effort could she steady her voice.

He thought a moment. "Yes, he said he was lonely and—I'm not sure but I think he's poor. He would send me out to see things but he wouldn't go with me. He had been in a hospital and hadn't got his strength back, he said. He told me that when he was well and making money he had had a housekeeper. He called her Bel. He said her little child made him nervous. He had to send her away."

"Bel?"

But the young man was not interested in the housekeeper. His eyes brightened. "He's writing a play. He says there is one tragic moment in every life, the thing that makes a man or breaks him."

"Did he tell you what moment that was—in his life?"

"No. He read me parts of his play but it was way over my head. I'm only a laborer. I'd understand it in pictures. He read some poems and I understood them. I thought they were wonderful; they were all about you." He smiled at her and asked almost timidly, "You do think they are fine, don't you?"

Her face was white as she smiled, "I thought his short stories were"—she hesitated then used his adjective, "wonderful."

"Do you think he might have been happier if he had been able to follow a writing career instead of being—as he said—forced into business?"

She looked fixedly at her questioner. "I want you to tell me what you have in mind. You came to see me; now what? Are you going back to your father or—to Canada?"

"Oh, I've volunteered in the army. I leave for Canada tomorrow. In the Canadian army, I mean. I go to Toronto for training. Our government is rushing us over to England. I want to get in as quick as they'll let me. It's going to take all we've got to stop Hitler."

She leaned forward and laid her hand on his. "I am so proud of you for doing that. If I were a strong man that is what I would do."

His face reddened a little and the warm smile returned.

Then as though it were Joseph to whom she were speaking, "We haven't time to discuss it, but I want to say this to you. When we read the papers or hear lectures, we get the idea that all this war and evil are complicated. To me Hitler and all his kind represents what I see as the Anti-Christ stalking over the earth, murdering the weak and helpless. The bullies in life. Someone stronger than he must thrash him as we thrash all bullies. There is the ideal of Christian goodness which we try for even though we fall far short. God and the Devil. You have to take sides—clean-cut, no compromising. My brother fought and died against that same kind of bully. I am so proud of you because you are not afraid to face evil and fight it."

She withdrew her hand and moved restlessly in her chair. Her heart was beating fast and hard; she felt as though it were throbbing in her throat. She must get him out of the house before Sandra should come. Desperately, with a longing that nearly overpowered her, she liked this young man and wanted to be kind to him. She wanted to take his hand, put away his hat and bring him into her home, warmly welcome. She wanted to seat him at her table and let him know the sweetness and charm of their family supper. She wanted to put clean sheets on Joseph's bed and know him to be sleeping there respected, admired, wanted.

He had an aching need of something in his life and she could supply the need. She was trembling as she forced herself to stand on her feet. She must not. She must not. There were Sandra and Nan. Any minute her daughter would come in.

"I am so sorry I cannot ask you to spend the night here. I am so sorry."

He rose. He reached down for his hat. "Thank you very much for letting me come in and see you. I would have liked to see your little girls. My father says there was a baby—though I suppose she is not a baby now."

"No, she is growing up."

"I know all about Joseph. My father says he is a brilliant and remarkable person. I don't think I'd have courage to face him from what my father says about him. I hope the United States helps us out in this war. Of course they are helping now. My father worries for fear Joseph might have to go."

Her hand on the back of the chair helped steady her.

He took a few steps toward the door. She breathed hard, then she jerked up her head and followed him. When he reached the door he stopped and turned around with something of embarrassment in his face. "I hope you don't think it was wrong for me to come here, Mrs. Donovan. I'm not a pusher-in generally. I see how I've upset you. I'd go away feeling better if I thought you didn't mind."

They were standing in the hall. "No, I'm glad you came. I thank you for coming. I only wish I could be to you what I would like to be. I cannot. Believe that. What I want to do, I cannot do."

There was a relieved expression in his face. He looked down at the hat in his hand. "I don't stand a big chance of coming back; the first over get the works, you know, but could I ever see you if I came back—after the war?"

"Yes." Her voice was weak; she could not say anything else.

He was out on the porch. He stood a moment then looked back at her.

"Come here, John." She laid both hands on his shoulders and kissed him. "Please remember that I like you and I'm proud of you. Someday I'll see much more of you. You will come back to us."

She watched him as he passed down the street. He walked aimlessly as a man does who has no immediate destination in view.

CHAPTER XXIV

As Mary closed the door she glanced up and saw Miss Simmons standing at the head of the stairs. For a moment they looked at each other then, without speaking, Mary reentered the parlor, went through to the sittingroom and dropped down on the sofa as though all energy and strength had suddenly deserted her. She lay without moving a muscle. Could she get her numbed and battered mind used to the revelations made to her by that boy in time to act her usual part before her children?

Above her head, the music changed; now they were repeating the Schubert Impromptu. Was it minutes or hours later when she heard Sandra's step on the porch and the happy note in her laughter as she called, "Thanks, Professor Waring."

The door was opened and lights flashed on. "Mother?" The girl came in looking lovely, flushed and happy. "Professor Waring brought me home in his car." She was pulling off the green felt hat.

Mary Donovan sat up. Immediately Miss Simmons and Nan joined them, just as Sandra asked, "Are you sick, Mother?" They all stood looking at her. She gazed directly into Miss Simmons' eyes as she said, "No. I got a little overtired putting up that wet-wash. I must have fallen asleep so supper will be a little late."

Miss Simmons coughed twice, cleared her throat and with no authoritative note in her voice said, "Hanging up a wet-wash must be the very devil of a job."

Never had the lights seemed brighter and never had the hearts of her two daughters seemed gayer than through that supper hour. First, they hilariously crossed Tuesday off the calendar. Only two more days to go, then, "Friday and perhaps Joseph will be here and the play!" Nan drew the pencil mark through the date.

Sandra was calling out, "Hey there, you! Go back and put those spoons where they belong." Nan, standing before the table pretending to be unable to decide, laying forks here and there and finally looking up under the long lashes and shaking her head charmingly, "Setting a table is the very devil of a job." Their laughter rang out. This or that was the very devil of a job.

As she served the supper there was in Mary's mind a sense of relief; she had got her guest out of the house in time but as plainly as though he stood before her, was that coarse miner with the pompadour brush of hair, the rough voice, the half-Slavic face and the honest eyes. She wanted an entire night to think about that Elizabeth who put her boy in a "very religious family" to be brought up. There was some integrity in that young man and was that his father's sensitiveness in the eyes?

Sandra turned suddenly, "Mother! You look exactly as though you were going to cry into your tea and you're not listening to a word. The next time Kit's 'all stiff' I'll hang that wash myself."

"Or," Nan smiled, "Harriet and I'll do it."

"Miss Simmons, please." But Mary smiled.

Nan changed the subject. "Will you use rouge, Sandra? Will you bring me home some? I'd like a regular splash of it, just once. Miss Simmons has started another cap for me. It's the very devil of a job." And they were off again into gales of laughter.

It astonished Mary to see how Sandra, the young lady, and Nan the child could reach some common denominator of perfect companionship. She surmised how quickly the girl could change and reach that same companionship with Professor Waring.

She was in her room when the clock struck twelve, separating every word of information that young man had given her about her husband, placing the bits together to form a picture. When the picture was as plain as she could make it, she sat looking at it, completely oblivious of her surroundings. There, in the privacy of the night, she could weep over the tangled threads of life.

She woke with sunshine slanting into her room. She hurried down into the kitchen, thinking, "Joseph will have received my letter and have had time to answer. I'll get a sensible letter this morning."

At the breakfast table, she spoke to Sandra, "I haven't seen a newspaper this week. Please bring one in tonight." Always Miss Simmons had argued that it was unnecessary for Mary to subscribe.

Sandra answered quickly, "The paper is full of nothing but war, Mother. The same thing every day—German troops advancing. They're still bombing London. President Roosevelt has signed the bill appropriating four billion dollars for planes and for the army. We're sending destroyers to help Britain. That's about all. Enough I'd say."

"I happen to enjoy reading the paper for myself. Civics class headlines don't interest me."

As she went about her work through the day, Mary's mind was feverishly active. She wished she could think through to the rock bottom of one question: just what was the value she attributed to this social position she coveted for her daughters and her son? She reasoned—it has nothing to do with money and it has everything to do with money.

Neither she nor her parents had ever discussed money, or acted either niggardly or as wastrels with money. They had lived graciously, generously, simply, modestly, charitably; with time for study, time for music and art, time for loving and entertaining, all without ostentation or display. That is the way one might fervently wish that every human being on this earth might live. Only an infinitesimal number of people were so privileged. Her family's comfortable reservoir of money had made it possible. She saw that clearly. But through the generations steady hard work had gone into maintaining that reservoir. Her grandfather, the mill-owner, her grandfather, Judge Kent, her father and her brother, Lawrence, how doggedly they worked. But they didn't work like groveling slaves; their work was an outlet for their magnificent energy, their buoyancy of spirit, their zest for life.

Recently Lawrence had published an article which had fascinated her. He had stated that within ten years after the Pilgrims settled on their New England shores, they had become the strongest, most energetic people on the face of the earth *because they were the best fed*. They cleared the forest and from the soil brought diverse crops, they ate wild turkey, fruits and soon fresh vegetables. They pushed westward, cleared more land, on and on to the Pacific, always adding—what? Meat, fruit and fresh vegetables. The best fed people in the world. The masses of poor on the earth, toiled with weak bodies for a handful of starch! She smiled at that lecturer who had told them education didn't lessen crime. How eloquent and superficial these lectures were. He didn't mean education, he meant book learning. Poverty produced crime enough because poverty produced weak, hungry, unbalanced minds and bodies.

When she sent Nan back to school she was so restless that she put on her coat and walked out into sunshine, beautiful after the storm of the previous day.

She walked for about a mile, away from the avenue, through many short streets where, block by block, the houses became smaller, shabbier, until she came to the cotton mills, the industry started by her great-grandfather. Long since ownership had passed out of her family but she still held stock. There were the long brick or stone buildings extending for half a mile and there were the rows of detached and semi-detached houses for the "hands."

When she was a little girl she had known the houses painted, the grass plots mowed, the trees bearing rich fruit—apples, pears, plums and grapes, the flowers pretty before the front windows. They were largely English, Scotch and Welsh inhabitants in the beginning. Then came the poor, the underfed, from eastern Europe, then the Italians. Then came a "ten-year" depression and the wheels stopped turning and there had followed want and disease. She had watched it happen.

She had watched something else happen. She had seen the children of these "poor" sent to school, some to college. What had she seen? The District Attorney of their county, an honored and respected "first citizen," now living in one of their fashionable suburbs, a big, hearty, well-fed man, was a grandson of one of those immigrants. She could fill a gallery with such portraits.

Now, in 1941, the wheels were turning again, the torn, dirty curtains at the windows were replaced by white, starched ones; some women were sweeping up the untidy yards. The children went to school with washed faces. Those children would go to college, to New York and Chicago. Some would be ashamed of their fathers and mothers; some would burst with pride, knowing they started eating the good food, going to the schools, only a little later than their old New England neighbors.

She walked slowly past the long factory listening to the hum of machinery which ought to have been music in her ears.

The wheels were turning after ten frightful years. But she wondered how any person with a soul could be happy knowing the wheels were turning, not because of prosperity, but because of war.

She started to climb the long hill. She wondered why people forget that the Devil was a fallen angel. A fairy story? An old myth? Of course; also an everlasting truth evolved from the travail and suffering of man during the ages of his sojourn on earth. All the patriotism, bravery, noble sacrifice, sacrificial love, understood by the angel, were used by the Devil to destroy man's food, his home, his children and his hope.

The wheels were turning and she hurried a little until the sound of their whirring was dim in her ears.

She walked slowly along the beautiful avenue, a little tired now, the April sun warm on her face. The real wealth of the world was to be destroyed—children, strong young men, food, minerals, forests, the fertility of the ground.

Had she learned anything in these ten years? Had she learned what it was from her heritage she wanted to save, to treasure and pass on to her children?

In spite of wearying work, rented rooms, reduced income, she knew quite well that she was still numbered among the so-called aristocrats of their city, county and state. Important people always spoke of her as Mary Kent. Not long since, that most important and formidable Lucy had come in to see her. Mary had brewed and served tea while Lucy chatted with Sandra. When her daughter had gone on, Lucy had bent to plant an affectionate little peck on Mary's cheek. "You know, my dear, Louise Farnsworth was my best friend. When that beautiful girl is eighteen, I'm to have the privilege of introducing her formally to society." Mary had smiled and avoided discussion.

Now, as she walked slowly along the avenue she asked herself, what did she want for that daughter?

As to the circus antics of either American or foreign millionaires, the fashionable divorce mill at Reno, the vulgar if not criminal escapades of movie stars at one end of the scale, they were all as remote from what she wanted as the drunk behind the bars of their city jail was at the other. Sometimes she studied the pictures in the evening paper of so-called celebrities in café society. The smugness apparent in their vacantly grinning faces! The cheap snobbery! Or was she unkind in her judgment? Were they merely puppets with shrewd business men pulling the strings behind the scenes? At any rate they meant nothing to her.

When she approached the little white house with the green blinds a feeling of warmth seemed like a flood rising in her, even into her throat. For a moment her lovely eyes held in them something of the laughter of her girlhood. Through ten years, the legs of lamb, the roasts of beef, the bags of oranges, the fruits from the trees her father had planted and the green vegetables from the garden had never been absent from her table. Her children were well fed. They went to school with strong bodies. How plainly she could hear her father's strong, hearty voice at the dinner table as he asked the blessing, never mumbling the words but always saying them as though for the first time; so simply, "God bless this food to our use and us to Thy service, for Christ's sake, Amen."

She walked through the empty rooms—home. After hanging away her coat, she stood before the mirror smoothing her hair. She wondered why her eyes showed no trace of the tears she had shed alone in her room the night before. That boy little knew how much he had told her. He little knew how she had hungered to know something of the picture that his disjointed words had given her. Sad or bitter, she had longed to know. There was something in her heart today of the old sweetness. Her husband might be, in the eyes of society, worthless, neurotic, a failure, or a hundred worse things but she knew he loved her. It was all useless, hopeless, the strings were tangled beyond any hope of straightening and yet there was the sweetness.

There was that uneven thumping step on the porch, a childish voice calling, "Mothey?" She turned with a bright smile to Nan.

CHAPTER XXV

While Mary and the child ate their supper, Sandra telephoned. She would be home fairly early. The last rehearsals were going badly. "He blew us up. He told me I was one degree above a drip." A happy, infectious laugh came over the wire. Then Mary heard an anxious note, "Is everything all right, Mother? There's nothing—new?"

"Nothing at all. I had a refreshing walk and was so busy with my thoughts I forgot to buy a paper. Bring one in."

She was disappointed when Sandra came in a little after eight carrying a large bundle but no paper.

"Oh, I'm sorry I didn't get it. Bother the war, I guess my mind was on the play. I hate to ask you—but these darned skirts are too long. I'm bound to trip on them and ruin the play. Could you turn them up for me if I slip them on so you can see how much? Queen Victoria and her cronies were ashamed of their ankles but, just because of their modesty, I don't want to break my neck."

The beautiful weather held over to Thursday and by afternoon Mary had measured and hemmed the skirts and had found it no mean job. She pressed the dresses and laid them carefully over a sofa.

She had stepped out on the porch to speak to Nan who was playing in the sunshine when Miss Simmons came hurrying down the stairs, carrying a suitcase. She brushed past Mary murmuring something about going to attend a political conference. "Sorry to miss the play. I'll be back by Sunday night, going to do my housecleaning during the week." Before stepping into the taxi she turned to Nan. "You may go in and play those small records any time you want to." Then, in her flustered haste she bumped her head getting into the car. Mary saw how red her face was as she adjusted her hat. Miss Simmons flustered and rushing was an amazing sight!

As she passed through the parlor she stopped to shake up a pillow here and there, straighten a chair, wipe some dust from a mahogany table. Then she heard a car grind to a stop and saw a gray sedan at her door. A big boy sprang out, leaping rather than running.

"Mrs. Donovan, Sandra sent me for the dresses and to say she is not coming home for supper."

She fetched them, thanked him and watched him drive away.

She pushed aside the curtains and stood looking toward the street. Three women were passing. Mary watched them, thinking about them. How old were they? She judged in the forties, one older. All three had graying hair with similar permanent waves, with similar purple rinses, with similar black dresses, short fur jackets and each wore a tiny flowered hat which sat coquettishly over one eye. They carried expensive bags and tripped along in thin-soled, high-heeled shoes.

She saw the parlor at the Woman's Club filled with such women listening to lectures on this and that. Juvenile Delinquency. Did people use words today as scapegoats? Two fine big words like Juvenile Delinquency acted partly as an opiate. They removed the problem pleasantly into some intellectual area of remoteness, something for professionals to deal with or lecture about. "Oh," she thought, "there is such fine stuff under all that superficial veneer of fashion." She remembered Mattie's saying so often, "Someday they'll scrub the paint off, roll up their sleeves and go to work to save humanity."

Dear Mattie. She was thinking of her when suddenly the street appeared very beautiful to Mary. Sometimes something like a miracle happened—oh, she had more than once noticed it. There came a combination of light, an atmosphere, a flash of crimson and purple in the sky and the very pavement grew rosy. Some tangible beauty seemed to sing through the air. Now, such a moment came and she watched it down the street under the arch of elms. Then slowly the sky paled.

She was looking across when she saw Judge Carter come down his drive. He too was carrying a suitcase. He set it on the drive and walked across the lawn to stand under his magnificent magnolia tree looking up as the gardener began to strip off the winter packing. He stood with raised head as a tall young man joined him. Hunt must be home. She had understood he had been in Mexico all the previous summer. Now she saw the chauffeur bring the car from the back, saw Hunt take the wheel, his father sit beside him. The chauffeur was left standing beside the drive.

Mary parted the curtains but dropped them quickly as they almost stopped in front of her house. Both leaned forward and looked toward her door. Then the car started up again and they disappeared down the street.

As she turned back into the room her hand seemed of its own accord to swing out and knock over a treasured vase. She picked it up and saw the lip edge was snapped off.

Nan called, "What was that?"

"Mother was careless and broke a vase."

She was so intent on fitting the broken piece and wondering if she could mend it that she hardly noticed a florist's delivery car stopping in front of her house. When she answered her bell, a boy thrust a huge package into her hands, called, "Donovan" and was gone.

Setting it on a chair, she and Nan undid the wrappings, revealing a mass of Easter lilies. There was an envelope addressed to her. She tore it open and read the words on the card, "For Mrs. Donovan from George Campbell Waring."

They stood gazing into the beauty of those great white bells. She was disturbed and not at all pleased by the gift. They arranged the flowers on a small table, then she smiled at Nan, "I guess we're all play-acting. I'll be glad when we strip off our wigs and costumes and wash off our make-up."

At the table Nan asked, "Is Professor Waring a friend of Uncle Lawrence's?"

"No, dear, they never saw each other. Why?"

"I thought that might be why he puffed up Sandra's play and sent you Easter lilies."

Her mother's head dropped into her hands as she laughed and when she looked up her eyes were wet. "Oh, Nan, what would I do without you?"

Nan looked annoyed. "That wasn't funny. Why did you laugh?"

"What do you mean by 'puffed up' the play?"

"Harriet says he probably did. She says Sandra did have a big idea. Only a garden could make Queen Victoria and her gardener equal friends. The queen would rather be there than in her palace in England. I told her it was Sandra's own idea to make it an Easter play because she talked the idea over with me. She borrowed the words,

'In the beauty of the lilies Christ was born across the sea,
With a glory in his bosom that transfigures you and me:
As He died to make men holy, let us die to make men free—'

Wait 'till you hear her say that—just the words with no music —it'll make you tingle. She did the whole speech for me, privately, upstairs."

There was a rapt expression in the thin little face; her eyes glowed as she reached out a bony hand and touched her mother's arm. "Sandra says she'd rather write one verse like that than be all the greatest actresses in the world rolled into one. I couldn't decide. What do you think, Mother?"

"I think Sandra's right. The great actresses must have great lines to say. Still, we need them both, don't we?"

"That's what Harriet thinks; we need them both."

"Miss Simmons, please."

"She's sick and tired of being called Miss Simmons. She says to call her Harriet but never Hattie."

Mary smiled and watched the bright eyes. They opened very wide as she looked up, "Mothey, do you know why Sandra can write plays?"

"She's talented?"

"Yes. Harriet says she inherited my father's gifts. He was a very wonderful writer; much better than Uncle Lawrence because he makes it all up. He never has to borrow. Did you know that?"

"Yes, I knew that." She had spoken as though that father had been dead for a hundred years. Mary rose and began to remove the dishes.

Nan made her laugh often through the following hours. In an angelic mood, she wiped dishes, limping back and forth to the pantry where she set each piece of china down carefully.

Before Mary got upstairs she was undressed. "I said my prayers, Mother. I prayed God not to let Sandra be a bust. She said a bust was worse than a drip."

"Well, don't you do any worrying about her. When one loves to do something one is apt to do it well."

Again laughing, Mary let her wear her very best clothes to the play. She felt the small hand clutching hers tightly as they stood in the lighted hall watching the ushers, smart-looking boys, and girls in pretty, long dresses. They patiently waited their turn. Nan was patted on the head and then they were following a girl in a white dress all the way down the center aisle to the front row completely unconscious of the stir in the audience as they passed. Here and there some woman turned to another and lifted an eyebrow. Behind them as Mary and Nan removed their wraps, one woman said to another, "Plucky?"

"Perhaps there's nothing to it. People always think the worst."

"Did you see tonight's paper?"

Mary did not know they were staring at the back of her head. Tonight, it was a very pretty head for she had worn no hat and her hair never appeared lovelier.

The lights in the hall were dimmed. Mary smiled at Nan as she felt the wiry fingers digging into her arm and caught the quivering tone in her voice, "They're going to start, Mothey."

Half conscious that the vacant seat beside her was being filled, she turned with surprise at hearing Hunt Carter's voice saying, "Good evening, Mrs. Donovan." She returned a quick nod and smile then gave her attention to the stage.

Like most of the audience of parents and friends, she expected to be pleased, entertained and perhaps slightly bored. Instead she was astonished. Undoubtedly, Professor Waring had "puffed up" the play, but he had puffed it up to good purpose because it was clever and what was more refreshing, it was amusing.

The man had talent. Quite aside from the witty lines there was a professional touch to the details of lighting, change of scenery (there were but two acts), the entrances and exits, those banes of amateur performances. The settings were charming, a welcome change from the usual arrangements of the well-known furniture which often brought guffaws from the audience.

During the intermission many people left their seats. Courteously Mary turned to her neighbor, wondering a little at the rather strange coincidence of his being seated next to her. "You're home for Easter?" In a quick glance she had observed the boy's development into manhood. There was maturity as well as something of distinction in his bearing. He was looking at her with a friendly but penetrating expression in his deep-set eyes.

"Yes, I came yesterday morning." He did not ask for Joseph and she noted the omission.

He leaned forward and smiled at Nan. "Hello, there, Nancy. You're getting to be a big girl."

The child flashed one thoroughly unfriendly glance in his direction, then stiffened and leaned far back in her seat, as nearly behind her mother's shoulder as she could get. A little impatiently Mary jogged her. "Nancy, Hunt spoke to you."

The small mouth set determinedly and Nan looked straight ahead in stubborn silence.

Mary briefly and deprecatingly explained Nan's recent feud with Hunt's little brother, the detested Willie Carter. Hunt unsmilingly remarked, "The Carter brothers seem to have a genius for making mortal enemies of the Donovan sisters." He leaned forward and spoke nearly to the back of Nan's head, "I'm sorry, Nancy. If I'd been home I'd have walloped him myself. Can I buy you a new one?"

Nan looked straight in front of her, too near tears for her mother's comfort. Mary whispered, "Better give up, Hunt."

There was a deep pink in Mary Donovan's cheeks as she watched her daughter on the stage. Even she, the mother, could almost forget Sandra in the character she was portraying. For many reasons the performance left her both proud and uneasy.

The applause was prolonged but Nan jumped to her feet. "Remember, Mothey, we are to go back-stage right away."

With a quick nod to Hunt, they hurried to the stage door but already the narrow passageway was choked with boys and girls. Somehow they edged their way in, managed to speak to Sandra, Nan thrilled with glimpses into dressingrooms. Slowly, stopping for friendly words with acquaintances, they found themselves again at that convenient side door. Outside, Mary was surprised to find Hunt at her side.

"My car is down at the gate. Please let me take you home."

"Oh, no thanks. Go right back. You will want to see your friends."

He insisted. They started down the long lane between parked cars, where the uneven ground caused Nan to stumble and fall. Hunt leaned down, put his arms about the slight form and settled her against his shoulder, accommodating his pace to Mary's until they reached his roadster. There were hardly a dozen words spoken until they reached home where he carried Nan to the door. "I'm going back to the hall, Mrs. Donovan."

"Thank you, Hunt. You've been very kind tonight. It was quite a coincidence that your seat was next to ours."

"It wasn't a coincidence, I planned it." Then he leaned forward and looked at the little girl. "Will you say good night, Nancy?"

Her smile was a little feeble but she said, "Good night, Hunt."

"That's better. You know *I* didn't steal your cap." He turned and ran down the steps, jumping into his car as he said aloud, "I did a hell of a lot worse."

Mary saw him make a rapid turn and disappear up the road into the darkness. She took Nan directly upstairs.

"Mothey?" The voice was tremulous. "Do you feel bad too?"

"About what?"

"What they did to Sandra. They made a big, fat old thing out of her; then they covered her up with old black clothes and a horrid wig."

Mary explained about character-acting but Nan was unimpressed.

She demanded, "Why isn't Joseph here when Hunt's home?"

"Do you know it's nearly midnight? I'm putting the light out; now, not another word. We'll talk it all over in the morning."

She left the door ajar and walked softly down the hall. At Miss Simmons' open door she stopped. She still wanted to read the President's speech and Miss Simmons wouldn't mind if she borrowed the paper. She went in and snapped the light on over the table. There was the neat pile of papers kept "just in case there is an article I need to refer to."

She found Monday's paper, settled herself and started to read when she was interrupted by the ringing of the telephone.

It was Sandra. There was a detailed explanation. Gladys Odell lived about five miles out on the Boston Road. Professor Waring and the leading people in the cast were all invited out for a celebration to meet someone from the Workshop and some important drama critic and they wanted her to come.

Sandra sounded strangely upset, undecided, and excited.

Mary answered calmly. "If you want to go, I would."

"But I can't quite decide. Is everything all right?"

"All right? You mean here? Of course. Nan's asleep—"

"Mother, you know where I am. I'll go."

Mary hung up the receiver and stood scowling a moment then she got a sweater and returned to Miss Simmons' room. Now, she noticed that under the few local papers, there were several Boston dailies of recent date. With interest, she read their editorial comments on the speech and on other matters. She was idly turning the pages when a headline caught her eye; "Two Harvard Students May Be Involved—" She shivered a little—something about a girl committing suicide. Her hands were not quite steady as she searched through Tuesday's paper, Wednesday's paper. Another headline; "Sleeping Tablets Bought by Harvard Student—"

She was startled at the sound of her doorbell. Hurriedly, she descended the stairs and opened the door. She looked her surprise at seeing the tall, stoop-shouldered form of Judge Carter.

"Good evening, Mary." He followed her into the sittingroom as she lighted a table lamp. He looked a bit tired and disheveled. "I've come to you direct from the train—from Boston."

When, conscious of a sudden weakness, she dropped down on the sofa, he crossed the room and sat close beside her. Never in all the long years in which the knowledge of his love and deep devotion had been hers, had the warmth of her admiration so ardently expressed itself. Rugged, strong, tired and always, always lonely. She laid her hand on his. "I knew nothing until an hour ago. I have been reading the Boston papers. You went—because of Joseph?"

"Of course—as though it had been Hunt."

She looked up into his eyes. "What a friend!"

It was an hour later when he left. Before going upstairs she must have absent-mindedly turned out the light for when Sandra came home she found the parlor dark.

CHAPTER XXVI

Hunt Carter parked his car far out in the road, zigzagged across the lot where cars were moving in seemingly every direction and approached the lighted doorway. Almost at once he saw the group in the midst of which Sandra stood, bare-headed. She was step-ping into one of the cars when he approached close to the running-board. She turned and saw him.

They looked steadily at each other; then he asked, "Can I speak to you alone a moment, Sandra?"

She did not hesitate but jumped out, walked quickly some twenty feet then turned and looked up into his face. For the many minutes in which they talked neither pair of eyes seemed even to waver.

At the wheel, Professor Waring smiled as the other cars pulled out leaving them. He asked carelessly, "Who is he?"

"Hunt Carter, Judge Carter's son," one of the boys had an-swered. Now he added, "I think he's going into his father's office. Well, I don't suppose we can leave the leading lady behind. Blow the horn, Professor."

But the professor did not blow the horn. He waited with ap-parent indifference but his eyes were sharp as he looked at the tall young man who walked back with Sandra to the running-board. He saw the quick motion of the hand he held out, saw Sandra take the hand, heard the words, "If Dad gets back tonight, I'll telephone you."

She slipped into the back seat with two other girls and was silent through much of the drive.

Out in a comfortable old home on the Boston Road, the drama critic had been speaking of character-acting to the gay group perched on divans, in easy chairs or reclining on the rug in front of the burning logs in the Odells' fireplace. There were delicious toasted sandwiches, hot coffee, beer and, judging from the array of bottles which Sandra noticed on a side table, plenty of whiskey and soda. The nonsense and wit and repartee enchanted Sandra.

Once she noticed Professor Waring and an interesting-looking man, talking earnestly as they stood by a desk apparently examining a manuscript.

There was always another round of drinks, more cigarettes or candy and, instead of growing dull, eyes brightened; but at last they reluctantly went upstairs for wraps and soon were outside getting into cars. How it was managed Sandra never knew; but somehow she found herself alone in Waring's car. A few miles down the road one of the cars passed them; the other had long since disappeared.

They came to a fork and instead of going straight on, he turned a sharp right. "Let's go up over the hill. It's such a fine night. Warm enough?"

"Yes, but it's after one—"

"Your mother won't worry?"

"Oh, no. I told her we would be late; only—"

"Only what?"

"I might have a telephone call. I ought to be home." She could have added, "I'm very tired." But she did not know she was very tired.

They had emerged from a thickly wooded section and come out near the brow of a hill where the valley, now bathed in a silver radiance of moonlight, lay stretched out before them. He drew to the side of the road, braked the car and snapped off the ignition. "How's that?"

Her eyes swept across the valley. "Makes me feel like whispering, it's so quiet after you stop the engine."

"What's that young bean-pole's name? Carter? Did he have something definite about Joseph?"

"Not exactly."

In his eyes which were watching her intently, there flashed a glint of laughter. "I suppose, having been brought up across the street from each other, you and this Hunt Carter are old friends?"

"Not exactly."

"Joseph's friend?"

Her lovely eyes opened wide as she seemed to be looking far

into the shadows down the road. She was thinking more deeply
than he knew. She answered simply, "I think they have always
liked each other."

He changed the subject abruptly. "Happy tonight, Sandra?
You liked the people? The atmosphere? The talk?"

"I loved it." She turned to him, laughing, and there was an
excited note in her voice. "Do you know what that did to me
tonight?"

"Tell me." His voice was low and tender.

"It just fired me with ambition. I can't quite explain because
it wasn't very definite but somewhere in myself I felt a terrific
urge to get out in the world and do things. I don't mean run
around to see things. I mean study, learn a lot. I'm so beastly
ignorant. Perhaps someday if I do well in college, I might get
to be a professor of English—Uncle Lawrence says there is no
prejudice against women if they are equal to men in brains. I
suddenly felt ashamed of not being through High School when
I'm seventeen. Miss Simmons never stops reminding me of my
indolence."

She went on half breathlessly, "I could have been through a year
ago if I had got down to working. The trouble was Mother
couldn't possibly swing it, financially. She's nearly killed herself
working and saving money to meet Joseph's expenses. I either
had to wait until he was finished or go out to live with Uncle
Lawrence and I couldn't bear leaving Mother and our baby. Besides I do love sports and I'm as strong as Joseph. I think my
perfect health is partly due to playing tennis with you. Then I
loved our plays." She repeated with a little laugh, "That's what
it did to me—made me ashamed of my indolence and long to get
somewhere and be somebody and belong to people like that."

His eyes had never wavered from gazing at her face. Carelessly
he stretched his arm across the back of the seat and turned a little
more toward her. "You're going to get somewhere. You're going
to be a great deal more of a someone than anything you have in
mind."

For a moment he seemed uncertain of himself as with narrowed eyes he thought deeply before speaking. He turned to put up the window as the chill night air blew in, half muttering under his breath, "Damn that bean-pole!"

She did not quite catch the last word but she saw he was laughing as he replaced his arm and again looked into her face. "I didn't bring you up on this road to show you either moonlight or scenery, Sandra. I didn't intend to talk about what we both want, for quite a long time yet. We've been mighty happy just working together and being together, haven't we?"

There was an expression of slightly flustered surprise and happiness in her face as she glanced at him and smiled, "Yes, I have."

"Perhaps I never told you how I happened to take this little job here, last year—the little job which seems destined to change the course of my life. These Odells. You will learn someday that the world is filled with powerful nobodies. Mrs. Odell, Jakie, they call her, is the sister of what the American public worships, a movie magnate, a Croesus—well, let's not go into that. Year after year, increasingly, the people with no roots, no background, no real culture—whether movie stars, writers, actors or painters— make a lot of money; then they seek out the fine old bits of America where culture has been inherited, treasured and guarded for generations. They buy themselves in, stay until there are too many of their kind, corrupt the place then leave it a shambles."

She spoke eagerly, "But new blood is desirable, isn't it?"

"You're thinking of new blood of a different kind. It's a long story and we'll discuss it some other time. Anyway, I was at loose ends, came here for a week end with the Odells, quite calculatingly, and some member of the school board met me and—you know the rest.

"I, like many professional men, began my life by teaching to further my education. I thought it rather fun to take the job for a few months. In June, I left, as you know for California, stayed out there all summer. Twice I wrote a resignation, twice I tore it up, telling myself I was the damnedest fool I ever hoped to meet. Do you know why I tore them up?"

She looked at him wonderingly and he smiled into her eyes,

"Because of you, Sandra. Your face. I had to cross the continent to see your eyes looking up into mine again. I had to see you on the tennis court, work with you in a play, just be with you day after day."

His hand lay caressingly on her shoulder. "I didn't intend to tell you this at Easter; I wanted to get through the year but to-night I've made an important decision. I signed a contract today to go out to Hollywood."

Her head bent slowly over her hands which were clasped in her lap. She spoke quietly. "Of course that's wonderful for you. About everyone I know has said we were unbelievably lucky to have a person so talented as you. I can't imagine what it will be like to have you gone."

She did not see his brilliant eyes watching her. He spoke softly, "You care?"

"Why, everyone will care."

"To hell with everyone. Only you and I matter."

Her head was resting against his shoulder because he had brought his arm and shoulder to her head. She sat as still as though she had turned into a statue. "Sandra, you have been sitting here actually planning to be a school-marm like the damnedest little blue-stocking that Massachusetts ever produced." He laughed lightly. "Don't you ever look into the mirror? While you're brushing and combing that mass of glorious hair do you look out of the window and watch robins pulling worms out of the earth? Do you close your eyes or are you saying your prayers while you're undressing?"

For a moment she looked confused, then she laughed merrily. "I guess I've been told so often that I'm exactly like my grandfather that I've grown up feeling like him and feeling I look like him. I'll show you his picture. He was big and bluff and strong and wonderful, and everyone loved him and called him 'Old J.R.' But he was far from handsome. What looks I have I get from Mother and I happened to get what they call the Farnsworth hair." She sounded even merrier as she added, "When I get to thinking too much about my hair they tell me blondes fade young."

His laugh rang out in the night. "Your mother has done a good job." He added with seeming irrelevance, "Did she like her lilies?"

"Oh, yes. She loves flowers."

"I'll tell you a secret. I'd give—well most anything except you—to be able at some proud moment to call your mother my friend. You can't see her with my eyes. One sees aristocrats of lineage but not so often aristocracy of soul. I acknowledge humbly there is such a thing as a lady. I acknowledge she is very beautiful but—" he was drawing her closer—"I also admit she is an enigma to me. I don't understand her life, her beauty, her background and her present life. But what wouldn't I give to know she was my friend." He laughed, "Then I could thank her for Sandra."

He spoke with sudden earnestness. "I've told you about everything there is to tell about the mess I made of my young life, marrying an impossible fool at twenty-one, finishing college after marriage, two children that have never meant anything to me. I've come to the end of that rocky road. I asked my wife for a divorce and as she's met another steadier and, God grant, stupider guy and wants to marry him, she's already in Reno. I pay for it all and that will keep me strapped for a while. She'll have the children and at last I'll be free to live—actually live."

She sat silent, listening intently.

"Free! You can't even conceive what that word means to me." When he stopped as though he were inwardly savoring the coveted state, she asked hesitatingly, "When will you go? Before the end of the year?"

"I'll have to. I'll clean up my work first; someone else can manage the examinations—routine sort of thing. I want to get into my own work before July. However, I'll be in New York more or less through the winter. You'll be having your *one* serious year at Wellesley. You heard that *one?* This contract can't put a continent between us for a year. We'll meet in New York."

He waited but she did not speak. Again she seemed like a small still statue, a scarcely breathing, taut little figure. Once his hand caressed her hair and lay gently a moment against her cheek. He felt a sudden trembling through her body and said, "Did you ever own or come in contact with a thoroughbred colt? You're more like one than like anything I ever saw in the world. I've seen young beauties and just touch them and they tremble from head to foot." He leaned over and touched her lips. "Sometimes I've watched you and seen some little flicker of your eyelids and always thought of one of those colts."

These were no wet, slobbery, awkward caddish boy kisses. He was gentle and seemingly wise and sometimes he spoke lightly and laughed and sometimes there was a fervent earnestness in his voice. "I'm taking it for granted that you understand. Next spring you will be eighteen. Then we can be married. Sandra, will you give me your promise that you'll keep yourself just as you are now, until then?"

She did not speak and her head bent a little farther over her hands.

"You know, my darling, you have everything. God has lavished gifts on you. You can act. That in itself, if you were as plain as a board fence, would insure your future. You have brains, quick, receptive, humorous, everything a man craves and longs for in a life companion. Then you have what you don't know you have." He slipped his hand under her coat and caressingly the hand moved from her waist over her slender hips, up under her breast where he held her closely as his lips pressed hard on hers. He murmured, "Will we talk intelligently to each other? You're too smart to want any hypocrisy. You have sex with a capital 'S,' darling. That full red mouth, a body full of strength and health and warmth."

He began to pour out his love for her in a mixture of teasing and adoration. He told her she was a sleeping beauty, a woman in body and a child only in her ignorance of love. Damn it! When she wrote a play, it was about gardens and democracy.

Clever? No barnyard calf could have been more stupid. He was blinder than any proverbial owl. His nearness, the touch of his clothes, the slight smell of whiskey, his voice close in her ear, his hands on her body shook her from head to feet.

For over a year, he had made her his friend. She had sat at his feet, mentally and spiritually drinking in wisdom, worshiping as at a shrine.

Once, when she had expected happiness, honor and comradeship, she had been treated like a "piece of baggage" by Hunt Carter. How deep that wound had cut only her mother had suspected. She had turned to this clever, intellectual, admired friend, not with reason but with passionate longing. Proud? No words could measure her pride in his friendship. Romantic? She had steeped her mind and heart in a romance but it was a romance of her own imagining, untouched by reality.

He was to be, eternally, her teacher and her friend. In their rehearsals when he had arranged a costume, fitted a wig or deftly explained make-up, the touch of his hands had meant nothing to her. When he went away for vacations, to California for an entire summer, she felt no longing for his physical presence. She was not in love with him.

Love had not touched her and yet not one muscle of her body or one tense nerve could have reacted against him. So long she had figuratively made herself into a piece of clay for his hands to mold, that she seemed to have no separate will when she was with him. She had longed for his respect; she had worked for his praise. Even in aspiring to go out into the world and succeed she had nebulously dreamed of his pride in her.

Now, he was stripping her of that pride. Again she was merely a pretty blond girl that a man wanted to fondle. The passionate physical contact filled her again with a sense of cheapness.

Of course he was sincere. Of course he loved her. He spoke gently, tenderly, "I had no intention of saying all this tonight, darling. I meant to wait until the end of the year and, in the meantime, hoped to make a friend of your mother. You know we must talk everything over with her and work for her consent. And," he laughed, "we must never let anyone's consent or opposition make any difference to us."

She lay limp and trembling in his arms and he fatuously interpreted her silence as acquiescence.

He drew her back into her own part of the seat and straightened up. "Damn it, we must go home. From what I've heard of your father and now Joseph, I think we'd better not give these gossip-mongers any more ammunition than we can help."

She made no intelligent answers. She had no intellect, no mind. She was simply a trembling, physical thing enveloped in a fog. She hated darkness and loved floods of light. Everything about her seemed murky black. Her father. She shivered and he asked, "Cold?"

"Oh, no."

Once, sudden tears spurted from her eyes but he did not notice for, conscious of the late hour, he was driving hard and fast.

When he came to the white house he got out, walked up the steps and, in the shadow of the doorway he held her close, kissing her lips again and again.

He was gone. Alone, she stood crying a moment; then, with the fumbling motions of an old person, she found her key and let herself in.

The parlor was dark. Strange. Mother always left the parlor lighted when she was out. There was a bright light at the head of the stairs in Miss Simmons' room. "Mother." Her voice was shrill, beseeching, "Mother."

Mary Donovan came hastily across the room. "I didn't hear you come in, dear." There was a whining cry. "I'm afraid we've waked Nan."

The child's voice, high-pitched, called, "Mothey, I've had a bad dream."

In another moment, Mary was leaning over the little girl's bed.

"My leg aches, Mothey." Mary arranged the pillow, smoothed the sheets and quilts then rubbed the leg as Sandra stood in the shadow leaning against the wall of the dark hall.

"Mothey, you didn't tell me why Hunt can be home and not Joseph."

"I can't stop to talk tonight, Nan. Close your eyes now and go to sleep."

She left the door ajar. Before she went out to Sandra, she stopped a moment listening to the child's whine,

"Where's Joseph?"

PART V

FATHER AND SON

===

CHAPTER XXVII

Joseph Donovan was standing at the back of a lecture hall where several groups of students were among the hundreds of men and women attending a forum in Boston in the middle of January in the year 1941.

The principal speaker was a witty fellow, amusing his audience with personal reminiscences. "Do you know what we discussed over cocktails and at forums, in our clubs and dormitories, when I was a student at Harvard, fifteen years ago?"

He told them that the "liberals" and "literati" then prided themselves on being the Great Debunkers of America. "This was a country ignorantly worshiping the machine and the money-maker. We shouted hysterically to each other and to the world that 'things' were despicable; everyone who was prosperous was an enemy to true civilization. This was especially true to those of our number living on income accrued through the hard work of fathers and grandfathers. Anyone who respected the conventions of their forefathers was an ignoramus; anyone who spoke in praise of the Victorian era or the Puritan tradition (they seemed inter-changeable appellations) exemplified the common twelve-year-old mind of the country. We shouted for freedom like our Revolutionary fathers but not the same freedom for we yelled for sex freedom. Well, we got it."

There was laughter and applause before he went on. "We wanted to see the end of religious and social reformers, the end of all prohibition and when the dullards at the helm of this ship of state did not listen to our voices, we, the superior clay, packed up and went to Europe to live."

The boys laughed and leaned forward to listen. "Fifteen years ago—even ten years ago—and now? A visitor here today, can hardly believe his eyes or ears. The 'debunked' Victoria has given way to Helen Hayes' beloved Queen; scorn of the 'mass-mind' has changed to study and sympathy for workingman and child. Now we are the greatest geniuses at business in the world. America is the only fascinating place in the world for an intellectual to live in. We not only began writing books like *The Grapes of Wrath*, showing our sympathy for the ignorant and unfortunate and confused, we actually brought out Longfellow and Whittier to be seen in plain view on our shelves beside Whitman and Poe.

"We began reading American history and listening to music by Americans. Now, in season and out, we discuss American Art. We suddenly got religion—not the worship of America but a worshipful appreciation of what America stands for—the equal rights of man. When we pass a factory where are massed, in the parking space, hundreds of cars, the property of the workmen, we do not sneer 'things': Instead we ask, where, in what other country in the world, can you find workmen enjoying that prosperity?

"I'm here to tell you, young men, that before months pass you are going to be asked to shed your blood for the ideal that this our America stands for."

Quite honestly he acknowledged our glaring failures in our efforts to establish the equality of man. He acknowledged the unforgivable mistakes of the British but he had just returned from London and when he described the heroism, the humor, the courage of the people there during the bomb raids and ended, "These inheritors of the Magna Charta are holding our first line of defense," a deep silence held the audience. Secretary Stimson had that day said that the United States would be in grave danger of invasion by air if the British Navy were destroyed or if it surrendered.

He brought this European war out of Europe and set it on their doorstep.

He eloquently and with deeply felt sincerity accomplished his purpose. The men and women who had gone to hear a lecture on current topics had come away knowing themselves to be an integral part, not distant spectators, of the events. They had been told that the crisis in Britain was but sixty or ninety days off; already we had become the arsenal of democracy; already we were sending ships and planes and weapons. We were at war.

The boys flocked out in groups of three or four, some silent, half stunned by their sudden acceptance of the imminence of the peril; others excited, talking hard and fast to relieve their minds.

Of course for a year or more they had discussed war. There had been even that amusing group calling themselves, "Veterans of Future Wars"; who had put on a funny skit, joking about battlefields and death. Didn't boys always find plenty of fun—fun about undertakers, jokes about "stiffs" and endless stories of graveyards? Was it because of some deeply felt, age-old consciousness that they were the likely victims of early death that they daringly brought the subject out onto the stage where it could be ridiculed? We're not afraid of the big, black wolf so we sing and dance around him?

Joseph Donovan was one of the silent ones. Even in the hall while he was following every word of the speaker, his mind and heart were reaching out to his mother. Not only with tenacity but with singleness of purpose he had followed a clear-cut pattern in his life. He would not be twenty-one until the coming fall and by that time he would be started in his law course. True, from statistical standpoints he had never known anything but hard times. He had seen men selling apples on corners or, later, working in WPA squads on the streets, as mills stood silent with empty yards and closed gates. He had known nothing else.

Yet he thought of himself as one of the most favored of the earth's inhabitants. The loss of the old Farnsworth place, the change from luxury, ease and social life to the little white house with the green blinds had meant nothing to him but pleasure. He had his mother. He had his mother all day instead of part of the day. She was always close. He had Sandra and then they had a baby. His father had so often been absent that his final departure was only an acceptance of a deep hurt to his affectionate heart.

On his bicycle, in streetcars, on trains, he could go wherever he chose unhampered; but all vehicles turned soon enough and took the straight path home. He loved that home. Only tonight did he suddenly find that out. Passionately he loved that white house, that garden, the long avenue under the beautiful elms, and the busy city.

He was one of the most fortunate boys in the world. He had breathed the air of freedom; he knew the stimulus of work, the fun of play.

Through the dirty slush on the Boston sidewalk, the boys' feet made their way, some toward subway entrances, some toward streetcars. They did not all live in college dormitories, expensive clubs or even cheap boarding houses for many came daily from homes. Their jackets were turned up about their ears for the wet snow sifted down in slanting lines as the raw wind drove it now steadily, now in hateful gusts.

Sharply, Joseph Donovan saw pictures. He saw his mother's head bent over her account books, over the dress or blouse or undergarment she was making, saw her hands pushing the electric iron, mixing dough. He also saw them, slender and small, lifting the heavy silver ladle as she ceremoniously served the stew; saw them lifting the silver tea pot as she poured at supper. He saw her standing at his window putting up the shade, opening the window wide; felt her lips on his forehead and heard her good night.

But there was something else he was trying to get at. How had she put it? What had she said to him during the Christmas vacation? What had she said that day when he had come in using violent language as he cursed Hitler and all Germans? The submarines were sinking ships, night and day; boys like himself, women and children were dying horrible deaths, drowned in icy water. Night after night the German planes bombed British cities; schoolhouses were wiped out in broad daylight with all their innocent victims. The archfiend of the world, Hitler.

She had thought deeply. "Joseph, if we allow ourselves to think of Hitler as the author and perpetrator of all this evil, this war like the last will only be followed by a breathing spell before another war of the same kind. It is the age-old battle of Evil against Good. You can call it the Devil against the God of love if you wish or the carnal against the spiritual if you like that better.

"What I see is the well-meaning people of the earth—well-meaning but complacent and selfish—allowing evil to flourish in themselves. Greed, lying, materialism, frivolity, class hatred, inequality. Some of these evils, to a greater or less extent, flourish in every man and every nation. Freedom-loving people become weak, spineless, smug, self-righteous, and the evil in the world, always watching and waiting for an opportunity, arms and strikes. It is so much bigger than one nation pitted against another, so much deeper, so much more terrifying. We'll destroy Hitler but will we ever keep fighting until we destroy what he represents?"

He hadn't quite got her idea then but now, on that slush-filled street, he saw it. With a yearning nostalgia he wanted to see her, to enter the little white house and talk to her. With some sudden insight he saw what would be lost to all mankind if the war came to our shores. He saw what the ideal of Christian America stood for. Only an ideal, partly realized but nearer to realization than in any other part of the world. It was like a vision.

He had slowed his steps as he thought. Surrounded by his comrades, his heavy shoulders, his big blond head, even that large Kent nose stood out prominently. A group of students who had lingered in a restaurant now caught up to his crowd. A hand touched his shoulder.

"I say, Donovan."

He turned, starting violently as though wakened from a dream. "Hello, Hart."

"Say, Donovan, I tried to find you at the hall but couldn't locate you. I was late leaving the house and just before I got away there was a telephone message for you. I took it."

Joseph stopped, turning to look into Hart's face. "What was it?"

"It was your father talking."

"My father!" He was going to add, "That couldn't be" but caught himself in time.

"Yes. He was disappointed not to speak to you but said to tell you he would be at the Parker House until twelve o'clock tonight. He wants to see you."

An avalanche of jokes followed the delivery of the message. "The old man's brought the horsewhip; how many checks did you draw, Jo? Bet it was the fat blonde." They became funnier and funnier as consternation was plainly visible in Joseph Donovan's face. Desperately he made a turn at the first opportunity, followed by howls and a few well-aimed snowballs.

In front of the hotel Joseph stood looking up for a moment at the lighted building, still a little dazed, an uncomprehending expression in his eyes; then quite suddenly he shrugged his broad shoulders, an entire change came over his countenance and the wide smile spread across his features.

He murmured, "The dope. That ass, Hart! Of course the message was from Uncle Lawrence!"

He cleared the space between him and the door in a couple of strides, his face illuminated with eager pleasure and happy anticipation. It was Uncle Lawrence of course.

CHAPTER XXVIII

Joseph stepped inside the door to glance quickly about the corridor. There was no tall, gray-haired Uncle Lawrence in sight so he went directly to the desk. "I want to see Dr. Lawrence Kent. From Chicago. I think he came in this afternoon, at least sometime today."

No one by that name had been registered, and Joseph turned away, perplexed. He thought, "Of course it's that boob, Hart. He's probably got even the name of the hotel wrong. It's late to start scouring all Boston and Cambridge but gosh, suppose

Uncle Lawrence were leaving on a night train. Damn it. I don't want to miss him."

He walked about the main lounging rooms of the hotel trying to decide on some course of action. The sensible thing was to call Hart and see if by any chance the idiot's memory would bring up the name of some other hotel.

He was hurrying toward the telephone booths at the end of a long corridor when he glanced through the doorway into a reading-room. A few rather elderly men were sitting about in the snug warmth reading papers and magazines. In the far corner a dark-haired man lowered his paper and glanced up over his spectacles toward the door.

Joseph saw him rather hazily and without interest as he hurried on. Then he began to slow his steps. Queer enough. Something about that man seemed vaguely familiar, reminding him of some-one—no—he guessed it was merely one of those slight resemblances.

He extracted the nickel from his pocket and was pulling the door of the booth shut, ready to call his number when he stopped, scowling. He suddenly knew what was familiar about that man's face. He smiled as he thought that the man in the spectacles read-ing the paper had looked for all the world like his own little Nan. Funny—the way he looked up with that twist of the neck just as Nan did.

Then with a start he pushed the nickel back into his pocket and jerked open the door. His heart began to beat hard and fast and he felt as though his head were whirling. That message was right. The name of the hotel was right. He was the idiot. It was his father!

He retraced his steps slowly, very slowly, coming nearer and nearer the readingroom and he felt like a sick girl. His legs seemed weak and unsteady and nothing he could do, neither long breaths nor damns, could affect the thumping of his heart. He'd better get hold of himself before he went in there. He never did.

Feeling as though he were walking in a fog, he entered the room, crossed over the thick carpet and stood a moment, moistening his lips. Again the man looked up, then with an exclamation jumped to his feet.

If he were jittery, he did not show it. Joseph could not know how long he had been schooling himself, getting ready for this moment. He held out his hand, held the boy's for a moment, then with his most engaging smile, he spoke quietly, "I'll say it for you —the last person on earth you expected to call you. The last person you would expect to be talking to tonight."

"I'll say!" There was an awkward pause and his father suggested he get rid of his jacket and cap. "And take this chair." The leather-covered chair was drawn closer.

It was as though everything inside the boy were swelling to the bursting point. The memories, the old feeling of the ten-year-old youngster came back. How he had adored this father. How he had tried to imitate him. He, big, hulking, clumsy Joseph had tried to step lightly and gracefully like him, speak like him, use his words and gestures. Even at college, he found himself trying to light a cigarette and flick the match the way his father did.

There was something, unrealized by him, beatific in his wide smile tonight. It was as though some unrecognized ache, some secret disease were brought into the open and cured; something of hidden longing which had been buried for years were suddenly satisfied; some hidden grief assuaged. He could scarcely see his father's face through the mist of his happiness.

The charming voice was doing all the talking and Joseph was astonished for apparently there was nothing in his career at college his father had not followed. His scores, his races, his defeats and the why and wherefore of them—he discussed them all sympathetically. Again and again he was stopped by an annoying, deep-chested cough.

"You've got a bad cold."

He smiled and, with that quick wave of the hand, "This climate, you know; beastly." He passed it off lightly. "Gets me, as always, in the chest. It's nothing. I finally throw it off."

They got on the subject of the lecture at the hall and his father agreed with everything as Joseph reported it but it seemed to change his entire expression.

The deep-set hazel eyes burning beneath the reddish-hued lids fastened piercingly on the boy's face and there was angry bitterness in the words, "My God, Joseph, we've been in this war for years now. We're only waiting for some plausible excuse to offer the people before we start sending our armies over to follow our ships and planes."

Joseph began to speak rapidly with his father's fluency now. He began explaining his mother's ideas—the age-old struggle of Good and Evil with Evil always aggressive, ready to watch for weakness and strike and the smug softness of the well-inclined. "Mother says we can always conquer evil but when we win one battle we go blind and turn our backs." He leaned over smiling, "Remember how Mother always quoted Tom Paine? 'Tyranny, like Hell, is not easily conquered.' Remember?"

His father was silent, listening, and the burning eyes scarcely wavered.

Joseph dropped his own eyes and looked at his hands as he went on, "We're the guys who get it in the neck. We know that. We'll all go again. You know by experience. Mother went through it all once before. You know—Uncle Gordon. But this is different. You actually believed you were doing a finishing job, actually thought it was for the last time. We know better now. Mother knows. It'll be only one round. We'll win the battle but the war goes on." He smiled. "I guess I was rather homesick to see her and talk to her tonight. I remember one Christmas when I heard everyone talking about Jesus being the Prince of Peace. I asked her about that verse, 'I came not to send peace, but a sword.' You know I would find that." He stopped to smile but his father's eyes were not smiling. "She said she wished the bells would ring that out instead of the other. It's the whole point—you've got to fight all Hell to get rid of Tyranny."

There was silence then he looked up and smiled, "We'll all go. We know that but no one wants to, Father. I hope they won't bring on their silly parades and bands—just let us wade into the Hell and get it over."

Long since the elderly men had disappeared and now the room was well-nigh emptied. Joseph looked at his watch. It was after one o'clock. He jumped up. "Holy Mackerel! I hope you weren't catching a train? You're staying here?"

The answer was so smoothly evasive that Joseph did not quite understand. He was apologizing, "I've kept you up so late—and with that cold—"

Again the quick charming laugh, "Newspaper men don't sleep, you know—" There was the characteristic gesture of the hand, that wave that seemed to brush away lightly any absurd idea. Then the hand rested affectionately on the boy's shoulder. "Thank you for coming. I'm so happy that you could make it. I wanted very much to see you—" Was it the racking cough that stopped him?

"But," with consternation in eyes and voice, "but, of course, I'll see you again. Tomorrow? Can't you come over and have dinner?" He was remembering his extravagance earlier in the month and the alarming flatness of his purse at the moment. He could borrow, his credit was still good. He repeated, "Can't we have dinner? How long will you be here? I'll telephone you at noon time." With each sentence some pleading in his voice increased.

"Oh"—his father stepped back—"I don't happen to be staying here—at the hotel. I'm with friends for a day or two, just a quick business trip."

Joseph had pulled on his jacket and stood with cap in hand. "Oh, can't I—that cold of yours is bad—" He was going to say, "Take you in a cab?" but he remembered his lack of money so he changed to a lame, "It's such a bad night." Then, his eyes eager with interest, "Are you on a New York paper?"

His father seemed quite ready for that question. He answered pleasantly and with a frank smile, "Not at the moment. The depression flattened some of us, you know. At the present moment I'm picking up a bit of hard-earned cash with a publisher, while they're looking over a book manuscript I've finished. I'm selling some textbooks for them." He smiled and then, before Joseph could ask more questions, he again pressed his shoulder. "Thanks for coming. It has been a great pleasure to me."

They shook hands and Joseph started across the room. At the door he turned and saw his father standing with head bent slightly forward watching him with an expression of intense yearning and sadness in his eyes.

Joseph waved his hand, smiled and walked out through the corridor, seeing nothing but the door ahead. Then he turned up his collar, pulled down his cap and plunged into the wet snow.

CHAPTER XXIX

The January storms closed in on the eastern coast; for days the snow fell, the bitter northeast winds blew relentlessly and the streets became difficult to navigate. Then came mid-day hours of brilliant sunshine and sudden thaws when the gutters ran in rivers and one wondered which brought more discomfort, the storms or the thaws.

Through the hours of study, of physical training, of loafing, of either work or fun, the fog cleared from Joseph's mind.

This was not the disappointment of a little boy momentarily sad because his hero had, for a short time, disappeared over the horizon. This was not the little boy who at four o'clock had forgotten what caused the tempest at two o'clock. This was a hurt.

This was a man's hurt. First there was that question of his father's appearance. Why did Joseph find his mind pushing back that word "shabby"? He had been too excited to see details. A woman would have seen the rubbers worn as old as rubbers can get; would have noticed the soiled back of the collar and the frayed cuffs although the suit was carefully brushed; would have observed the white hair thickening about the temples although at first glance it was still a dark head. The lamps in the readingroom were designed to throw a brilliant light on the book or newspaper, not on the face; yet keen eyes would have seen the blotched skin, lines etched by illness, worry or dissipation, the sunken eyes; would have seen that the man was sick.

It was actually days after the meeting that the thought came to him, "Why we never once spoke of Sandra or Nancy and he never *asked* about Mother."

They had discussed public affairs and his college career and his future in law. It never occurred to him that his father might have managed that, steered the course of the conversation where he wished to confine it. Why, there was little Nan! Why hadn't he told him about the resemblance which caused him to come back to the readingroom. How on earth did it happen that Sandra's name was never mentioned? Great guns! Sandra!

The thought of Sandra always brought relief. At the present he was without any steady girl and he was already planning to have Sandra out for Commencement week. She had absolutely floored him at Christmas time. That radiant, dignified, proud person, tall and graceful and, he thought, beautiful. He had found it necessary to work at keeping any silly note of affection out of his voice. "Come on, Sandy, old girl. There's no one else around so I'll have to take the family spinster to the movies." Or he would put a dance record on the old phonograph, roll up the rug and call, "You'd better take what pleasure you can get while you're young, Sandy." He remembered his mother saying that they shook the house.

He made several attempts to write home about his father. He tore them up. They were mere words, either hollow or too light or too heavy. Why did he have this feeling of disloyalty to his mother? What would the knowledge of this meeting do to her? Why couldn't he just tell it naturally? He wasn't used to this analyzing, this indecision. He was miserable. How would he describe his father? Wouldn't it be better to borrow some money and go home for a Sunday and tell her?

He grabbed his pen, ended his letter with the usual affectionate words, jumped up, sealed the envelope and went out and dropped it in the postbox. With a sense of liberation he assured himself he would either go home or write fully next week.

He postponed the telling when writing the next week and the next. He shrugged, "I'll wait now until Easter vacation. It will be different when I can sit down and tell her step by step how it happened."

Through February, life went on in its routine way and the weather performed in its routine way. Joseph wrote home, "All the king's horses and all the king's men couldn't keep these streets clear. As Miss Simmons once remarked 'it's the very devil of a job.' "

Miss Simmons. He often sent humorous, affectionate messages to her. Twice, during the recent fall, she had come to Boston for week ends and arranged by letter beforehand that he should lunch with her at the College Club.

He had explained to his roommate, Kurt Foster, "I'm lunching with something institutional. I'll come out of that building and walk timidly down Commonwealth Avenue reduced from what I consider a man to a little boy saying 'Yes, mam' and worrying for fear I got crumbs on the floor.

"You being a scummy product of the curbstones of New York City couldn't understand the place she fills in the so-called granite structure of New England. Residing in our house, she spreads respectability over a block."

There was a smile in Kurt's eyes as he turned from his desk at the opposite side of the room, stretched, and lit a cigarette. "She's the master-mind who hounded you through your reading and studying so the infant could be in a class at Harvard with regular men?"

"In large part; everyone I knew had a hand in that. Incidentally, she offered to fork up dough if I needed it at any time and that's broad. I haven't needed it, having you around; still one remembers with gratitude and goes to the College Club, gets stared at by fifty or a hundred women, remembers to talk nicely, to whisper instead of shout and, gosh darn it—enjoy the Presence."

The rejoiner, "In some ways you're a nut about women—all

women," was perfectly satisfactory. Joseph, himself, when he considered the subject at all, thought he probably was a nut about women—about his mother, his sisters, Miss Simmons and his girls. The faces of the last class, numerous and somehow fleeting, were getting to look in his mind like the composite face of a crowd.

Walking across the room, Kurt stopped at his desk. "You know, Jo, to be serious, you actually believe in them. I wouldn't trust any dame, young or old, married or single around any corner. Someday, if I don't watch you, you'll do a hari-kari over some chorus girl. That little red-headed trick at the Tavern. I heard her giving you a hard luck story one day and you've been doubling the tips and looking at her like a brother ever since. I think she needs the money for syphilis treatments. You're a nut." Then as usual to relieve the seriousness, "Of course as long as I'm here I'll watch over you but God help you when you get out in the wide world without my fatherly protection."

"Do you think it's my handsome Apollo-like nose that will get me into trouble or my sylph-like grace or my super-Clark Gable sheer masculine fascination that brings them flocking?"

"Well at that—that ear-to-ear grin of yours has something in it."

"Teeth perhaps?"

Levity was their salvation. When Hart yelled across a crowd, "Say, Donovan, what did your father do to you that night?" Joseph grimaced, "He kissed me. All the Frenchmen do, idiot."

Levity helped when it couldn't cure.

Kurt had lingered beside Joseph's desk. He picked up a framed picture of Sandra and stood studying it as Joseph went on writing. When he set the picture back in place he smiled, "I hope to Heaven you're so dead broke you can't afford a breakfast when she gets here."

"Probably will be; but even at that I won't be throwing her to the wolves."

A fat little fellow with carroty red hair ambled into the room. "Here's the dope you wanted for your mother, Donovan, about the elms."

Kurt leaned over to listen as the short fat finger pointed out paragraphs. He told them that in Europe they called it the "elm death," that it was introduced to America by infected beetles. He showed how a fungus invaded the water-conducting system of the tree, how the beetles tunneled into the dead bark. Carefully he explained all the measures known for protecting the trees before New England and other states should be stripped of their beauty as it was now of the horse chestnut. They were all tree lovers and Kurt was naturally scientific. "How far can these beetles fly?"

"No more than five hundred feet in search of food. You might find them in your wood pile so you've got to make an annual clean-up of breeding places, cut all dead wood out of all trees, water elms in dry weather; then, if they are diseased cut them down."

Joseph groaned, "There's two of the most beautiful ones at my mother's old home that have got to go. It's tough. Thanks a lot, Burns. I'll send it on."

"Will your mother get on the job and raise money to pay for protection? Wake up the people now? The ones who'll groan to high heaven when it's too late?"

They sat back in tilted chairs, feet on desks and discussed trees and forests, then went on to hunting and dogs until they found themselves hungry and started out to get dinner. They enjoyed talking endlessly about any subject if it were far enough removed from the topics required for examinations.

There came the deceptive days of March. One day the sun shone with seductive promises of spring. Pouring beneficently on the Commons it caused men to open their coats, women to unfasten their furs and bare their throats to its rays. Then, when girls were loitering before shop windows looking longingly and speculatively at the display of spring hats, out from the northeast came the biting wind and, as though with devilish glee, the old ocean pounded against the rocks at the shore, gales swept through the city, sidewalks were again obliterated and men and women hurried about seeking any shelter.

On that late Friday afternoon, a freak storm had veered away down the coast, leaving behind it a sensation of relief and security.

Great patches of blue became visible in the western sky, the blue made more striking by contrast with the crimson-tipped clouds. In a narrow Cambridge street not far from the University, a girl stopped before a house, gazing at it with great interest. She did not know anyone in the house; she did not know who lived there. She was looking at it because she thought it was such a beautiful house.

It was small and obviously old, built of red brick with deep-set windows composed of nearly square, tiny panes of glass which at that moment reflected the crimson and blue of the sky. Perhaps it was the doorway that fascinated her most of all for over it was a perfectly proportioned arched window.

She looked long at that door thinking it neither too large for the house nor too small to suggest hospitality. How the brass knocker with the eagle's head shone and how pure a white were the tied-back muslin curtains at the window!

Snow was banked high along a low white picket fence and hung in heavy masses on the shrubs but she was a girl with an imagination and she could picture how pretty the place must look in summer when the grass was green and the garden was in full bloom. She knew quite well that Boston gardens were summer gardens coming to maturity under the heat of July and August sunshine just as she knew her southern New York gardens in their lovelier spring beauty.

Where the snow was cleared she laid one hand on the gate and let her imagination run riot. Imagine living there with a college professor husband. She half closed her eyes and began to furnish the interior with soft rugs, old pieces of mahogany—of course family heirlooms—an old clock on the stairs, book cases stacked with leather-bound. . . .

She was as startled as though she were a thief caught stealing the place when the door suddenly opened and a tall old man, wearing a muffler wrapped about his shoulders and neck nearly to his ears and carrying an enormous green flannel bag came hurrying down the walk.

She was stepping back through the snow when he reached her. He asked courteously, "Were you—had you come to see me?"

He was very nice, even nicer than the house, she thought; a gentleman. She found her voice. "No, sir. I was admiring your house. It is beautiful. I think it is perfect."

"I'm glad you like it." Perhaps he was far keener of eye, far more discerning than she would have thought from his age for he added, "Can I help you in any way?"

She asked quickly if he could tell her how far she was from a certain street and number which she mentioned with the familiarity one usually connects with one's own street and number.

He directed her with the utmost care; then, raising his hat, walked away. She turned and started very slowly in the opposite direction, stopping often to look about, going on, then stopping again. She would never reach much of anywhere at the rate she was moving.

She had not seen the elderly gentleman as he approached the distant corner meet a tall young man, look up with several characteristic jerky bows, smile and murmur cordially, "Good day, Donovan. Nice after the storm."

The young fellow touched his cap, smiled with pleasure and came on down the street. The old man was so distinguished a person that Joseph would never have known him personally except through his uncle.

He was thinking of that as he neared the next corner; still thinking of it when his eyes rested on the figure of the girl loitering along the way.

Even from the back one would apply three adjectives in describing her—little, poor and queer. Perhaps the professor had seen that. She would take a few steps, stop to grasp a fence, bend her head until her shoulders were hunched, then start out again almost zigzagging on the sidewalk. One doesn't meet intoxicated girls in the middle of the afternoon in a highly respectable neighborhood.

He had overtaken her when she turned and looked directly up into his face. For a moment he drew back as though he had been struck a blow; then some enormous excitement showed in his face; his brows were drawn into an incredulous frown as he stepped close to her and leaned down. He almost whispered, "Bel!"

Her dark brilliant eyes, seeming at the moment almost as large as her thin face, looked up at him, her whole countenance intense, even the muscles of her face quivered with emotion as she asked, "You know me?"

"Of course. I'd know you anywhere."

"Although I'm so old?" She seemed to be exulting in the knowledge, repeating again and again, "You knew me."

He hurled questions at her. What on earth was she doing in Cambridge? How in all creation did she happen to be walking down the street—only a few blocks from where he lived? What was she doing? Was she painting? Giving an exhibition? Where did she live?

She answered none of them clearly until he pressed the last question so hard that she finally answered, "I live way over in Boston. I was taking a day off, sight-seeing."

"Off from what?" He wanted her entire history immediately. Couldn't they go somewhere and have tea?

She asked speculatively, "Your house?"

"Holy Mackerel! No! There's a drugstore across the corner and booths, you know. What about it? I hope you don't have to hurry."

She did not take to the drugstore idea. An expression of great satisfaction spread over her face and her eyes gleamed as through the gathering dusk she watched him. There was a sweet coaxing quality in her voice as she asked, "What about you? It's Friday night. Have you any dates?"

He had no dates of consequence, nothing he couldn't change. She appeared quite suddenly to light on a solution. "Why can't you come home with me? I want to show you—something. I'll give you a surprise party. I'm quite a housekeeper nowadays. I'll cook us a little supper and I have some wine. We'll celebrate."

Had she suggested endowing him with a fortune he could not have looked more excited and happy. He would have to telephone his roommate, would she mind stopping a moment in the drug-store?

She sat whirling around and around on a stool, such a funny-looking little thing. He smiled tenderly, thinking, "Odd as Dick's hat-band" as he entered the booth and got Kurt on the wire. Would Kurt excuse him at the meeting? He explained, "Dinner with an old friend."

Kurt asked, "A dame?"

"A dame."

"What age?"

"Indefinite, Papa."

"Dangerous, son. I don't like the jubilant tone in your voice. You're excited. I know you. This is no 'just a dame.' Watch your step and get in before twelve. I'll sit up for you, my boy."

"O.K."

Out on the darkening street, he looked down at her. "Seems to me you've grown smaller. I'm afraid of stumbling over you."

She was hanging onto his arm with both hands, her eyes fairly glistening. "I warn you, it's a long trip."

It was a long trip. They journeyed, jostled by crowds for over an hour before they stopped before a bare-looking building in a neighborhood of cheap tenements. They climbed stairs to her apartment. She took a key out of her pocket, inserted it in the lock as she tossed her head, "It's all I can afford, Joseph, but it's quite nice inside."

She still held the door, looking up into his face. "Do you hear that?"

"Sounds like a kid."

"It is. It's my baby. Come in and see him."

CHAPTER XXX

Looking through the most rosily tinted glasses would not have caused the apartment to appear "very nice inside" at that particular moment for there was an instant altercation with some one named Mrs. Jansen.

"I said three hours and you've been gone five and a half. Jansen and the boys will be on me for their dinner, growling if it's a minute late."

As amazing as anything in the place was the woman. There was so much of her. She sat broad and squat on a stool, her gray head an insignificant apex of a cone composed of sloping shoulders, billowing skirts and large feet spread out in carpet slippers. On her lap was a pan filled with potato parings while various tins held other vegetables she had been preparing for dinner. Her face was broad and flat, her pale eyes sharp as she looked Joseph over.

Besides the woman and her kitchen paraphernalia, there was a wide couch bed at one side of the room, an easel and all kinds of artist-material stacked in a corner while the remainder of the floor space was filled with a child's play-pen. It was not so much a matter of wonder that there was little standing room left as that so much could be crowded into the box-like room.

"And I kept him awake every minute so you'd get a good sleep tonight after your outing." She belligerently addressed Joseph. "I sent her out myself. She'd seen the Museum but she'd never seen the Library. Look at her. There isn't a picking on her. She's eating her heart out in this room day and night. I sent her but I said three hours." She was gathering together her pans and peelings and hoisting herself up heavily.

Bel helped carry all the things across the hall, murmuring apologies and fervent thanks. "Oh, Mrs. Jansen, I'm so grateful to you. I've had a wonderful afternoon, entirely thanks to you." They disappeared into the opposite apartment.

While all this was going on, a small dark-haired baby boy was struggling to his feet, clinging to the edge of the pen while his eyes followed every movement of his mother. When she came near him he held up his arms, grabbing at her skirts, then promptly losing his balance, falling to the floor but happily starting to climb up again.

Alone in the room, Joseph looked at the child. He was a little fellow with silky dark curls, small features and very dark eyes. One would know he was Bel's child by the shining darkness of those eyes. Now he was on his feet, swaying and clinging to the rail as he watched the open door. He was neither talking nor crying nor whining; merely vocalizing shrilly.

Bel came in and with movements swift and quiet hung away her wraps, took Joseph's cap and jacket, straightened chairs, set the boy on the couch, folded the play-pen and in a few minutes transformed the place. Now one noticed the softness of coloring in the room, the pictures, the simplicity that hardly escaped bareness, the something "very nice."

As she moved, she talked incessantly. "Mrs. Jansen has a heart of gold. She loves my baby. Once when I was sick she took him right into her place for three weeks and every day she nursed me like a mother." It wouldn't take her long to prepare the baby's supper and get him settled for the night. Joseph must look at the kitchen. It was a pity that it was dark so he couldn't understand how much sunshine came into the rooms. The baby's bedroom had southern exposure and sometimes she laid him stark naked right in the sun. Mrs. Jansen had old fogy notions about getting out on the street. She thinks it keeps people sane to walk on the street. Imagine! If that kept people sane we'd empty our asylums! She, Bel, thought the street was noisy and dirty. Here it was quiet and clean. There was this sittingroom with sunshine and just see her little kitchen and bath. He must like it, just walk about and look at everything.

It sounded like an invitation to roam freely over an estate. He did look into the bedroom where he saw the crib, one poor little bureau, a chair and a clothes-horse filled with diapers. There was no rug. He came back and sat down on the couch by the baby. Cautiously he touched the dark hair and found it softer than anything he remembered touching before. He asked, "How old is he?"

There was an hysterical quality in Bel's laugh. She came to the door feeding-bottle in hand. "I hoped you'd be original, Joseph. That is the first question everyone asks about a baby. He's over a year old."

"Is this original? Is he small for his age?"

"No. He has small bones but he is tall."

"Is it too *un*original to ask his name?"

Why is she so jittery about questions, he wondered.

"His name is Roger. I named him for my father. I never saw my father but I liked the name."

He had no courage to ask, "Roger what?"

While she stood explaining so little about the baby, he looked at her, seeing details now that the coat was removed. She wore a straight, very short and narrow brown wool skirt and over it, reaching halfway to her knees was a lighter brown smock made of wash material. It was dull and unattractive, buttoned up to her chin but flowing out formlessly below. The outfit did nothing to relieve the pallor of Bel's skin.

The baby was clutching at the buttons of his coat. Joseph picked him up carefully, knowing enough from his memory of little Nan to feel the area beneath for dryness. Bel watching, said, "He likes you."

Now the child was jumping, clutching, gurgling and wriggling and Joseph could hardly hold him. "You know, Bel, he's excitable like you."

She had come back, watching him with feverishly bright eyes, as he added, "I remember my father saying that you were excitable."

She lowered her head and stood very still with hunched shoulders and asked in a strained voice, "Your father—said that?"

"Yes."

"When?"

He explained. Didn't she remember that night of the storm when she had to go all alone to New York? His father thought she was too excitable a young girl to be traveling alone? Didn't she remember?

There was something in her eyes now that startled him. Slowly she smiled but it was a sad little smile and without a word she returned to the kitchen.

He called, "If I can help you, tell me what to do."

"Take off his clothes."

Smiling and quite excited himself, he managed his clumsy fingers and removed the blue rompers, the shoes and socks. He helped with the bath, laughing with her at the antics of the child. She wrapped him in a bath towel, then sat down on the couch to put on his nightclothes.

Joseph watched. "He's awfully pretty, isn't he?"

"You think so? Mrs. Jansen says he is."

"I guess you like him?"

There was silence. He looked from the baby up into her face and found her eyes filled with tears. She wiped them on the corner of the bath towel.

"The whole trouble is, I love him, Joseph, and I can't give him up, no matter how hard I try." She set the baby in Joseph's arm, showing him how to tilt the cup of milk.

While he was managing this feat, the door opened and, still in man-size carpet slippers, Mrs. Jansen crossed the room and entered the kitchen. As she returned, with eyes narrowed to mere slits, she watched Joseph holding the baby.

When the door clicked behind her, Bel looked out, smiling, "Isn't she the heart of gold? She brought two big pieces of apple pie and two pieces of cheese, two doughnuts and two pickles."

He grinned, "And two tons of curiosity with the pie?"

"Why should she? I explained you while I was in there."

As he conscientiously tilted the cup he found himself wishing he could have heard Bel's explanation. When she came to take the baby, he grinned, "But you didn't introduce me."

"Why should I?"

"Gosh! I'm not up on etiquette." All the levity on the tip of his tongue he held back, as Bel settled the baby in his crib, darkened the room and softly closed the door. He was thinking, "Holy Mackerel! What Kurt could do with this scene!"

Again she began that fast and furious talking. He must set up her drawing table; the tablecloth was in such and such a drawer; he could find the knives, forks and spoons while she cooked; it was late for dinner and he must be starving so she wouldn't stop to cook too much; they would open a package of potato chips and a can of peas; she was sure she had a jar of chicken noodles but she must have eaten them; she was on a diet so she would broil this lamb chop for him; she didn't eat meat often.

He watched the small, thin lamb chop broiling, knowing it was the only one and not knowing what to do about it, or about anything else for that matter. He couldn't suggest they divide the chop for it was so small he could have eaten it in one mouthful while he was waiting for a helping of meat.

She had thought she had a bottle of wine but she couldn't find it but she did have rum. Her smile was twisted and her excitement and nervousness showed in every action and word. "I love rum in my tea, don't you? Or do you always have a cocktail?"

He explained that he was nearly always in training and was about to suggest milk but he thought just in time of the baby. That need was probably measured to a half pint. Oh, no, he didn't care what he drank with meals as long as there was good drinking water.

While he tried to control his voracious appetite, ashamed of the way he was cleaning off the dishes, she nibbled on potato chips, her eyes so bright, her excitement so great, even her happiness in having him there so apparent that he found himself with but one wish—to add to her pleasure.

She brought the rum to the table and, after pouring tea, she tilted the bottle, pouring rum into her cup as though she were adding hot water.

"Great guns, Bel! You take a little tea with your rum."

She added sugar and as she stirred she half closed her eyes and smiled at him. "You know, whiskey's terribly expensive but I know a place where rum is cheap—cheaper than gin. With cigarettes, I can work half the night. Let me fix some for you?"

She finally gave up trying to persuade him and he gave up trying to fool her too much about training. He was still hungry when she took the dishes out to the kitchen.

When she turned out the kitchen light and came in, he was looking at her working material in the corner.

Of course he would not remember what she used to paint? Of course he remembered. Didn't he put his heel through her picture? Wasn't that the beginning of their friendship? She was such a good sport about that accident.

She looked happy. "We are friends, aren't we, Joseph? We've always liked each other, haven't we?"

"Sure."

"That's why I can talk to you."

"Do I remember? I remember that house on the cliff and the rain and the grandmother called Marta."

"Oh, yes. She lives in France now; but she wasn't a grandmother." She looked thoughtfully into his face. "Let's not remember. Let's just be ourselves."

No one ever understood her abstract ideas. Such literal-minded fools—the men who sold pictures. Now she would show him what she meant. Excitedly, she hauled out an enormous canvas and set it up against the easel.

He burst into a very roar of laughter but checked it as she motioned toward the bedroom. "The baby. It's usually so quiet here."

"Gosh, I'm sorry." They listened but there was no sound from the bedroom so in a subdued voice he said, "That's wonderful. Now, you've found your line, Bel. Why, she could speak."

It was Mrs. Jansen in gray gingham dress, calico apron, carpet slippers, a beneficent smile on her broad face and a motherly light in the pale eyes.

"Oh, no." She leaned toward him with burning, angry eyes. "That isn't art, Joseph. That's photography. It's nothing but accurate detail. There's no idea, no soul."

"I think there's Mrs. Jansen's soul. Have you shown this to a dealer?"

Like many of his questions she left it unanswered as she brought out two smaller canvases and stood them up. He was quiet now, his face sober and earnest. He took a long breath and let it out audibly. "Well, Bel, I admit I don't know anything about art but if these aren't beautiful I'll eat my hat and half my wardrobe."

She sat up with back held stiffly. "That's my baby. I couldn't foolishly spend money for photographs so I did them. I showed them to you because Roger likes you. No one else has seen them."

She walked back to the table and poured more rum in her tea and he wondered how much of a nut she really was. Could it be her mind was slightly deranged? He began to feel decidedly uncomfortable; not that he had felt comfortable for a moment since he had entered that door. He sat awkwardly on the stool as she sprawled on the floor near him.

She set her cup down and fumbled nervously as she tried to light a cigarette. He leaned forward and held the match. She took a few puffs then, laying her arm across his knees, she rested her body against him. Suddenly she closed her eyes and buried her face against his leg. Her thin little body was shaken with sobs.

Caressingly he smoothed her wild hair, patted her shoulder, begging her to stop crying, beseeching her to tell him the trouble.

She sat up, wiped her eyes and smiled, "That was so wonderful, Joseph. You will never understand—to feel your hands—gentle hands."

She took a long drink then talked again of her painting. He argued. Why not do that kind of painting if she could sell it and make a name and a living? If her abstract ideas were above the average intellect why not come down to the general level? "To my level?" he laughed.

But try as he would and did, he could not pin her down to any rational arguments for or against being practical. She talked incessantly of art, of beauty, and always of her baby. The baby was beautiful. He had seen the hands—like little flowers and feet more beautiful than the hands. Did he know that men and boys were far more beautiful than women and girls? Women had lumps and bunches and protruded here and there. She shuddered. She, herself, was very much nicer undressed than dressed. She had quite a pretty body but she didn't have a pretty face. If she could have been beautiful! She would have sold her soul to be so beautiful that a man could not help but fall in love with her.

The longer he looked at her and listened to her the younger she appeared. She looked up, "Am I getting to be very ugly, Joseph? Can you remember me before? When you first saw me this afternoon, did I look plain and ugly and old?"

He knew she had only looked little and poor and queer so he lied gracefully and praised her bright eyes and wild curls and said the longer he stayed the younger she seemed to grow.

Again she laid her face against his knee and smiled, "You are such a sweet boy. You don't know it but I love you. I love you so deep down that it's a horrible pain. But—you don't know why I love you. It isn't for anything you think."

Half a dozen times he tried to tear himself away but always she begged, "Only a few moments longer, Joseph. You promise but I'm so afraid you won't come again."

He swore he would come again within the next week but he must not now stay until morning. "What will your friend, Mrs. Jansen think?"

"Mrs. Jansen? Think? I guess if you knew all she's had a chance to think, you wouldn't worry about tonight. Don't bother about Mrs. Jansen."

At the door he promised again. He would come. Was there any way she could manage to go out to dinner? No, it was the time of day she couldn't be away. Well then, would he be allowed to bring in some stuff to cook? Wouldn't that be fun?

She looked up at him. She swayed a little as she stood and he wondered if she were a little drunk. Still, he remembered her zigzagging across the sidewalk in the middle of the afternoon. She reached up and pulled his head down toward her, her hands hard and tight against his neck.

At first she kissed his cheek but when he tried she would not let him get his head up. Somehow, trying not to hurt her, he unfastened her arms.

She was crying as she turned away. "You can't understand, Joseph. I'm so lonely. You can't understand."

"Understand what, Bel?" He was bewildered, but he lacked the courage to ask where Roger's father was.

He stood a moment watching her cry, then he said gently, "Good night, Bel. I will come again soon."

He found his way, trying to step lightly, down flight after flight of stairs, thinking, "Damn Kurt. I bet he's deliberately sitting there with his clothes on, waiting." It wasn't funny.

Jogging along in the streetcar for which he had had a long wait, he remembered that she had no telephone, that he had not looked at the number on the house and that he did not know Roger's last name. He could not write or telephone but he could easily find the house.

As, after his visit with his father in the hotel, he had been miserable trying to push back that word "shabby," now he was miserable trying not to remember too much; trying not to remember those sad answers which his mother had returned to his questions as he grew from a little boy into his High School years.

Bel. It was all vague about the past. The point was that, as usual, he had jumped into deep water and now he'd better consider how to get himself out. She had a year-old baby, she was poor and she was a nut. "Odd as Dick's hat-band." Who was Dick? What did the hat-band look like?

Across from him in the streetcar, a couple of workmen looked at him curiously as he grinned to himself. He was thinking of Kurt. He'd better get his explanations ready. "Yes, Papa, it is rather late—old friends get to talking." The trouble was Kurt was the son of a very distinguished New York surgeon and together with plenty of money and aristocratic family connections, that father had endowed his son with a scientific mind. Kurt was not a nut. He dealt with hard facts and he was always one step ahead of Joseph.

But he could be funny. They had collaborated on a couple of

skits which had gone over well. What they couldn't do with this! Call it, "Dinner Engagement." Mrs. Jansen and the potato peelings, the pie, the rum, then the art. Kurt knew something about art—painting souls!

The grin faded from his face and he turned up his collar and tried to get down farther into his jacket for the car was cold. He knew he would never describe his dinner engagement and fun would be the last thing he would ever get out of that memory.

CHAPTER XXXI

Time had defeated March. They tore a sheet off the calendar on their desk. April. The rough old back of winter was broken but there would still be plenty of bad days. Nevertheless, caps and hats were off for good and jackets gave way to sweaters and one might wonder what the textbooks were for at college because one heard no talk morning, noon or night except of the crew, the baseball team or the war.

Still the men who were expecting degrees read books, crammed information and facts into their memories, burned midnight oil and wore puckers of worry in their foreheads.

And Joseph could not work. Narrowly Kurt watched him. Between the two friends there was something never known before —a disagreeable silence. There was something worse—misunderstanding.

In their past, whenever Joseph declined an invitation and Kurt suspected he was "strapped," out of his more affluent allowance he would toss some bills across to him. "Here, son. No money could compensate for the loss of your company."

Joseph would look at the bills. "I suppose your usual usurious rate? Twelve percent?" Yet the loans had always been returned.

It was on the first of April that the check from his mother came as usual. Gently and apologetically she asked him to be careful because there had been some unexpected repairs to make on the house.

On the second day of April, Joseph asked Kurt if he could lend him twenty-five dollars. Kurt was sitting at his desk and the light shining on his book left his face in shadow. He did not answer or look up. Joseph waited; then slowly his face grew red.

Minutes passed; five minutes, ten minutes. Try as he would Joseph could not make the words on the page before him register in his brain. Words blurred into mere printing. He was still staring at the black marks when Kurt jumped up and walked quickly across the room to the door. He turned and spoke scathingly, "Damn you. Are you such an ass, such an idot that you don't know you've gone hay-wire? You can squander your mother's money but I'll be damned if I'll finance you! Just go to hell!"

He did not return until late when Joseph had turned out the lights. Without speaking he undressed and got into bed and in the morning there was nothing but a painful silence between them.

Before breakfast, Joseph wrote a letter to Miss Simmons, addressing her at her school, asking her for money. He felt sick and his breakfast was tasteless in his mouth.

Hay-wire. He knew that. He did not have to be told. He was going hay-wire and he could not stop himself. He had promised Bel he would bring her that money Friday afternoon.

He had kept his promise to come to see her that week following his first visit. He had promised again and again and he had kept his promises. The long trip was familiar to him now. He was at home in the poor neighborhood, known to the grocer and butcher. With ponderous thought he had become accustomed to considering the amount of money in his pocket and the days to go and the price of oranges, chops, butter and fresh vegetables. Time after time he walked through the street carrying a large paper bag, perhaps with celery sticking out of the top, and mounted the flights of stairs always to see dark eyes peering over the banister.

He knew well enough that doors were softly opened, eyes peeked through narrow apertures. He shrugged his heavy shoul-

ders. When the door of her apartment closed behind them, there
was a gurgle of excitement and pleasure from the little boy in
the play-pen, a violent wriggling until he pulled himself up to
the rail then a squirming into strong arms as he was picked up
and swung to the ceiling.

Three weeks of this and her feverishly bright eyes, her plain
thin face came between him and the printed page. He saw her
biting her lips and blinking away tears. Even above the noise of
a swing band when the radio was going full blast he heard her
voice, "Oh, Joseph, you are keeping us alive. We would starve
without you." Long since he knew that Mrs. Jansen had given
her that chop. But now he knew that Mrs. Jansen could not pay
all that back rent. Bel had received a dispossess notice.

On Thursday afternoon, without speaking, Kurt threw a letter
onto his desk. He saw the name Harriet Simmons in the upper
left-hand corner. He slit it open, took out the note and check.
It gave her pleasure to know that he came to her when in some
temporary need. If he would accept the small amount as a gift
that would give her pleasure; if he wanted to return it, please take
his own time. In the many years in which she had lived so close
to them, he and his family had become integrated into her otherwise lonely life. Their interests had become of vital concern to
her. He must think of her as one deeply interested in his present
and future welfare.

He looked at the check and found the amount was double what
he had asked for. It would go a long way toward easing that back
rent. He murmured, "Grand old Institution!"

On Friday he cashed it and placed the money in his pocket.
Desperately he had been striving to discipline his mind and get
caught up with his work and he had had some success. He had
hoped to get to Bel's in the late afternoon but it was nearly six
o'clock when his day's engagements were finished and he could
start. Roger would be asleep and he was afraid she might be worrying for he had not gone to see her or sent her any word during
the week.

This was Friday. One week from today he would be home for his Easter vacation. One week. He could leave Thursday or Friday. A great warmth surged through him as he thought of his mother, the white house, Sandra and little Nan. He visualized it all. After the girls went up to bed, he and his mother would go into the kitchen where she would prepare a midnight snack. A homesick boy or man never longed to see a parlor, no, he smiled, just to get into the kitchen with his mother. It was while sitting with her at the round table that he could talk and tell her about everything that had happened to him and even laugh hilariously over his girls. She seldom asked questions except with her eyes and smile.

The car was still a mile from his destination when there was trouble. An Italian with a pushcart filled with fruit must have calculated badly while crossing the street. His cart hit the moving car and all his polished apples, his grapes, his oranges and bananas were strewn over the pavement, halting cars and stopping traffic. Was it funny? People stood up, looked out of windows and laughed heartily as a policeman ordered the Italian to get the cart out of the way; boys scrambled dangerously under the trolley stealing the fruit.

There was a long delay before the car moved on. Joseph looked about at the faces, mostly smiling pleasantly as though they had been partakers in a delightful event instead of witnessing the losses of a poor man. He was feeling more sensitive about poverty than he had two months ago.

He left the car at the familiar corner and, even as he walked the half block, a quiet glow of satisfaction spread over his face. Just one week and he would be sitting beside that table in his own kitchen telling her everything. He would go back to that night when he had walked through the slush and seen his father. Somehow he had perfect confidence that his mother would understand it all. She would help him solve his problem.

The shabby upper hall was empty. There was no thin face peering over the banister. With his strong fingers he beat a tattoo on the door and almost instantly he heard a scrambling within,

then something being knocked over and Bel's voice, "Joseph?"
"O.K."

She opened the door, then switched on the light. At a glance
he saw that she had been lying on the couch in the dark. There
was the crumpled pillow and the old brown blanket thrown in a
heap, partly on the floor. Immediately she began to fold up the
play-pen and tidy up the room and, as she moved about with
nervous, jerky motions, he saw her for the first time without the
narrow skirt and familiar loose brown smock.

There was the body of a fourteen-year-old girl—except—what?
Although her back was straight and her legs and arms slender,
her chest was flat and hollow and—was it her slip too tight across
the middle? He was embarrassed by the sight of her. She had
said women and girls had lumps and bumps in the wrong places,
protruded in improper spots. One glance and he did not look at
her again.

He picked up the folded pen and placed it against the wall as
she hurried out some diapers which were lying on the floor.

"Were you asleep?" He looked into her face now and knew she
had been crying. It was strained and drawn and haggard.

Even as she answered she darted toward the bed, picked up the
loose sheets of a letter, stuffed them into an envelope which she
retrieved from the floor and then put it all in the drawer of her
work table. She turned to him. "I was trying to sleep but I
couldn't. I thought you weren't coming."

"You knew I would come. I promised. I have the money;
enough to tide you over."

She was stepping into the narrow skirt, pulling up the zipper
at the side. It got caught and she jerked and tugged making it
worse.

"Hold on there. Take it easy."

The more she forced it, the worse it stuck.

"Here, let me. I see the trouble." His head was so close to her
body as he manipulated the zipper that he felt the warmth from
her. With awkward fingers he eased the catch. "There it comes."

He backed away quickly and walked about the room, already

jittery himself, as she reached for the same old brown smock, stuck her thin arms into the sleeves then began buttoning it up as always close under her chin.

He had turned his back and wallked into the kitchen, snapping on the ceiling light. "Anything for dinner? It was so late the store was closed."

She stood beside him. "No. I hoped—" She stopped abruptly, then went on slowly. There was nothing dramatic about her speech but every word fell like weights of lead into his mind and heart. "No. I have eaten every scrap you brought in last Friday. If I could stop being so hungry. Sometimes I'm so ravenous I could chew on the pantry shelf. I can stand it as long as I have cigarettes but when they give out and I have no rum I can't stand it. But if I ever touch the baby's milk I'll kill myself." It was as though she had screamed and told him she couldn't pretend any longer. She dieting! Always nibbling a little, while he cleaned off the plates! In the same dull tone she asked, "You haven't had dinner?"

"No." He laughed, "Which shelf will we begin on?"

She rose to the challenge bravely. "You, being the giraffe, start at the top. I, the mouse, will nibble from the bottom."

He opened doors. "I expect that's about the way the pantry shelves look in France and Belgium and Poland after those beasts, the Germans, have visited them. Oh, no. I'm not sure they wouldn't envy us. Here's evaporated milk and a box of macaroni. With salt and pepper wouldn't that be tasty? There's a pinch of flour in this bin. What would it all make? Isn't there a delicatessen store within a mile?"

"If you have any money to buy it, some chopped meat, an onion or a can of tomatoes with the macaroni would be delicious. I could be cooking this." She turned the box of macaroni over and over in her hands.

It was nearing nine o'clock when he returned with a large brown paper bag in each arm. He had calculated nicely, leaving himself one dollar and carfare to get home. Mounting the stairs he told himself quite gleefully, "I'll take the Presence at her word. I'll

write for more. Now I know how a beggar feels. I know how
a thief rationalizes his conduct. I may empty Kurt's pockets while
he sleeps. Or there's the clubhouse till; what was I treasurer a year
for if not to know how to open that? It probably isn't too difficult
to become anything on this sordid earth, if you once accept the
role. A beggar is probably quite contented and happy after he
cuts all the ties that link him to ambition, respectability or society. I'm getting more of an education than a Harvard degree
promised and getting it inside of a month. Gosh a-mighty! If
I ever get to be a judge like my grandfather Kent, I won't be
entirely ignorant of the human beings I'm judging."

His eyes were eager, his wide smile, as Kurt said, had something
in it when he set the packages on the kitchen table. That last
ten dollars which he had planned to stretch over the week had
produced even tea, packages of cigarettes and a bottle of rum.

She stirred the macaroni, then looked at the articles he was
setting out. Her face was white and pinched and sober.

He touched her shoulder, giving it a little shake. "Come on,
cheer up. The drought's over, the rain has come. Rent can be
paid, food plenty, baby sleeping like a top. That's a silly expression. No one does anything like a top."

She smiled, "Yes, they do. They go round and round and round
—like my mind—round and round and never get anywhere. It's
a very sensible expression."

She had already set the table. When it came to serving, he took
the large spoon from her hand. "I'm the host tonight." Accurately, he divided the macaroni and meat balls, one spoonful in
this soup plate, one in that. "No more dieting. *You'll* lick your
plate from now on just the way I do."

"And the rum?"

"What did you think I brought an extra quart of milk for?"

She leaned toward him, raised his hand in both hers and kissed
it again and again. He remembered the first night he had come to
the apartment and how wildly she had kissed him when he was
leaving.

What was the matter with him, anyway, tonight? He'd better

get hold of himself. He hated his knowledge that she was hungry —for food, and for what else? He hated having seen her in her slip without the old smock hiding her. Almost rudely he jerked his hand away. Then he threw his arm roughly about her shoulders and pulled her in toward the table.

"Allow me." With mock ceremoniousness he held her chair but pushed her so hard down into it that she landed heavily.

She scowled angrily, "Don't do things like that to me."

There was embarrassment for a few moments as they ate. He tried not to see her devouring the food as he enjoyed his own.

She had cleared away the used dishes and was sipping her hot tea and rum, lighting one cigarette from another, when he looked at his watch. "Holy Mackerel! I'll have to run. I had planned to get here by seven, give you the dough, pick up something at a lunch counter and be home before ten. I've got to get in a couple of hours of work before I go to bed. Here it is nearly eleven already."

She looked up soberly into his face. "Don't go just yet, Joseph. I want to tell you something tonight. I don't think you'll ever have to come again."

CHAPTER XXXII

A feeling of unbearable misery suddenly overwhelmed him. He tried to speak lightly. "Gosh, Bel, I don't come because I have to. No one is compelling me to come. I'm here because we're friends and just at the moment you're down on your luck."

"Down on my luck!" Her tone was so bitter, so sharp, it fairly cut the air. She jumped up, cleared away the remaining dishes, folded the cloth and pushed the table against the wall.

He had seated himself in her one easy chair. Never would she take it while he was in the room. She began to walk up and down in the narrow space; up and down, her shoulders hunched in that queer manner but not a word did she say.

Finally he spoke gently, "You must have been crying like the dickens before I came. You mustn't do that, Bel. I thought you were made of sterner stuff."

As though she had not heard him, she began to speak. "Boston doesn't let either its own babies or babies from outside starve. I think Boston is a good city to live in. I've been finding out about their infants' homes and the way they place children with private families. I'm sure that, if a baby were placed in a nice home, he would be wanted and loved and he would grow up never knowing the difference. He would go to school, grow to be a big boy able to earn his living and it would never matter much who brought him into the world."

He stared at her incredulously. "You're not thinking of giving Roger—"

She did not reply and now her annoying way of ignoring questions she did not wish to answer, infuriated him.

"You're crazy. You're talking like an idiot. You told me you couldn't part with him. Just because you're all-in today, feeling down, don't go jumping off the deep end."

He leaned forward and tried to grasp her hand but she jerked away. His voice rose angrily, "I won't stand for a foul play like that. You're just hitting bottom, that's all and you'll be up again before long. Are you too damned lazy to go through with what we planned? Have you asked Mrs. Jansen? I'll scrape together enough money to pay her for looking after him while you get out and hunt for a job."

He drew a long breath and went on, "You've got talent, Bel. You can paint photographs if that's what you want to call them. Get to work and paint them and earn your living." He was ready to shout as he finished, "You're talking like a damned quitter. I'd wash dishes in a restaurant. I'd clerk in a five-and-ten but I wouldn't give Roger away like a loaf of bread or a pair of shoes."

He dropped his head into his hands, his elbows on his knees. There wasn't room for two to pace the floor and she had pre-empted the space. He twisted and turned. Once he laughed harshly, "I might put his name up for my House. There's room for

two in my bed and there are men there who know less." Slowly
a deep red spread over his face. In his eyes was the same level look
that could come in his mother's. He spoke in a hard, thoroughly
unsympathetic tone,

"Now that we've hit bottom, suppose you tell me what in hell
Roger's name is anyway? I've been coming here for weeks, sharing your life with you, trying to help you. As far as I know
you think I'm a damned fool. What do you call yourself?"

She stood near the couch with her back toward him, her shoulders still hunched as though she were warding off a blow. But
her silence only enraged him. What was she to him anyway?
He looked a very simpleton in his own eyes as he gazed angrily
at her ugly old brown smock and wild hair. If it only had been
a love affair there would have been some justification for the mess
he had been making of his life for the past month but he felt that
his pity was turning to loathing. What was she to him? Nothing.
She could even give that boy away.

"I say, who is his father? If he's dead, say so. If he isn't, why
in hell can't he help you?"

She turned slowly and looked at him. She dropped onto her
knees and laid her face against the edge of the couch and again,
as he had seen her once before, she shook from head to feet with
racking sobs.

The color left his face and his anger cooled and he watched her
with the old pity as she took the hem of her smock, wiped her
eyes and without lifting her head from the couch, answered, "I'll
tell you his name. As you say, we've hit bottom. I'm awfully
sorry for you, Joseph." She turned and placed her hands on his
knees. "I'm so sorry for you."

She stopped as though thinking deeply, then she smiled. "Do
you know, Joseph, it has been a strange and exciting experience for
me to know a boy? Do you know that boys are sweet? I never
knew boys." Her voice was almost a whisper. "I hope Roger will
grow up to be a sweet boy. I won't see him. I suppose he really
has no name but if he could take it, his name would be Roger

Donovan. I know it's terrible to tell you, but here it is. Your father is Roger's father."

Once, years ago, Mary Donovan had stood at her bedroom window and watched her husband disappear into the blinding snow. There had been a look in her face that suggested gray granite. Now in her son's face there was exactly that look.

Bel clutched at his knee. "Don't, Joseph. Don't look like that."

He spoke clearly and quietly. "Go back to the beginning, Bel, and tell me what I don't know. I like things from the beginning. Make it the truth, please."

She threw herself against the couch and sometimes he bent over close to get every word.

"I could tell you all the facts but that wouldn't be the truth. The worst truth is that I love him. I've always been his slave." She motioned toward the table. "That letter—came from him today. He is sick. He's almost killed himself finishing a book which he has been writing for years. He's been drinking again and he's lost his job and he's too sick to work. I want to be with him to take care of him. He won't even give me his address and I've no money to go to New York and try to find him. Three months ago he brought me here. He knew this house and left me here with Roger and he intended to send me money. He couldn't stand the baby another day. He had to get it out of his sight."

He did not break a long silence but sat with eyes fixed on her face, waiting.

She went on, "You think he took me when he left your mother. People said that. He didn't. She sent him away. She sent him away to die. I followed him. That was ten years ago. You say you remember the night of the storm when he went with me to New York? Of course he made me love him. He got me a job so I could work near him. You can't understand love. You know nothing about it. I can remember when I was sitting at my desk, working, he would pass by and merely press my shoulder with his hand and I could live on that for weeks.

"He could have had me body and soul any time but he was

only good to me. He said I must work and go straight and be a lady. He was only a friend. He never loved me.

"It was after your mother sent him away—he was having a hard time, quarreling with Marta who had only wanted his money. He began to go down and down. I begged him to let me come and live with him. I washed and cooked and waited on him day and night and I promised I would never have a baby. I swore I would never have a child if he let me come and live with him. How could you know what that means? Oh, Joseph! All the horrible things I did! I don't know why I'm still alive. And then —and then I had this baby, Roger.

"He couldn't look at him or endure him and his nerves got on edge when he cried. Do you know why?"

She stopped so long that Joseph wet his lips and asked, "Why?"

"Because of you. He was so proud of you. He talked to all the important men he knew—and he knows plenty of important people—he talked and talked about you. Don't you see he couldn't stand other children? To disgrace you?

"I began to be so scared. I knew—I was sure that sooner or later he would creep back to your mother. She had never divorced him. Did she know he would come back to her? I was sure of it. I knew what he would do. I knew he was thinking of her every minute of the day and night. He'd go back again—creep back on his belly, I would tell him. Oh, I was sure of it. I did the wrong thing."

He couldn't ask what she did; he simply sat waiting.

"I got pregnant again. Like a fool, I thought—another child and he'll get a divorce and marry me for he can't let a family go. When he knew I was pregnant he brought me here. It's because I expect another baby—"

With scarcely a movement of his eyelids he watched her.

"I wrote him, I've been writing almost every day, to his old address hoping my letters will get forwarded. I've begged him to let me come back to him. I can help him get on his feet again. You don't know how kind and tender he can be, how he can steal your heart and soul and make you love him. You don't know that he can be so cruel that the Devil would envy his sarcasm and evil, bitter nature.

"I heard nothing from him except a little money in an envelope every week, then, one night in late January he rang the bell. I almost fainted. I thought if he saw Roger now—so pretty and sweet. He asked me to keep him in the other room and he stayed only two hours.

"It was a terrible night, a blizzard and he was sick with a bad chest cold. He went out in the evening saying he would be back. I sat here all night waiting until morning. I'm still waiting. I haven't seen him since. Today I got this cruel letter—just some money. He said he was sending me nearly his last dollar and he hoped I'd found some way of looking out for myself. I probably will never hear from him again."

"When do you expect this baby?"

Her eyes appeared again like two glittering points of light in her plain, pinched-looking face. She ignored his question and went on, "He's worked years and years on this book and I've always told him no one would publish it. They wouldn't dare because everyone in their world would recognize Marta. New York's a big place but it wasn't big enough for those two. I think that's why Marta went to France. She was afraid of him—"

He interrupted, "When do you expect this baby?"

"In August."

"I'll get my degree in June and there won't be much trouble about my getting some kind of a job. I can earn a living. I'll be of age. I'll borrow money to keep you going. Will you hang on until then, Bel? As soon as I get a job I'll take care of you." Perhaps he saw the depth of the water into which he was plunging but he did not hesitate. "If there's no other way to get things right for Roger, I'll marry you, Bel."

She gazed at him, her lips apart, with that burning brightness in her eyes. Then, slowly, a smile played about her lips as she shook her head from side to side. "You are a sweet boy, Joseph. I wish I could have seen your mother just once."

His voice was not the voice of any "sweet boy" as he said, "We'll just leave my mother out."

She stared at him until he again asked impatiently, "You agree with my plan? You'll promise to take good care of Roger and hang on? I'll get the money."

Almost never was there any color in her sallow face. Now, her entire countenance suffused with red. "We'll just leave your mother out! We'll just never be allowed to mention your sister's name! We'll just take your father's money and his pity and his disgust—and his hate. Now we'll take your money and your pity—and your disgust and hate."

She was breathing audibly. "We'll get even with life. We'll pay him off by marrying you. That would be the last drop of bitterness life could offer him." She laughed, quite hideously to his ears. "You are such a child, you don't begin to imagine what I mean when I say I love him. You are a simpleton. Don't you know I'm young? You should see me when I get fixed up with rouge and lip stick and a red dress. I need lots of red. I can get other men. Why don't I? Because I love him. I want to live with him. I want to take care of him."

It was horrible. He watched her almost gasp for breath.

"*You—*" she laughed aloud, "*you* ask me to take good care of Roger, to hang on. I love that baby because it is his child. I'll take care of his child and I'll never belong, either body or soul, to anyone but him. You are such a child, such a fool that you don't know I've been saving you because of my love for him. Just leave your mother out! Never dare to mention your sister's name!" Then with startling suddenness her entire attitude changed. She held her hands tightly pressed to each side of her face, staring fixedly at the opposite wall.

Now she was watching him with a strange cunning in her eyes. She pulled herself up to her feet and as she walked up and down she often glanced at him. Once, she passed him, and he looked up and was startled at her expression.

"You pride yourself on keeping a promise, don't you, Joseph?"

"What are you getting at? What do you want?"

"I want you to promise me you will protect Roger."

"O.K. That's what I'm getting at. I intend to."

Still she walked. "Please allow me to speak of your mother for a moment. I know her. I know her as though I had spoken to her, as though I had seen her. I know she has a beautiful face. I've known her for eleven years. I've thought of her day and night. I'm the only person in the world who understands exactly how she loved Tom Donovan, why she married him in the face of the opposition she had, why she didn't divorce him and why she would wait for him to come back. I only want to say to you that if she could look into my heart she wouldn't despise me."

He made no comment.

Still she walked, her eyes narrowing cunningly. "Joseph, your father adores you. It was because of you he couldn't stand this family. Perhaps if you went to New York and saw him and talked to him, you could persuade him to get a divorce and marry me, to *save you*."

He looked steadily at her, so steadily that her eyes dropped. She turned her head away as he said, "You're a damned fool if you think I'd do that." He added, "You say I don't know anything about love. I've learned a hell of a lot about it tonight. Perhaps I'll go to New York to see him; perhaps I'll get down on my knees and beg him to marry you to save Roger or to save me. Perhaps! You can be damned sure I won't. I've made up my mind. I'll take Roger and I'll support you but there won't be any love connected with it." The stony expression of his face was worse than any anger.

He stood up. "It's somewhere near morning. I'd better not look at my watch." He stood thinking. "This is Friday—or rather Saturday morning and you have food enough for a couple of days. I have to work over the week end and I can't cut Monday. I'll be back Tuesday night."

He walked to the door. "Better try for some sleep. Good night, Bel."

His hand was on the doorknob when she whispered, "Just a moment." She came near him and looked into his eyes. "Joseph,

I have a terrible headache." She walked to her table drawer, opened it jerkily and rummaged around until she found a small notebook, out of which she extracted a crumpled bit of paper. She looked it over carefully. "You have a little money? I don't want to touch those bills for the rent."

"Not much."

"That little drugstore at the corner is open all night and these tablets only cost fifty cents. If you would take a little more time and get some for me—or give me the money—I would be eternally grateful. I'll come down with you. I won't mind going."

He reached for the paper. "You'll do nothing of the kind. It's three o'clock."

Rather reluctantly she handed him the crumpled slip of paper. He studied it, looking perplexed, for on it was scrawled in her handwriting, a long number above her name, Bel Dynitch, and down in the corner, the name, Benny.

She was watching him sharply. "It's old, Joseph, a prescription given me by a New York doctor—long ago. It's all right. You can't run to a doctor every time you want headache tablets. When you go in, ask for Benny. He knows me."

He scowled, "That's against the law. A prescription from a New York doctor is illegal in Massachusetts. Besides, I suspect this was a special drug the doctor gave you for something more than a mere headache and it couldn't be used over and over even in New York. The whole business is illegal, Bel."

"I know all that, Joseph. I'd better go myself."

She fixed the catch on the door and they quietly descended the stairs together. At the street door, with the paper in his fingers, he tried to joke. "Sounds like bootlegged stuff to me. Gives them to you cheap? Does Benny get you the cheap rum also? You know the Massachusetts laws are strict. We'll probably both land in jail."

She did not laugh but crouched back in the corner of the vestibule. "Yes, he gets me the rum too. He knows when I come to him I need it." Jerkily she stepped forward. "Give me the paper. I'd better go myself."

"You wait here." He walked off rapidly, found the drugstore, asked a sleepy-looking individual if his name was Benny, got a smiling nod in reply, handed him the slip of paper and was given a box of tablets. "Thanks." He took the fifty cents of change in return for his last dollar. Benny remarked pleasantly, "It's rather late." Joseph grinned, "Yes," and walked out.

She was standing in a dark corner. When he handed the box to her, her wiry little fingers closed on his hand. "Please let me, Joseph." She raised his hand to her lips.

It was as though some dam were bursting in his chest giving way to a flood of pity. He put his arm about her and pressed his face against her hair, the hair that always appeared dry and wild and always disarranged and he was surprised to feel it soft as silk beneath his cheek.

He murmured, "Keep your chin up, Bel. It's a hell of a twisted road but we'll come through all right. We only need a little time."

She did not answer his good night. As he walked rapidly away he thought he heard those terrifying sobs again.

Above, the stars were growing pale in the faint light from the east. The air crisp and cool, yet with the promise of spring, was welcome after the close air of the apartment. He raised his face enjoying the feel of the fresh wind.

Once he thought of the bootlegged sleeping tablets but only with relief, knowing they would assure Bel a good sleep.

CHAPTER XXXIII

On Sunday morning he wrote that note to his mother, completely unconscious of the brevity of the scrawled lines.

He wouldn't visualize her on the following Monday morning, stepping out onto the porch, raising her face to the spring breeze, as she waited for the postman to make his way down the avenue. Long before that hour he had forgotten he had written the note.

He had spent Saturday and Sunday poring over his books. Now

he must not fail. Now he would go without food or drink to catch up in his work.

Kurt was watching him. He saw him on Monday morning, lying in his bed sleeping heavily and looking so dead tired that he hated to wake him. However he watched the clock and knew when there was no more than time for shower, dressing, breakfast and the quick walk to the lecture hall. He shook him vigorously, "Get up you lazy lout. There's just time to make it if you don't dawdle."

He did not dawdle. He was on the sidewalk, books under his arm, when a sharp whistle and the calling of his name caused him to look back to the door. It was Kurt, also with books under his arm, ready to start out. He ran down the steps speaking as he came. "There was a telephone message for you. The fellow wouldn't wait for you to come. It was some foreigner I'd guess from the voice. I could hardly understand him but I got him to spell the name. J-a-n-s-e-n. He kept repeating, 'Tell Joseph Donovan to come right away. It's bad.'"

"What's bad?" He spoke irritably.

"Damned if I know. I tried to get him to wait for you but he said something about Mama. I tried to make him tell me 'what' bad' but he kept repeating like a parrot, 'Tell him to come.'" Kurt turned away. "I'd forget it. You'd better hurry or you'll be late again. You're a fool if you cut today."

Kurt started off briskly but Joseph stood on the sidewalk looking at the pavement. He began to walk slowly. He stopped. He came back, an alert, angry, almost desperate expression in his face. At the curb was parked a small Ford coupé, Kurt's car. He looked at it a moment then he whistled shrilly and ran down the block. "Kurt."

He seemed to look through him and past him as he blurted out "I never asked you before. Give me your keys. Let me use the Ford. It will save time."

There was a moment of hesitation then Kurt put his hand in his pocket, brought out the keys and tossed them into the outstretched hand.

"Thanks." He ran back to the Ford. He was sitting in the driver's seat, inserting the key when a second strapped bundle of books was tossed over his lap into the seat and Kurt stood beside him. "Move over, I'll drive."

Joseph's face flushed angrily. "I won't hurt your damned car. I've got to go."

Kurt was edging in. "Move over. I'm driving." He gave a brutal shove, settled in the driver's seat and started the ignition. "Now don't make mistakes. That wastes time. Say right or left *before* we're on a corner. That's all you have to do. You can keep your mouth shut otherwise. You don't have to tell me one damned thing." Then mockingly but quite jovially, "You've got a chauffeur. Pretty nifty, I'd say."

He did not keep his mouth shut. Except for his concentration on the route, his mental faculties seemed blurred into one question: What's bad? Had she put Roger out in the sun and let him fall off the fire escape? He remembered afterward how definitely that one fear clutched at him as he tried to explain the situation to Kurt.

Once in a while he breathed aloud, "Well, we made it," as Kurt, caught behind a truck, impatiently swung out, regaining the right side of the road in the nick of time; as Kurt slipped through a yellow light, "Couldn't stop without endangering the neck of my passenger"; as Kurt took a cut through a play-street, "Kids all in school."

More than once Kurt asked, "You're sure our destination is this side of Albany?"

Mechanically, Joseph said, "Left, right, straight on," then, "Stop at that apartment house, the one standing all alone."

Kurt crossed the traffic in a wide curve and drew up at the curb. "I'll be right here waiting, making notes of the landscape gardening. I love scenery. If you want me, I'm here. I hope your kid's safe."

Joseph took the flights of stairs two and three steps at a time. When he reached the upper hall the door of the Jansens' apartment opened, first a crack, then wider and Mr. Jansen's face looked out. He motioned toward the opposite door. "Mama's in there."

Lightly this time, Joseph's fingers beat his usual tattoo on the door. There was no sound from within. He turned the knob and the door gave. There was Mama sitting broad and squat on the stool her narrow eyes fastened on the figure lying on the bed. She looked up at Joseph and nodded several times.

There was no play-pen in sight and he would remember the fear which clutched at him now with certainty as he asked, "Where's Roger?"

"In there with Papa." She nodded toward the door.

"He's all right? Is he—"

She nodded again. "He's good with Papa."

"Bel?" He was coming toward the bed. He looked down. The slight figure was covered with the brown blanket. Her eyes were closed and she seemed to be deeply sleeping. He spoke scarcely above a whisper. "She isn't well. Has she been sick?"

Over Mrs. Jansen's face came a curious tremor as though the muscles were twitching. She was hoisting herself up from the stool—no easy task. On her feet, she stood a moment breathing heavily, then she walked to the work table. She spoke loudly, "We can't wake her up. Papa couldn't sleep because of Roger's crying in the night. For an hour he cry. Then he stop. Then again he cry and Papa says to go in and see why Roger cries all night. I found the door open. I shook her. I did everything. I can't wake her up." All the time she was talking she had been holding in her hand the small box which he had purchased at the drugstore Friday night. He was staring at it. It was empty. When he took the box from her hands, he dropped it. While he was picking it up from the floor, he asked, "When did you see her last?"

"On Saturday. I lent her my electric iron. She had cleaned house, washed and ironed all the clothes. She came in and thanked me for the iron. She was very nice and kissed me and said she was very tired. I scolded her for doing so much hard work in one day. She said she would rest on Sunday. All day Sunday it was very quiet. Now I have a terrible fright."

"When did you find the box?"

"Right away when daylight comes—lying on the floor."

He walked to the bed and leaned over, his face almost as white as the face on the pillow. "We must get a doctor right away."

She laid a hand on his arm. "I think not. She breathes all right, you think? Doctor might make a terrible lot of trouble. Perhaps she wake up soon."

"You don't have a doctor? Someone in the neighborhood who knows you?"

She shook her head. "We go way down to clinic. Mostly for teeth. There are dozens of doctors. I think not."

"Wait here a moment. I have a friend in a car downstairs. Let me talk to him." From the front door, he called, "Kurt, come up here." On the way up the flights of stairs he explained, every detail about his purchase of the bootlegged headache tablets.

Soon Kurt was sitting on the stool, his fingers on the thin wrist, then his head laid down on the chest. Behind him stood Mrs. Jansen, an agony of fear in her pale eyes.

Kurt rose. "She may be all right. We can't take chances. I'll get someone." At the door, he turned and looked at Joseph. "It may take me some time, Jo. You stay right here."

As he ran down the stairs, Mrs. Jansen looked at Joseph. "He's a doctor? That boy?"

"His father is a famous doctor in New York. It's going to be his line too. He knows more than I do. He would know what to do."

She looked relieved. "He was not scared."

"He didn't seem to be. He'll find someone we can trust. He knows lots of people."

She replied, "I am very glad. Doctors make much trouble."

Kurt walked rapidly to the corner where he looked into the drugstore. The telephone booths were near the lunch counter and already people were milling in and out for hot coffee and sodas. He crossed to a saloon where he handed a bill to the bartender.

"I want to use a phone. You know, a private conversation." The bartender winked.

In a back room, he waited and gave numbers and waited again. He was following his father from home to hospital. "If he isn't operating, he can be disturbed. Tell him it's his son talking from Boston and connect me right away. Make it quick." Again, "It's Kurt, Dad. It's something serious. Jo and I are in a jam. Give me the name of any Boston doctor you know and can trust, then you telephone him while I'm getting to him. God, Dad, someone is dying here too. You've got to come. Don't wait for a train. Did I ever ask you to do anything like this before?"

More long waits. The entire business of numbers to go through again. "Harriet Simmons. Which school? Give me the number." More waiting as perspiration ran down his face. "Of course she can be disturbed. Tell her it's an urgent call from Boston." He wiped his forehead as he waited, muttering, "If she's teaching the Angel Gabriel to blow for the Resurrection, she'll have to come." "Miss Simmons? It's Kurt Foster, Joseph's roommate—you remember?" Over and over he gave careful explanations. "You will save his mother if it gets out? Those damned reporters grab everything if it's about a Harvard student. I don't want you to come now but I might need you later. You will understand if I call at the house. I want the name and phone number of that judge who's so devoted to the family. Yes, talk to him. Yes, it's damned serious. There's a girl dying of sleeping tablets that Joseph gave her. Please watch out for his mother and sister. Yes, I'll call you tonight."

He was mopping his face when he settled with the bartender. He ran back to his car and turned toward the center of the city. The shortest cut to Beacon Street. His father had promised to phone an elderly physician, an important man of sound judgment who was doing little practice now as he was writing his memoirs.

Kurt would fetch him. Of course his memoirs would be concerned with education, hospital connections, important discoveries, or, he muttered, "consultations over the liver of a king or president or other potentate. Such trivia as a woman on the top floor of a tenement dying from an overdose of sleeping powders! What a nerve I have to bring him here. This affair is good for an obscure line on a back page of a newspaper—nothing more if they keep our names out of it."

On the ride back to the apartment, beside him sat a thin little man with white hair and a white vandyke beard. He looked so frail that Kurt was scared into driving steadily and carefully. Once sharp eyes were turned on him as the elderly man said, "Of course one stands by a pal. The boy a little wild perhaps?"

Kurt exploded, "Good Lord, please understand. He's a prince if there ever was one. He's no more to blame for this than you are."

"Calm down, please, and watch your driving. You missed the curb at the corner by a hair's breadth. My arthritic neck doesn't like too sudden an application of the brakes. How is your father's health? Good, I trust?"

"He's very well, sir."

At the foot of the stairs, Kurt looked at what he thought of as "the weak little shrimp," with consternation. "Good Lord, I forgot those stairs. There's no elevator."

"You're out of breath, boy, take it easy. I've climbed mountains in distant countries and tenement stairs in Boston all my life. Those are my two hobbies—the view from mountaintops and the women and children at the tops of tenements." All the time he was talking he was going steadily up the stairs. On the third flight he asked pleasantly, "You say you expect to practice medicine? In New York?"

Behind him, Kurt answered meekly, "Yes, sir."

"I hope you won't confine your practice to Park Avenue women. You will always find elevators but you may also find yourself grown rich and old before your time—with boredom."

Kurt relaxed. Perhaps the "half pint's" memoirs would turn out to be interesting reading.

When they opened the apartment door, Mrs. Jansen was sitting on the stool and Joseph was bending over the couch. For an instant the horror in his eyes gave way to relief when he saw the doctor. There was an imploring note in his voice. "Can you hurry, sir? She must be very weak. I can't see her breathe."

The doctor set his bag on the table. Some ten minutes later he turned from the bed. "She is dead."

During their long wait, Joseph had found the crumpled slip of paper which Bel had replaced in the small notebook and now, Mrs. Jansen handed that and the empty box to the doctor. He examined them both, then slipped them into his pocket even as he spoke quietly, "Will you two boys wait in that other bedroom? This good woman will get me clean towels."

Back and forth from bathroom or kitchen to the bed the doctor passed pursuing his investigation, extracting all kinds of information from Mrs. Jansen by questions so casual and gently spoken that she hardly knew she was being interrogated. Her fear of "trouble-making doctors" seemed to vanish as she related all she knew of Bel's coming there, her life, her habits, her talents, her baby and the exciting meeting with this young man and the boy's sympathy and kindness.

Did Bel come alone months ago? No, a New York man brought her. It was "terrible." He wanted to get rid of her but he did send her money but not enough. He belonged to a wife and family. That was the "terrible" trouble. Did she know his name? No, Bel was very close about telling anything about him.

Did the good Mrs. Jansen know that Bel expected another baby? She did. It was "terrible." Now would she take him across the hall and let him see the little boy called Roger, and Papa?

In a very few minutes he came back alone and seating himself on the only chair in Roger's room, he laid a pad on his knee and continued talking in the same quiet way.

"Kurt, will you get the stool and another chair? We'll sit down and talk it over and see what's to be done."

First he answered Joseph's anxious question. "No, those two hours while Kurt was getting me made no difference. It was quite too late to save her. Before I make out the death certificate, I wish to clear up many details. The young woman is pregnant— about five months and that is always serious." His eyes were sharp now, turned to Joseph. "Exactly when—before this accidental meeting in March, on a Cambridge street—when had you seen this young woman before?"

There was something pathetic, even painful in Joseph's embarrassed smile as he said, "It was the day after my ninth birthday when I saw her first, then it was the next summer when I saw her working in a drugstore at home."

For a fleeting second a half smile played about the doctor's lips and Kurt smiled broadly as he volunteered, "We've got half the college as witnesses."

Ignoring that point, the doctor's face grew grave. He repeated earnestly the very words Joseph had used so jokingly to Bel. "The Massachusetts laws are strict. Illegally, you purchased the tablets that were used to kill her, at three o'clock in the morning? I want the whole story—every detail—no omissions. Would you prefer to have Kurt go out or do you want him here?"

Kurt was sitting on the window sill, his elbows on his knees. He looked up in surprise.

Joseph said quickly, "I want Kurt to hear everything."

The doctor smiled, "I thought so. Now will you relax and get that stony look off your face, Joseph? You can't help the girl any longer. She is past all help. Now, suppose you gather yourself together and help yourself."

He spoke as pleasantly as though at a social meeting. "I was once a guest at Judge Kent's house in my youth. I am nearly your grandfather's age and I remember the family very well." Still pleasantly he went one, "I can assure you the officials won't question my authority and I can take care of the medical aspects of the case." Then he looked up sternly, "Joseph, do you know the man who brought Bel here?"

The boy's haggard, white face turned crimson. Twice he half choked, "Yes, sir, he—"

The doctor interrupted, "Just a moment. I think it will be easier if you tell it all in your own way; that is, start either at the beginning—back there when you were nine years old—or start anywhere you please but tell me everything."

As though giving him time, the doctor talked on, "Of course if some reporters get together—this drug clerk, Benny, will only be interested in protecting himself." As though thinking aloud, "We're going to need legal skill and influence." Turning to Kurt, "You talked to Judge Carter? I know *of* him—William Higginson Carter."

He opened his pad. "Now you may start at any point you choose, Joseph, but tell me everything."

He turned to Kurt with a delightful glint of humor in his eyes. "If you practice medicine as long as I have, Kurt, you will find extraordinary, astonishing new things in Nature every day; but nothing in human behavior will surprise you."

CHAPTER XXXIV

"Where's Joseph?" The querulous tones of Nan's voice followed Mary Donovan on that Friday night as she stepped from the child's room into the hall where Sandra was standing in a shadowy corner near her own room.

Sandra never crouched but there was something suggestive of cowering or at least shrinking in her position now. While Mary stood with her hand on the stair rail, Sandra ran quickly into her own room. She did not put on the light.

For a moment Mary listened, heard some groping, then went back to speak to her daughter. "What's the trouble, Sandra?" Sandra groping in the dark was unthinkable.

It was Mary who switched on the light but the girl had turned her back murmuring, "I'm just dead tired, Mother. I want to talk to you tomorrow but now I want to think and—get to sleep."

"You're in trouble?"

"I'm all right. Only I want to tell you something tomorrow. Not now."

Mary looked steadily at the girl's back. "Very well, dear." She was pulling the door to. "If it's about Joseph—"

Sandra whirled around. "You've been in Miss Simmons' room, reading those nasty Boston papers. Oh, I'm so sorry. It's all right now, Mother. Hunt told me tonight. His father's been out there. He thinks everything's settled and his father may be home already and Joseph may come any time. I'm so sorry you saw those papers. No horrid gossip got into our own home papers. You may be sure of that. We were trying to save you, Mother. We didn't want you worried."

"That's the last thing I ever want you to do. Judge Carter stopped in on his way from the night train."

"Oh!" She gazed into her mother's face. "Then it is all right? I was sure neither Joseph nor Kurt had a thing to do with it."

"Was that what was troubling you?"

Sandra turned away. There seemed to be a catch in her throat as she answered, "I want to sleep, Mother. I want to talk to you in the morning."

"Very well, dear."

Mary turned out the hall light and, in her room, she sat on the edge of her bed, slowly undressing, as she thought of the things Judge Carter had told her. The events of one week. One week. Oh, no. It did not begin with that confused letter of Monday morning. It began way back when her son began asking, almost begging for more money. The name of that suicide—Bel.

There was no anger, no fury, no slightest urge to *do* anything. Her hands were cold and wet and hung weakly over her knees. The sense of coldness, of weakness seemed to be creeping into the innermost parts of her body yet her thoughts were clear and, with the penetrating coldness of a legal mind, she assembled every bit of evidence, sorted and pieced together until she saw—what?

Distantly she heard the clock in the sittingroom chime one, two, three. She heard footsteps in the upper hall, a creaking of the stairs in spite of soft bedroom slippers. She called, "Sandra?"

"I want a little milk, Mother. Please don't come down. I am hungry." She repeated, "Please don't come down."

"I won't." She pulled up the quilts and turned her face into the pillow. She must try to sleep.

She had been so intent on listening to the clock, and to Sandra's footsteps on the stairs and, because her window was now on the other side of the house, she did not hear other steps coming up the avenue; uncertain footsteps, sometimes shuffling as though the feet were so heavily weighted the owner could scarcely lift them; footsteps coming slowly up the avenue, stopping, then coming on, softly shuffling around the house, back toward the side door, back farther toward the woodshed door.

Sandra had set a glass on the round table in the kitchen. She was opening the pantry door to get the milk when she heard the rattling of the latch at the woodshed. She stood still, holding her breath, listening. The door was being opened.

"Joseph!" She had spoken aloud and almost with the word, she crossed the room, turned the key in the lock and flung open the door.

The brilliant ceiling light in the kitchen streamed out into the shed, illuminating the figure crossing the floor. It was her father. The footsteps, for the sound of which Mary Donovan had yearned through years, had come up their walk and passed their window and she, unknowing, was falling into a deep sleep.

To the girl, there were sharp memories of early childhood when she had gazed so disconcertingly at the stranger who was always appearing and disappearing; there was the child-sadness, unspoken but acute when he went away "for good."

There was more, much more. There was an accumulation of shame, of deep-rooted indignation. Because she could not understand the truth, this man, like a character in a play, had become, in her mind, the author and perpetrator of every sadness in her mother's life. When she saw the knuckles of Mary Donovan's hands skinned and bleeding, she subconsciously blamed him; when she saw her hanging out a wet-wash or leaning over an ironing-board, she blamed this man. When Hunt treated her like "baggage" or Mazie spoke of her as "that blonde from across the street," unknowing to herself, she blamed him.

Was there something even deeper rooted in her mind? Forgotten completely? A dark hall, a man acting "queer" trying to catch her, terror, as on hands and knees she had crept away and scurried into her bed?

Cruel? Unjust? It was unconscious cruelty. Now she stood in the doorway looking at him. Pitiable. Shabby. He stood before her, an abject creature, humble, smiling an ingratiating smile as he said,

"Sandra?"

She blocked the doorway and he did not advance toward her. Under the slouched brim of his hat, his hollow eyes looked dull and dim. She did not know that he looked like a drinking man who needed whiskey desperately. He spoke again, "Will you tell your mother?"

She did not speak and he repeated, "I want very much to see your mother."

She spoke in her beautiful voice, the tones and articulation of which were not unlike his own in their former clearness. "You cannot see my mother. It would upset her. She is having trouble enough. Please go away."

His half smile was pitiful. "Won't you let her decide that? Will you tell her I am here?"

"No, I won't. Please go away. Please go back wherever you came from."

His hand was pressed against the woodshed wall. Now he leaned his shoulder against that wall. "Is Joseph here?"

His dull eyes were fastened on her face. She stood erect, slim and proud in her bearing and lovely to look at, the light behind her making a radiance of her hair.

"No, Joseph is not here."

Now the muscles in his cheeks were twitching. His voice seemed to be weaker. "I've hitch-hiked all the way from New York to Boston to get to Joseph. I've hitch-hiked all the way from Boston here to follow him. They said he had gone home. I've got to lie down."

"I have some money. I'll give you all I can find if you'll go somewhere else and not make my mother miserable. I must save my mother."

She was turning away when he called hoarsely, "No, don't get it. I wouldn't take *your* money. Will you just go away yourself, close the door and lock it? You surely won't mind if I rest here for a few minutes. I'll be gone before daylight."

She closed the door and turned the key. She turned out the light and made her way to the stairs. First her legs, then her entire body began to shake. She clung to the banister, creeping up step by step. Feeling with her hands, she found her way along the wall in the dark hall until she reached her room. She turned the lock in her own door, groped for her bed and lay down.

Now the last vestige of her self-control was gone and her body was racked with sobs as she lay shaking. She knew she had been, according to her own standards, a bully. She knew she had been cruel. She did not know the night had tested her far past the limit of her endurance. And the worse thing was; she could not endure herself.

CHAPTER XXXV

There is much to be said for a northern spring. In more temperate sections of our country, spring seems slowly to creep in and we hardly notice the transition from cold to summer heat; but in the north there are seasons when everything seems to burst into new life, beauty and song overnight.

Mary Donovan waked after scarcely two hours of deep, refreshing sleep. The sky was still gray but in the east a rosy light was tinting the breaking clouds. Carrying her shoes in her hand, she went through the upper hall, glancing into Miss Simmons' room and noting the perfect order of the newspapers on her table.

She saw Sandra's door closed. She looked into Nan's room where the little head with its chestnut curls lay peacefully on its pillow. With great care she closed that door.

Downstairs, she mechanically began doing all the little things she did every morning of her life. Kit, freed of her "stiffness" for the last few weeks, had washed and ironed and cleaned until the house was, as she said, "shining for Easter."

The blessed routine. Easing the shades up noiselessly, setting the breakfast table, going in and out of the pantry for coffee, eggs, bacon and bread. She walked through her rooms, watering her plants, straightening pillows, setting chairs in place, putting books and magazines back on shelves. Long before her own was ready, she smelled Mr. Ryder's coffee. He occupied the room over her kitchen. Was his routine blessed to him? He would rise, cook his breakfast, make his bed and presently, quiet as a shadow, he would pass her window on his way to his work. He completely separated himself from their life yet he was a comforting part of it.

As she drank her coffee, a lovely light was flooding in from the east windows. As she loved the world hushed with snow in winter, so she loved the "hush" in her head in this early morning hour, the pleasantness of quiet, the ceasing of the tongue's eternal wagging, the feel of the white calm of the mist across the lawn slowly burning away under the glistening gold of the sun's rays.

From her desk in her room upstairs, she had brought down a note received from one of those cousins, twice or thrice removed, who had bought her old home. They were inveterate travelers and now she noted this letter had come from Oregon. It was brief; would she look after their elms? They had read of the diseases attacking the trees. Send them all bills.

In the midst of her reading, she heard a sound which caused her to look up quickly toward the window. It was the first robin's note and she thought it sounded as though he were in the old apple tree. She went to the window. Here and there the winter birds were still flitting about—the white-throat, the song sparrow and even a junco, there was the robin singing and there was the pink of the apple blossoms and there was some answer to the doubts of man.

She pressed her face against the pane and looked toward the elms. Soon dense flower-clusters would line those twigs with tawny-red blossoms, to be followed by the winged fruit that would one day, sail off on the spring breeze.

She saw some movement through the shrubbery and presently two men appeared in the open lawn. They carried ropes and on their legs were the spiked braces of tree-men.

Hastily she slipped on her tweed coat and went out. A car stopped at the curb and a man wearing a leather jacket stepped out and joined her. They had talked together several times before because he was the scientist directing the work in their part of the country.

A man of few words, when he spoke it was always to the point. They were up early? The men were merely finishing some checking so they could get off because of the Easter holiday. She would not lose more than the two trees but they must come down.

They stood a moment in silence as she remembered a young girl standing with her father beneath that tree, cupping her hands and shouting to the man above to "hold on," as her father had called, "hold off." There was the large treated area which now carried the deadly fungus. "Elm death."

She stood with light-shod feet on the cold, damp earth, the soil that soon would burst into a million blooms. She stood with folded arms watching them until they all drove off in the foreman's car, then she slowly re-entered her quiet house.

Milk wagons were stopping before houses, bottles rattled. Cars were beginning to pass but few people were as yet on the street.

She was in her parlor, turning to enter the hall when a taxi came into view driving very fast and stopping abruptly at the curb in front of her house. Instead of moving she watched every detail as though physically incapable of stirring. The door of the car was flung open and Joseph's blond head, then his heavy shoulders came into view. He was standing on the curb paying the driver. Then he reached in and helped Miss Simmons out of the car. There was some further reaching for bags, the taxi started away and they turned toward the house.

They stood a moment speaking to each other then Joseph picked up the bags and followed Miss Simomns up the walk.

No. He was following more than Miss Simmons. Mary Donovan did not stir. Her clear mind was taking note of the fact that

Miss Simmons was carrying a baby in her arms. Was that incongruous? No. Mary knew that that deep-bosomed woman should have been carrying babies in her arms for many years.

She watched them come nearer and nearer. Again Joseph set down the bags and Miss Simmons handed him her keys. They spoke together. Mary knew what they were saying. They must be quiet; they must not wake anyone; they must not burst in on Mary. No, they must "save her."

As they stopped on the porch, Mary could see the child. At the edge of his bonnet she saw hair dark like his eyes. He was a pretty child, wrapped now in a new blue blanket, a very pretty blanket.

The key was turned in the door and they entered the hall. There was some whispering, then Miss Simmons stole upstairs while the door into the parlor opened not five feet from Mary. "Joseph?" He started; but the quietness, the composure in her voice instantly reassured him. "I have been watching you coming."

She laid her hands on his shoulders and kissed his lips; then her hand reached up, smoothed his hair and rested a moment against his cheek; then—only for a moment—just a little, she broke; then she raised her head and forced a smile. "The girls are asleep. Let's go into the kitchen."

She was warming the coffee and making toast. Presently she poured a cup. "Drink that. I will have some too."

She told him briefly that Judge Carter had stopped in last night and described the week to her. She smiled, "You look as though you had been on the rack for a month."

"You should see Kurt. I expected to get the works but he took it with me. I want to sleep."

She was conscious of the way his eyes seemed to be devouring her face. She sat forward and laying her hand on his, said, "You have brought the baby home? Has Miss Simmons taken it or is she planning to put it in a home?"

A deep crimson flush, an angry flush spread over his face and neck. "Mother, that's my baby. I mean of course, not by birth —but he's mine. No one on earth can have that boy. Miss Simmons wants him but she can't have him. I don't know how in hell I'm going to manage it, but I'm going to keep him and take care of him. I want to bring him up and give him a chance."

"Oh." She watched the flush fade from his face and something less understandable take its place. That something she had noticed the minute he had entered the sittingroom. It was an expression never seen on his face before. She did not know it was the stony, set expression that once had been on her own face.

"Joseph, let's take things one at a time. Here and there are little points I wish to be sure of. If I ask what you don't wish to answer, say so. First, were you in love with the artist, the girl who committed suicide?"

"Hell, no. I had to help her. You would have helped her, Mother. I kept telling myself you would have done what I did."

"Was she, to you, a pretty girl, attractive?"

"I think she was cute years ago but she was skinny and plain and old-looking and wild at the last, but" he emphasized the word, "but, I can't get her face out of my mind one minute day or night. It's always there between me and everything I look at. That's why I couldn't study."

"That will take time. Was there a funeral?"

"Yes. Everything was attended to and Dr. Foster paid for everything. It was just one thing after another, day and night, questions, interviews, interviews and questions. Kurt is a wreck. Dr. Foster, Judge Carter and the doctor who came when she died —they managed everything—inquest, post-mortems—she died from the sleeping tablets I bought for her."

He described Mrs. Jansen. "Bel used to say she had a heart of gold. She certainly had—the way she protected me." Then without waiting for more questions he plunged into that something he must get off his mind before he could begin to feel right—his visit with his father. When he finished she asked the one question he dreaded, "How did he look?"

"I think he looked sick." He could not bring out the word "shabby."

She stood up and walked to the window with her back to him

as she asked, evenly, "What do you want to do first, I mean now?"

"Sleep, Mother. I'd like to sleep for a week in my own bed."

She came back smiling and laid her hand on his shoulder. "Slip up before the girls come down. I'll tell them you're here and keep them quiet. Then I must speak to Miss Simmons."

He stood for a minute, his strong arms tight about her shoulders, his face against her hair, then he was gone. She let tears wet the fingers she held tight against her eyes but only for a minute; then she dashed cold water onto her face. She was smoothing her hair when she heard the soft thud of slippers and Sandra came in. "I know, Mother, I heard him. Joseph's home."

Her talk with Miss Simmons would have to wait. The baby must be sleeping, it was so quiet up there. Miss Simmons would be unpacking.

Sandra was pouring herself some coffee. "Nancy doesn't want to get up so I fetched her some books and fixed her up in bed. I'll take up some milk and toast, then can I talk to you?"

"Of course but not over half a cup of coffee. We'll take care of Nan then we'll eat a good breakfast."

Sandra went back and forth to Nan whose cold had reached the worst sniffly phase and as Mary cooked the bacon and eggs she glanced toward the east windows. All the heavy grayness had been obliterated from the sky, the clouds had disappeared and in their place was a clear, soft green-blue as a background for the apple blossoms while far above the sky was one vast expanse of indigo. Perhaps this Easter Sunday would be, in their lives, somewhat like that sky, clear and settled after the removal of the menacing clouds.

She was thinking such thoughts as Sandra finished her breakfast and began, "Mother, you've always told us there was one thing you wouldn't tolerate in one of your children. I've been thinking about it all night and now I want you to tolerate it."

Mary looked puzzled. "What on earth am I such a tyrant about?"

"You say you won't allow one of us to run away from trouble. Always stand up and face the thing and fight it out right where you are. I want to run away. I've got to run away. I want you to let me take all my books and go out to Uncle Lawrence's and study there, then come back and take my examinations so I can get my diploma. Then I want to go to Chicago University instead of Wellesley next year and live with Uncle Lawrence and Aunt Cathey."

Mary studied the face before her. "Why?"

"Because I'm engaged to Professor Waring. I don't want to be. I can't face it. I can't manage it and I'm going to run away."

"Suppose you tell me exactly what happened and when it happened." She watched narrowly the dilated, unhappy eyes of her daughter as she described the party, finding herself alone in Professor Waring's car, the stop on the hill and what followed.

She had not finished; she was hopelessly trying to explain her own stupid acquiescence, when the telephone rang. Mary waited for her daughter to jump up, as was her custom, and run to answer it. Nine times out of ten the calls were for Sandra. Now she sat with a scared, stricken look on her face and did not move.

"Won't you answer?"

"Please, Mother, you—"

As Mary hurried from the room, Sandra followed her, almost gasping, "Mother, I haven't told you. Something terrible happened in the night—I must—"

Mary was picking up the receiver. "Yes?"

A secretary was connecting someone. "Mary?"

It was Dr. Porter's voice.

"Oh, good morning, Doctor Porter."

"Mary, could you be ready to come to the hospital with me in about fifteen minutes?"

As quick as though she saw them all safe; Joseph sleeping, Nan in bed, Sandra close to her elbow. Surprised and bewildered she answered, "Why yes, but—"

"What for? Get a good stiff grip on yourself, Mary, and take it just as quietly as you can. It's Tom. He was picked up on the street just before daylight. He was in my neighborhood—perhaps he was trying to get to me. Anyway they brought him here. I took him to the hospital about two hours ago. I had some calls to make and now I'm going back. I want to fetch you. Now keep a stiff upper lip and I'll stop for you in about fifteen minutes."

A few minutes later, as she stood near the front windows watching for the doctor's car, Sandra, crouched in the corner of the sofa, her head bent in abject shame, told her mother how she had sent her father away in the night.

The car drew to the curb. Mary spoke quietly, "Take care of everything while I'm gone, dear. We'll talk later."

She closed the door softly behind her as she went out.

CHAPTER XXXVI

When they drove into the hospital yard, Mary remembered how the brown brick buildings had looked that July Fourth when she had come there with Mattie Briggs. She remembered the hot, sultry day and how young and alert, how full of responsibility she had felt that morning. Now the sky was indigo blue, the spring breeze was fresh and the sun poured into the court, yet she felt almost numb and as though she were walking blindfold as she followed Dr. Porter through corridors into an elevator.

He led her to a small single room at the end of a hall. There was a screen inside the door and a nurse was coming out.

Dr. Porter touched her shoulder then turned to leave her. "I'll be back in a few minutes."

She stood alone behind the screen. "I hope his eyes will be closed so I can see him first." Twice she pulled herself up to take those necessary steps and twice she waited trying to feel quiet and steady.

His eyes were open, watching the door. One could almost measure the deepening of the expression of anxiety, of dread, of longing as he gazed at her. "Mary?"

She walked over and quickly laid her face down against his

cheek while her hand pressed his forehead. She did not speak because she could not.

He raised his hand and touched her hair. "It's the end, Mary."

No more than she could stop her heatbeats, could she stop the scalding tears that wet his pillow. "I'm so sorry, Tom, about last night. If I'd only known. I wanted you to come home—not here."

"This is better."

She walked about the room, biting her lips, digging her nails into the palms of her hands, swallowing hard until she gained her usual self-control. She pulled a small chair up close to the side of the bed and leaning over laid her hand on his.

"Tom, don't give up. Let's fight together." She smiled, "I'll help you. Don't give up. You see I want you to come home."

Couldn't she hear that there was scarcely a tone of his clear, beautiful voice in the weak, husky sounds with which he tried to speak? "There are things I want to say to you, Mary. I hope I have a little time. Tell me first about Joseph. I was trying to get to him when I found out—I got to the apartment—they said he had gone home."

"Yes, I know. I know everything, Tom." Quickly and clearly she told him the story. Once he interrupted, "Go back, Mary. How did Joseph know about—"

"About Bel?" She spoke the name quietly and told him of the accidental meeting on the street. She told him of the doctor, of Kurt's father and the only name she left out was that of Judge Carter. "It's all over and finished and now we must all try to forget. It won't be easy." She tried to force some lightness into her voice. "I see plenty of hurdles to get over but we've climbed out of some low places before and we can all do it again. The first thing is to get you well so you can come home."

She had not seen him, as Sandra saw him, standing in the wood-shed, unshaved, unkempt, wearing his shabby coat and slouched hat. Now he was in a clean room, a clean bed, a clean hospital shirt, his hair brushed and face shaven. In those two hours Dr. Porter had done for Tom all that was in his power to do, including a preliminary physical examination of heart and blood.

Mary saw the whitening hair, the blotched skin drawn tight over the cheekbones; felt, as though it had been in her own body, the pitiful exhaustion; but there was something of which she was more keenly conscious—the restless hands and eyes and the entire countenance in which there was not one vestige of peace.

He looked past her at the sunshine pouring in through the narrow window, then murmured, "This is the last spring, Mary."

"Oh, no, Tom." She tried to keep her voice light and cheerful as she told him of the beautiful early morning, the apple blossoms and the first robin singing. She saw that look of yearning deepen in his eyes as he moved restlessly. She could hardly hear his words.

"Joseph talks about that house—that place just the way you do. Joseph—" He stopped abruptly and closed his eyes.

Almost as suddenly he opened them, stared hard as though at the opposite wall and asked sharply, "There must have been a good lawyer and the influence of your Kent-Farnsworth tribe to help Joseph?"

She spoke eagerly, "It was his own innocence that counted, Tom."

"Carter? Was it Carter?"

She bit her lips, "Yes."

"Always taking care of you—"

He turned on the pillow and looked directly into her eyes. "Mary, why didn't you divorce me and marry him? You would do almost anything for the sake of your children."

Her eyes held the steady direct look which in Sandra could be so disconcerting. Now in Mary's eyes the expression seemed to brush aside any suggestion of evasion. She spoke gravely, "That's one question I do not have to answer, Tom." Her voice trembled as she added with passionate tenderness, "You know the answer. You've known it from the day I met you. You've known it for twenty years."

His lips twisted bitterly. "It was when I doubted that—when I didn't believe you—I thought it was your pride and your principles and your children and your determination to go through with it—"

Her hand was laid firmly on one of his, stopping for a moment the nervous movement of the fingers. She felt a sudden, violent tremor as he asked, "What did they do with that boy? That baby?"

"He will be taken care of, Tom."

"How?" Then he laughed bitterly, "I couldn't endure him; I couldn't bear to look at him but even at that I don't want him put in an orphan asylum. Could they find a foster home for him?"

"He has found a home, Tom."

For a moment he looked into her face. "Where? You've taken him?"

She nodded. "Joseph and I will take care of him."

He rammed the knuckle of his forefinger in between his teeth as he clamped hard on it for a moment, then he turned his face away. "My God!"

She laid her head down on his arm and they were both quiet for a long time. Neither had spoken when an intern and nurse came in. She walked about the room as they attended to temperature and pulse.

He was impatient and annoyed at their ministrations, curt in answering questions, irascibly repeating, "Just let me alone"; but, when they withdrew he spoke meekly, almost humbly, "I only wanted to lie down. Porter was a friend in need—one of your friends, Mary."

A few moments later he startled her by asking, "Would it be right to bring the little girl, Nancy, here? I have wanted to see her."

"If you want to see her, I shall bring her. Of course. You will be surprised to see how much she is like you. She has your eyes, your complexion and some of your mannerisms." She found it difficult to steady her voice and try to ask casually, "You know she is lame?"

"Lame! How lame? Why is she lame?"

She was biting her lips again as she thought, "God help me."

She needed a moment to grope for words and she felt his eyes watching her anxiously as she answered, "One leg didn't develop just right and she has to wear a brace." She told him that there was a possibility of her being helped. Lawrence was very fond of her and he was always on the lookout for some relief from the difficulty.

She was still speaking when Dr. Porter and a nurse came in.

At noon time she said gently, "They will want you to rest, Tom." She smiled, "Tomorrow is Sunday—Easter Sunday—and I have a large family to feed. I'll go home now and see about marketing, then I'll come back."

His eyes never left her face. He whispered, "Lean over." She leaned over and, with difficulty, he raised his hand and touched her hair. "My own Mary, you are still beautiful. You are young." How many times, in their bedroom, had there been such moments. He looked deep into her eyes then his hand dropped. "Love—it passeth understanding." She turned away as he said weakly, "I just wanted to feel your hair."

She lingered. At last he spoke, "You will bring Nancy and Joseph? Tell Joseph I want very much to see him." A tremor seemed to pass through his body. "Don't let Sandra come."

She called a taxi and drove through the streets. At home, she made out a marketing list. "Sandra, I'll trust you to use good judgment and do all the errands. Take Nan with you."

She had made adequate explanations to them all and had spent some time upstairs with Miss Simmons, putting at her disposal every convenience of her home. As she was leaving her room she looked back and smiled, "I don't think either of us have time now for—thanks or—"

Miss Simmons' voice cut in authoritatively, "Just remember you are not made of iron. There are people here who need you. You'd better get some rest."

She went downstairs and found Joseph looking much refreshed after hours of sleep. She told him more of his father's condition than she had explained to the girls. She ended, "He wants most to see you. Will you call a taxi and we can go together."

He stood a few feet from her. There was that expression—that stony look in his face—disturbing—something she couldn't understand in the face of the boy she had always understood. He looked directly into her eyes. "No, Mother, I am not going to see him."

"Joseph!" She went up to him and smoothed the side of his hair. "Joseph, I don't know you. Of course you'll come to the hospital with me. He may—not live, dear. He has asked to see you. I can take Nan tomorrow. Come, call the taxi."

He turned away out of reach of her hand. "I'll call the taxi but I won't come with you."

She stood watching him for several moments as the color slowly left her face. "Very well, I'll go alone. Think it over, son. Perhaps you'll follow later. I'll pick up a sandwich somewhere and hope you'll sort of look after things here. I won't be back for supper."

He had returned from the phone when he asked, "Is it all right for Sandra to go? She has been crying her eyes out and wants to see him."

Mary was pulling on her gloves as she answered, "No. I'm afraid not. Not Sandra. He wants to see you."

He walked through the hall with her and helped her into the taxi, remarking, "I want to go over to Hunt's later. And, shall I get our own car out of storage? I hope the tires are all right."

"Yes, I intended to call the mechanic this week. That would be a great help." She was holding the door of the taxi open; now she leaned out and spoke earnestly, "Think twice, son. I hope you will come to the hospital later."

His eyes looked directly into hers. "No, Mother, I'm not coming."

She closed the door and they drove away.

She saw Tom look with pitiful yearning still toward the door after she entered the hospital room. "You didn't bring Joseph?"

She passed it off. "You are still so weak. He is getting the car fixed up for me. It will be good to drive again instead of calling taxicabs."

She had hardly taken off her coat and hat when he tried to raise himself on his elbow. He fell back as she hastened to his side.

"Mary, can you find out what they did with my clothes? There are papers and keys—don't wait."

She found the clothes, the keys and the papers from an inside pocket. "Try not to exert yourself, Tom."

There was all the old impatience in his face and voice. "Damn them. All they know is to stick needles in your arm. I don't want to sleep. Punch this pillow up. That's it." He was gasping for breath. "I'll get sleep enough. Now listen, Mary."

She pulled up the chair, her eyes frightened as she watched him. He was jerking his neck, trying to pull his head back with the old restless, fretful motions. She knew how he wanted to fling that head about, pace up and down the room with that light, quick step. She could hear the tap of his shoe on the floor, she could see the grace of movement when he turned on his heel, the old fire in his eyes.

He was handing her keys. "Mary, off and on for ten years I've been writing a book for you. You'll find all those poems also. They're for you. You can do anything you damn please with them—burn them before you look at them, if you want to. I've told you everything—everything—every way I earned money—"

"Oh, Tom, please. I know, I understand—everything."

His hands were flung about, grasping the quilt, twisting it, flinging it away. He needed a cigarette pack. She could see him open it, light one, flick the match.

"And—Mary—those family photographs. You cried, remember? Well, I've sold two more. You'll get the checks. About the book—" he smiled, "I told you I'd do that."

He stopped speaking and closed his eyes but there was a horrible twitching in his face and throat.

She laid her hand on his forehead and asked gently, "Where did you stop in the book?"

He tried to laugh. "I stopped it—" He had to wait for hoarseness to pass and he finished so weakly she could hardly hear. "I stopped it on that morning I walked into your father's office. You know the rest. I had to write it so you would know—"

"I understand, Tom. I understand everything. Please try to rest."

His eyes were closed and she felt the muscles slowly relaxing as her hands lay on his and again he breathed more quietly. Once he asked, "Will you lay your head down, Mary?"

She did not know what he wanted but she laid her head down on his arm. The room was quiet. Far down the hall, she could hear voices but they seemed far away.

She knew he was sleeping. She sat beside him hardly stirring and when a nurse looked in she motioned to her to go away. When he opened his eyes, he looked at her and smiled, "You didn't go home. You—and Joseph."

She smiled back, following his unspoken thoughts. "Two people who have always loved you." She added almost gaily, "I remember telling you once, when he was a baby, that you were going to be surprised some day to find how much you cared."

She was surprised now to see some complete change not only physical, for he was lying quiet, relaxed, breathing easily; but more astonishing was the expression in his eyes. The yearning was there but something of that anguished look was gone.

At supper time she took her tweed coat and went out. She walked over to the business streets. Saturday night. Everywhere there was bustle and life and movement. Many of the stores were open, eager to take in the dollars; for the factories were running, making war goods, and again the wanted dollars were filling the pockets of the men and women milling in and out of the open doorways.

She walked as far as her bank. Across the corner was Fuller's Drug Store. She made her way through the traffic, streetcars, automobiles and baby carriages. She went up the steps and entered. For a moment the blaze of light almost blinded her as she looked about. Over there in the corner, a young couple was leaving a boot. She slid into it, picked up the card and tried to read. She would order a sandwich and a cup of coffee.

She looked across at the soda counter. As though it were yesterday she could see three young boys enter, grab the vacant stools, whirl and wind their feet about the pedestals. She saw the girl come over to Joseph, saw his wide smile, his excitement.

A blond girl took her order. She drank the hot coffee, tried but couldn't swallow the sandwich, paid her bill and went out.

All through the evening he slept. Near midnight she found a taxi and went home.

It was between five and six on Sunday morning when the phone rang. An intern asked, "Do you want to come, Mrs. Donovan?"

The sun was just beginning to light up the pink of the apple trees. The buds were beginning to swell on the magnificent magnolia over in Judge Carter's lawn. Not until May would they burst into full bloom.

The hospital was full of that smell of early morning cleaning. Old women were mopping floors, hand-carts stocked with towels and sheets were being pushed up and down halls; the smell of food was in every corridor.

His eyes were on the door. She was hanging away her coat when he asked, "Joseph?"

She sat down beside him and he spoke irritably, "Joseph?"

She laid both her hands on his and held them. She saw him close his eyes and for the first time in her life she saw tears on his cheeks. But then he was weak; his eyes were dull and lifeless. The fires were nearly burned out.

Once in the early morning he had lain so long with closed eyes she thought he was sleeping. She was looking toward the window when she remembered how Mattie Briggs and she had laughed when Mattie remembered that she had left biscuits rising.

"You are smiling, Mary."

She started. Then she told him about Mattie and the biscuits. He smiled, "You always loved a joke, Mary. We used to do a lot of laughing. You had laughing eyes."

She thought he seemed quite a little stronger. He was quiet, breathed easier and soon fell into what she thought must be a good sleep. She sat with her hands close on both of his then she laid her head down on his arm. He liked that.

The hands under hers had relaxed for some time before she

raised her head and looked into his face. She would always remember that the slight smile was on his lips.

It was near eleven when she came out of the hospital. She walked to the street. It was too far to try to walk all the way home but she wanted a few moments in the air.

It was Easter Sunday and the church bells were ringing. Above her head the sky was a vibrant indigo blue. Through all the air there was that curious singing beauty of light that she loved. The streets were well filled with people going to various churches, resplendent in their Easter finery. She admired the new hats and the pretty clothes on the children.

She walked down through the business streets to the trolley. She was in no hurry to get home. It was good to be out among people.

It was on Tuesday of that Easter vacation of Joseph's that his father was buried in the Kent-Farnsworth burial lot. There had been a good picture and an article of unusual length in the newspaper; quite the kind of an article that a boy might be proud to read about his father. He had been a writer of distinction, publishing stories and articles in such and such magazines. He had been an editor of such and such periodicals and had done brilliant work on their own paper. The writer of the article understood that he had nearly completed a full length book before his untimely death.

On Wednesday, Joseph Donovan packed his bag and returned to college. "Kurt will be there and we can get in four days of hard work."

Across the arbor at the side porch, the branches of the early rambler hung heavy with their weight of crimson blooms; weeks since, the trees had been in full leaf, the lawn velvety smooth and lovely in its first brilliant green. It was June; and again the sunlight filtering down through the branches of the elms traced beautiful patterns on the pavement. The college year had ended and Joseph Donovan was home.

Miss Simmons had packed her bags, left her room in perfect order and Joseph had driven her to catch the night train for

Boston. She would spend the summer on her sister's farm in Maine.

Mary Donovan was watching for his return from the station. She saw the car but he did not stop at their door but went on and turned into Judge Carter's drive.

It was late and her daughters as well as the little boy, Roger, were sleeping soundly upstairs. She was busying herself in the kitchen when she heard him closing the garage doors.

She smiled as he stood in the door looking at her. "Joseph, I believe you're going to be a bigger man than your grandfather. Your head almost reaches to the top of that door."

"Any cold milk?"

"I baked some of those thick molasses cookies you like."

They sat together at the round table.

"Rather nice, Mother. Judge Carter says I have a place waiting in his office when I come back. He has an idea that Hunt and I will want to go into a law partnership—some day. He and Hunt have planned it together. Rather nice?"

"I should say very nice if—when the time comes, that is what you want."

"Mother, about Sandra. Can't you see what a difference there is in her since those weeks out in Chicago with Uncle Lawrence? A hell of a difference. That's what she needs and what she's got to have. I want you to promise me." He reached for a second cookie. "Kurt will be in medical school. They're going to need doctors when we get officially into this war. He says he is going to ask Sandra to come down for dances and football games. You let her go, Mother. Kurt's a good guy and he's a gentleman. But I don't want her to go with only a navy suit and a few blouses. I wish you'd see that she has pretty dresses and—you know, all the other little things. Spend money on her."

Mary laughed. "Spend money on her? Oh, Joseph, what you don't know!" She looked down at her plain black dress, picking up a fold of the skirt and twisting it in her fingers. "How I hate this black—or dull gray—or navy for that matter—the badge of the unimaginative. I was looking through that catalogue with the colored illustrations, changeable silks, changeable like the colors in the sky, those Scotch tweeds, violet, sand and green all seen through a warp of blue just like autumn colors in our hills." She laughed, "I found my mouth watering. I was positively drooling. I'll spend money on her."

He looked at her steadily, unsmilingly as she repeated; "I'll spend money on her. Lawrence claims the privilege of paying for Nan's operation. He wants that entire responsibility."

It was on the following morning when he again stood on the porch, a newly packed bag at his feet. He had swung a little boy up to the ceiling; he had rubbed his cheek against Nan's hair as she sat on the floor in the bay window with the child, still excited over the new treasure and enjoying playing "little mother" to him; and now he turned to the tall girl at his side. There was some mistiness in her violet-gray eyes as she watched him. He joked, "These country yokels must be blind, leaving this poor spinster on our hands. Guess you'll have to be your brother's only and best girl."

"All right, I'll accept my fate. I'll even promise to answer all your letters."

"You'll do a hell of a lot better than that; you'll write three to one; and remember I don't want you to tell me who's elected governor; I want you to tell me how many teeth Roger has, what Nan has learned on the piano, what Mother said—you get it?"

"I get it."

He walked into the parlor and met his mother coming in from the sittingroom. He took a few quick strides up and down the room. "Hunt's following me at the end of the month. Judge Carter agrees that we're wise to get in on the ground floor, get officers' training and be ready when they need us. The sooner we get at it all, the sooner we'll be through and home again."

She was watching his face. "Joseph, if by some strange chance you should ever meet John Donovan, be good to him. I think if you should come to know him, you would like him."

He made no answer.

She laid her hands on his shoulders. Quickly his strong arms tightened about her and his face was pressed against her hair.

When she drew back and looked up into his face, there was

pleading in her eyes. "My son, I want you to do something for me. I want you to say these words every night of your life. 'Forgive us our trespasses as we forgive those who trespass against us.' "

He looked at her with gray, bleak-looking eyes. "I might say it, Mother, but I won't feel it."

"You will someday, my darling. You and I loved him. You will forgive him as we both hope to be forgiven."

"I'm not you, Mother."

She smiled, "No, but you're woefully like me. You will say it. That's all I ask now."

There was the sound of an automobile horn as Hunt Carter arrived to take Joseph to the station.

At the curb Mary watched them put the bags in the car. Sandra, at their insistence, slipped into the front seat between the two young men, and Joseph with a last quick smile looked back into his mother's eyes. Then she walked back to the porch.

Mary Donovan stood alone, looking far down through the beautiful "abbey arches." It was one of those glistening, singing, perfect June days.